continued . . .

For Those Who Fell

"Careful plotting and realistically messy detail . . . Dietz expertly jumps from one theater of combat to another, one side to another, to show the opponents planning but then improvising as plans go awry." —*Publishers Weekly*

"The usual fast-paced adventure we have come to expect in the series and from Dietz." —*Booklist*

"An excellent story, well written and rich in detail, that sets the scene both militarily and against the background of a galaxy-wide war . . . It is a great tribute to William Dietz's skill that he is able to make [the story] seem possible and believable." —SF Crowsnest.com

"William C. Dietz raises the bar of excellence for military science fiction with every book he writes . . . a superb action-packed thriller." —*Midwest Book Review*

"If you . . . take comfort in reading about mayhem on an interstellar scale, then this is probably a good bet for hours of slack-jawed, drooling entertainment." —*The Agony Column*

For More Than Glory

"Dietz has created an intricate tapestry of local and star-faring culture with top-notch action sequences." —*Publishers Weekly*

"Plenty of conflict and mayhem . . . rewarding." —*SF Site*

"Thoughtful . . . plot conscious." —*Chronicle*

"Exciting military SF fare. Series readers and *Starship Troopers* fans will want this." —*Booklist*

BONES OF EMPIRE

WILLIAM C. DIETZ

ACE BOOKS, NEW YORK

THE BERKLEY PUBLISHING GROUP
Published by the Penguin Group
Penguin Group (USA) Inc.
375 Hudson Street, New York, New York 10014, USA
Penguin Group (Canada), 90 Eglinton Avenue East, Suite 700, Toronto, Ontario M4P 2Y3, Canada
(a division of Pearson Penguin Canada Inc.)
Penguin Books Ltd., 80 Strand, London WC2R 0RL, England
Penguin Group Ireland, 25 St. Stephen's Green, Dublin 2, Ireland (a division of Penguin Books Ltd.)
Penguin Group (Australia), 250 Camberwell Road, Camberwell, Victoria 3124, Australia
(a division of Pearson Australia Group Pty. Ltd.)
Penguin Books India Pvt. Ltd., 11 Community Centre, Panchsheel Park, New Delhi—110 017, India
Penguin Group (NZ), 67 Apollo Drive, Rosedale, Auckland 0632, New Zealand
(a division of Pearson New Zealand Ltd.)
Penguin Books (South Africa) (Pty.) Ltd., 24 Sturdee Avenue, Rosebank, Johannesburg 2196,
South Africa

Penguin Books Ltd., Registered Offices: 80 Strand, London WC2R 0RL, England

This is a work of fiction. Names, characters, places, and incidents either are the product of the author's imagination or are used fictitiously, and any resemblance to actual persons, living or dead, business establishments, events, or locales is entirely coincidental. The publisher does not have any control over and does not assume any responsibility for author or third-party websites or their content.

BONES OF EMPIRE

An Ace Book / published by arrangement with the author

PRINTING HISTORY
Ace hardcover edition / October 2010
Ace mass-market edition / October 2011

Copyright © 2010 by William C. Dietz.
Cover art by Don Sipley.
Interior text design by Kristin del Rosario.

ISBN: 978-0-441-02088-1

ACE
Ace Books are published by The Berkley Publishing Group,
a division of Penguin Group (USA) Inc.,
375 Hudson Street, New York, New York 10014.
ACE and the "A" design are trademarks of Penguin Group (USA) Inc.

PRINTED IN THE UNITED STATES OF AMERICA

10 9 8 7 6 5 4 3 2 1

*To my dearest Marjorie, with thanks
for all of her help, advice, and forbearance*

ONE

The city of Imperialus, on the planet Corin

THE CITY OF IMPERIALUS HAD BEEN CONSTRUCTED within the embrace of an ancient crater, where it was at least partially protected from the winds that scoured the area each fall. But the "blow," as the locals referred to it, was still months away, and the temperature was beginning to climb as Trey Omo and his team of street toughs entered the section of the metropolis called Port City.

A thousand years earlier, back before Imperialus had become the capital of the sprawling Uman Empire, Port City had been the *only* settlement on Corin. And not much of one at that. But those days were gone, and the slum around the bustling spaceport was populated by people who were too poor to escape the endless noise associated with the facility. They lived in poorly maintained five-to-ten-story buildings, many of which were hundreds of years old and built on the rubble of structures that dated back to the first Imperial epoch. There had been repeated efforts to spruce the area up, but thanks to the forces of greed, corruption, and institutionalized incompetence, Port City always reverted to form within a matter of years.

That meant the citizens of District Five, as it was officially known, were tough, cynical, and eternally wary of strangers. So when Omo and his assassins entered the slum, word of their arrival spread like ripples on a pond, and it wasn't long before the local power structure went on the defensive. Criminal gangs pulled their members in off the streets, merchants doubled their security, and it was as if the entire population was holding its breath, waiting to see what would happen next.

That was fine with Omo, who didn't want to do battle with the locals but was perfectly willing to do so if that was necessary. *His* job was to set up an ambush, wait for Isulu Usurlus to land the following day, and kill him before the Legate and his official motorcade could clear Port City.

It was a routine operation insofar as Omo was concerned. A straightforward political assassination not unlike half a dozen others he had participated in over the years. His team consisted of thirty people, who had been divided into three ten-man squads, two of which were commanded by trusted noncoms, with the third being led by Omo himself.

The first task of the day was to finalize the way the ambush would be organized, and having scouted the area a few days earlier, Omo had a pretty good idea of where he wanted to place his men. But in order to fine-tune his plan, it was necessary to inspect each location to make sure his first impression was correct, then take control of it. That might require some muscle, however, which was why half of Omo's squad accompanied him as the beat-up delivery van arrived in front of a ratty apartment building and pulled over to the curb. "Check your weapons," Omo said gruffly. "But keep them out of sight. We don't want trouble if we can avoid it."

Once his men were ready, Omo opened the passenger-side door, got out, and led the toughs across the broken sidewalk and into what had once been known as the Grand Imperialus Hotel. However, as Omo and his team crossed the lobby, there was nothing "grand" about a space in which the poorest of the poor could rent a three-foot-by-seven-foot section of dirty floor for fifty centimes per night. A pathetic accommodation to be sure, but one that was superior to sleeping on the streets, where all manner of predators roamed the darkness.

It was never a good idea to stare, not in Port City, so the scraggly-looking specimens who were standing, sitting, or lying around the lobby were careful to look elsewhere as the toughs made their way back to a bank of elevators and took control of the only one that worked. It carried them to the second floor, where Omo led his men down a graffiti-decorated hall toward the east side of the building.

At the end of the passageway, the group was forced to turn left. The air around them was thick with the cloying odors of cooking, backed-up toilets, and the sickly sweet scent of incense. The mixture caught at the back of Omo's throat and reminded him of the public "stack" in which he'd spent his early years.

And there was no escaping the incessant babble produced by dozens of competing vid sets, a child wailing somewhere nearby, and a shouting match between a man and woman. All punctuated by the occasional bleat of a distant siren, the gentle rumble generated by a shuttle as it passed over the building, and the constant slamming of doors.

Having arrived at what he judged to be the correct spot, Omo came to a stop. Then, after gesturing for his men to take up positions to either side of a door, he rapped on the much-abused wood and waited for a response.

There was a thirty-second pause during which scuffling sounds were heard—and Omo sensed that someone was peering at him via the door's peephole. The assassin smiled stiffly, held a gold Imperial up so that the person within could see it, and waited to see which emotion would win: greed or fear.

Omo wasn't surprised when a series of *click*s were heard, and the door opened just far enough for a man to peek out. He had thin wispy hair, deep-set eyes, and hollow cheeks. "Yeah?" he inquired cautiously. "What do you want?"

"I want your room," Omo answered simply. "I'll give you two Imperials for it. But you have to clear out now and never come back."

Two Imperials was a lot of money in Port City, and Omo could see the eagerness in the other man's eyes. "*Three* Imperials," he responded cagily. "Give me three Imperials, and the room is yours. We need time to pack though."

"Okay," Omo replied reasonably. "Three Imperials it is. Plus ten minutes to pack. Then, if you aren't out of there, my men and I will throw you out."

The man was frightened but determined and ran his tongue over dry lips. "I want the money in advance."

"Here's a third of it," Omo replied as he held his hand out. "You'll get the rest in ten minutes. Start packing."

The gold piece disappeared so fast Omo could barely detect the movement of the other man's hand—and the door was about to close when he placed a boot in the gap. "Oh, no you don't," Omo cautioned. "Leave it open."

The man withdrew, and the door swung open, giving Omo a clear view of what had originally been a hotel room with attached bath. Now it was home to a family of five, including the man, a rail-thin woman who was feverishly stuffing belongings into pieces of mismatched luggage, and three children who were busy getting in the way.

Makeshift bunk beds took up one wall, a mattress occupied part of the floor, and a vid set was perched on top of a cage containing three chickens. But beyond the squalor, three vertical windows could be seen—each of which was worth at least one Imperial to Omo.

A full fifteen minutes passed before the man, his emaciated wife, and their brood of grubby children collected the rest of their money and left the room, each carrying as much as he or she could. Once the family was gone, Omo went over to the filthy windows and looked out through the one that was open. It offered an unobstructed view of the narrow street that the Legate's motorcade would be forced to negotiate on the way to the Government Zone. "It's perfect," Omo said, without turning his head. "Honis and Dybel will stay here to guard the room. I'll send a rocket launcher and two men over within the hour. Are there any questions?"

"Yes," one of the men said. "Can you send some beer, too?"

That got some chuckles from the others and a grin from Omo as he turned to face them. "No," he said firmly. "But if the mission is a success, I will buy the beer tomorrow night. And there will be women, too. . . . But you must remain sober until then. Understood?"

Omo wore his hair military short, had a face that looked as if it had been carved from weathered stone, and a slash for a mouth. There were men strong enough to oppose him—but none was present in the room. The mercenaries nodded soberly. They liked Omo and respected him.

Then, as if in response to an earthquake, the entire building shook, and a near-deafening roar was heard as a spaceship took off less than a mile away and began to claw its way up through Corin's gravity well. Those who lived in Port City barely noticed.

Aboard the passenger ship Far Star

The *Far Star* was half a mile long and could carry five hundred thousand tons of cargo plus two thousand passengers and crew, along with everything required to keep them happy during long, boring weeks spent in hyperspace. Time during which they were free to enjoy the amenities available in their beautifully appointed cabins, participate in activities organized by the vessel's cruise director, or shop in the onboard arcade.

All of that was more than adequate for most people, the single exception being Xeno Corps Officer Jak Cato, who was playing cards in the locker room located adjacent to the engineering spaces on Deck 4. He hated the social posturing, petty backstabbing, and boring conversations that passed for fun on the upper decks and preferred to spend his time below.

Of course there was another reason to venture down into the bowels of the *Far Star* as well, and that was the opportunity to play cards with the vessel's crew, all of whom had proven themselves to be delightfully ignorant regarding the police officer's special talent. That wasn't too surprising given Cato's failure to mention that he was a member of the Xeno Corps, or "the freak show," as its detractors referred to the organization.

Because had the other three people seated at the table known that Cato could effectively "read" their emotions, they would have not only been outraged, but demanded that he return the 546 Imperials he had won from them and their shipmates during the last four days. It was money Cato was going to need once the *Far Star* put down on Corin.

The game they were playing was called Roller, which involved rolling dice to determine how many cards were dealt from a deck of sixty-three, then using them to assemble a winning hand. It was a complicated process that demanded a good memory, keen judgment, and a certain amount of luck.

However, thanks to Cato's ability to "sense" excitement, fear, anger, and a host of other emotions, he had been able to take more rounds than he lost while being careful to let the others win enough games to keep them coming back. Now, as the middle-aged engineering officer seated across from him assembled a new hand, he could "feel" her sense of jubilation. Should he fold? And avoid a loss? Or let her win?

Such were Cato's thoughts when a hand came to rest on his shoulder. The voice was female and very familiar. "It's five o'clock, Master—and time to get ready."

Cato frowned. "Okay," he said irritably. "Wait outside . . . I'll be there in a moment."

CeCe Alamy colored slightly, took a full step back, and quickly withdrew.

Meanwhile, the engineer projected a sense of concern but was careful to keep her face blank. Cato knew she was afraid he would leave before the next round of betting began, and the pot grew substantially larger. And he might have let her have the win had the voyage been one or two days longer. But, since the *Far Star* was going to put down the next day, there was no reason to suffer the loss.

Cato produced a smile, put his cards facedown on the table, and scraped a double handful of coins off the table. "Sorry about that—but duty calls. My boss is hosting a fancy dinner tonight and expects me to be there. Thank you for your hospitality and keeping this rust bucket running. I think I speak for all of the passengers when I say well done!"

That produced a round of chuckles as Cato took his winnings and withdrew. Alamy was waiting in the corridor beyond. Her hair was piled up on the back of her head the way the wealthy girls on the upper decks wore theirs and held in place by the silver pin Cato had given her back on Dantha. She had large luminous eyes, a straight nose, and full lips. The dress she wore was simple but elegant, having been sewn by Alamy herself. Cato was not only annoyed by the interruption but dreading the evening ahead as he paused to tuck his winnings away. "Who are you anyway?" he demanded irritably. "My mother? Or my slave?"

The words were intended as a joke, but as blood rushed to Alamy's face, Cato regretted them and rushed to make amends. "I'm sorry, CeCe—that was a stupid thing to say."

But it was too late. Cato "felt" the full extent of Alamy's shame as she looked down at her feet. "I'm your slave, Master—and I apologize for giving offense."

"*No*," Cato replied emphatically, "you *aren't* my slave, not really. We'll get that straightened out later on. And stop calling me 'Master.'"

Except that Alamy was supposed to call him "Master," having been purchased for twelve hundred Imperials on Dantha, in the wake of Governor Nalomy's death. It was his intention to free her, however, just as soon as they found a place to live on Corin and he found time to deal with all of the paperwork. "I'm a total and unforgivable jerk," Cato said sincerely as he reached out to take her hand. "Come on. . . . Let's go up to our cabin, where I promise to dress up like a Hiberian Zerk monkey so Legate Usurlus can show me off."

Though not enough to neutralize the way she felt, the mental image was enough to make Alamy smile, and Cato was quick to take advantage of the opening by walking side by side with her as if she were free, and insisting that she pass through doors first. The result was that by the time they entered the Class III cabin the government was paying for, they were on speaking terms again.

True to her very efficient ways, Alamy had already assembled the basic elements of Cato's dress uniform and laid them out on the bed they shared. The arrangement wasn't a necessary aspect of the master-slave relationship but wasn't all that unusual either, especially where wealthy individuals were concerned.

The next forty-five minutes were spent showering, shaving, and dressing. Cato's uniform consisted of a helmet, which he would be forced to hold in the crook of his left arm while standing, sculpted body armor, and a knee-length kilt. The subtle plaid was supposed to remind observers that the Xeno Corps was technically part of the 3rd Legion, although that organization wasn't all that proud of the group and would have been happy to hand it off to some other outfit had there been any takers. A pair of high-gloss combat boots completed the outfit.

That was the basic kit. But Alamy, who had been born free but raised in a slum, was a stickler for all of the little things that had to do with rank and status. So she made sure that the flashes that denoted Cato's rank as a Centurion were equally spaced on his shoulders, the brightly polished medals that had previously been stored at the very bottom of his footlocker were perfectly aligned on his chest, and the length of gold braid that looped under his left arm was properly secured.

The braid marked Cato's status as an aide to a senior officer, in this case Legate Usurlus, who, though of sufficient rank to command a Legion, hadn't done so for many years. As Usurlus liked to put it, "I fight battles in the Senate and its surrounds, which though quieter are just as dangerous."

The comment referred to the fact that Usurlus was related to Emperor Emor and had long been one of his troubleshooters. The latest assignment had been on the planet Dantha, where it had been necessary to remove a corrupt Procurator from office and reestablish the rule of law. A task that brought the patrician and the policeman together and had everything to do with Cato's presence on the ship.

"There," Alamy said, as she took two steps back. "You

look very handsome." And it was true, in her opinion at least, because Cato had a nice, if somewhat battered, face. Plus, his body, with which she was intimately familiar, was tall and strong. So much so that he frequently drew admiring glances from other women, many of whom were free and therefore more eligible than she was. Still, Cato had been true to her so far as Alamy knew, and that would have to do.

"I wish you could come," Cato said, as his eyes met hers. "Then you'd know how painful these dinners are."

"I *do* know," Alamy responded tartly. "I was one of Governor Nalomy's servants, remember? Now mind your manners. No swearing, no belching, and don't stab things with your knife. It isn't polite."

"Okay," Cato agreed good-naturedly. "But only if you kiss me."

Alamy raised a quizzical eyebrow. "You could order me to kiss you."

"True," Cato allowed, "but there would be a price to pay."

"There certainly would be," Alamy agreed as she stepped into the circle of his arms.

Cato "felt" the strength of her affection for him as her lips gave under his, knew he should free her, and wondered why he hadn't. *Corin,* he thought to himself, *I'll do it on Corin.* Then, helmet in the crook of his arm, it was time to leave.

The two-bedroom suite was the finest accommodation the *Far Star* had to offer. The servants had withdrawn by that time, leaving their master to inspect himself in the large bathroom mirror. Legate Isulu Usurlus was vain, he knew that, and felt no guilt regarding the matter. The man who looked back at him had carefully tousled blond hair, gray eyes, and an aquiline nose. Tiny lines had begun to marshal their forces around the corners of his eyes, however, and stood ready to bracket his mouth. He saw them as enemies that, having been allowed to establish a beachhead while he was on Dantha, would have to be defeated on Corin. A process he looked forward to after months of privation on a backwater planet.

Usurlus was dressed in a white toga, a pleated kilt, and a pair of gold-colored sandals. The only signs of his rank were the silver and gold bracelets on his left wrist, the family crest on the pin that held the toga in place, and the way he carried himself. Which was to say with the confidence of a man who was completely sure of his place in Imperial society.

Having satisfied himself that he was presentable, Usurlus left the suite and stepped out into the corridor, where his chief bodyguard was waiting for him. Dom Livius was a big man with a prominent brow, a fist-flattened nose, and a pugnacious jaw. Like his predecessor, who had been murdered on Dantha, he was an ex-legionnaire and a dangerous man. Usurlus smiled at him. "Livius! What are you doing here? We're on a spaceship. Take the evening off."

"Thank you, sire," Livius responded doggedly, "but if it's all the same to you, I'll come along. It's true that we're on a ship, but so are two thousand other people, and I have no reason to trust them."

"All right," Usurlus conceded, as the two men made their way down the corridor. "Suit yourself. . . . But the main danger will come from Rufus Glabas, who claims to support Emperor Emor while secretly consorting with the Hacia combine. Then there's Porica Lakaris, who hopes I will marry her brainless daughter, and Catullus Skallos. A man who, if my information is correct, has feelers out to the Vords in case the despicable creatures conquer the Empire.

Fortunately, none of them are likely to attack me with anything more pointed than words."

"If you say so, sire," Livius responded cynically. "But I'll be there just in case."

"As will Centurion Cato," Usurlus observed. "Assuming Alamy has been able to round the rascal up and make him presentable. Between the two of you, I will feel quite safe."

The Galaxy Room was a rectangular space, which—thanks to the sensaround built into the bulkheads—appeared to be floating in space. That was an illusion, of course, since it was impossible to see anything from the vantage point of a ship traveling through hyperspace, but it was effective nevertheless. So much so that Cato experienced a brief moment of vertigo as he entered the room and made his way back to the point where a bar had been set up with a spectacular nebula in the background. It looked like an exploding star shell—and glittered with reflected light.

Fifteen or twenty other people were present, all dressed in their evening finery, and of higher status than a mere Centurion. But, thanks to the respect routinely extended to soldiers, the other guests were polite, if somewhat distant. And that was fine with Cato, who planned to maintain a low profile throughout the meal and make a quick escape the moment it was over.

Fortunately, a retired *Praefectus Castrorum* and his wife were present, and like most staff officers, the Prefect was ready to hold forth at length regarding the sad state of the military in general and the 3rd Legion in particular, he having served in the 5th, which to hear him tell of it, was the finest group of men ever to take the field. It was boring stuff, but whenever the Prefect was talking, Cato wasn't required to, and that suited him just fine.

The Prefect was droning on about the finer points of

logistics, something he felt the 5th Legion was especially good at, when Usurlus entered the room, closely followed by Livius. Suddenly the center of social gravity shifted from lesser lights to the Legate, and Cato was free to drift away as an orgy of ass kissing began.

Finally, once the greeting process was over, and Usurlus took his seat at the head of the glittering table, Cato and the rest of the guests were free to do likewise. That was when Cato discovered that he was sandwiched between a paunchy merchant named Skallos on his left and a thirtysomething widow on his right, the latter being the more interesting of the two. She was attractive in a slightly worn sort of way— and very scantily dressed. That, at least, was a good thing, since she had a very nice figure.

The meal began, as such affairs always did, with obligatory toasts to the Empire, the Emperor, and various other notables, some of whom Cato had never heard of before. Eventually, as their glasses of wine were being refilled, the widow put her left hand on Cato's right knee.

She smiled unapologetically when he looked at her. Cato would have said something at that point had Usurlus not preempted him. "Did all of you have an opportunity to meet Centurion Cato?" the Legate inquired smoothly.

Naturally, all eyes swung over to Cato as the widow found bare skin under the kilt and sent her hand up his thigh. "Good," Usurlus continued, as if all of them had answered in the affirmative. "Now, those of you with a keen eye for military detail may have noticed the small X-shaped device located just above Centurion Cato's medals. That signifies membership in the Legion's Xeno Corps, an organization formed to cope with non-Uman criminals—some of whom have very unusual capabilities.

"Take the Sagathi shape shifters, for example," Usurlus said, as his eyes roamed from face to face. "As you may have heard, they can impersonate any being having roughly the same mass they do. So how to catch them? Well, that's where empaths like Centurion Cato come in. Because they can sense what we can't.

"In fact, since Cato is with us tonight, perhaps he would be so kind as to give us a demonstration of his abilities. Tell me, Centurion Cato. . . . What is Citizen Belo feeling right now?"

The man in question was seated on the other side of the table. And what he was feeling was scared, although Cato had no way to know why and didn't care. He was angry at Usurlus for using him as a source of cheap entertainment and uncomfortably aware of the widow's hand, which had traveled halfway up his thigh and was about to enter dangerous territory.

So rather than remain where he was and be forced to deal with the pleasurable but possibly embarrassing results of his dinner companion's advances, Cato slid his chair back and came to his feet. Then, happy to escape, he circled the table as if it were somehow necessary to close with Belo in order to "feel" his emotions.

Once in place, Cato placed his hands on the businessman's shoulders, closed his eyes, and frowned. "Wait a moment. . . . Yes, yes, yes . . . There's no doubt about it. Citizen Belo is hungry!"

That got a good laugh, and the sense of relief that emanated from Belo was almost palpable. But rather than release Cato from his social agony, Usurlus was determined to push on. "Very good, Centurion Cato," he said dryly. "Although I think it's safe to say that Citizen Mima's lapdog could do as well!

"Perhaps a more difficult test of your capabilities is in order. I want you to move to your left. I will say a word as you pause behind each person—and you will communicate what they feel."

Everyone in the room had influence of one kind or another, so the proposal was fraught with danger, and Cato's forehead was populated by tiny beads of sweat. If thoughts could kill, Usurlus would have been dead many times over, regardless of the big bodyguard's presence.

But thoughts *couldn't* kill, which left Cato with no choice but to go along, albeit in his own way. Meaning that rather than give factual reports, the kind that could get him into trouble with the Legate's guests, Cato chose to provide innocuous readouts and run the risk of triggering his host's ire.

So when Cato took his place behind the Prefect's wife, and Usurlus said the word "marriage," the empath responded with the word "joy" rather than "boredom."

A few minutes later, as he stood behind Rufus Glabus, Cato replied with "hope" when Usurlus offered the word "future," even though the politician sitting in front of the Xeno cop was radiating a sense of doom. And, predictably enough, Glabus nodded in agreement.

And so the charade went until it was time for shipping magnate Catullus Skallos to respond. The trigger word was "Vord," and rather than the dread most people in the room felt regarding the gaunt-looking aliens, Skallos projected something akin to eagerness. But, consistent with his previous readouts, Cato gave voice to the same emotion the rest of the guests had registered. And, as Cato made eye contact with Usurlus, he knew the Legate was onto him.

Mercifully, the process came to an end five minutes later, and when Cato returned to his seat, it was to discover that the widow was flirting with the middle-aged bureaucrat to her right. A development that left Cato free to eat as course after course of food began to arrive. There were some pro forma interactions with Skallos, but not many, for which Cato was grateful.

Eventually, after what felt like a century of boredom, the meal came to an end, and the Legate's guests lined up to thank him as they left. Cato slipped three hand-dipped chocolates into the empty dispatch pouch on his belt, knowing how much Alamy would enjoy them, and was almost out the door when a heavy hand landed on his shoulder. "Not so fast," Livius said, as Cato came to a halt. "The Legate would like to speak with you in half an hour."

Cato swore as only a veteran legionnaire can.

Livius grinned unsympathetically. "What did you expect? I've never heard such a load of bullshit! Tell me Centurion Cato—what am *I* feeling now?"

"You're happy," Cato answered resentfully, "because you're a rotten sonofabitch."

"You got that right," Livius agreed cheerfully. "Be there, Cato. . . . Don't make me come and find you."

And with that, Cato was allowed to leave the sensaround for the corridor outside. Alamy was going to be pissed. He was in trouble again—but not for stabbing his food with a knife.

Having waited for thirty minutes, Cato made his way to the suite that Usurlus occupied, where he paused to straighten his uniform before pressing the button next to the door. He heard a distant *bong*, followed by a *click*, as Usurlus gave a verbal order.

Cato opened the door, took six paces into the cabin, and came to attention. His eyes were on a spot located six inches over the Legate's head. "Centurion Cato, reporting as ordered, sir!"

Usurlus was seated in a well-upholstered chair with a drink in his hand. He was dressed in shimmery synsilk pajamas and apparently ready for bed. "Put that ridiculous helmet somewhere and have a seat," Usurlus said. "Would you like a drink?"

Cato put the helmet on a table and took the chair across

from Usurlus. He had already consumed two glasses of wine and was determined not to backslide where his drinking problem was concerned, so he answered accordingly. "No, sire, thank you."

"So," Usurlus said lazily, "did you enjoy dinner?"

"Yes, sire," Cato replied. "I did."

"You're a terrible liar," Usurlus observed as he took a sip of his drink. "And I'm an expert where lies are concerned. You hated it, didn't you?"

There was a pause as Cato nodded reluctantly. "Sir, yes, sir."

"And your responses to my little game? Were any of them truthful?"

"Yes, sire. When you said, 'music,' Citizen Tersus felt a sense of foreboding. His wife plays the harp."

Usurlus chuckled. "In other words, he likes harp music as much as you like dinner parties."

"Yes, sir."

At that point there was movement beyond a half-opened door followed by the sound of a woman's voice. "I'm going to take a bath," she announced. "Are you coming?"

Cato thought the voice was familiar. Was it the widow? The one who had been sitting next to him during dinner? Yes, he thought it was.

"That sounds like fun," Usurlus replied as he turned toward the bedroom. "Save some hot water for me!"

Then, having turned to Cato, Usurlus was serious. "And when I said, 'Vord,' how did Citizen Skallos respond?"

Suddenly Cato realized something that should have been apparent all along. Usurlus had been using him all right— but for a purpose other than entertainment. "Citizen Skallos felt a sense of eagerness, sire. . . . Verging on excitement."

"And the others?"

"Dread, sire."

"And for good reason," Usurlus mused out loud. "You

fought them—so you know. The Vords are warlike, their empire is still in the process of expanding, and we're in their way. Emperor Emor is trying to negotiate with them, but they have taken control of two rim worlds and clearly have an appetite for more. I think Skallos is trying to cut a deal with them. An insurance policy if you will—just in case they win."

"So what will you do?" Cato inquired.

"I will give his name to Imperial Intelligence," Usurlus answered, "and request that they keep an eye on him. We live in a complicated world, Cato—and there are very few people we can trust."

Cato sensed that the meeting was over. He stood, bent to retrieve his helmet, and was about to turn toward the door when Usurlus spoke again. "Give my regards to Alamy—and tell her that she's doing a good job."

Most people of the Legate's rank wouldn't have known Alamy's name, much less sent a message to her; but Usurlus wasn't most people. And, come to that, what did the message mean? What "job" was Usurlus referring to? There was no way to know as Cato said, "Good night," and withdrew. Would Alamy be interested in a bath? Cato hoped so—and went to find out.

The city of Imperialus, on the planet Corin

The journey from Dantha to Corin was Alamy's first trip on a spaceship, and as the *Far Star* was cleared to land in the city of Imperialus, she felt a tremendous sense of excitement. Because never, even in her wildest fantasies, had Alamy imagined that she would travel to another planet, much less the Uman Empire's capital. Yet there she was, stretched out on an acceleration couch in the main lounge side by side with Cato, as the liner entered Corin's gravity well and began to shake as she entered the upper atmosphere.

There were hundreds of people around them, all staring up at the overhead, where the ship's progress could be monitored via a dozen large screens. The center picture showed clouds, the partially obscured brown landmasses beyond, and patches of blue that marked major bodies of water.

As she looked down on her new home, Alamy felt fear seep in to replace some of the excitement because so many things were unknown. Would Cato free her? Would he still want her? And what would she do if he didn't? Alamy had been employed in a sandal factory before her father died, and her stepmother sold her into slavery, so she had no skills to speak of. It would be difficult to survive in a city like Imperialus were Cato to abandon her—so perhaps slavery would be better.

Cato, who could "feel" Alamy's emotions, even if he couldn't access her thoughts, reached over to squeeze a hand. He knew she was worried, and understandably so, but he had concerns of his own. Potentially serious concerns regarding the trip from the spaceport to the government zone where Usurlus lived.

Though not an expert where Imperialus was concerned, Cato had been stationed there twice and knew the city well enough. The streets could be dangerous, especially in slums like Port City, which was why wealthy citizens and important government officials flew from building to building in private air cars.

But, according to Livius, a motorcade had been laid on to transport Usurlus and his party from the spaceport to his home. The idea was to give the vid nets a photo op and a reason to report on the Legate's return, plus his success in battling corruption on Dantha, an accomplishment that Emor's surrogates would hold up as an example of what a good job the Emperor was doing. Which was why Usurlus couldn't refuse to ride in a motorcade even though it was going to follow a predetermined route through one of the Imperial city's most dangerous slums.

There would be bodyguards, of course, led by Livius, with Cato acting as second-in-command. Such was his duty. But the fact that Alamy would be traveling with the motorcade added to the sense of foreboding Cato felt and raised the stakes even higher, as the ship slowed and thunder rolled across Port City. Moments later, the ship was down, the dice had been thrown, and Cato knew that the rest would be a matter of luck.

TWO

The city of Imperialus, on the planet Corin

ONCE THE FAR STAR *WAS ON THE GROUND, IT TOOK* more than two hours for her passengers to disembark, and that included Legate Isulu Usurlus, who traveled with twenty-seven trunks, some of which had to be packed prior to being loaded on a truck for transshipment to his high-rise home. Fortunately, the motorcade's schedule had been set to allow for a lengthy disembarkation process, so that wasn't a problem.

The convoy was to include four policemen on gyro-stabilized unicycles, two armored stretch limos, plus a so-called war wagon that was supposed to bring up the rear. The vehicles and the personnel who were going to ride in them were assembled next to one of the spaceship's enormous skids near the VIP ramp.

The group consisted of people from three different organizations, including the city's police force, the Imperial Security Service (ISS), and the bodyguards who were part of the Legate's household. So the first problem was that of command, which Livius solved by declaring himself to be in charge and staring down every man who looked as though he might object.

With that settled, and time ticking away, Livius laid out his plan. The unicycles would go first, sirens blaring, to disperse traffic. The limos would follow, roofs closed, with the war wagon bringing up the rear. Attackers, if any, would expect Usurlus to be in one of the limos, so Livius planned to put him in the last vehicle instead.

Not counting the policemen or Cato, the chief bodyguard had fourteen people to defend the motorcade. By putting five in each car and four in the war wagon, he intended to make sure that each element of the convoy could defend itself if it were cut off from the rest.

There was barely enough time to review radio procedures and check weapons before Usurlus plus Alamy and six personal attendants arrived on the tarmac. Ten minutes later, sirens wailing, the convoy of black vehicles left the relative security of the airport and entered the maze of streets that constituted Port City.

Alamy was in the first limo, all the way in the back, sitting next to a couple of the Legate's servants. They were talking about how good it was to be home again as she peered out through bulletproof glass. Alamy had been reading about Imperialus in an effort to prepare herself for life in the city and to impress Cato. So as the motorcade pushed regular traffic out of the way, she knew that Imperialus occupied roughly five hundred square miles of land and boasted a population of more than fifteen million people, which meant that affordable living space was at a premium.

It was a problem Cato would have to confront very soon. She knew her master had been forced to borrow money in order to purchase her, and, having paid the debt prior to lifting from Dantha, was almost broke except for the money made playing cards with the *Far Star*'s crew. The upshot was that things would be tight.

Was that why he hadn't freed her? Alamy wondered. Because he wanted to save some money first? Maybe . . . But what if he was forced to sell her in order to pay his bills? That possibility filled Alamy with a sense of dread as Port City closed in around the car.

Having placed himself in the lead limo, which could be expected to come under attack first if there was an ambush, Livius had asked Cato to ride in the heavily armored war wagon with Usurlus. Then, if the motorcade was cut in two, each segment would have an experienced leader.

Now, as the convoy burrowed even deeper into the slum, groups of bystanders could be seen. They stood on street corners, where they cheered, waved enthusiastically, and held up freshly printed signs that had Emperor Emor's smiling countenance on them. "All of them have been paid," Usurlus said cynically as he stared out through a rectangular gun port. "That's the only way someone of my rank can draw a crowd. Still, that's good for the local economy," he added dryly, "and it's nice to see that the Office of Public Morale is doing its job."

Cato wasn't so sure. The whole charade seemed pointless to him, but he'd never been interested in politics even though he knew such things were important.

Meanwhile, a half dozen spherical media drones were cruising along fifteen feet above the motorcade, taking everything in. So they were in a good position to witness the full extent of the destruction as pre-positioned charges went off, and entire buildings tumbled into the street. Both were occupied, which meant that more than a hundred people were dead before the actual battle began.

The first rocket aimed at limo one hit, the resulting explosion rocking the vehicle from side to side, but heavy armor prevented the projectile from penetrating the interior. The doors on the right side of the vehicle were bent inward and jammed, but Livius discovered that those on the left were still operable and hurried to exit. "Come on!" he ordered. "Our job is to go back and defend the war wagon."

Four security men followed Livius out into the roiling dust as incoming small-arms fire began to ping the limo and the doors slammed shut. Alamy had never been in such a situation before, but it was obvious that the attackers were going to inspect the vehicle as soon as they could and would probably kill everyone inside. "Quick!" Alamy said. "Lock the doors!"

The other women were frightened but used to following orders and quick to obey. Alamy heard a series of *click*s as she crawled forward, slid in behind the wheel, and discovered that the engine was still running.

She had never driven any sort of motorized vehicle before; but she'd seen others do so and understood the controls. So Alamy locked the driver's side door, and was about to kill the engine, when the dust began to clear, and three men appeared in front of her. They were firing assault weapons, which sparkled as they raked the windshield. The bullets couldn't penetrate the glass but left milky white divots where they hit. Alamy feared that one or more of them would eventually punch through.

The act of putting the limo in gear and stomping on the accelerator was more a matter of impulse than careful planning, but the results were the same. Tires screeched as the vehicle lurched forward; two of the assailants went down and were subsequently killed as the car rolled over them. Then it crashed into the pile of debris that had been dumped into the street and came to a violent stop.

Alamy's heart was beating like a trip-hammer as the third assassin appeared to her left and began to fire at the driver's side window. That was when she spotted a row of buttons labeled ANTIPERSONNEL SYSTEMS and touched each one of them.

Alamy felt a sense of satisfaction as grenades sailed up into the air and exploded. A piece of shrapnel cut the gunman down as inky black smoke poured out of two dispensers located under the chassis and electrical discharges crackled all around the limo. Then, with nothing else to do, Alamy felt scared.

Livius was vaguely aware of the explosions behind him as he and four of his men sprinted back toward limo two. He was sorry that it had been necessary to leave the women on their own, but protecting Usurlus was his first priority.

Livius had traveled only fifteen feet when he heard a loud *whoosh*, and a rocket hit the limo just as the second security team was getting out of it. The explosion killed three people and left another on the ground clutching his right thigh. A fifth officer was down on his knees, trying to help the casualty, when automatic-weapons fire swept the area. It was coming from *both* sides of the street, and even though his men were firing back, Livius knew all of them were going to die if they remained out in the open.

"Get in the limo!" he shouted, and there was no need to repeat the order as a bullet punctured a man's throat, and blood sprayed the road behind him. He went down clutching the wound in a futile attempt to stop the bleeding. Having spotted the action, an ITV camera drone swept in to get a close-up, took a bullet through its casing, and exploded.

All of the survivors were inside the limo by that time, including the individual who had been wounded in the rocket attack and hit *again* as he was dragged to safety. The vehicle shook like a thing possessed as another rocket hit it—and bullets continued to rattle against the limo's heavily armored skin. "Put some counterfire on those bastards!"

Livius ordered. "Who's the best shot? Give him the sniper's rifle and open the moon roof."

There was a supply of both weapons and ammo under the floor, and it wasn't long before an ISS agent named Cantos was targeting assassins in the buildings to the right. He was a true marksman, and soon thereafter the rate of incoming fire began to slack off. Livius took the opportunity to contact the war wagon. A quick glance at his watch told him that about six minutes had passed since the attack had begun. "Livius to Cato," he said into the lip mike. "What's your status? Over."

The moment the demolition charges went off, and entire buildings fell into the street, Cato realized that they were up against professionals rather than a few wild-eyed fanatics. Knowing that the assassins wanted everyone to bail out, he insisted that they remain inside the war wagon while preparing to exit should that be necessary. Which was why Usurlus was wearing body armor and, at the Legate's insistence, was armed with a submachine gun (SMG).

Given his day-to-day demeanor, it was easy to forget that the Legate was a general, who, given the competent manner in which he handled the SMG, hadn't forgotten his early training. That at least was a positive as a rocket slanted down from a neighboring building, hit the roof, and exploded. The round failed to penetrate the war wagon's armor. But the angle, plus the point of impact, combined to tip the vehicle over.

As he was thrown down, Cato realized that the bottom of the vehicle was exposed and wondered if it was armored. Probably, given the possibility of remotely detonated bombs, but he had no way to know for sure. "Give me a status report," Livius demanded. "Over."

"They blocked the road behind us," Cato answered laconically, "and a rocket dumped the war wagon onto its side. But everybody's okay at this point. Over."

Livius took note of the last part of the message and knew it was Cato's way of saying that Usurlus was alive without revealing which vehicle the Legate had been riding in. Because even though their transmissions were scrambled, there was always the possibility that their attackers had the capacity to decrypt the radio traffic somehow. "Okay. . . . My team and I were forced to hole up in limo two. We'll join you ASAP. The ISS is sending a quick response team, ETA five minutes. Hang in there. Over."

If Livius was in limo two—then what about Alamy in limo one? To say nothing of those with her. Cato wanted to know but couldn't ask. He was about to respond to Livius when one of the team members interrupted. "They're right outside! Trying to cut their way in!"

Even as the man spoke, a spot on the back door began to glow orange, a fiery jet stabbed through, and the assassin began a cut that ran down toward the ground. It was scary, but the clock was ticking, and help was on the way. Cato turned toward the man behind the wheel. Though still in the driver's seat, the man was slumped sideways because the truck was lying on its side; he was trying to release the harness that held him in place. "Fire some grenades," Cato ordered. "That should discourage the bastards."

The driver flipped a switch and stabbed a button. Nothing happened. He stabbed it again. "It looks like the system was damaged. Sorry, sir."

Cato was just about to go back and fire through one of the gun ports when Usurlus triggered the emergency escape hatch mounted at the center of what was normally the floor.

Then, having swung his feet through the opening, he was outside firing the SMG.

Cato swore, followed the Legate out, and immediately came under fire from two assassins who materialized out of the swirling dust. The policeman was armed with a shotgun. He fired—and fired again.

One assailant threw up his hands as a full load of double-ought buckshot snatched him off his feet. The other assassin seemed to twirl as a couple of slugs hit him in the shoulder and turned him around. A third shot finished him off.

Turning to his left, Cato spotted Usurlus. The Legate was standing next to the war wagon, firing short, controlled bursts at a target the policeman couldn't see, as incoming bullets spanged all around him. "Grab that crazy bastard," Cato ordered grimly, "and get him inside."

All of the security men had exited the war wagon by then—and two of them took Usurlus from behind. Within a matter of seconds, he was stripped of his weapon, hustled to the open hatch, and stuffed back inside.

Cato was about to join the Legate inside the war wagon when a thrumming sound was heard, two heavily armed ISS air cars arrived overhead, and gunfire lashed down. There weren't all that many assassins left to shoot at, but Cato heard a whining sound and turned to see a unicycle coming straight at him. The rider was wearing civilian clothes and was clearly not a policeman, so Cato began the process of bringing the shotgun around and hoped there would be enough time.

The man on the cycle was guiding the one-wheeled vehicle with his knees, which left both hands free to fire identical pistols. Cato heard a bullet whisper past his ear and felt another tug at his sleeve as he fired. The buckshot hit its target, blew the rider out of his seat, and dumped him onto the pavement. The unicycle flashed past, hit a pile of rubble, and did a full somersault in the air before crashing to the ground.

*   *   *

Trey Omo wasn't dead. Not yet, anyway, although he could feel his life's blood draining out onto the pavement around him. He wasn't especially surprised. Not after a lifetime of combat. Dying was disappointing, though, especially just one year short of the retirement he had promised himself and the peace that might have followed.

Omo heard gravel crunch under someone's boots, blinked to clear his eyes, and saw the man with the shotgun loom above him. So he ordered his right arm to move, was pleased when it obeyed, and the pistol came up off the ground. That was when the shotgun spoke, Cato "felt" Omo die, and the battle came to an end.

Heart in his throat, Cato turned and hurried past the point where Livius was talking to one of the newly arrived security men. Limo one was pockmarked where hundreds of bullets had hit and covered with a thick layer of dust. Cato's knuckles made a rapping sound as he knocked on the driver's side door—and he could hardly believe his eyes when the window slid down. Because there, seated behind the wheel, was CeCe Alamy. Tears were rolling down her cheeks. "You're alive."

"Yes," Cato answered as he opened the door to take her into his arms. "And so are you."

Usurlus appeared out of the still-swirling dust as a chorus of sirens was heard, and an ITV media drone hovered above. He was unarmed but accompanied by three bodyguards. His face was drawn and serious. He nodded to Cato and Alamy as if meeting them for the first time. "Hello," Usurlus said vacantly as he surveyed the destruction all around him. "And welcome to my world."

It was dark by the time all of the wounded had been removed to hospitals, the dead taken to the district morgue, and the initial phase of the investigation completed. Legate Usurlus and his party were gone by then, leaving Cato and Alamy to find a hotel and get some sleep.

Having rescued their trunks from limo one, Cato hired a local to transport them to an arterial about five blocks away, aboard what normally served as a vegetable cart. Then, having paid the man fifty centimes, Cato hailed a ground cab. The driver was somewhat less than pleased when he saw how much luggage he had to deal with, but he managed to cram most of it into the vehicle's trunk while swearing under his breath. The final case went into the back with Alamy, which forced Cato to sit up front next to the driver. "Take us to the Fonta Hotel," he instructed, hoping that the hostelry was still there.

"Got it," the driver said as he pulled away from the curb. Traffic was heavy, so it took the better part of twenty minutes to crawl past the brightly lit spaceport and cross the river that separated the south side of the city from the more prosperous north. District Four was generally referred to as Far Corner because it was a long commute from the city center, which was where all of the governmental and corporate office buildings were located.

Far Corner was a lower-middle-class neighborhood, but still respectable, and the area where Cato hoped to find an apartment. Not so much for himself, because he could survive just about anywhere, but for Alamy. And that was strange because of the nature of their relationship. The truth was that, in the normal order of things, most slave owners wouldn't care whether their property was comfortable or not. But Cato did, and that meant finding somewhere decent to live.

The Fonta Hotel had seen better days, but that was just as well given the need to keep expenses down. A creaky android came out to greet the couple and help with their luggage. The red uniform the machine wore was a bit threadbare but otherwise presentable.

Cato paid the cabbie, took Alamy's hand, and led her into a dark, shabbily furnished lobby. The woman behind the reception counter had multiple bod mods, including a forked tongue, which had been very much in style six years earlier. Alamy watched in fascination as it flicked in and out. "Good evening," the clerk said pleasantly. "What can I do for you?"

"We need a room," Cato replied. "For one—maybe two nights."

"Excellent," the woman responded. "And how would you like to pay? With a chip? Or cash in advance?"

Cato had a credit chip embedded under the skin of his right wrist, but there was nothing in the account to draw upon. "That'll be cash," he said. "How large a deposit do you need?"

"Ten Imperials should cover it," the woman said as she eyed an ancient monitor. "Room 204 is available and looks out onto the street. I'll print a keycard."

The couple were up in their room fifteen minutes later. It was worn, but reasonably clean, and was a welcome sanctuary after the assassination attempt. Cato took Alamy into his arms and kissed her. "The women in limo one told me what you did. That was very brave."

Alamy looked up at him. Her eyes were huge in the dim light. "I was scared."

"So was I," Cato replied. "And we had every right to be."

"Who were they?" Alamy wanted to know. "And why did they want to kill Usurlus?"

"The investigation will take time," Cato predicted. "Five of the would-be assassins had nearly identical tattoos. All of them featured two snakes wrapped around a ring and facing each other at the top. Sound familiar?"

The design *was* familiar and for good reason. As one of Procurator Nalomy's kitchen slaves, Alamy had been required to serve the governor and her guests. In that role she had seen the family crest displayed on silverware, fancy china, and napkins. "The Nalomy family was behind it!" Alamy exclaimed.

"Exactly," Cato agreed. "Or so it appears, although I suspect that Senator Tego Nalomy and his staff will not only deny the connection but produce a fancy story to explain the tattoos. It makes sense, however—and Usurlus will have to be very careful indeed."

"What about *you*?" Alamy wanted to know. "You had a role in bringing Procurator Nalomy down as well."

"I'm small fry," Cato replied dismissively. "I doubt the Senator even knows my name. No, you and I have a bigger problem to confront, and soon, too."

Alamy smiled. "What's that?"

"We need an apartment," Cato replied, "and it's going to be hard to find."

"That's true," Alamy allowed gently. "But that's tomorrow—and this is tonight."

Cato kissed her, and a siren wailed outside somewhere, but neither one of them heard it.

Slaves weren't allowed in the dilapidated restaurant without their owners, so Alamy was waiting outside the door when Cato arrived. It was humiliating, but Cato seemed to be completely unaware of the problem as they entered the room together. Could he switch his talent off? Or was it on, and he just didn't care? There was no way to know.

After they had been seated, and ordered breakfast, Alamy placed two sheets of paper in front of Cato. Having requested a list of rentals in the Far Corner area from the desk clerk, and assured him that she was acting on Cato's behalf, Alamy had gone through hundreds of listings looking for what she judged to be the sort of place he might like. And, having a pretty good idea of how much money her owner had to spend, which apartments were worth taking a look at.

"You never cease to amaze me," Cato said enthusiastically. "Once breakfast is out of the way, we'll go in search of our new home. Something with running water, I hope!"

The list was a good start, but six hours later they had inspected more than a dozen properties, and Cato was depressed. They were standing on a side street, next to the overcrowded apartment building they had just left, with nothing to show for a day's worth of searching. So when a street tough spotted two people who clearly didn't belong in the area and came sauntering over, Cato was in no mood for a clumsy shakedown. Though of medium height, the man was muscular and armed with a length of pipe decorated with fake gemstones. They glittered in the late-afternoon sun and would clearly inflict some very nasty wounds were the makeshift club to make contact with bare flesh. "Hey, citizens," the thug said ominously, "you need a guide? You give me five Imperials, and I'll show you how to get out of here alive."

"Tell you what," Cato countered as he raised his left hand palm out. "You give *me* five Imperials, and I won't send you to jail."

The badge that had been "printed" onto the surface of Cato's skin glowed blue and was an unmistakable sign of authority. The street tough looked surprised, immediately began to back away, and turned to run.

Cato glanced at Alamy and shook his head. "This isn't Dantha," he cautioned. "You'll have to be careful here."

"I'll keep that in mind," she replied dryly. "There's one more place on our list. Shall we take a look?"

They took a look, but the basement apartment was no better than all the rest, and Cato's pocket com began to beep insistently as they returned to the street. Alamy watched him answer and saw a frown appear on his face as the person on the other end of the call did most of the talking. Finally, having uttered a series of "Yes, sirs," and "No, sirs," Cato ended the conversation with a terse acknowledgment. "Tomorrow morning, 0800 hours, yes, sir."

Then, having clicked the com closed, he said, "Damn it! Of all the rotten luck . . . There are thousands of officers in the Legions, and I get Tuso Inobo."

"Who is Tuso Inobo?" Alamy inquired cautiously. "And why don't you like him?"

"He's a Primus Pilus, or senior Centurion," Cato answered grimly. "And I don't like him because he's stupid, unimaginative, and ambitious. And that's a bad mix of qualities for any senior officer to have."

Alamy was still in the process of learning all of the nitty-gritty details about the way in which the Legions and the subordinate Xeno Corps functioned, so she didn't understand. "So you are going to report to this Inobo person? I thought you were part of the Legate's staff."

"No," Cato answered bitterly. "Usurlus has a hold on me but only until we get a chance to meet with the Emperor. That's when the Legate plans to use me as part of an effort to tell Emor how dangerous the Sagathi shape shifters are—and request more funding for the Xeno Corps. Something my organization would be glad of. In the meantime, I'll be on detached duty, reporting to the senior Xeno Corps officer in the city of Imperialus, and that's Inobo."

Alamy was in love with Cato but understood his faults and sensed there was something about his relationship with Inobo that he hadn't shared. "I understand why you don't like Inobo," she put in, "but how come he doesn't like *you*?"

Cato's eyes flicked, then came back. "I shot him in the ass."

Alamy's eyes opened wide. "You *what*?"

"It was more than ten years ago. We were on a stakeout," Cato explained. "Members of a rival gang arrived, broke into the warehouse we had under surveillance, and a gunfight erupted. We went in, and I was about to shoot one of the bad guys, when Inobo stepped in front of me. That's when I shot him in the ass. He never forgave me."

Alamy felt a desire to laugh but managed to hold back. But Cato "sensed" her true emotion and produced a boyish grin. "You don't feel sorry for me, do you?"

"No," Alamy admitted, as a smile claimed her face. "I don't."

"Okay," Cato allowed, "maybe the bastard does have a reason to dislike me. . . . Although it's pretty stupid to step out in front of someone who's about to fire a gun. In any case, I have to report for duty in the morning, and we need a place to live."

"I'll keep looking," Alamy promised, as the two of them started downhill. "If that's okay with you."

"I'd be grateful," Cato replied, and Alamy hoped it was true.

It was early morning, and a storm front was crossing over Imperialus. As Cato followed a steady stream of people up out of the subway station, he discovered that it was raining even more heavily than it had been twenty minutes earlier. Fortunately, the military base that took up all of District One, and was generally referred to as "Imperial Prime," was mostly underground, where the Command Center was safe from anything short of a direct hit from a nuclear bomb.

It had been a few years since his last visit, but there hadn't been too many changes, so once Cato cleared security, he was able to make his way to the part of the complex that was home to the 3rd Legion's staff officers, having made only a couple of wrong turns. From there it was a relatively simple matter to ferret out the office labeled XENO CORPS, CORIN, which, like the organization it served, was a relatively small affair.

Being a good ten minutes early, Cato took advantage of the opportunity to visit the men's room, where he ran a final check on his Class II uniform. Then, as he was unable to put the moment off any longer, it was time to confront Inobo in his bureaucratic lair. Hoping to get the unpleasantness over as quickly as possible, Cato crossed the hall and entered the office. A reception desk blocked the way. The noncom seated behind it looked up, and said, "Good morning, sir. . . . What can I do for you?"

"I'm scheduled to see the Primus Pilus at 0800 hours," Cato replied.

The other legionnaire's eyebrows rose incrementally— and a look of what might have been pity appeared in her green eyes. "Ah, yes," she said as she glanced at the screen in front of her. "Centurion Cato. He's expecting you. It's the door on the right."

Cato thanked her, made his way around the fortresslike desk, and paused outside the door labeled PRIMUS PILUS INOBO. Then, having rapped on the frame three times, he waited for permission to enter. It came the way he expected it to, as a one-word command. "Enter!"

Cato opened the door, took three paces forward, and crashed to attention. "Centurion Cato, reporting as ordered, sir!"

Even though Cato's eyes were on the picture of Inobo shaking hands with some dignitary or other that was hanging over the other officer's head, he could see his old enemy well enough. Inobo's relatively small head rested on a large muscular body. His skin was the same shade of brown as Cato's, and his head had been shaved to show off a dozen lines of scar tissue that originated just above his forehead and ran back along the top of his skull. Cato knew that each "kill row" had begun as a carefully administered cut, which, having been infected with kaza dung, had been allowed to fester for weeks so as to produce the hard ridges that the variants born on Kenor were so proud of.

Below Inobo's smooth forehead, safe within bony caves, two coal black eyes could be seen, both of which were filled with undisguised malice. The officer's nose had been pounded flat, his lips were pursed in an expression of eternal disapproval, and even though he hadn't said anything yet, his jaw was already at work.

"Well," Inobo said deliberately as he flicked an imaginary piece of lint off his immaculate uniform. "Jak Cato, a Centurion now, who would have believed it? But shit floats, everyone knows that, so I guess it was only a matter of time before you bobbed to the surface. Not via the regular promotion process, of course, because that would be impossible given your record, but via a *meritorious* field commission granted by a Legate who never goes to war."

Inobo's chair produced an audible sigh as he leaned back in it. "But who knows?" he asked rhetorically. "Maybe the next group of assassins will get lucky and polish Usurlus off! Where will you be then, Cato? Did you ever think of that? Back to Section Leader, that's where. . . . If you're lucky enough to keep your stripes.

"Meanwhile, I'm supposed to put you to work," Inobo added reflectively, "so you can wait in line to kiss the Emperor's ass. Fortunately, I have the perfect job. . . . We lost Centurion Sispus three weeks ago. The silly bastard followed half a dozen Ur suspects down into the sewers under Freak Town and never came out. You'll take his place. Any questions?"

Cato, his eyes still focused on the photo, had one. "Sir, yes, sir. What squad?"

Inobo had anticipated the question. He smiled evilly as he gave the one-word answer. "Bunko."

Cato felt his already depressed spirits plummet even further. Members of the Xeno Corps' bunko squad were charged with pursuing alien con artists, who, owing to their unusual capabilities, were often hard if not impossible for the municipal police to track down. More than that, the bunko squad was often used as a bureaucratic dumping ground for police officers who were considered to be misfits, fuckups, or screwballs. The assignment was clearly intended to punish Cato for past crimes, brand him a loser, *and* block the possibility of advancement.

Cato felt the anger start to build, and because Inobo could "feel" it as well, the Primus nodded agreeably. "That sucks, doesn't it, Cato? Maybe you'd like some of me. If so, come and get it."

That was what Inobo wanted more than anything else, Cato realized. A reason to court-martial him. So even though he wanted to accept the invitation, the Centurion managed to restrain himself.

Inobo nodded knowingly. "Very good. . . . Maybe you *have* learned something over the years. That will be all, Centurion Cato. See Section Leader Shani. She'll fill you in regarding the squad's current caseload. Now, get the hell out of my office and stay out of trouble. I'll have your ass for breakfast if you don't."

Cato said, "Yes, sir," and did a neat about-face. Four paces later, he was outside the office, having closed the door behind him. The receptionist looked over and grinned. "Welcome back, sir."

"Thanks, I think," Cato replied. "I'm looking for Section Leader Shani. Where would I find her?"

"In jail," the noncom replied casually. "Where else?"

THREE

The city of Imperialus, on the planet Corin

AS WAS HIS HABIT, USURLUS AWOKE ABOUT 10:00 AM.
He just lay there at first, luxuriating in the comfort of his
own bed and the sound of Satha's steady breathing. It felt
good to be back on Corin. And not just because of the physical pleasures that were available on the Empire's most important planet but also for the excitement of being at the
center of things, where a nimble politician could make a
difference.

The thought was sufficient to make him want to get up.
He was careful to slide out of bed without waking his favor-
ite slave. On his way out of the bedroom, Usurlus paused
to peer out of a porthole-sized window and saw that it was
raining. Then he made his way into the bathroom and a
shower large enough to accommodate a party of six, something it was called upon to do every once in a while.

Then, after a hot shower and half an hour spent in front
of a big mirror, it was time to don a robe and make his way
into the dining room. The Legate's staff knew he was up and
knew what he wanted—a cup of hot caf, a poached egg, and

a slice of dry toast. They were waiting as he sat down. A voice command was sufficient to activate the wall screen.

Political junkie that he was, Usurlus spent most of his time watching the news channels. And he wasn't surprised to see that all of them were busy rehashing the attempt on his life the day before. That was satisfying in a way since it served to let everyone know he was back and still worth assassinating.

But some of the other news stories were somewhat disquieting. It seemed that the warlike Vords had taken control of a rim world called Therat, a planet which, though at the very edge of Imperial-controlled space, was populated by Umans. It was a test, a way to gauge the Empire's temperament, and, therefore, important. That was the way Usurlus and many others saw it. But rather than send a fleet to confront the aliens, and force them to back down, Emperor Emor had agreed to diplomatic talks!

It was a shocking development that Emor's traditional supporters disapproved of, and the so-called pragmatists like Senator Nalomy supported, thereby turning conventional alliances inside out. Still, Emor was a tricky bastard, so chances were that he had good reasons for talking to the Vords. Or so Usurlus hoped as he finished his breakfast, gave a voice command, and began to play the last twenty hours of com calls on the wall screen.

Given the assassination attempt, there were lots of them, including requests for interviews from all of the major news organizations and expressions of concern from family, friends, and associates. That was to be expected.

What wasn't expected was the absence of any message from the Emperor, who was a cousin, after all, and the person for whom Usurlus had traveled to Dantha. Although there *were* expressions of concern from people Usurlus normally thought of as the opposition, including members of the so-called Combine, a group of powerful business interests. All of which was very confusing.

Usurlus touched a button, and Livius appeared as if by magic. "Make all of the usual preparations. I'm going out."

Livius nodded. "Yes, sire. And your destination?"

"The Senate."

"Yes, sire. The cars will be ready in thirty minutes."

The worst of the rain was over by the time Usurlus and his body double stepped out onto the carefully landscaped veranda forty minutes later. It was necessary to circle the rooftop swimming pool before the two of them could access the landing pad, where two identical air cars were waiting. One would carry the *real* Usurlus, and the other was for the android that looked like him, a strategy calculated to make the Legate that much harder to kill.

Four bodyguards were present—two for each Usurlus. Livius and a young man named Tupus waited for the Legate to board car one before joining him in the passenger compartment. Then, once both vehicles were ready, they took off. Car one banked away for the short trip to the Senate, while the other turned east as if headed for the spaceport and was soon lost in traffic.

The pilot in control of car one was an old hand at navigating the city's crowded skies and gave the sixteen-hundred-foot-tall Imperial Tower a wide berth, knowing that anyone who violated the security zone around it was likely to be shot down. The cylindrical building was not only the government's most important office complex but housed Emperor Emor's living quarters as well.

From there the pilot had to thread her way between a succession of high-rise towers and cope with the heavy air traffic that was typical of the city's wheel-shaped corporate and governmental zones, before coming in for a landing on an artificial island at the very center of Lake Umanus.

Having been cleared to land, the pilot put the air car down on a pad, waited for her passengers to disembark, and immediately took off again. Only the Emperor, and Senators themselves, were allowed to park vehicles there.

A covered walkway led Usurlus and his bodyguards toward the building that loomed ahead. The dome-shaped roof was sheathed in real gold and supported by dozens of marble columns, one for each of the worlds that had banded together to form the Empire more than a thousand years before.

Usurlus was well-known within the Senate, and the assassination attempt was only hours old, so the Legate had to stop and chat with more than a dozen officials, politicians, and staff members before entering the rotunda.

The men had to pass through a security checkpoint, and the bodyguards were required to check their weapons. The next half hour was spent talking with various people in the high-ceilinged hallways, and while nothing specific was said, Usurlus got the feeling that his initial impression was correct: The overall situation had undergone a dramatic change of some sort. It seemed as though his contacts were nervous, unsure of themselves, and admittedly pensive though none could say why.

In an effort to find out what might account for the uncertainty, Usurlus made his way down two levels to the senatorial baths, where the man nicknamed "the oracle" was generally in residence between 1:00 and 2:00 PM.

Because Livius and Tupus weren't allowed to enter the dressing rooms or the baths, they had no choice but to make themselves comfortable in the staff lounge while Usurlus entered and went straight to his locker.

Ten minutes later, clad in nothing more than a white towel, Usurlus padded out onto the blue tiles that circled the pool. Both men and women were present, some of whom were nude, either because they *wanted* to be seen or didn't care.

Usurlus fell into the first category and, having let his towel drop, eased himself into the hot water. Then, once he was acclimated, Usurlus followed the pool's curve back toward the grotto where Senator Paulis typically held court. Paulis was a big man, with a significant paunch and thighs like tree trunks. His entire body was covered with wiry black hair, and he sat with a towel across his lap.

Besides his ability to predict the political future, Paulis was a moderate, and therefore a man who was well positioned to communicate with both of the major political parties. As Usurlus arrived, Paulis was surrounded by a group of younger politicians, all hoping to hear one of his famous stories.

"Look what we have here!" Paulis proclaimed. "The man we welcomed home with bullets instead of bouquets. I noticed that you donated ten thousand Imperials to help the families of those killed or injured in the attack. Well done, my boy. . . . You have the makings of a Senator."

"Thank you," Usurlus said as he found the bottom with his feet. "It's good to be back. . . . Even if my reception was less than friendly."

Paulis turned his beady eyes toward his audience. "Perhaps you youngsters would be kind enough to give the Legate and me a moment alone. I sense he's ready to share all of his secrets, which I will pass on to you the moment he leaves."

That got a laugh, followed by a certain amount of splashing, as the Senator's admirers departed. A couple of them were rather comely—and Usurlus watched them swim away. "I see some things never change," Paulis rumbled as he dabbed his forehead with a hand towel. "You still have an eye for beauty."

Usurlus smiled as he turned to look at Paulis. "And your advice is still sought by all. Tell me, Senator. . . . What the hell is going on? I haven't been back for very long, but judging from what I've seen and heard, strange times are upon us."

Paulis looked around, as if to be sure that no one could hear, and nodded sagely. "All of us play our various roles, but the Empire rotates around the Emperor, just as planets must circle their suns. So if a sun becomes unstable, the entire system suffers."

"What are you saying?" Usurlus demanded. "What's wrong?"

Paulis shrugged. "Consider the last few months. . . . The Vords take possession of Therat, so what does Emor do? He agrees to negotiate. Meanwhile, a small group of separatists take over a small town on Regus IV, and he nukes them! For what? A century of legionnaires would have been sufficient to bring the rebels to their knees. And there's more, much more, none of which makes any sense."

Both men were silent for a moment. "So," Usurlus said thoughtfully, "what could explain such unpredictable behavior?"

"I could be wrong," Paulis allowed soberly, "and I hope I am. But it's my guess that Emperor Emor is insane."

The words seemed to hang suspended in the air, and Usurlus felt a chill run down his spine. Suddenly, what had already been a bad situation seemed immeasurably worse.

Like all of the neighborhoods around the circumference of the crater, Far Corner was divided into the lower slope, the middle slope, and the high slope. But unlike upper-class areas like North Hill and Crater View, residents of Far Corner couldn't ride public transportation any higher than the middle slope.

That created a situation in which what might have been premium real estate up along the rim of the crater was less valuable than property lower down, mainly because the people who lived there had to own private air cars or climb hundreds of steps to reach their homes. Not a pleasant process in the rain, which rattled on the umbrella Alamy held overhead and drained just beyond her shoulders. She lacked appropriate footwear, however, so her feet were soaked, and her shoes made occasional squeaking sounds as she battled ever upward.

Looking for a place on the high slope was a desperate strategy. She knew that, but having explored the lower slope with Cato, and the middle slope by herself, Alamy had come to the conclusion that if an affordable apartment existed, it was somewhere above. So, with three listings in hand and a crusty meat pie for sustenance, she had set out to conquer the heights.

The price was right on the first apartment, but it was too small, and dreary to boot. The second property was perfect in every way, but had already been taken, much to Alamy's disappointment. So she wasn't holding out much hope for the *third* rental, which was even higher than the others and slightly over budget.

Alamy paused, eyed a street sign, and took another look at the address on her printout. She was close, *very* close, so as she paused to catch her breath, she turned to look down on the city. It was still raining, and mist obscured the downtown area, so there wasn't much to see.

In order to reach what the owner called Arbor House, it was necessary to turn left off the public stairs, open a rustic gate, and follow a narrow path between a raised knee-high flower bed on the right and a well-clipped hedge on the left. Then, as Alamy passed under a vine-covered trellis, she saw the house uphill on the right. The outside was covered with white stucco, the structure was three stories tall, and the roof was covered with red tiles. She liked it right away but could see why it would cost more and knew the owner would be able to get full price from someone else. But she had come a long way and wasn't willing to give up without at least speaking to the landlord.

Alamy was about to climb the final set of stairs to the main entrance when she heard something squeak to the left and turned to see a middle-aged woman emerge from a thicket of shrubbery. She was pushing a heavily laden wheelbarrow, which produced another *squeak* as she came to a stop. "Hello . . . Can I help you?"

"I'm here to look at the apartment," Alamy explained. "Are you the gardener? It's beautiful!"

"Yes, I am," the woman replied. "I'm glad you like it."

"Is the owner home?" Alamy inquired. "I sure hope so after all of those stairs."

"You could have called ahead," the woman suggested unsympathetically, "then you'd know."

"That's true," Alamy agreed, "but my master and I arrived from Dantha yesterday. He has a pocket com, but I don't."

"So you're a slave," the woman commented evenly. "Your master must trust you a great deal. Choosing a place to live is no small thing."

Alamy felt a combination of embarrassment and pride. "Yes, I guess he does. He's a policeman and had to report for duty."

"Well, then," the woman said, "you should take a look. Come . . . I'll show you around."

Alamy followed as the older woman limped up the stairs, led her along the front of the house to the north side, and up even more steps to a landing. Then, having palmed the door lock, she led Alamy inside.

The apartment consisted of a large living room that looked out over the city and a kitchen that took up most of the far wall. There wasn't a lot of furniture, but what there was appeared to be in fair condition and would make for a good beginning. "There's a half bath over there," the woman said helpfully, and when Alamy went over to open the door, she was impressed by how clean the room was. "I like it," Alamy said honestly. "But I wish there was a bedroom."

"There is," the woman answered. "But to reach it you have to climb the stairs in back." The woman pointed, and now that Alamy looked more closely, she saw a set of spiral stairs back in the corner. "Go ahead," the woman said as she rubbed her right thigh. "I'll wait here if you don't mind."

Alamy made her way up the circular stairs and found herself on the third floor. It was a bedroom all right, with a full bath and a freestanding stove in one corner. All of which was quite charming. But the amenity that put everything else to shame was the sliding glass doors that opened onto a small terrace and a sweeping view of Imperialus.

Then, as if determined to impress her, the clouds that obscured the city began to part, and the sun appeared. Alamy could see the lake, the rotunda's gleaming dome, and the river that divided north from south. And there, grouped around the lake, were dozens of high-rise buildings, with the Imperial Tower standing head and shoulders over all the rest. The view was absolutely gorgeous, and would be equally beautiful at night, when the city's lights were on. Conscious of the fact that the gardener was waiting for her, Alamy took one last look and returned to the floor below.

"So," the woman inquired, "what do you think?"

"It's lovely," Alamy answered honestly. "But my master can't really afford it. Not unless we could get the rent down a bit. Is the owner here? I might as well ask."

"Well, how much *can* he afford?" the other woman wanted to know.

Alamy had been bargaining for things all her life and knew that to disclose how much money Cato had was to break the first rule of financial negotiations. But she also knew it was a fixed amount and saw no harm in being open about it. "My master can afford fifty Imperials a month," she said. "Which is ten short."

"I'll make you a deal," the woman offered. "If you could give me some help with shopping, and clean the first floor once a week, I'll rent the apartment to you and your master for forty-five Imperials a month. I live alone, you see, and I'm on a limited income, so servants are out of the question. What do you think?"

That was when Alamy realized that the woman in the dirty clothes owned the house. "I think it's wonderful," she replied enthusiastically. "Thank you! There's one thing though. . . . A favor I would ask."

"And what's that?" Madam Olivia Faustus inquired indulgently.

"Don't tell my master about the chores," Alamy replied.

Faustus looked at Alamy. The older woman had gray hair, pulled back into a bun, and knowing brown eyes. "So it's like that, is it? Are you sure he'll free you? And do the right thing?"

"No," Alamy admitted, as her eyes went to the floor. "But he's kind, and funny, and brave."

"Those are good qualities," Faustus agreed. "And I hope he's smart, too. . . . Smart enough to realize what a treasure he has. You have my word. And I'll feel safer with a policeman about. Now, what's your name, dear?"

"CeCe Alamy."

"Well, CeCe," Faustus said, with a wave of her hand. "Welcome home."

The Military Detention Facility (MDF) was located within the sprawling base commonly referred to as D-1. MDF's administrative functions were located in an unimaginative three-story structure located at midslope and having unob-structed views of the lake. But the "tombs," as the prison-ers referred to them, were located underground in order to limit the prison's footprint and enhance security at the same time.

So that was where Xeno Corps Officer Yar Shani was locked up, on Level 3 of the female "stack," where about 150 other minimum-security prisoners were housed. It was torture of a sort, because like all Xeno Corps officers, Shani could "feel" the emotions seething around her, and given the nature of where she was, that meant the policewoman was subjected to a nonstop bombardment of hate, anger, and fear. She could shut quite a bit of it out, of course, but that required continual effort, which was exhausting. Especially given her hangover, the pain generated by cuts and bruises suffered during the brawl, and the residual nerve spasms left over from the stunner bolt that had been used to subdue her.

So Shani was sitting on a fold-down metal bunk, knees drawn up to chest, battling both the emotional environment and the negative feedback from her own body as a uniformed jailer appeared outside her cell door. The ten-year veteran had a leathery face and a brusk "don't screw with me" de-meanor. "Front and center, Shani," the woman ordered. "Let's have a look at you."

Shani could sense the jailer's bored disinterest as she swung her boots over onto the duracrete floor and made her way forward. That was when the older woman compared her face to the one on a small pocket comp, confirmed a match, and returned the device to its holster. "All right," the jailer said. "Turn around and back up so I can put the cuffs on."

Being a cop herself, Shani knew the drill. She did an about-face, brought her wrists together, and stuck both hands out through a rectangular opening. "So what's up? Am I out of here?"

"Looks like it," the woman said noncommittally, as the flex cuffs wrapped themselves around the inmate's wrists. "A Xeno officer is here to collect you."

"Which one?" Shani wanted to know as she turned toward the door. Because if it was Inobo, then he would rip her head off before the inevitable disciplinary hearing, when he and a couple of other officers would remove it *again*.

"Beats the shit out of me," the jailer responded, as she waved an electronic wand at the door, and it slid open. "You can come out."

How many times had Shani said something equally unfeeling to people she had arrested? A thousand? Probably. It went with the job. Because to feel was to care, and to care was to compromise one's objectivity, and to compromise one's objectivity was to court a violent death.

Shani's boots made a rhythmic thumping sound as she followed the gleaming corridor past prisoners who knew she was a cop and hurled insults at her. "Screw you, bitch!" "Come back soon, cop!" "What's your hurry, freak?"

An elevator was waiting at the end of the hallway. It was so small that no mob of rioting prisoners would be able to reach the surface unless they were willing to travel two at a time. The women stood shoulder to shoulder as the door closed, a loud whine was heard, and the platform began to rise. Less than a minute later, it jerked to a halt. Having been ordered to exit, Shani marched down another narrow corridor to Interview Room 3.

As Shani entered the room, she was relieved to see that someone other than Inobo was seated on the other side of the metal table. She had never seen the man before but noticed he was old for a Centurion, a fact that suggested he had come up through the ranks. That impression was reinforced by the row of medals stamped into the upper-left-hand quadrant of the officer's clamshell-style body armor. Whoever the officer was, he'd been places and done things.

What Shani could "feel" told her even more. Strangely, given the fact that he was a Xeno cop, the Centurion couldn't shield his emotions. Because if he'd been able to do so, he certainly would have. Especially the momentary surge of sexual interest he projected as she entered the room. However, that was replaced by a very businesslike feeling of determination as Shani crashed to something akin to attention. She couldn't place her hands down along her thighs since they were cuffed behind her, but he knew that. "Section Leader Yar Shani reporting as ordered, sir!"

Cato eyed the woman in front of him like what she was: a professional soldier as well as a police officer. She had short black hair that fell straight around her ears as well as bangs that hung all the way to a pair of big brown eyes. They were focused on a point somewhere behind him. There was a yellow-blue bruise on her left cheek, her upper lip was swollen, and her right earlobe was missing. A wound suffered years earlier while battling a serial rapist. A scumbag who, according to Shani's P-1 file, had subsequently been gelded with his own force blade. A considerable testimonial to the officer's strength, agility, and skill.

But was she smart? Or just a troublemaker in uniform? Which was to say the kind of cop Inobo believed *him* to be? It was too early to tell. "Remove her cuffs," Cato ordered. "Then you can go." The jailer freed the restraints, slipped them into a belt pouch, and left the room.

"At ease."

Shani moved her right foot sideways and clasped both hands behind her back. Her eyes were still focused on a point directly above the officer's head, and her face was empty of all expression. "My name is Cato," the Centurion said. "Jak Cato, and I have been ordered to assume command of the bunko squad. It isn't the most glamorous group in the

Corps, as you know, having been sent there after a series of screwups in Xenocide. But I take the assignment seriously—which means *you're* going to take the assignment seriously. Do you read me?"

Shani said the only thing she could say, which was, "Sir! Yes, sir."

"By this time," Cato continued, "you have concluded that I must be in a shitload of trouble, too. Because why else would I be in charge of bunko? And there's some truth to that. . . . The difference is that if they bust me, it will be to Section Leader, and if I bust you, it will be to an infantry slot on a planet you haven't heard of. And I'm guessing that you want to be a cop. Is that true?"

"Sir, yes, sir!"

"Okay, then," Cato said mildly. "Let's make this a fresh start. Sit down and tell me what took place in the bar. You beat the crap out of a civilian before his buddies jumped you. Why?"

Shani sat down. Their eyes met. Something jumped the gap. Both of them knew it, and both of them were determined to ignore it. For the moment at least. "I'd had three drinks, sir. . . . That's when a civvie came over. He asked if I was a Xeno freak."

"So you were wearing civilian attire?" Cato inquired.

"Yes, sir," Shani confirmed. "I told the civvie no, that I was a member of the Xeno Corps, and flashed my badge to prove it. That was when he asked if I could 'sense' what he was feeling, and I said no, because it's impossible to know how a pile of shit feels."

Cato grinned sympathetically. "And then he took a swing at you?"

"Yes, sir," Shani replied. "I came off the stool, blocked his arm, and kicked him in the balls. He grabbed what hurt, fell to his knees, and was crying when I kicked him in the head."

Cato frowned. "Was that appropriate?"

Shani shook her head. "No, sir. The pile of shit had already been neutralized by then."

"That's correct," Cato replied sternly. "Plus it was stupid. As you learned when three of the civvie's friends beat the crap out of you. But I'm going to send an officer to that bar to find out if there were any law-abiding citizens who might have felt that your actions were appropriate. Then we're going to run a check on the other people in the fight. Chances are that at least a couple of them have criminal records. If so, we'll be able to argue that you kicked the pile of shit in the head because you 'sensed' his buddies were about to attack you. I have a feeling that Inobo won't buy it, but if the other officers on the board do, you'll get off. Which, all things considered, is more than you deserve."

Shani felt a profound sense of gratitude, which Cato was quick to pick up on. He smiled tightly. "You're welcome. Now let's get the hell out of here. We have work to do."

The Nalomy estate, 356 standard miles east of Imperialus, on the planet Corin

The sprawling villa was perched on a hilltop, where it was not only subject to the cooling breezes during that latitude's long, hot summers, but had sweeping views of the family's compound, the whitewashed town in which staff and hundreds of slaves were quartered, and ultimately the vineyards for which the clan was justifiably famous.

But the wine produced by the Nalomy family was little more than a profitable hobby since their most important source of income was the money derived from the business of politics. A two-way affair in which more than a dozen members of the clan provided their skills as council members, mayors, senators, and even governors in return for not only the salaries and perks associated with those positions but the money that could be made through influence peddling, insider trading, and contract fixing. All were crimes that carried heavy penalties if caught, but the Nalomys had excellent attorneys, and only a few members of the family had been sent to the prison planet named Sand over the past fifty years.

There had been one significant loss, however, and that was the death of Governor Uma Nalomy, Senator Tegor Nalomy's only child. A beautiful if headstrong young woman who was not only the person the elder Nalomy loved most other than himself, but was being groomed to become Empress eventually, when she had been set upon by a mob of angry citizens who had literally torn her apart.

The thought of that, and the memory of the small casket that contained little more than his daughter's severed head, was enough to start the tears flowing down Senator Nalomy's carefully biosculpted cheeks as he stood on the porch that circled the main house and looked out over the well-cultivated land. Property that would now go to a less-than-promising nephew in the wake of his death.

The reality of that served to rekindle the anger Nalomy felt toward Legate Isulu Usurlus for bringing his daughter down. A man who, by all rights, should have been killed in the carefully choreographed Port City ambush but had miraculously survived thanks largely to the efforts of a Xeno cop named Cato. The fact that the two men were still alive was nothing less than maddening.

But not for long, Nalomy promised himself, as a Tas bird rode a distant thermal higher into the sky. Because he was a patient man, and would *never* give up his quest for revenge, not so long as there was a breath in his body.

Nalomy's morose thoughts were interrupted as a tone sounded in his ear. He never took calls directly, preferring to have them screened first, so he knew the call was important. A single voice command was sufficient to open the circuit. "Yes? This is Senator Nalomy."

"Of course it is," the man on the other end of the call replied confidently. "This is Emor. . . . I'd like to get your opinion on something."

Nalomy was not only startled, but amazed, since Emperor Emor and he had never been on especially good terms. A schism that had widened during the months since his daughter's death. Yet here, on a com call, was Emor, seeking some sort of guidance. Perhaps the senatorial wags were correct. . . . Maybe the old fart *was* losing his mind. If so, Nalomy hoped to profit.

"Emperor Emor!" Nalomy said enthusiastically. "This is both a pleasure and an honor. I would be happy to help in any way that I can. What's the subject?"

"The Vords," Emor answered succinctly. "As you know, they took control of Therat, a planet that isn't especially important in and of itself but is part of the Empire. Simply put, the bastards are willing to discuss the matter, and as you may have heard, I'm willing to hear them out. The question is whether we should take a hard line, and threaten war, or sacrifice Therat to buy more time. As you are the leader of the Core World Combine, I would be interested in your opinion."

The Core World Combine was a group of Senators who generally favored a strong central government, wanted special rights for the founding worlds, and generally opposed equal representation for the rim worlds since that would dilute the Senators' considerable power. So if Emor was checking to see how much support there would be for letting the aliens have Therat, it was a good indication of the Combine's steadily growing influence and a sign that the Emperor was crafty rather than crazy.

"It would be an honor to provide an opinion," Nalomy said smoothly. "Generally speaking, my associates and I oppose spending the Empire's money to defend planets that continually whine about the tax burden imposed on them while demanding equal representation. So, much as I sympathize with the people of Therat, I believe that most members of the Combine would understand the need to sacrifice the planet as part of a strategic plan directed at strengthening the Empire's defenses. Because I assume that once our Navy is in position, it will send the Vords packing."

"Yes, of course," Emor replied vaguely, as if already bored with the subject. "You have been most helpful, Senator. . . . And I appreciate it. Tell me, how's your daughter? Well, I hope."

Nalomy frowned. What was this? A cruel joke? Or evidence that the rumors regarding Emor were true? There was no way to know, and given how powerful the Emperor was, Nalomy knew it was important to watch his tongue. "My daughter is dead, Excellency. . . . Murdered by a mob on Dantha."

"Oh, that's right," Emor replied hurriedly. "How stupid! I hope you'll forgive me."

"Yes, of course," Nalomy lied.

"Well, then," Emor replied awkwardly, "I'm sure we'll talk soon. Good-bye."

That was followed by an audible *click* as the connection was broken. Nalomy's wife was dead, but his mistress was very much alive and clad in little more than a very revealing toga as she stepped out onto the porch. "Oh, there you are," she said. "Lunch is ready. Who were you talking to?"

"A very strange man," Nalomy grated as he turned to follow her inside. "And one we need to replace."

FOUR

The city of Imperialus, on the planet Corin

IT HAD BEEN A LONG DAY, AND BY THE TIME CATO got off the subway and let the rush-hour crowd carry him up to the surface, he was dog tired. But rather than head for the hotel and some well-deserved rest, he had a long climb in front of him. Because the apartment Alamy had found for them was upslope. *Way* upslope, judging from the directions she had given him via their prospective landlord's pocket com. A selection that wasn't going to work.

So as Cato boarded the crowded escalator that would carry him and hundreds of other citizens up through the midslope area, he was trying to figure out how to say no without making Alamy feel bad, and berating himself for assigning her such a difficult task to begin with. She was still very young, had been raised on a nowhere planet, and had no knowledge of Imperialus. Sending her out to find an apartment had been half lunacy and half desperation.

The climb from the escalator terminal to the upper reaches of the crater's rim did nothing to make Cato feel better, so by the time he spotted the plaque that read ARBOR

HOUSE, he was both exhausted and grumpy. But Alamy was waiting to greet him, and the look of excitement on her face was such that any complaint regarding the climb would have seemed churlish, so he forced a smile instead. "Come on!" Alamy said excitedly. "I can't wait for you to see it."

The sun had already started to set as Alamy escorted Cato in through the garden, and there was something wonderfully domestic about walking arm in arm with her as she described her day. "So," Alamy concluded, "this was the last place on my list. What do you think so far?"

"I think it's a helluva climb—but it's a nice-looking house. Almost *too* nice. Are you sure we can afford it?"

Cato could have said "I," and Alamy took note of the fact that he hadn't as she looked up at him. "It's only forty-five Imperials a month!" she announced cheerfully. "Madam Faustus likes the idea of having a policeman around the place—so she's willing to give us a break."

That was true, of course, but Alamy had chosen to omit mention of the chores she had agreed to do to help offset some of the rent, fearing that Cato's pride might get in the way. Even though she was his slave, she was his lover, too, and might become something more one day. All of which made for a confusing mix of hopes, fears, and sometimes-conflicting motivations.

Cato took note of the flight of stairs that led up to the second floor but didn't say anything as Alamy opened the door and waited for him to precede her. He was both surprised and pleased by the size of the living room/kitchen combination, as well as the presence of some furniture, and the nicely appointed half bath. It was definitely better than anything they had seen on the lower slopes, and the price was right.

There was a problem, however, and a rather obvious one at that. "Where would we sleep?" Cato wanted to know. "I don't see a bed."

"Follow me," Alamy replied, with a smile on her face. "The bedroom is upstairs."

"Of course it is," Cato replied good-naturedly, as she led the way up the spiral staircase and into the room above. The western horizon was awash in pink light as the sun sank below it, and the rest of the city's lights came on. The combination was so stunning it brought Cato to a complete stop as he looked out through the front window. "My God, Alamy," he said. "It's absolutely beautiful!"

It was the reaction that Alamy had been hoping for. She felt a flush of pleasure as Cato pulled her close and turned to kiss her on the mouth. The moment lasted a good thirty seconds, and when it was over, he looked down on her admiringly. "You are absolutely amazing. . . . Both of us will have thighs like tree trunks before we move out, but it will be worth it, and I promise not to complain. Not much, anyway."

Alamy laughed, another kiss followed, and one thing led to another. Finally, wonderfully spent and still wrapped in Alamy's arms, Cato kissed her cheek. "Thank you, Alamy. . . . This is the nicest home I've ever had."

Alamy felt the same way, but for different reasons, which was a subtlety that not even a skilled empath could detect. The sun had set by then, stars twinkled in the sky, and two of the city's fifteen million citizens were happy.

Clouds screened the dimly seen sun as it cleared the crater's rim and continued to inch higher in the sky. As Usurlus left the air-conditioned comfort of his home and made his way across the veranda toward the waiting air cars, he could taste the bitter, ozone-laced air, hear the incessant roar of traffic, and feel the city's energy pulsating all around him. All of which was normal. Unfortunately, Usurlus couldn't shake the feeling that something was wrong, *seriously* wrong even though he couldn't put a finger on what the problem was.

Livius was waiting next to the first of two cars, along with a robotic body double who, the Legate suddenly realized, looked at least a year younger than he did! The fact that his body was aging brought a frown to his face as he said, "Good morning," and entered the vehicle that bore his family's crest.

Minutes later Usurlus, Livius, and a bodyguard named Maximus were airborne and on their way to the sixteen-hundred-foot-tall Imperial Tower. The cylindrical building was thicker at the bottom than the top, and in addition to serving as the Emperor's main residence, provided office space for the officials who actually ran the government's day-to-day functions.

Given its importance, the tower was always at the center of an airborne traffic jam, but rank hath its privileges, and the Legate's car was given a Class 2 priority, which meant his vehicle was allowed to swoop in onto the twenty-second floor after circling for a mere thirteen minutes. A very speedy landing indeed.

The entire floor was dedicated to the task of launching and retrieving official vehicles, but was always crowded nevertheless, and subject to what could only be described as organized chaos. Although the air car was allowed to put down in a VIP slot, the pilot was required to take off the moment that the official and his bodyguards were clear of the blast zone, so another vehicle could land in it. An administrative robot was waiting to lead Usurlus and his security detail into a brightly lit lobby.

The android was six feet tall, equipped with a face that was intended to be reassuringly Uman without being memorable, and spoke in a well-modulated voice. "Good morning, Legate Usurlus," the machine said politely. "My name is Civius. Please let me know if there is anything I can do to make your visit to the Imperial Tower more pleasant. The Emperor's secretary knows that you are here—and is looking forward to meeting with you. Please follow me."

With bodyguards in tow, Usurlus entered a high-speed elevator already occupied by a government official with a head-shaped artificial intelligence tucked under one arm, a heavy-gravity variant carrying a Kelf functionary on his back, and a hovering security drone that buzzed ominously as the platform rose.

Secretary Arla Armo's office was located only four floors below the Imperial residence, a surefire indicator of how important she was. Usurlus could have contacted the official from the comfort of his home. But by visiting her in person, he hoped to take advantage of a half-hour opening if there was one and slip in to have a few words with the Emperor. Then, if everything went well, he would bring Cato to a subsequent get-together.

The elevator slowed and coasted to a stop. Two security men were waiting to greet the foursome as they exited. Livius and Maximus were required to surrender their weapons, pass through a detector, and enter a lounge where a dozen of their peers sat waiting for clients to complete their business and leave.

Meanwhile, Civius led Usurlus past an imposing reception desk, down a short hall, and into a tastefully decorated office. Air cars, robo transports, and maintenance sleds could be seen beyond the slightly curved windows, with the tops of other skyscrapers probing the sky all around.

Secretary Arla Armo was a middle-aged woman of average height, who rose as Usurlus entered the room and circled her massive desk to greet him. The forward part of her head was shaved in the style expected of women on Opara III, leaving what remained of her hair to fall straight in back. She had wide-set eyes, a small nose from which her gold wedding ring dangled, and high cheekbones. The smile appeared to be genuine—as was the brief embrace. "Legate Usurlus," Armo said warmly, "this *is* a pleasure! Welcome home and please accept my condolences regarding those who lost their lives during the assassination attempt. The Emperor was very upset."

Not so upset as to call me, Usurlus thought to himself as he nodded soberly. "Thank you. . . . Those of us who survived feel fortunate to be alive. And the fact that someone wants to kill me adds to the urgency of my visit. I hope to see Emperor Emor as soon as possible."

"Yes, of course," Armo acknowledged as she returned to the other side of the desk. "Please . . . Sit down. I will give you the earliest appointment that I possibly can. Unfortunately, the Emperor has been very busy of late owing to the Vord landing on Therat, a nasty uprising on Partha, and the upcoming Emperor's Day celebration. Festivities begin tomorrow. Will you watch the processional?"

Usurlus knew that Armo was referring to the traditional parade in which a litter would carry the Emperor through the streets of Imperialus followed by angen-drawn wagons loaded with costumed revelers whose job it was to bombard the crowds with coins, trinkets, and toys for the children. The event was part politics and part hedonistic carnival. The latter was fine with Usurlus although he had no intention of celebrating the occasion with the plebes. "Yes, of course," he lied as he sat down.

"Good," Armo said as she touched a screen, and the Emperor's calendar appeared in front of her. It was almost entirely blank, and had been that way for the last month or so, but she couldn't share that with Usurlus, or anyone else for that matter. Even the slightest hint that the Empire was largely running itself would not only start a widespread panic, but almost certainly trigger a coup attempt and an all-out attack by the Vords. All of which were things that she and other high-ranking officials were hoping to avoid. Unfortunately, as each precious day passed, and the situation grew worse, it was hard to see how they were going to put things right without telling the truth. But for the moment, the charade would have to continue. "You're in luck," Armo said brightly. "There's a one-hour opening on the tenth of Tremen."

"But that's more than two months away!" Usurlus objected. "I'll be honest with you, Arla. . . . I came here hoping to see Emperor Emor *today*. Can't you slip me in somewhere? I would be happy to wait if that helps."

"That's very considerate of you," Armo allowed, as she pretended to inspect the calendar in front of her. "But there wouldn't be any point in waiting. The Emperor's schedule is not only full—he's double-booked in some cases. But here's what I'll do. . . . If someone cancels during the next week or so, I'll slip you in. It could be on rather short notice, however, so be ready to respond quickly." That wasn't going to happen, of course—but it would keep Usurlus on the sidelines for a while.

Usurlus sighed. "Okay, Arla. . . . Thank you. I'll be ready if you call."

After a couple of minutes of small talk, Usurlus left. Armo's chair sighed as she rose and turned to look out the window. Traffic continued to swirl, a long line of silvery security drones snaked by, and one wall of the high-rise across from her morphed into a new set of video mosaics. Each "tile" played a commercial intended for the high-net-worth eyeballs in the Imperial Tower. But the secretary saw none of it. The Empire was coasting, and eventually it would come to a stop. What then?

*   *   *

Alamy was still asleep when Cato tickled the bottom of her feet. She pulled her legs up into the fetal position and made a pitiful noise, in hopes that he would stop, but it didn't work. "Come on," Cato said as he bent to kiss her cheek. "It's time to go out and meet people."

Alamy groaned, yawned, and made use of a hand to shield her eyes. "Go out and meet *who?*" she wanted to know.

"Why the Emperor, of course," Cato answered genially. "This is Emperor's Day—which means that he will be carried through the streets of Imperialus. So this is a chance to see all of the silliness, marvel at how crazy our fellow citizens are, and find a good meal somewhere. Imagine that! You won't have to cook."

Alamy wasn't a citizen, not since she'd been sold into slavery, but it would have been mean to say that, so she didn't. Besides, the outing was clearly a response to her requests to see more of the city, which was very nice of him. "You're right," Alamy said as she swung her feet over onto the floor. "The Emperor would be very upset if we weren't there to greet him."

"That's the spirit!" Cato said as he brought her a piping-hot cup of tea. "Here . . . You can take this into the shower."

The tea, as well as the act of serving it to her, constituted still another gesture. Alamy rewarded Cato with a kiss before making her way into the bathroom. It was, she decided, going to be a very nice day.

Cato watched her go, marveled at how beautiful Alamy's naked body was, and remembered making love to her the night before. It had been a wonderfully urgent session, satisfying to both of them insofar as he knew, and a reminder of the important task he had been putting off. He knew he should free Alamy—and felt guilty about his failure to do so. And guilt was new to him.

Back before Dantha, and before Alamy, Cato never felt guilty. And why should he? If he spent all of his money in a succession of bars, got drunk, and woke up next to a woman he didn't know, there was no punishment other than a terrible headache, a bad taste in his mouth, and a period of enforced poverty.

But ever since Alamy had become part of his life, there was someone else to not only take care of but answer to. Even if she was a slave—and theoretically subject to his slightest whim. Was that why he'd been slow to free her? Because to do so would force him to confront yet another level of commitment? Yes, possibly, although Cato wasn't sure of anything anymore.

Cato smiled in reaction to his own confusion, heard the water in the bathroom stop, and went downstairs to pour himself a cup of caf. The questions could wait. A new day lay before him, and he was determined to enjoy it.

Much to Cato's surprise, it took the better part of two hours for the two of them to board a crowded subway train, ride it into the center of the city, and force their way through a mob of people to the point where they could claim a three-foot-long section of curbing. The mood, which Cato could "feel" in a way that Alamy couldn't, was ebullient bordering on giddy. People were laughing, dancing to the tunes played by street musicians, and sipping alcoholic drinks they carried with them.

Having positioned themselves to see the Emperor, it was necessary for Cato and Alamy to wait as hucksters, con artists, and pickpockets worked the crowd. Cato was off duty, and wanted to remain that way, so rather than scan the area for criminals, he chose to focus on Alamy instead. Even so, the police officer had to flash his badge at the more-intrusive hucksters in order to drive them away.

Finally, after a wait of more than twenty minutes, a peal of trumpets was heard as the first elements of the annual processional appeared. They were members of the elite Praetorian Guard, a military unit created to protect the Emperor, and whose members were drawn from the many legions.

The guards wore gold helmets with red crests, glossy black clamshell-style body armor, plaid kilts, and calf-high boots. They carried energy rifles crosswise over gleaming saddles so as to have them available at a moment's notice. The genetically engineered animals (angens) they rode were *huge*, uniformly black, and draped with bulletproof fabric. Their hoofs made a distinctive *clop*, *clop*, *clop* sound as the detachment passed, and children fortunate enough to stand in the front row stared at the enormous beasts in slack-jawed amazement.

The Praetorians were followed by a succession of angen-drawn wagons. They were loaded with costumed individuals, who were busy throwing coins and trinkets to the crowd. Cato caught a flying decim and gave it to Alamy just as a cheap necklace hit him in the shoulder and fell to the ground.

Alamy bent to retrieve the item, but wasn't fast enough, as greedy hands snatched it away. She laughed as a roar of approval went up from the surrounding crowd. "Here he comes," Cato predicted. "Emperor Emor."

Alamy stood on tiptoes, trying to see over the heads to her right, as a phalanx of armed security drones swept in over the crowd. Cato knew their sensors were set on maximum sensitivity and that the machines would kill without hesitation, even if that meant slaughtering innocent citizens who had the misfortune to be standing next to a would-be assassin. The machines made an ominous humming sound as their shadows rippled over the spectators below—few of whom had any idea of how much danger they were in.

But there weren't any assassins waiting to kill Emor. So no mistakes were made as the drones continued on their way. Meanwhile, as the Emperor's richly decorated palanquin hove into sight, it was subjected to a barrage of Imperial red flowers purchased for that purpose. Other flowers had already been thrown, of course, thousands of them, some of which were piled on top of the litter's flat roof. It was supported by four beautifully carved posts, each resting on the flat bed below, where the most powerful man in the Empire was partially visible behind gauzy curtains.

Four heavy-duty androids held the horizontal poles that kept the conveyance aloft, and when they took a deliberate step forward, it was always in perfect unison. The whole thing was meant to be impressive, and was, as the palanquin arrived directly in front of Cato and Alamy.

Then something unexpected took place as a cool breeze found its way between the surrounding skyscrapers and slid past the Imperial litter on its way to Lake Umanus. That was when the curtains flew, Cato caught a momentary glimpse of the Emperor, and was shocked by what he saw. "Alamy," he shouted. "Look! It's Fiss Verafti!"

As the curtain fell back into place, Alamy looked and caught a glimpse of a rather ordinary-looking man, whose features were known throughout the Empire. But she knew that a Sagathi shape shifter could morph into a likeness of any living thing having roughly the same mass that he or she did, and that like all of his kind, Cato could "sense" such creatures regardless of physical form. So if he said the being on the palanquin was Verafti, then she believed it, even if the Sagathi was supposed to be dead.

Alamy heard Cato swear, turned to see him lunge out

onto the street, and was barely able to grab his belt as a drone swooped in to confront the potential assassin. A cluster of gun barrels could be seen protruding from the machine's bulbous nose, and Alamy feared that one or more of them were about to fire, as she was forced to yell in order to be heard over the crowd noise. "Show your badge! Let the drone see it!"

Cato had already thought better of his plan to rush the Imperial palanquin and arrest Fiss Verafti. And as the drone appeared in front of him, he knew he was in trouble. So he raised his left hand, "willed" the badge to appear, and was grateful when it did.

The people who had been standing around the couple had withdrawn by then, leaving them to confront the drone alone, as the hulking robots carried their burden up the street. The drone hovered for a moment, as if deciding what to do, before finally sailing away.

Cato released a breath and was surprised to learn that he'd been holding it. "Damn! That was close."

"Yes," Alamy agreed, as the crowd swirled around them. "It sure was. Are you sure about Verafti?"

"Very sure," Cato answered darkly. "Even though we found a Sagathi hand back on Dantha, there was no body to go with it, and now we know why! The bastard cut the damned thing off and left it for me to find. Then, with no one looking for him, it must have been easy to reach Corin."

Alamy's eyes grew larger as the persistent roar of the crowd grew more distant, and they were left standing in an ocean of trash. "Oh, my God!" she said, as the full weight of Cato's words hit her. "Verafti murdered the Emperor!"

"That's the way it looks," Cato agreed grimly. "But nobody's going to believe me—and Verafti has the Emperor's entire security apparatus to protect him."

Alamy frowned. "What about the other Xeno cops on Corin? Why didn't *they* notice Verafti?"

"That's a good question," Cato replied thoughtfully. "And one that I can't answer. Not yet anyway. Come on. . . . We need to find Legate Usurlus and tell him. He's the one person who might believe us. That's why he brought me here after all . . . So it's worth a try."

Far above the crowded streets, in high-rise condominiums and apartments throughout Imperialus, the city's movers and shakers were in the process of celebrating Emperor's Day in their own ways, and Usurlus was hosting one such gathering in his luxurious home. His guest list included what appeared to be a random gathering of politicians, government officials, and corporate executives. But each person had been invited because of what he or she knew, or *who* they knew, which was often more important. So each individual was an ingredient in a social mix that might or might not produce the result Usurlus was hoping for, some sort of explanation for the political malaise that could be felt all around him.

So that's where Usurlus was, a half-empty glass in hand, when Livius appeared at his side and waited for the Legate to finish a conversation with a powerful business executive. The man was boring, so Usurlus was glad when the interaction was over and he could turn to Livius. "Yes? Is there a problem?"

"Cato is here, sire," the bodyguard replied gravely. "With Alamy. He wants to see you and insists that the matter is urgent."

Usurlus frowned. He knew that Cato hated parties and everything associated with them, which meant that the issue was urgent indeed. "Tell them to wait in my study," Usurlus instructed. "I'll join them when I can."

Because Usurlus had to pause and visit with various

guests as he crossed the crowded living room, it took the better part of ten minutes to slip into a hallway and follow it back to the study, where Cato and Alamy were waiting. They looked out of place in a room that managed to be both simple and elegant at the same time. The walls were covered with a tightly woven textile manufactured on Thoa, floating shelves supported carefully chosen art objects, and the dark hardwood floors seemed to glow as if lit from within.

A glass desk occupied one end of the rectangular space, and the visitors were seated on the skeletal chrome chairs that were arranged in front of it. Both of the visitors rose as Usurlus entered—and he waved them back into their seats. "This is a pleasant surprise," Usurlus said as he rounded the desk. "Livius said the matter is urgent. . . . And it must be since Officer Cato has a well-known aversion to parties."

"It *is* urgent," Cato replied earnestly. "Alamy and I were on Privia Street, watching the processional, when a breeze blew some curtains out of the way, and I got a good look at the Emperor. Only it wasn't Emor! It was Fiss Verafti. The bastard is alive!"

Usurlus felt something cold trickle into his bloodstream. If Verafti was alive, and posing as the Emperor, that would explain a great deal. But that was impossible. Wasn't it? He eyed Cato skeptically. "You're absolutely sure?"

"Yes," Cato replied unhesitatingly. "I would stake my life on it."

"That could be the case," Usurlus mused thoughtfully. "Because if we were to level such an accusation and be proven wrong, neither of us would survive for very long. I like Emor, and respect him, but he's absolutely ruthless. And if it appeared that we were trying to remove him from the throne, he would have us killed."

"He *was* ruthless," Cato replied flatly. "Until Verafti made a meal out of him and took control of the Empire."

"Point taken," Usurlus said, as the fingers of his right

hand drummed on the glass desktop. "It wouldn't stand up in a court of law—but there is some anecdotal support for what you say. Of the thirty-seven people who came to my party, more than half had reason to meet with Emor on a regular basis. But, as far as I can tell, not one of them has done so within the last month and a half."

"Verafti is afraid that he'll give himself away," Alamy observed. "But he couldn't avoid the Emperor's Day processional. He *had* to show himself or cause people to wonder why he didn't." Then, fearful that she had been too forward, she blushed. Neither man seemed to take notice.

"That's correct," Cato agreed. "And if he's been in hiding, that would explain why none of the local Xeno cops spotted the change. They haven't seen him and weren't supposed to."

"That makes sense," Usurlus agreed. "Who's in charge of your detachment anyway?"

Cato winced at the thought of taking the problem to his superior officer. "Primus Pilus Inobo, sire."

"All right then," Usurlus said as he came to his feet. "I'm of the opinion that the best way to handle this matter is through official channels lest we be accused of plotting a coup. Make an appointment with Inobo. I'll explain the situation, and we'll let him take it from there."

The prospect of sharing anything of consequence with Inobo filled Cato with dread, but he had a tremendous amount of respect for Usurlus's political acumen and gave the answer that was expected of him. "Sir, yes, sir."

As Tuso Inobo's official ground car pulled up in front of the Temple of Truth, he felt nervous, and with good reason, since it was no small thing to meet with a Legate. Especially one as influential as Isulu Usurlus was said to be.

But, even though such a face-to-face meeting could be

interpreted as a measure of his importance, it could be risky as well. Especially since Inobo's steady climb to the rank of Primus Pilus had been accomplished by keeping his head down, avoiding the types of decisions where things could go seriously wrong, and looking for ways to curry favor with his superiors. So the last thing Inobo wanted to do was allow himself to be drawn into the sort of political machinations Usurlus was known for—where he might be forced to take sides in a contest he didn't understand.

And making an already difficult situation worse was the fact that Cato was involved and would be present at the meeting, too. For Cato was frequently in the wrong place at the wrong time—and something less than reliable where difficult situations were concerned.

Inobo got out of the car and made his way across the street to the black-granite building located at the center of a large traffic circle. Unlike the high-rise structures that surrounded it, the temple was only three stories tall. And, as if to emphasize the sanctity of what went on inside it, the building had no windows. That, combined with its polished surface, gave the structure a somewhat ominous appearance. Inobo felt a chasm form at the pit of his stomach as a pair of curved doors opened to admit him.

The lobby was large and spacious, and the air was verging on cold as Inobo made his way over to a gleaming reception desk. Surprisingly, given the austere setting, an actual Uman being was there to greet him. The Civil Servant Corps uniform looked a bit tight on the woman, as if she had gained weight since it had been issued to her, but there was nothing wrong with her smile. "Good morning, sir," she said cheerfully. "How can I help you?"

Inobo gave his name, plus a conference number, and was instructed to follow an airborne usher. The shiny metal ball floated four feet off the ground and was the source of a gentle whirring noise as it led the Primus Pilus onto one of four lifts. The platform rose with more speed than Inobo thought was necessary, before coming to an abrupt stop on the second floor, where the globe-shaped robot led him off.

A few moments later, Inobo entered a wedge-shaped room to discover that both Usurlus and Cato were there waiting for him. That in spite of his effort to come early, thereby allowing the Legate to arrive last yet still on time. All he could do was apologize. "Sorry I'm late, sir."

"But you aren't late," Usurlus objected as he rose to greet the officer. "I was damnably early—which is a rare event, I assure you!"

After a brief forearm-to-forearm grip, Usurlus waved a hand in Cato's direction. "You know Centurion Cato, of course. . . . May I take this opportunity to tell you what a fine police officer he is?"

"Yes, of course," Inobo replied noncommittally. He was aware that Cato was on Corin at the Legate's request but was surprised to hear Usurlus speak of him so warmly, and suspicious as well. Was Cato blackmailing Usurlus? *Forcing him to say positive things? Yes,* Inobo decided. *Nothing else could explain it.*

"Well, then," Usurlus said, as the three of them took seats around a conference table that was shaped like the room. "Let's get this meeting under way. Proctor Theno? Are you ready?"

The proctor was an AI who, through various iterations of himself, was presently presiding over more than two dozen such meetings, all of which had one thing in common—a need for a government-sanctioned witness that couldn't lie, couldn't forget what had been said, and couldn't be bought off. That made Inobo even more nervous since he knew that whatever was said to him, and the way in which he responded, would be on record for however long the Empire lasted. Proctor Theno's melodic voice seemed to originate from nowhere and everywhere at once. "I am ready. . . . The session has begun. Please proceed."

"Thank you," Usurlus said as he looked Inobo in the eye. "Before Cato and I can begin, some history is in order. You may or may not have read the report I wrote on the subject, but I suspect a refresher would be useful, and it makes sense to capture the information in the official record as well."

Inobo knew that a report written by Usurlus was included in Cato's P-1 file but had never taken the time to read it, so he was careful to limit his response to a nod that was immediately captured by more than a dozen vid cams that were built into the walls.

Cato had clearly come prepared because his account of what had taken place on Dantha, including his pursuit of a shape shifter named Verafti, was succinct and professionally neutral. The account concluded with the discovery of Verafti's hand and what looked like sure evidence of the murderous Sagathi's death. And, based on what Inobo could pick up from Cato's emotions, he was telling the truth.

Usurlus nodded in agreement as the narrative came to an end. "So that was the end of it, or so we assumed, until yesterday. Cato, please tell Primus Pilus Inobo what you observed."

Inobo listened intently as his subordinate described the processional, the errant breeze, and his brief glimpse of Emor. Then, as Cato made his incredible announcement regarding the Emperor's *true* identity, it was all Inobo could do to keep from laughing. A reaction that, while appropriate given the far-fetched nature of Cato's allegation, would be politically inadvisable, given his subordinate's relationship with Usurlus. With that in mind, Inobo chose his words with care. "That's a very serious accusation if true. What would you have me do?"

"I want you to launch an official investigation," Usurlus

replied soberly. "Perhaps Cato was mistaken. I hope he was. If so, it should be easy to establish. All that is required is for you and let's say two subordinates to take a quick look at the Emperor. If he's Uman, you'll know right away. If he isn't, that will be apparent as well. Then, depending on your findings, the appropriate actions can be taken."

It wasn't that simple, of course. There was no way to carry out such an inspection without the Emperor's agreement. And by approaching the Emperor's staff with such an outlandish request, Inobo would not only draw attention to himself but invite Emor's wrath. Along with possibly dire consequences.

But he couldn't ignore an official request from a Legate even if he believed that Cato was either mistaken or running a con of some sort. So he would have to pursue the matter. But carefully—very carefully. "Yes, sir," Inobo said, with what he hoped was the right note of sincerity. "I'll do my best."

FIVE

The city of Imperialus, on the planet Corin

THE SUN WAS OUT BUT HIDDEN ABOVE A GREASY layer of smog, which the light breeze from the west seemed powerless to drive away. The result was an unrelieved simmering heat and a lot of short tempers, especially down on the city streets, where police officers were required to work. District Seven, which was generally referred to as the X Quarter, was no exception.

The teeming neighborhood, which was home to more than 150,000 non-Uman sentients, was located in the southwest section of Imperialus, sandwiched between District Six to the east and District Eight to the northwest. Its main claim to fame other than the diversity of the sentients who lived there was a crime rate second only to that of Port City, where the Usurlus motorcade had been ambushed. And, as was the case in all of the Empire's ghettos, the denizens of D-7 made it a practice to prey on each other.

That was why Cato and Officer Yar Shani were walking the crowded streets, looking for the Ur con man who had sold lethal Dream Dust to the quarter's pushers, and through them to dozens of unsuspecting addicts, six of whom had been killed over the last two weeks. "I don't know why we bother," Shani said disgustedly, as they stepped out of an Estengi whorehouse. "Why not let this Sesu guy do all of the work for us? Most of D-7's addicts are thieves, prostitutes, or worse. We're better off without them."

"I hear you," Cato replied as he paused to let his eyes adjust to the light. "The problem stems from the word 'most.' The rest are innocent of anything other than a physical addiction. They deserve our protection."

Shani wasn't so sure of that, but having been rescued by the Centurion and given a second chance, she was in no position to argue. So she blanked her emotions, and said, "Yes, sir."

"Save the 'sir' stuff for when other people are around," Cato replied. "We're working as partners at the moment— and you know this city a lot better than I do. So the last thing I need is for you to 'yes, sir' me as I make some damned fool mistake."

Shani, who had already taken a liking to Cato, felt her respect for the Centurion increase even more. Most officers, especially those right out of the academy, thought they knew everything. "Yes, sir. . . . I mean sure," she replied. "So what's next?"

Cato was about to reply when a voice spoke through the plug in his right ear. "This is nine-four. I have shots fired and two officers plus an unknown number of civilian casualties at the scene of a code 64. I need backup, plus medical units, and I need them *now*. Over."

Cato knew that a code 64 referred to a shooting, but there was no way to know what the circumstances were as he touched a button on the right side of the sculpted half helmet typically worn during warm weather. What looked like a transparent visor appeared in front of his face. It was light green in color and shimmered with reflected light. Section Leader nine-four's location had already mapped itself onto the Centurion's heads-up display (HUD), along with a glowing cursor that pointed the way. "This is eight-one with eight-five," Cato said. "We will respond. Over."

All sorts of emergency radio traffic began to pour in through Cato's earplug as the staccato sound of gunfire was heard, and both he and Shani began to run. Because they were empaths, both officers could "feel" the emotional slipstream that flowed past them as they followed glowing cursors across a street and through a busy shopping arcade. The police officers were running, so some of the onlookers were simply curious, but others reacted to the uniforms with resentment verging on hate.

But Cato had no time in which to analyze the emotional environment as he accidentally sent a stall owner sprawling, jumped a Cloque baby basket, and ran pell-mell toward the sound of gunfire even as battle-related transmissions continued to pour in. Radio discipline had deteriorated by that time as nine-four and his street cops fought what sounded like a one-sided battle. Cato heard the sound of an explosion followed by swearing. "God damn it to hell! The bastards have grenades. Put some fire on that upstairs window. . . . No, the one to the right. Got him! Nice work."

Then a second voice chimed in, and the situation took a turn for the worse. "Kevo is down. . . . There are only three of us now. We're trapped on the second floor and running short of ammo."

Suddenly, Cato was on the scene, as both he and Shani exploded out of a pedestrian pass-through, to find themselves in what looked like a war zone. Half a dozen airborne drones were on-scene, feeding live video to the news nets, as people all over Imperialus tuned in to watch.

Three police cars were parked in the middle of the street. One of them was on fire, and the others had been riddled with bullets, although the vehicles' armored skins had been sufficient to stop most of the projectiles. That was why Section Leader (SL) nine-four was crouched behind one of the cars, directing the battle from there. Sirens could be heard in the distance, but traffic was thick, and Cato knew that five or ten minutes could pass before additional units arrived.

A fully automatic assault weapon began to fire short three-round bursts from the tenement on the opposite side of the street, and bullets pinged off the cop car as Cato and Shani took cover behind it. A single touch was sufficient to dismiss the HUD. The SL turned to look at them, and Cato saw relief in the other man's eyes and "felt" a sudden surge of hope as the noncom spoke. "It's good to see you, sir. . . . Some Trelid merchants were running a hawala in the building across from us, an Ur gang decided to rob it, and ran into armed resistance. By the time we arrived on the scene, a full-scale battle was under way!

"Corporal Isser took a team in to put a stop to it, but some Ur reinforcements came out of the woodwork, and my people were trapped. I have seven effectives here on the street, and I could send a second team inside, but there are a whole lot of civilians in there, and it's damned hard to tell the good guys from the bad. So if we go in, there's bound to be a lot of collateral damage. I sent two drones in, but both are MIA."

Cato nodded. He knew that a hawala was an underground bank set up to evade Imperial taxes, fund criminal enterprises, and make the sort of high-interest loans that many residents of the quarter had no choice but to accept. "Understood. Use your people to seal off the area, keep the suppressive fire going, and give me your sidearm."

Nine-four looked surprised. "My sidearm? What for?"

"Because Officer Shani and I are going in there," Cato replied matter-of-factly, "and we're going to need some additional firepower."

Shani grinned wolfishly as she pulled the car's door open in order to access a riot gun—and having accepted the additional pistol, Cato stuck it down into the small of his back. Two extra clips went into his belt pouch as his partner checked her newly acquired weapon to make sure it was fully loaded.

When Cato's eyes met Shani's, it was like looking into a mirror. He smiled. "Ready?"

Shani answered by pumping a shell into the chamber of her shotgun. Cato grinned. "Okay. . . . Follow me!"

The police officers ran a zigzag pattern across the body-littered street as bullets flattened themselves against the grimy pavement and kicked up bits of duracrete all around. Then they were momentarily safe inside the doorway of the building, where a dead Ur marked the path Corporal Isser and his team had taken into the building.

Like all of his kind, the Ur had a low forehead, squinty eyes that could deal with lots of harsh sunlight, and the upward-curving tusks that marked him as a male. His head was resting in a pool of blood. "I can 'feel' some friendlies just inside the door," Shani commented. "No hostiles."

Cato nodded in agreement, pushed the blood-smeared door open with his right foot, and went in with his pistol at the ready. But there were no enemies to deal with, just a group of terrified Trelids. They came in various sizes depending on age, but all had sleek heads and fur-covered bodies. Most members of the group had been partially shaved, both as a way to keep cool and to emphasize their individuality via the elaborate patterns carved into their fur.

One of the residents explained that they were trapped between the warring criminals on the floors above and the cops outside. Cato motioned for the group to stay where it was, brought the HUD down, and eyed the diagram that would lead him to Isser. Then, having oriented himself, Cato drew the second pistol. With a weapon in each hand, he preceded Shani up a set of filthy stairs.

A dead Trelid lay six risers up, her eyes staring sightlessly at the distant ceiling, as occasional bursts of gunfire were heard from the level above. "We coming down!" a male voice shouted in heavily accented standard. "We live here. . . . No shoot!"

"Careful," Cato cautioned as he gained a landing and turned to aim both pistols at the group of Trelids who were descending the next flight of stairs. He knew that one or more of the refugees could be a perp and "scanned" the ethers for emotions that might telegraph a threat. There weren't any, but Cato was well aware that some "norms," as empaths thought of them, had a natural ability to shield their emotions. So it was important to be careful.

Meanwhile, having allowed the shotgun to dangle from its sling, Shani was following the clearly terrified residents with her pistol. And, as they passed within two feet of her gun barrel, she shot one of the females in the head.

Cato looked on in horror as a mixture of blood and brains sprayed the individuals around the dead Trelid. Some of the survivors screamed as they thundered down the stairs. "Are you crazy?" Cato demanded as he lowered his weapons. "You shot a civilian in cold blood!"

Shani looked at him. He could "sense" that she was hurt rather than angry as she hooked a boot under the body and rolled it over to expose an ugly-looking disrupter. Though worthless beyond ten feet, such weapons were devastating close in and perfect for intimidating a small group of civilians. Cato made a face. "Sorry, Shani. . . . How did you pick her out? I didn't."

"I got lucky," the officer replied simply. "I caught a glimpse of the rupter. Apology accepted."

"Okay," Cato said as he eyed the next set of stairs. "Let's clear the second floor and do it fast."

Shani grinned approvingly as the pistol slid back into its holster. "Now you're talking!"

Cato was halfway up the last flight of stairs when two

Urs appeared. The empath could "feel" their hostility and fired both pistols. Empty casings arced through the air and bounced away. They made a rattling sound as they hit the floor. Both aliens staggered under the force of the onslaught, and one of them managed to fire a burst of bullets into the ceiling as he fell over backward and landed with a *thud*.

Meanwhile, the volume of fire from the street below had increased, and bullets were punching their way in through the front wall, turning the upstairs hallway into a meat grinder. "This is eight-one," Cato said over the command frequency. "We're just short of the second floor and about to clear it. The units on the street will hold their fire. Over."

The incoming fire slackened, then stopped, as a new voice was heard. Cato recognized it as belonging to Inobo. "Cato? What the hell are *you* doing in there?"

"Enforcing the law," Cato answered laconically. "Stand by." And with that, he and Shani mounted the last few steps to the hallway, followed their cursors to the right, and began to close on Isser's position. Cato "felt" hate off to his right, made use of a pistol to gesture toward a closed door, and was rewarded with a loud *boom* as Shani fired the shotgun. A ragged hole appeared, the feeling of hatred ceased to exist, and the police officers were free to advance.

The graffiti-covered walls were riddled with bullet holes, empty casings lay everywhere, and Cato had to step over a dead policeman before he could go any farther. "Corporal Isser? This is eight-one. We're closing on your position."

The response was immediate. "Watch out, sir! The Urs know you're on the second floor. They—"

But Cato never got to hear what the Urs planned to do as a grenade rolled out into the hallway twenty feet ahead of him, went off with a loud *bang*, and produced clouds of billowing gray smoke. It appeared as if the would-be bank robbers had taken the device off a dead cop and hoped to escape under cover of the artificial fog.

Both Cato and Shani were blinded, but they knew what their opponents were going to do, and could "feel" the combined emotions of hatred and fear as the Ur invaders surged into the hall. The police officers sidestepped into an open apartment on the right side of the hall, thereby avoiding the massed fire that lashed out of the smoke as the stocky aliens lumbered toward them.

Shani fired first, blowing big holes in the wall, as she targeted adversaries she couldn't actually see. Then Cato joined in, firing his weapons in alternating sequence, as the Ur invaders came level with the open door. Bodies jerked and fell, thereby blocking the aliens immediately behind them. The slaughter was over twenty seconds later as the last Ur fell, Cato called reinforcements into the building, and medics rushed to give aid to Isser and the sole surviving member of his team.

Cato's face was grimy, his uniform was filthy, and he was bleeding from a superficial leg wound as he emerged from the building and entered the street. Nine-four was there to greet him. "Helluva job, sir. . . . Thank you."

"You're welcome," Cato answered evenly. "Here, I believe this belongs to you."

The Section Leader accepted the pistol and slipped the weapon into a shoulder holster as Shani placed the shotgun on the hood of a bullet-riddled patrol car.

That was when Inobo appeared. His uniform was spotless, and judging from the expression on his face, he was pissed. "You are in command of the bunko squad, Centurion Cato. . . . Please explain your presence in the middle of a street operation."

Cato thumbed the release on his pistol, caught the nearly empty magazine as it fell free, and tucked it away. Then, having removed a fresh clip from a belt pouch, he pushed it up into the butt of his weapon. "Sorry, sir," he said sarcastically, "I thought we were getting paid to stop crime."

Anger flared as Inobo opened his mouth to speak, but Shani preempted him. "Actually, sir, if I'm not mistaken, we nailed the guy we were after. . . . On the way out of the building, I stopped to take a look at the dead Ur who was half-blocking the doorway. We'll have to wait for a positive ID, but judging from the obvious physical similarity, I'd say the body is that of Hola Sesu. He's the perp we were chasing when the battle began."

Inobo's jaw worked, but nothing came out. Finally, having failed to come up with something to say, he did an about-face and left. Shani grinned. "I don't know about you, sir," the officer said as she turned to Cato, "but I could use a caf break."

Imperial Chief of Staff Rujan Rolari was a very busy man and for good reason. Because ever since Emperor Emor had begun to neglect his duties, Rolari had been forced to fill the vacuum. That meant he was very powerful, and had he been a more ambitious man, he might have used his position to further his own interests.

But Emor had chosen well, for his purposes anyway, since Rolari was loyal and more interested in process than power. Which was to say the sort of man who could be stationed in among the levers of power without fear that he would pull any of them.

So as another day began, and a constant stream of functionaries and androids came and went from Rolari's cluttered office, he was trying to stall. And that was no small task since the military wanted orders concerning the Vord invaders, the Ministry of Health was pushing for permission to inoculate the entire population with a new strain of disease-fighting nano, and the Senate had yet to approve the tax increase the Emperor had submitted a month and a half earlier.

As busy as he was, Rolari would never have agreed to see Inobo had it not been for the record of a meeting between the police official and Legate Usurlus that the Primus Pilus had submitted days earlier. A truly amazing electronic document in which the Legate and a Xeno cop claimed that Emperor Emor had been replaced by a Sagathi shape shifter! That was a ridiculous allegation, of course, but Usurlus had a reputation as a mover and a shaker, especially in wake of events on Dantha. Not to mention his familial connection to Emor.

So what if Usurlus took his theory to the Senate, where those who opposed Emor would take advantage of the opportunity to cause trouble? Such were Rolari's concerns as a robotic assistant announced Inobo's arrival—and the police officer was shown into the room.

Inobo was frightened as he entered Rolari's office, grateful that no other empath was present to witness his discomfort, and amazed by what he saw. Heavy curtains had been pulled as if to seal the room off from the rest of the world, and a holographic representation of a partially completed artificial planetoid floated off to the left. A daybed had been placed against the left wall, a heavily laden U-shaped desk blocked the path directly in front of him, and a floor-to-ceiling bookcase stood to the right. Its shelves were loaded with printouts, mineral samples, and electronic components. All of which were presumably related to some project or other.

The man himself was standing with his back to the door talking to a dimly seen full-sized telepresence as Inobo came to a stop. It was then that he noticed the absence of guest chairs. A clear signal that Rolari didn't encourage visitors and, when forced to tolerate one, wanted to get rid of them as quickly as possible.

As the conversation ended, and the telepresence exploded

into motes of light, the Chief of Staff turned to face him. Inobo found himself looking into a pair of extremely serious brown eyes. Rolari's bowl-shaped haircut, bladelike nose, and stern demeanor made him look more like a Reconstructionist cleric than a government bureaucrat. And the tight, high-collared gray tunic worn over black trousers did nothing to soften that impression. That was when Inobo realized that there wasn't any chair *behind* the U-shaped workstation either. "So, Primus Pilus Inobo," Rolari began without preamble, "it's your contention that Emperor Emor is dead, having been replaced by a shape-shifting sentient named Verafti."

"No, Excellency," Inobo replied as he delivered a jerky bow. "I believe no such thing. . . . But once Legate Usurlus and Officer Cato made that allegation, and requested action, it became my duty to pass the matter up the chain of command and seek resolution."

Rolari nodded. "Yes, quite so. The essence of the request being that a panel of three police empaths be permitted an audience with the Emperor for the purpose of verifying his identity?"

"Yes, Excellency, that is correct."

"The Emperor is a busy man," Rolari said judiciously. "*Too* busy for such patent nonsense. Still, we must do everything in our power to battle negative rumors, so I am going to pass the request along to His Excellency for a final decision. Assuming that he approves, a date will be set that is consistent with the Emperor's busy schedule. Do you have any questions?"

Inobo shook his head. "No, Excellency."

Rolari raised an eyebrow inquiringly. "Really? Then why are you still here?"

Fiss Verafti, who in his role as Emperor Emor was Lord of the Suns, Giver of Laws, and Defender of the Empire, was gnawing on a Uman arm bone. It had been lying on the black-marble floor for days, but he was hungry, and a piece of gristle was still attached to it. Like all Sagathies, he had a triangular skull that narrowed to an abbreviated snout that was filled with razor-sharp teeth. They made grating sounds as they scraped the last bit of leathery flesh from the Praetorian's humerus.

Then, with the bone in hand, Verafti made his way over to a display case, where the priceless Hammer of Thesus was kept, and made use of the humerus to smash it open. The hammer, which was said to be the same one that Emperor Thesus had so famously carried into battle, was equipped with a three-foot-long wooden shaft. Having been forced to sacrifice one of his hands on Dantha, Verafti knew the hammer would be difficult to swing, so he morphed into a likeness of Emperor Emor, thereby giving himself *two* hands.

That accomplished, it was a simple matter to drop the bone onto the floor, raise the hammer, and bring it down. There was a satisfying *crack* as the humerus broke in two. That was the shape shifter's cue to change back into his native form and suck the marrow out of both sections of the bone. That took a while, but tasted good, and left him feeling momentarily satisfied.

The last piece of bone made a clattering sound as it landed among the debris scattered across the once-pristine floor. The mess would have been offensive to the *real* Emor but didn't even register on Verafti's consciousness since he regarded tidiness as a waste of time.

No, his interests were centered around hunting, eating, and mating. The latter had everything to do with why he had traveled to the Imperial world of Corin. Because it was there, somewhere within the hundreds of thousands of documents that Emperor Emor had access to, that Verafti hoped to find information that would lead him to Affa Demeni.

Or, if she'd been killed, to visit the place of her death and send a hundred Umans into the afterlife for her to feed on. But, after more than forty nights, he had yet to find anything solid to go on. He knew Demeni had been captured in the jungles of Sagatha, thrown into prison, and eventually escaped by taking the place of a Uman corpse that was being shipped to the xenobiologist's home planet for burial.

Then, by following police accounts of murders carried out by what they assumed was a serial killer, he'd been able to track his lover to the planet Hava, and from there to Corin. That's where the trail seemingly went dead; although after many long days spent at Emor's computer console, Verafti had been able to identify a possible hiding place. And that was the planet Therat, where, according to local police reports, a space yacht had been found sitting near a remote farm.

There were no people aboard the vessel, none who were alive, anyway, although Uman remains were present. DNA testing had subsequently confirmed that the well-gnawed bits and pieces scattered around the inside of the yacht belonged to a wealthy couple who had departed Corin for Therat weeks earlier. And because the owners' pilot was missing, police were of the opinion that *he* was responsible for the grisly murders, but Verafti had a different theory.

He was of the opinion that Demeni had taken the pilot's place on Corin, killed the Umans during the lengthy voyage to Therat, and eaten them. Mainly because that was what *he* would have done. And that was why Verafti had agreed to negotiate with the Vords regarding Therat's status. He might want to visit the planet in the very near future, and an all-out war would make that impossible.

Still, there was no way to be sure, so rather than run off to Therat, Verafti was determined to pore over all of the relevant files in case there was evidence that pointed in a different direction.

Meanwhile, as time passed, it was becoming more and

more difficult to maintain the role he was playing. Weeks had passed since anyone other than maintenance androids had been allowed to enter the Imperial residence, governmental problems were piling up, and Verafti didn't have the foggiest notion of how to cope with them.

A chime sounded, and Verafti turned in the direction of the sound, as Chief of Staff Rolari's face appeared on vid screens throughout the residence. "Good afternoon, Excellency," the image said unctuously. "I'm sorry to bother you, but there is what may be an urgent matter requiring your personal attention. Might I have permission to speak face-to-face with Your Imperial Majesty?"

All of the cameras in the residence had been turned off weeks earlier, leaving Verafti free to pick up a priceless Mirathian egg-jewel from the mess at his feet and hurl it at the nearest vid panel. The shape shifter's aim was good, and the screen shattered, but Rolari's doleful countenance continued to eye Verafti from other vantage points throughout the sprawling residence. The imposter had seen that look before and knew that if he wanted more time in which to find Demeni, he'd have to find a way to placate Rolari, a man who, though annoying, had been a useful tool in the wake of Emor's death and would have to be tolerated for a while longer.

So he made his way over to a screen, where the camera would show nothing more than the blank wall behind him, selected one of three togas that were draped over a bust of the goddess Prilleus, and morphed into a naked Emor. Then, having wrapped the garment around his torso, he gave two voice commands. "Camera on. . . . Com circuit on."

A chime sounded, Verafti saw Rolari react, and knew he was on-screen. "It's no bother," Verafti said engagingly. "I appreciate the energy with which you pursue your considerable responsibilities. Please join me in my office for caf tomorrow morning. We will discuss the matter then."

Rolari bowed, the screen snapped to black, and Verafti returned to work. Demeni was out there somewhere, she *had* to be, and he would find her.

It was late afternoon, and Alamy was waiting next to the seldom-used landing pad located on the hillside behind Arbor House as an air car with police markings swept in from the west and circled the area as if to make sure it was in the right place. Then, with the skill of a person used to putting her aircraft down in cramped quarters, the pilot dropped the car onto the faded X that marked the center of the pad.

The call had come in to Madam Faustus and been relayed to Alamy, who was busy cleaning the other woman's house at the time. There had been a gunfight. Cato had been hit and was being flown home.

The wound was superficial, or so Cato claimed, and the fact that he wasn't in the hospital seemed to support that contention. But Alamy was anxious nevertheless, and grateful when the skids touched down and a door swung open. That was when a female police officer emerged and stood to one side as Cato got out, as if ready to help him if that was necessary. She had short black hair, an athletic body, and a proprietary manner.

Then, much to Alamy's surprise, the air car's engines began to spool up, and it took off with blue lights flashing as it flew into an angry-looking sunset. "Alamy!" Cato exclaimed cheerfully, as she came forward. "This is Officer Yar Shani. . . . She was with me during the dustup earlier today. She had my back, and I figured the least we could do was offer her some dinner. I hope that's okay."

It *wasn't* okay, even if it should be, and for all sorts of reasons. Cato normally kissed her when he came home and clearly wasn't going to do so in front of Officer Shani, who was not only pretty but staring at Alamy with open curiosity. "Centurion Cato tells me you're from Dantha," Shani said evenly. "I can see why he bought you."

Alamy blushed, felt flustered, and managed a curtsy. "Yes, ma'am. Now, if you'll excuse me, I'll see about some dinner." And with that, she turned to hurry away.

Cato knew Alamy was upset but wasn't sure what he'd done wrong, as Shani took his arm. "This is a beautiful location," she said soothingly. "How did you manage to find it?"

Dinner would have been an unmitigated disaster if it hadn't been for Madam Faustus, who not only produced two steaks from her freezer but helped Alamy prepare two delicious side dishes while Cato and Shani sat on the roof and looked out over the city. "Don't worry, dear," the older woman advised kindly. "He's a smart man, and he'll make the right decision in the end."

Alamy hoped it was true, but had her doubts, as she carried a large tray up to the roof. Because as she served the food, it was easy to see that Shani was everything she wasn't. The other woman was worldly the way Cato was worldly, tough in the same way that he was tough, and as much a part of his work as the gun he wore. All of which were qualities that Alamy could never hope to compete with as a free woman, never mind a slave.

"This looks wonderful," Cato said sincerely, as the steaks were served. "I don't know how you managed to cook such a wonderful meal on short notice, but we're grateful. Where's your plate? Can I bring it up?"

"Madam Faustus helped me cook the meal, and I'm having dinner with her," Alamy temporized. "I'll be back to collect the plates later on."

Cato looked doubtful. "Okay, if you say so. . . . But I was

planning to tell Officer Shani some stories about our experiences on Dantha—and it's your job to keep gross exaggerations to a minimum."

"Fortunately, I'm an empath," Shani put in meaningfully, as her eyes locked with Alamy's. "So if Centurion Cato attempts to lie, I'll know. Enjoy your dinner."

Alamy nearly burst into tears and fled below.

Shani cut into her steak, took a bite, and nodded approvingly. "It was a difficult day—but this is a great way to end it."

"Yes," Cato agreed contentedly as he propped his leg up on a chair. "There are times when it simply feels good to be alive."

After weeks of reclusiveness, the Emperor was coming to work! Word of that miraculous event spread like wildfire, so that as Verafti stepped off the elevator and made his way toward the suite of offices located one floor below the Imperial residence, there were more people around than usual. All were hoping to catch a glimpse of Emor, so they could tell their friends and associates.

Verafti didn't know most of them, of course, but had learned that all he had to do was say something nice to keep most Umans happy, especially given who they believed him to be. So as he made his way across the elevator lobby and through the double doors into the reception area beyond, Verafti kept a smile on Emor's face and scattered greetings far and wide.

It was a very successful strategy, and one that allowed Verafti to breeze through the outer area and into his office without being sucked into the type of conversation that might give him away. He was intentionally ten minutes late, which meant that Rolari was there waiting for him, making it impossible for other officials to try to slip in. The office was at least three times larger than it needed to be, filled with all manner of expensive mementos, and organized around a massive desk that the real Emor actually used. Rolari was already on his feet and bowed deeply as the Emperor entered. "Good morning, Excellency, I hope you slept well."

Though predictable, Rolari was no fool, and Verafti could feel the Uman's agile mind churning through theories that would explain Emor's extended absences. Was the question related to sleep a tangential way of addressing the Emperor's health? And the possibility that he wasn't feeling well? Yes, Verafti thought that it was.

There was something more as well because Rolari was clearly staring at him, as if searching for flaws. Did the Uman suspect? If so, the shifter was about to take part in a very dangerous conversation—and might be forced to fight his way out. Verafti managed to produce a smile as he circled the enormous desk to the thronelike chair stationed behind it. "I slept well, thank you, and that's why I'm late. Please accept my apologies."

Verafti knew that any sort of consideration from the Emperor, no matter how minor, was sufficient to put most Umans in a good mood. And while probably incapable of being truly happy, even Rolari was susceptible to such manipulations. He produced a grimace that was intended to be a smile. "No apologies are required, sire. . . . I know how busy you are."

The chair sighed softly as it accepted Verafti's weight. "So," he began, "there is an urgent matter that you wish to discuss with me."

Rolari was about to explain when a delectable-looking slave girl entered the office holding a tray. Just looking at the Uman made Verafti's stomach growl, and he hoped Rolari couldn't hear the noise. Six nights had passed since his last substantial meal—and it would soon be necessary to feed again.

Once the caf had been served and pastries laid out, the girl left, and Rolari had an opportunity to speak. "Forgive me if I sound somewhat awkward," he began, "but the matter at hand is quite unusual—and I would understand if it were to upset you."

Emor liked caf, and Verafti didn't, but he managed to swallow a mouthful anyway. He raised an eyebrow. "Never fear, my friend. . . . Whatever the mysterious matter is, I will resist the temptation to kill the messenger." That wasn't entirely true, of course, since Verafti would gladly rip Rolari's throat out if such a thing was necessary, but the Uman smiled gratefully.

"Thank you, Excellency. The issue is this. . . . During the recent Emperor's Day processional, a variant named Cato was in the crowd and saw you."

Verafti felt a stab of fear. Naturally produced stimulants entered his bloodstream, his heart began to beat faster, and it took an act of will to hold the cup steady. Cato! Of all people. . . . The one Uman he was afraid of—and for good reason. Because the Xeno cop was not only brave and tenacious but a little bit crazy. And it was that "I don't give a shit—take no prisoners" attitude that kept him in trouble *and* made him more effective than many of his peers. So the fact that he was on Corin, and had been in the crowd, constituted *very* bad news. "Thousands of people saw me," Verafti said carefully. "What's your point?"

"Well," Rolari replied awkwardly, "Officer Cato is an empath, and having seen you, he claims that you are a Sagathi shape shifter named Fiss Verafti. I checked, and there *is* such an individual, or was prior to his death on Dantha. A circumstance that casts considerable doubt on Officer Cato's claim.

"Still," Rolari continued, "this Cato person has Legate Usurlus's ear, and he took the allegation to a police official, who brought the matter to my attention."

"I see," Verafti said gravely as he put the half-empty cup down. He knew Usurlus from Dantha—and had reason to fear the Legate as well. "So what do you propose?"

Rolari was still on his feet. He shrugged. "It's ridiculous, I know that, but if we don't put the matter to rest, rumors could begin to circulate. The opposition party would like nothing more than to raise doubts regarding your identity!

"So, to forestall that possibility, we could invite the police official and two of his Xeno cops to meet with you. I'm told that a single glance would be sufficient to establish your identity, so the whole thing would last no more than five minutes, and we could put the allegation behind us."

Verafti had no intention of submitting himself to such scrutiny but couldn't say that, and rubbed his chin as if giving the matter serious thought. "It's annoying, I'd be lying if I said it wasn't, but you're correct about the rumors. So instruct Secretary Armo to schedule the meeting for a couple of weeks out. I'd do it sooner, but there's the Vord thing to consider—not to mention the tax bill."

To the best of Rolari's knowledge, Emor hadn't done a lick of work on either one of those critical matters, but he couldn't say that, and didn't. "Yes, Excellency. . . . It shall be as you say."

"Good!" Verafti said as he came to his feet and circled the desk. "I'm glad we had our little talk. . . . I plan to work from the residence today. Please inform my staff."

Rolari, who had been hoping to get some real work done, bowed. "Yes, sire, please let me know if I can be of assistance." But Verafti was gone by then—so the offer went unheard.

SIX

The city of Imperialus, on the planet Corin

IT WAS JUST AFTER 3:00 AM, AND WITH THE EXCEP-
tion of computer-controlled delivery trucks, the streets of
Imperialus were empty of traffic as Senator Tegor Nalomy's
shiny black limo carried him out of the government zone,
through the corporate sector, and into the brightly lit X
Quarter.

In contrast with the rest of the city, the X was not only
open for business but vibrantly alive. The streets were
crowded with dilapidated pedicabs, speeding unicycles,
palanquins carried by slaves, angen-drawn vegetable carts,
taxicabs wrapped in gently morphing advertising, drug
dealers on roller blades, and even a few limos like Nalomy's.
Most were occupied by successful criminals rather than
politicians—however, some observers maintained that there
wasn't much difference between the two.

Nalomy knew that he shouldn't like the X, that it was
supposed to be beneath him, but the truth was that he glo-
ried in the rawness of the quarter and missed the days when a
younger version of himself had been free to stroll the streets,

explore the bars, and purchase whatever type of sex he happened to be in the mood for. There had been less money back then, and no power to speak of, but he'd been happier.

The memories of that time caused Nalomy to roll the window down an inch or so. Just enough so he could inhale the rich bouquet of broiled meat, the harsh tang of charcoal briquettes, and the pervasive scent of incense that clung to the X like perfume on a cheap whore.

As Nalomy took in the sights, smells, and sounds of the X Quarter, his driver took a hard right turn and steered the heavy limo down a narrow street hung with colored lights and lined with small shops that sold everything from groceries to electronics. Then, consistent with the instructions he'd been given earlier, the driver took a left and was forced to brake as a pair of Urs came forward to greet him. Neither appeared to be armed with anything more than cudgels, but the driver knew that appearances could be deceiving. Especially given the loose-fitting leather jerkins that both ruffians wore. "Who you?" the Ur at the driver's side window demanded gruffly.

"That's none of your fucking business," the driver replied haughtily, his right hand on the machine pistol resting next to him. "My employer has an appointment with Caliph Emsay—so open the door and let us in."

It was obvious that the Ur didn't like to be spoken to in that manner, and his left hand was already drifting back toward the small of his back as he mumbled some barely audible words into the boom mike positioned in front of his thick, rubbery lips.

But apparently the answer wasn't what the guard had been hoping for because rather than pull whatever weapon was hidden in the small of his back, he was forced to wave the vehicle through instead. "You go," the Ur said as he backed away. "But you be careful. I watch you."

The driver laughed dismissively and took his foot off the brake as a corrugated steel door rumbled up out of the way. Seconds later, the limo was inside what had originally been a factory but had been put to a variety of other uses during recent years. Now it served as home for a Cloque criminal named Chavor Emsay.

As the door closed behind his vehicle, Nalomy felt something akin to lead trickle in to fill the bottom of his stomach. Because powerful though he might be outside of the building, Emsay ruled the interior and had a reputation as a cold-blooded killer. Which was why Nalomy was there to see him.

Nalomy waited for the driver to open the door, got out, and took a quick look around. The ceilings were two stories high, there were gloomy corners all around, and the floors were made out of oil-stained duracrete. Other vehicles were parked near his, large pieces of machinery crouched here and there, and the noise from outside was so muted as to be barely audible. "Senator Nalomy?" a female voice said. "My name is Zether. . . . Please allow me to bid you welcome on Caliph Emsay's behalf."

Nalomy knew that the Cloque home world had been ruled by a succession of Caliphs prior to being brought under Imperial rule—which made the title Emsay had chosen for himself little more than an affectation. Did it have resonance with the local Cloque community? Yes, quite possibly, not that it mattered.

What *was* worthy of his attention was the crime lord's emissary. She was young, curvy, and dressed like the stripper she had once been. A look she had chosen for herself, or so

Nalomy assumed, since a display of bare skin would be of little interest to a Cloque. Her clothing consisted of a gauzy shimmer provided by a field generator concealed inside the elaborate necklace she wore. The device was programmed to reveal various parts of her anatomy in random order. At the moment, her left breast and right leg were on display.

Zether saw the way Nalomy was looking at her, took pleasure from it, and offered an arm. "If you would be so kind as to accompany me—the Caliph is waiting."

Nalomy took her arm and, with two bodyguards trailing along behind, allowed himself to be led through a maze of brooding machinery to the foot of a ramp, where a pair of heavily armed Ur stood waiting. "Your bodyguards must wait here," Zether said as she brought the group to a halt. "I can assure you that there is no one other than the Caliph within."

Nalomy directed a look to his security detail, gave a nod, and followed Zether up the ramp and into a room so palatial it would have done justice to Emperor Emor himself. Hundreds of yards of brightly colored synsilk had been artfully draped over poles that crisscrossed the high ceiling, previously drab walls were covered with Cloque tapestries, and most of the duracrete floor was hidden under expensive throw rugs.

And there, on the far side of the room, was what could only be described as a throne. Although the chair was a good deal larger than most thrones and had to be in order to accommodate Emsay's considerable bulk. Even though it was difficult to know what was hidden beneath the yards of gold brocade that covered the Caliph's body, Nalomy estimated that he weighed at least four hundred pounds. And, judging from the tiers of food arranged to either side of him, Emsay was destined to become even heavier. A fact that Nalomy took in and, like the politician he was, added to the growing store of data related to the crime lord. The fact that Emsay was fat meant he couldn't move freely and was dependent on his staff to carry out all of his wishes. A situation that rendered him potentially vulnerable.

Like all Cloques, Emsay had a round head, fan-shaped ears, and saucerlike eyes. Perhaps most noticeable, however, were the four tentacles that encircled his mouth and were used for eating. They were also employed during conversations with other Cloques, who relied on a combination of verbal speech and sign language to interact with each other. Now, however, Emsay chose to communicate via accented standard. "Greetings, Senator Nalomy. . . . This is an honor. Please forgive me for not getting up. My knees have been giving me trouble lately."

"Of course," Nalomy said politely. "I understand."

"Please have a seat," Zether said, and gestured to an ornate armchair that was positioned in front of Emsay's throne. Though covered with gold gilt, and upholstered with synsilk, the guest chair was located at least half a foot lower than Emsay's seat, leaving no doubt as to who was in control of the situation.

Nalomy sat down, and said, "No thank you," to refreshments, as Emsay plucked a tidbit of food off one of the trays to his right. Tentacles writhed as the pastry was stuffed into the orifice behind them. Emsay had a tendency to speak with his mouth full, so his words were slightly muffled. "So, it's my understanding that you have a problem and want it killed."

"Yes," Nalomy replied. He was conscious of how his words would sound on the evening news if the crime lord were to pass a recording along; but everyone knew that such things could be faked, and his body double was currently in a city hundreds of miles away, where it had given a speech the previous day. Not an ironclad alibi perhaps—but good enough to muddy the waters if there was an investigation. "I want to eliminate a Xeno Corps officer named Jak Cato."

Emsay nodded sagely. "Said officer is a known associate of Legate Usurlus, I believe. That makes such a task all the more perilous because Usurlus could and probably would seek revenge."

"You are very well informed," Nalomy commented, as his respect for Emsay went up a notch. "It's true that Usurlus could be a problem but only if he's alive."

The Cloque's tentacles began to writhe as he laughed. "Well said, my friend, well said. So you want me to kill *that* problem as well? I could certainly do so . . . In spite of the fact that the last attempt to eliminate him was a failure."

"Take care of Cato," Nalomy replied darkly. "Then, assuming everything goes as planned, we can discuss Usurlus."

"Agreed," Emsay said. "But such an assignment will be expensive because the police take care of their own and will try to avenge Cato's death."

"How expensive?" Nalomy wanted to know. "There's some truth in what you say, but Cato is a mere Centurion, and that should be taken into account."

Emsay was never happier than when he was negotiating a business deal and nibbling on Chor grubs. He popped one of them into his mouth, bit through the tough outer skin, and began to chew. "Money is but one form of compensation," Emsay observed, as little bits of food tumbled down onto his stomach. "We live in complicated times. Take the tax bill that is currently under consideration in the Senate, for example. The Emperor put it forward as a way to pay for additional police protection, which many of my fellow business associates and I feel is already sufficient. By putting more police on the streets, the government could disturb the delicate equilibrium that exists between self-righteous citizens and entrepreneurs such as myself. So, if you were to dedicate yourself to protecting my interests in that regard, I would consider that to be payment in full."

Nalomy listened with interest because if he could achieve his ends without spending thousands of Imperials, then so much the better. There were potential pitfalls, however— and it would be necessary to avoid them. "I can see your point," Nalomy responded carefully. "And I believe I can help or at least try to. But it's important to understand that the extent of my influence is limited—and that the measure may pass even if I and some of my colleagues oppose it. If that were to be the case, I fear you would be disappointed."

Emsay couldn't smile, not the way Umans do, but raised a reassuring hand. "Please rest assured that if your opposition to the increase is both ardent, and public, your part of the bargain will have been kept. And who knows? Perhaps I will find others to enlist in my cause!"

For one brief moment Nalomy felt a certain queasiness brought on by the possibility that the entire Senate could be bought off. But then he remembered his daughter, the manner in which her head had been delivered to him, and felt his doubts melt away. "I think we have a deal," Nalomy said as he came to his feet. "How soon will Officer Cato die?"

"Soon," Emsay assured him confidently. "Very, very, soon."

"And the method?" Nalomy wanted to know.

"Cato won't die in a hail of bullets," Emsay predicted with a wave of his hand. "I have other methods at my disposal. But why ruin the surprise? Watch the news. . . . Some of it will be good."

Finally, after six long hours of guard duty, Verafti was about to receive his reward, which was the freedom to leave the

Imperial Tower and do whatever he pleased. The situation was his own fault, of course, stemming as it did from the spur-of-the-moment decision to kill and eat one of Emor's Praetorian Guards a couple of weeks earlier, thereby obliging himself to fill in for the man lest he be missed.

Even though the kill had been the result of an impulse rather than a carefully crafted plan, he was none the worse for it other than being tired. Thanks to the second identity, he could leave the Tower and take care of various chores. Such as murdering Jak Cato and eating the bastard for lunch! Partly for the sake of revenge but to protect himself as well, now that the Uman knew he was alive.

So Verafti was two levels belowground, standing in a rank of twelve Praetorian Guards, as a long-winded Section Leader named Ponthus droned on about the need to look sharp while off duty and take all of the precautions necessary to avoid venereal disease.

Once the lecture was over, the guards were free to enter the locker room, where they could don civilian clothes and leave. Verafti hurried to do so, kept the interactions with his fellow legionnaires to a minimum, and was soon out on the street, where he could lose himself in the early-morning crowd. Thanks to the fact that he had full access to *all* governmental records, including those of the Xeno Corps, Verafti knew that Cato was in charge of the local bunko squad.

What he didn't know was where the Xeno cop was going to be on that particular day because the data banks didn't include daily tasking orders. But, given the well-publicized shoot-out that Cato had been part of, it seemed likely he was at home recovering from the leg wound he had suffered. So Verafti planned to go there, kill the worthless sonofabitch, and eat some of him. Then, after a day or so, he would have the pleasure of shitting Cato and flushing him down a toilet! It was, the Sagathi decided, going to be a very productive day.

*　　*　　*

Having cleaned the apartment, Alamy was about to go shopping with her landlady, but it was first necessary to take care of the genetically engineered pet Legate Usurlus had sent over. According to the note that came with the babble bird, it was for ". . . the purpose of keeping Alamy company," but she had her doubts. Usurlus could be thoughtful, there was no doubt about that, but Alamy had a sneaking hunch that the winged pet had been given to him, then regifted in order to get the noisy creature out of his elegant home.

It was about a foot and a half tall while sitting on its perch, had feathers that replicated every color of the rainbow, and was just smart enough to be annoying. It squawked in protest as she opened its cage and pointed the way. "Get in your cage, Rollo. . . . I have to leave."

Rollo cocked his head, regarded Alamy with a glassy eye, and made his case. "No cage. . . . I be good."

"No you won't," Alamy countered firmly. "There were Rollo droppings on the kitchen counter this morning. Now get in there."

Rollo hung his head in shame, made his way to the other end of his T-shaped perch, and entered the cage. Then, as he turned to look at her over one shoulder, he said, "Rollo sorry."

It was a great act, and even though Alamy knew it was an act, she might have relented had it not been for the doorbell. She went to the entryway, fully expecting to see Madam Faustus, opened the door, and was confronted by a man instead. The visitor was tall and, in keeping with the light drizzle, wore a long raincoat. A cap of tight curly hair covered his head, his eyes were brown, and when he smiled, some very white teeth appeared. "Hello," the man said pleasantly, "my name is Par Thonis. I'm looking for Jak Cato. Is he home?"

"This is his apartment," Alamy confirmed, "but he's at work now."

The man looked disappointed. "Yeah, that makes sense I guess, but I was hoping to surprise him. We served in the same outfit a few years back—and I saw him on the news. Is he okay? A reporter said he was wounded."

"Yes, he's fine," Alamy responded. "Or that's what *he* says anyway. I wanted him to stay home for a day or so, but he went right back to work. Would you like to come in?"

Thonis smiled agreeably. "That sounds like Jak. . . . Sure, I'll come in, but only for a moment. If you have a scrap of paper, I'll leave my number. Maybe the two of us can get together sometime soon."

"I'm sure Jak would enjoy that," Alamy said politely, and stepped out of the way. "Please come in. Can I take your coat?"

Verafti's ankle-length coat served to keep the rain off *and* conceal the two semiautomatic pistols that he wore in matching shoulder holsters. Because the Sagathi knew that Cato would not only be armed but was an excellent shot, as the criminals in the X Quarter had learned the hard way. So the last thing he wanted to do was remove his coat. Verafti smiled and shook his head. "No, but thanks for asking."

"I'll get something to write with," Alamy promised, and hurried away. Verafti had recognized her by then. Not by name, but by appearance, since she'd been a member of Governor Nalomy's staff on Dantha. More than that, she was an appetizing morsel that would more than fill the emptiness in his stomach.

Suddenly, as the multicolored bird in the cage began to squawk, an idea occurred to him. Why not kill the female, enjoy a leisurely lunch, and take her place? Then, when Cato came home, Verafti would be at the door waiting for the empath. The policeman would "recognize" him, that was true, but there would be a moment of hesitation. A second or two in which to shoot Cato in the face!

It was a good plan, an excellent plan, and Verafti was prepared to act on it when the babble bird spread its wings and made a commotion inside his cage. "Bad thing! Run! Hide!"

Alamy had a sheet of paper by then and turned to confront the angen. "Be quiet, Rollo! What's wrong with you anyway? Mind your manners."

"You mind *your* manners," Rollo replied contentiously, as his wings fluttered and the cage rattled.

It was obvious that the pet could see through his disguise somehow, but it was equally obvious that the young woman wasn't going to take the creature seriously, so Verafti was just about to morph into his true form when a knock was heard, and the front door swung open to admit a middle-aged woman. "CeCe?" she inquired. "Are you ready? Be sure to bring an umbrella."

Verafti hesitated as Alamy made the necessary introductions. "Madam Faustus . . . This is Par Thonis. He's a friend of Jak's. I'll be ready in a moment."

It would have been easy to kill *both* Umans, of course, but the situation was becoming more complicated with each passing moment, and Verafti had no way to know if other people were about. So he accepted the piece of paper and scribbled a random com number on it. "So where is Jak working today?" he inquired casually. "Not the X Quarter, I hope."

"That's exactly where he was headed," Alamy replied darkly. "A group of pickpockets have been working the Galaxus Hotel, and he's supposed to stop them."

"If anyone can do it, Jak will," Verafti predicted, and he gave her the note. "I won't delay you any longer. Please give Jak my best—and tell him that he has a beautiful wife."

Alamy blushed. "I'm not his wife—but thank you."

Thonis crossed the room, Rollo squawked and stuck his head under a wing, and Faustus was there to close the door behind the visitor as he left. "Somebody admires you!" she said cheerfully. "Jak had better keep a sharp eye out."

"Bad thing gone," Rollo observed as he eyed the room and blinked. "We lucky."

In spite of a reputation for crime, and the sleazy ambience for which it was known, the X was also an important center for commerce. Primarily because many of the wealthier non-Umans preferred to live there rather than put up with the social bias typical of the city's more fashionable suburbs. That made the X Quarter the natural place for non-Uman off-worlders to stay as well, both because many of the companies they worked for were quartered there, and for reasons of personal convenience.

All of which explained why the twelve-story Galaxus Hotel had been constructed in the heart of the district more than seventy years earlier and was still popular with the thousands of guests who stayed in it each year. Or those who weren't victimized by pickpockets anyway—since the Galaxus was a rich hunting ground for dexterous thieves. That was why Cato, Shani, and two other members of the bunko squad were present.

Cato was positioned in the manager's office, which was located on the second-floor gallery level, where a huge window afforded him a sweeping view of the reception desk, the sprawling lobby, and the Galaxy Bar off to the right. "Stay sharp," he said into his lip mike as he eyed the area below. "The people we're after are here. . . . All we have to do is identify them." There were double *click*s by way of a response as each member of the team acknowledged the scrambled transmission.

The process wasn't going to be that simple, of course, because the perps they were looking for had stolen more than five thousand Imperials' worth of money, jewelry, and other valuables over the last week without the hotel's security team figuring out how they managed it.

While the hotel's staff was well acquainted with the traditional "bump and grab" strategies that many dips used, these crooks had clearly come up with something new. None of the victims had been bumped, none had been accosted by a decoy, and none had been so foolish as to leave a garment, purse, or bag unattended while they stepped away for a moment.

A painstaking examination of the footage captured by the hotel's security cameras had been fruitless as well, leading management to conclude that the thieves were non-Uman sentients with exotic capabilities. Which was why the Xeno Corps' bunko squad had been summoned.

So as the hours passed, Cato and his operatives stared, and stared some more, in hopes of spotting a theft as it went down. But, much to their chagrin, two guests were victimized while they looked on! An embarrassing, not to mention frustrating, situation, which explained why Cato was feeling so exasperated when lunchtime rolled around.

Having dispatched Shani and a second team member to get something to eat, Cato ordered the third officer to keep watch from above while he went down to sit in the well-furnished lobby. The theory being that whatever was taking place was so subtle, it was virtually invisible from more than a few feet away.

Having chosen one of the few Uman-standard chairs to sit in, and being surrounded by Xenos representing half a dozen races, Cato was in a good position to understand how *they* felt when forced to enter the corporate or governmental zones. Because of the anti-Uman bias prevalent in the Quarter, Cato was on the receiving end of some disapproving looks and a flood of negative emotions. One Cloque business being even got up and left.

But that was to be expected as Cato sifted through the incoming emotions searching them for any trace of the greed, excitement, and fear that a pickpocket might project. There were traces of all three, of course, but none of the individuals within "range" exhibited enough emotional intensity to qualify them as suspects, leaving the empath without a suspect.

Cato did intercept something slightly suspicious, however, which came across as a sort of emotional buzz, like static on a radio. Though far from clear, the input was familiar since he experienced it every day. Because animals have primal emotions, as do some plants, and they're everywhere. And that made it impossible to move around without picking up what amounted to emotional background sound interspersed with an occasional spike of concentrated fear or satisfaction.

So, having detected a persistent emotional buzz, and with nothing else to do, Cato eyed the area around him, looking for the source of the input. That was when his eyes came to rest on a plant. It stood about four feet tall, had broad, shiny leaves, and was positioned behind a side table across from him and off to the right.

Being no botanist, Cato didn't have the foggiest idea what kind of plant it was, but as he took a moment to survey a larger area, he saw there were quite a few of them. It was understandable, really, since the lush plants were very pleasant to look at and brought a much-needed touch of green to a mostly beige-and-brown lobby.

As Cato's eyes came back to focus on the plant nearest to his chair, he was about to dismiss the matter and direct his attention elsewhere, when he noticed a trace of movement. Not by the individuals seated to either side of the plant, but by the object itself, as a vine inched out to caress the arm-chair sitting next to it.

The Trelid who was seated in the chair was busy talking on a pocket com and clearly unaware of what was going on as the tendril paused for a moment, as if to make sure that it was still undiscovered. Then, confident that no one was going to interfere, the plant sent its thin, nearly invisible vine slithering down along the side of the chair and into the open briefcase that sat beside it.

Cato, who could hardly believe his eyes, continued to watch in amazement as the tentacle-like extrusion probed the inside of the briefcase and was almost immediately with-drawn. The object that was removed, and pulled back to-ward the plant's beautifully glazed pot, looked like a jewelry case. But it could have been a wallet, a fancy minicomp, or half a dozen other things.

Were other similar plants stealing objects as well? Hav-ing been trained to do so by a sentient who came around to clean out their pots? One of the hotel's staff members perhaps? Yes, Cato thought so, and the Xeno cop felt a sense of grim satisfaction as he rose to leave. Rather than interfere with the theft he had witnessed, thereby warning the person or persons who were responsible for the scheme, he would set a trap for them.

Such were Cato's thoughts as the stolen case disappeared into the pot, he began to get up out of his chair, and a Trelid waiter passed in front of him. A bullet hit the Trelid in the back of the head, blew his brains all over the couple seated next to Cato, and set off a chorus of screams as the waiter and his tray crashed to the floor.

Cato was still in the process of rising when the lamp next to his elbow exploded into a hundred pieces, and his partner shouted a warning through his earplug. "The shooter is a Sagathi! He's above you!"

And that was all the time there was as Cato looked up to see a man vault over the rail that ran all the way round the second-floor gallery. There was a pistol in his right hand, and as his long raincoat flared out around him, the shooter morphed into his true form. A bipedal reptile with lots of teeth.

Cato shouted, "Verafti!" and began to reach for his gun, as the more agile guests scattered. The other Xeno cop had fired two shots by then. One hit a mirror, and the second blew a vase of flowers to smithereens, while the shape shifter remained untouched.

Thanks to the information obtained from Alamy, Verafti had been able to locate Cato with relative ease and stalk him for the better part of two hours before launching his long-range attack. The problem was that he couldn't sidle up next to his quarry the way he usually would without being detected and most probably shot.

That was why he had been careful to keep clear of the Xeno cops until half of the team departed for lunch. Then, having pulled one of two pistols, Verafti fired. He knew there would be a great deal of confusion when the Uman went down. That would give him the opportunity to shift shapes, exit the building, and make good his escape.

Unfortunately, the waiter had been killed in Cato's place, the second shot had been a hair too late, so the initial phase of the plan had been irretrievably ruined. But, as he flexed his knees in anticipation of the landing, the Sagathi was ready for claw-to-hand combat.

Verafti heard a *thump* as his feet hit the floor. Cato was still in the process of bringing his pistol up, giving the Sagathi the time he needed. He shifted his weight to his left foot and executed a sweeping leg kick. Cato swore as the weapon flew out of his hand, hit the floor, and skittered away.

But the battle was far from one-sided. As Verafti completed a full 360-degree turn, the Uman took the opportunity to step forward, grab hold of his opponent's arm, and bang it against a column. Verafti felt a moment of intense pain as the pistol flew free.

Having lost the weapon, Verafti made use of his right hand to reach out and grab a fistful of jacket. If he could pull Cato in and rip out his throat, the battle would be over. But as the Uman brought his hands up and took hold of his lapels, Verafti realized his error. It had been a mistake to revert to his natural form. His left hand was missing, and he couldn't control Cato with his right!

That was when the Uman kneed Verafti in the groin. But Sagathi males keep their sex organs safely tucked away *inside* their bodies, so a blow that might have disabled a Uman had no effect whatsoever, as Verafti snapped his razor-sharp teeth. They came within a quarter inch of the Uman's vulnerable neck.

That forced Cato to push his opponent away—thereby allowing Verafti to shape shift and go for his other gun. But as Verafti drew a pistol, Cato was swinging a lamp, and would have connected if it hadn't been for one of the hotel's ubiquitous security drones. It "saw" what its Central Processing Unit perceived to be a fight between two unruly guests and took immediate action.

Unfortunately, the robot chose to stun Cato first. His muscles locked up, he fell over backward, and crashed into a table. That gave Verafti an opportunity to fire at the most immediate threat. Two of four bullets passed through the drone's alloy skin and some of the components within. Electricity crackled as the machine lost its guidance system and spiraled upward, trailing a thin wisp of smoke. A beautiful 3-D representation of the Circinus Galaxy covered the slightly concave ceiling. The drone hit it dead center and exploded into hundreds of pieces, which rained down on the lobby below.

Those guests who hadn't escaped earlier ran for the exits as the debris continued to fall. Verafti grinned and swung around to point his weapon at Cato. The empath was lying on the floor, his face locked in a horrible grimace as he battled to regain control of his body.

But as the shape shifter's finger tightened on the trigger, Shani charged across the lobby, jumped up onto a table, and used it as a platform from which to launch herself straight at the killer. She hit Verafti hard, they landed in a heap, and the pistol went spinning away.

At that point, Verafti had a choice. He could stay and fight what would almost certainly become a losing battle or cut his losses and run, thereby living to fight another day. The decision was no decision at all.

Verafti was stronger than the woman, so as she repeatedly smashed a fist into his face, he was able to break free and morph into a likeness of Alamy. Then, changing faces as he fled, Verafti was able to jump an L-shaped couch and make for the front door. Shots rang out, but none of the bullets hit him as the doors parted, and he dashed outside. Twenty seconds later, Verafti was just another Trelid, sauntering through a seedy shopping arcade, looking for a new set of clothes. Sirens wailed, a cop on a unicycle raced past on his way to the crime scene, and life went on.

SEVEN

The city of Imperialus, on the planet Corin

LIVIUS DIDN'T ALLOW AIR CARS TO LAND ON HIS EM-
ployer's veranda unless the visit had been approved in
advance—but there was nothing he could do to prevent the
arrival of the aircraft with the word POLICE stenciled across
its boxy fuselage. It circled the building as if to be sure of
the landing pad's exact location before touching down. At
least the siren wasn't on, for which Livius was grateful.

The side door slid open, and a female dressed in civilian
clothes emerged. She was followed by Cato, who was clearly
the worse for wear and forced to lean on his companion for
support. Judging from all sorts of cuts and bruises, the officers had been in a fight. "I'm Officer Shani," the woman said
levelly. "A security drone stunned Cato, so it's hard for him
to walk. I told him to let me handle this, but he insisted on
coming along."

"Verafti," Cato croaked urgently. "He came after me
down in the X. You know what the bastard is capable of. . . .
You saw it on Dantha. Where's Legate Usurlus?"

"He's inside," Livius replied cautiously. "But the residence is secured, and my men are on duty. So there's nothing to worry about."

"Oh, *really*?" Shani inquired sarcastically. "Are *you* an empath? How do you know Verafti isn't posing as one of your men?"

Livius had seen firsthand what Verafti could do. His jaw worked, but nothing came out.

"Shani's right," Cato put in levelly. "We'll take a look. Once we're sure everything is secure, we'll get out. Believe me, I'd rather be home."

"Okay," Livius allowed reluctantly, "but there's something you should . . ."

But it was too late by then since both variants were already crossing the veranda, closely followed by two heavily armed street cops.

Cato's entire body hurt, and occasional muscle spasms threatened to bring him down, but he was determined to not only protect Usurlus but nail Verafti if the bastard was present. And, with only a dozen people to check, Cato figured the process wouldn't take long. But he was wrong because the *thump, thump, thump* of music could be heard before he entered the residence, which was packed with beautiful people.

Some of the revelers were partially dressed, but many were naked except for the garish body paint they had applied to each other hours earlier—paint that was beginning to wear off. Cato estimated that at least thirty people were present. Some were dancing, some were having sex, and some were unconscious on the floor. Those who could gave him blank-eyed looks and, judging from the emotions they projected, were completely unaffected by the presence of four strangers.

Livius had caught up by then and smiled bleakly. He had

to yell in order to be heard over the pounding music. "It started about 9:00 PM yesterday—and I suspect it will last until two or three in the morning. They usually do."

Cato shook his head in amazement. "Have all of the guests been here since the party started?"

Livius shook his head. "Hell no. . . . They come and go. In fact, five of them came in the door about fifteen minutes ago."

Cato nodded soberly. "That means Verafti could have infiltrated the place since the attack on me. Shani, check these people out. And be careful. I'll talk to the Legate."

Livius looked doubtful. "Are you sure that's necessary?"

"Yes," Cato answered grimly. "I am. You lead the way. And don't forget to pick me up if I fall down."

In order to reach Usurlus's private quarters, it was necessary to wind their way across the dance floor, step over a couple who were fornicating in the entryway, and follow a parallel hall past the study where Cato, Alamy, and Usurlus had met. A trail of discarded clothing led to an open door. Livius, who had no desire to enter his employer's bedroom uninvited, was careful to let Cato go first.

As the empath entered the room with weapon in hand, he was greeted by the sight of three people on a huge bed. The group included Usurlus, a younger though equally good-looking male, and a very athletic female who seemed determined to pleasure both of her companions simultaneously. The emotions present in the room were what Cato expected them to be given the nature of the situation, and it took less than two seconds to determine that all the members of the ménage à trois were Uman.

"Excuse me, sire," Cato said, as a thigh muscle began to spasm. "I'm sorry to bother you and your guests—but I'm here on police business."

*   *   *

Usurlus was far from pleased as Cato gave a brief account of the battle with Verafti and his decision to check the residence. But he knew that the Xeno cop was genuinely concerned for his safety, and that kept him from lashing out. "I appreciate your dedication to duty, Cato, if not your sense of timing," he said dryly. "We were just about to share a rather memorable moment when you barged in! So Verafti is no longer playing the same part that he was before?"

Cato took note of the way in which Usurlus avoided any mention of Emperor Emor, and he was careful to do the same. "No, sire. . . . I didn't say that. Given Verafti's capabilities, he can come and go at will. With that in mind, I think it's safe to say he will continue to take advantage of the identity you referred to."

"Okay," Usurlus conceded wearily, "it sounds as if we're right back where we were. Would you agree?"

Cato nodded. "Yes, sire."

"Then perhaps you should go home and get some rest," Usurlus suggested. "How do you like your new pet by the way?"

"Alamy is quite taken with it," Cato lied. "Thank you."

"It was my pleasure," Usurlus replied, which was true since he'd been thrilled to rid himself of the feathered beast.

Cato, who realized that he was still holding his gun down along his right thigh, returned the weapon to its holster and turned to go. The girl giggled, and the party continued as Cato staggered down the hall. Finally, after a long day on the job, he was headed home.

It was nearly dark by the time Alamy and Madam Faustus climbed the last few stairs and entered the walkway that led to Arbor House. The lights were on in the apartment above, so as Alamy removed the backpack that contained her landlord's groceries, she knew Cato was home. The prospect of seeing him made her feel warm inside as Faustus placed a gold Imperial in her hand. "That's for you, dear. . . . Girls need things from time to time. I'll see you tomorrow."

Alamy took the bag of groceries that belonged to her and made her way up the stairs to the apartment above. She threw the door open ready to receive a kiss and was stunned to see Cato and Shani sitting side by side on the couch. Both had cuts and bruises. "There you are," Cato said equably. "I was starting to worry."

Rollo trilled cheerfully. "It's dinnertime!"

"I went shopping with Madam Faustus," Alamy explained as she carried the bag into the kitchen. "Who beat you up? Or did you attack each other?"

"That's interesting," Shani observed archly. "The cat has claws."

"Verafti came after me," Cato replied, seemingly unaware of the friction between the two women. "And he would have killed me, too—except Shani threw herself at him!"

Alamy glanced from Cato to Shani and saw the look of triumph in the police officer's eyes. "Did you kill him?" she inquired coldly.

The look faded. "No, he got away."

Alamy frowned. "How did he know where to find you?"

"That's a good question," Cato mused. "We were wondering the same thing. He morphed into a likeness of *you* while making his escape."

Suddenly, Alamy felt dizzy and slightly sick to her stomach. "Do you have a friend named Par Thonis?"

Cato shook his head. "Thonis? No, I don't. Why?"

"Bad thing!" Rollo exclaimed loudly, and hid his head under a wing.

"Oh, my God," Shani said disbelievingly. "Did a man come here? Claiming to be a friend? And you told him where to find us?"

Tears were streaming down Alamy's cheeks by that time, and she nodded mutely.

"Why you stupid little bitch!" Shani exclaimed angrily as she came to her feet. "The entire team could have been killed!"

Alamy sobbed, ran for the front door, and made her escape. Shani was correct. She *was* stupid. The door slammed, and darkness took her in.

Because all Vords were color-blind, the clear blue sky and the way the golden sunlight glittered on Lake Umanus were completely lost on Ambassador Enig Serey Nusk as a Uman shuttle ferried him down to the surface of Corin.

But even if Nusk couldn't appreciate the city's physical beauty as he eyed the view screen in front of him, he could appreciate the city's grandeur. The domed building at the center of the lake, and the towering buildings that surrounded it, all testified to the power of the Empire the seven clans were going to crush. It would be an epic battle, one that would probably require a hundred standard years to win and cost millions of lives. And that would make the eventual victory all the more worthwhile because there is no glory without the giving of blood, and the taking of it as well.

The key is to take more blood than you give, the voice in Nusk's head put in tartly, as the pilot fired the shuttle's repellers, and the vessel slowed.

Nusk knew the "voice" well because the sluglike parasite that was half-wrapped around his neck had been paired with him almost immediately after birth so that the two of them could grow up together. The symbiotic relationship between the Vords and the parasitic Ya was at least twenty thousand years old and of benefit to both races. Thanks to the manner in which Heon could inject naturally produced chemical compounds into his host's circulatory system, Nusk could think more clearly, react faster, and recover from wounds that might have killed him otherwise.

But the bargain was far from one-sided. By aligning themselves with the Vords, the Ya had what they considered to be "mounts," meaning lesser beings to provide them a means of locomotion and nourishment. Although none of them spoke of it. They didn't have to since they were self-replicating and were therefore born with an understanding of why such a relationship was of value to them.

There was a solid *thump* as the shuttle put down, and the disembarkation process began. Nusk and his party of two advisors were something of a problem for the Uman officials in charge of the visit. Because the Vords were diplomats, after all, and, therefore, entitled to certain honors, but enemies as well since they had taken Therat by force.

So rather than being transported to the Imperial Tower via motorcade, the Vords were escorted off the shuttle and onto a private air barge. It was equipped with power chairs that could accommodate their gangly bodies and provided appropriate refreshments as well. The latter having been prepared with advice from the advance party, which had arrived more than a month earlier—and been forced to wait until Emperor Emor agreed to a specific date on which the talks would take place.

Nusk knew the discussions would fail since the seven clans had already voted in favor of war, but the interchange would be useful nevertheless. Because the talks would allow the members of his party to gauge Uman resolve—and gather whatever intelligence was available. Which was why one of his companions was a spy rather than a true diplomat.

Nusk and Heon were escorted up a ramp and into the official barge, where they were greeted by a Uman official who identified himself as the Imperial Chief of Staff Rujan Rolari. The words, which issued forth from the translator the official wore, were understandably formal. "Welcome, Ambassador Nusk—and advisor Heon. Please make your-selves comfortable for the short trip to the Imperial Tower. Emperor Emor is aware of your arrival and eager to meet with you."

I'm sure he is, Heon put in cynically, as Nusk bowed. *The fact that he agreed to meet with us signals how frightened the Umans are.*

Nusk wasn't so sure. In fact, he suspected that his Uman counterparts were pursuing a strategy not unlike his own and for similar reasons. *Don't underestimate our enemies,* he re-sponded. *The Empire they built did not come about by accident.*

Meanwhile, Nusk's reply to Rolari was equally formal. "Thank you. . . . Your capital city is very beautiful—and we look forward to our audience with the Emperor."

And to glassing the entire planet, Heon added, *so as to kill the very roots of your barbaric civilization.*

Verafti looked at Emperor Emor in the mirror and was satis-fied with what he saw. Having made the decision to meet with Ambassador Nusk and his parasitic companion, Verafti had gone to considerable lengths to play the part he had as-signed to himself, even going so far as to meet with Rolari and key members of the Imperial staff to ensure that all the niceties of protocol would be observed.

Having checked his appearance, he made his way over to the door that opened into the formal reception hall adjoin-ing the residence. Garbage skittered away from his highly polished shoes as the shape shifter marched across the trash-strewn floor to the point where all six of the Emperor's body doubles stood at attention. The robots had been activated by Verafti the day before and were programmed to obey the directives Emor gave them regardless of how strange such orders might seem. The shape shifter paused to reiterate the instructions given earlier. "Remember, you are to wait here and come when I call."

The identical robots replied in unison. "Yes, sire."

Satisfied that the machines would respond when summoned, Verafti opened the door and was quick to close it behind him. The reception hall had a high ceiling and paneled walls, which were hung with stern-looking portraits of Emperors past. A wooden conference table rested on a burgundy rug and served to split the space in two.

Imperial Chief of Staff Rujan Rolari and half a dozen Uman diplomats were seated on the south side of the table, while three long-faced Vords and their advisors were positioned directly across from them. All of the participants came to their feet as the imposter entered.

Once all of the introductions had been made, and refreshments had been served, Rolari read the agenda, to which everyone had agreed in advance. And that was when Verafti spoke up. "If Ambassador Nusk would be so kind as to indulge me, I would like to add a private meeting to the agenda, in the hope that if the two of us . . . Excuse me, the *three* of us, were to spend some time alone, we might be able to make even more progress. What do you say?"

Tell him "no," Heon put in before Nusk could respond. *The clans have spoken. Such a meeting would be pointless.*

Nusk knew that the Ya was probably correct, but he was curious as well. What did the Uman Emperor have in mind? Some sort of accommodation, perhaps? If so, that would be worth hearing. With that in mind, he made his response. "Of course. . . . It would be an honor."

You'll be sorry, Heon predicted darkly, but Nusk chose to ignore the comment as the formal discussions got under way. It was something of a farce since the Vords were referring to Therat as "a protectorate," as if to suggest that they were protecting the population in some way, while Rolari and his diplomats were calling the loss "a serious provocation." Such language sought to position the "incident," as they referred to it, as a minor annoyance rather than a violation of Imperial sovereignty.

Such positions were ridiculous, but they gave both parties some cover and served to make the talks possible. Verafti did the best he could to look interested but found it difficult to pay attention since the outcome made no difference to him. But finally, after what seemed like hours but was only forty-five minutes, the formal agenda came to an end as both sides agreed to schedule another meeting.

That was when nervous looks were exchanged, and everyone other than the two principals stood and trooped out of the room via the main entrance. Once the two of them were alone, Verafti was quick to seize the initiative. "So," he began, "that was a waste of time, wasn't it?"

Be careful, Heon cautioned. *He's trying to circumvent formal negotiations.*

"I'm not sure I understand," Nusk responded cautiously.

"I could be wrong," Verafti replied, "but it's my guess that you plan to attack the Umans no matter what they do."

Why is he talking as if he's a member of another race? Heon wanted to know.

Nusk had no idea. "No," he lied, "we are negotiating in good faith."

Verafti laughed. "Okay, if you say so. Tell me, Ambassador Nusk. . . . What does a Vord taste like?"

There was a moment of silence as Verafti activated a remote—and Nusk wondered if the translator was working properly. He was still working on a response when the door to the Imperial residence opened and six identical Emperor Emors entered the room. Heon said, *Run!* But it was too late as the robots grabbed hold of Nusk's arms and half carried, half dragged him away. The diplomat screamed for help, but there was no response.

"They can't hear you," Verafti explained matter-of-factly as he followed along behind. "The walls are very thick."

Then Nusk was inside the Imperial apartments, where the robots began systematically to strip away his clothes. They were quite efficient, so it was only a matter of minutes before Nusk and Heon were nude, and completely vulnerable. "I'll tell you what," Verafti said as he began to morph into his true form. "Why don't you hide—and let's see if I can find you."

Look for a door! Heon ordered. *Find a way out!*

Nusk took off at a jog. He opened each door he saw only to discover a succession of bedrooms, bathrooms, and closets. The diplomat's heart was beating wildly, his breath came in short gasps, and he had soiled himself by the time Verafti cornered him in the vast kitchen. A rack of knives was handy, so the shape shifter took one and held it away from his body. The long, narrow blade was used for boning, and was razor-sharp.

"I'm disappointed," Verafti said as he began to close in on the cowering Vord. "*Very* disappointed. It has been a long time since I enjoyed a good chase. I can sense your fear, you know, and I wish I had time to savor it, but the others are waiting."

Nusk uttered one last scream as light flashed off polished metal and cold steel sliced through Heon's soft flesh and into his own. The last thing he saw was blood spraying the area around him as he fell. As his body hit the floor, he saw the lights roll out of focus and wondered how such a thing could happen to him. Then he was gone.

Verafti uttered a growl of satisfaction, pounced on the body, and tore big chunks of bloody flesh off it. He was hungry, *very* hungry, and pleased to learn that Vords tasted good.

*   *   *

Rolari was anxious and for good reason. Having been disengaged of late, Emperor Emor had chosen to participate in direct negotiations with the Vords. So, which man was meeting with Ambassador Nusk? The erratic Emor, who might be mentally unstable, or what Rolari thought of as the *real* Emor? A man with a reputation as a savvy negotiator. There was no way to be sure—and the fate of the Empire could be hanging in the balance.

So Rolari felt a keen sense of apprehension as the long wait ended, the double doors swung open, and the two principals emerged together. "It was a hard-fought battle," Emor's body double said cheerfully, as both Umans and Vords stood. "But I believe significant progress was made. Would you agree, Ambassador Nusk?"

After a quick meal, and a hot shower, Verafti felt refreshed. Now, as he took a few steps forward, he faced a critical test. Nusk had been at least six and a half feet tall, and there was the parasite to re-create as well, so it had been difficult to muster enough mass to impersonate both at once.

But, regardless of species, it was Verafti's experience that sentients see what they *expect* to see. So if the new Nusk was a tiny bit shorter, and somewhat leaner than the original had been, the odds were good that no one would notice. And that appeared to be the case since neither one of the other Vords displayed any signs of alarm as he entered the lobby. That left the issue of language, which he planned to keep to a minimum as he worked to master the Vord tongue. "Yes, I agree," Verafti replied succinctly.

The meeting came to a quick conclusion after that as the Vords were taken back to the spaceport, and consistent with orders received from the being it believed to be Emperor Emor, the body double returned to the blood-splattered residence. Having completed its mission, the robot went to the storage room where he and his peers were kept, took his place in line, and switched to standby. His duties were complete.

It was a warm, slightly humid evening, so the windows were open on the chance that a refreshing breeze might find its way up the hillside and into the apartment. It was never entirely dark in the bedroom thanks to all the light generated by the city below. So as Alamy lay on her back and stared upward, she could see shadows crawling across the ceiling. Cato, who was lying next to her, made a gentle rasping noise with every breath he took. It wasn't loud enough to qualify as a snore, and the sound was reassuring in a way since it meant he was only inches from her.

Cato wasn't angry with her—that's what he maintained, anyway—but the two of them hadn't spent much time together since Verafti's attack. Cato avowed that was because he had to deal with the aftermath of the Galaxus Hotel battle and find the Kelf believed to be responsible for training the pickpocketing plants and collecting the loot hidden in their pots.

But Alamy had her doubts. She couldn't feel Cato's emotions, not the way the empath could access hers, but she was a woman. And women *know*. That's what Madam Faustus claimed anyway—and Alamy thought so, too.

It would have been easy to blame the situation on Shani, especially given the way the other woman was coming on to Cato and the advantages she had. Because Shani was both an empath and a cop—qualities Alamy couldn't hope to match.

But she knew Shani wasn't the problem. Not the *real* problem. That was located deep inside Cato. Part of the man was in love with her. Alamy was convinced of that. But another part was reluctant to make a commitment—and didn't have to so long as she was his slave. And Shani didn't require anything of Cato other than the absolute loyalty that cops expect of each other. Her life ran shift to shift, day by day, just like his did.

Such were Alamy's thoughts as one of the shadows that was creeping across the ceiling broke suction and fell. The slither flipped in midair and landed belly down across Alamy's face. She screamed, or tried to, but couldn't make a sound because of the way the rubbery flesh covered her nose and mouth. Alamy tried to rip the creature loose, but it was pancake-thin, and the suction was strong.

Rollo squawked loudly as one of the foot-long creatures dropped on him. It wasn't able to get a purchase, however, and fell free as the angen took to the air and sounded the alarm. "Bad things! Bad things!"

Cato was up by then, clad in no more than a pair of shorts, having been awoken by the way Alamy was thrashing around. He ordered the lights on, and what he saw made his skin crawl. Dozens of leechlike things were inching their way across the ceiling! They emanated a raw pent-up hunger and were flat enough to slide under a door had that been necessary. But it looked as though the creatures had been able to enter through the open windows.

But there was no time to take in more than that as Cato turned his attention to Alamy and the creature wrapped around her face. It was difficult to get his fingers in under the ridge of muscular flesh, but once he managed to break suction, the slither uttered a high-pitched squealing sound and wiggled in an attempt to free itself.

Dozens of tiny puncture wounds could be seen where the leech's hollow teeth had penetrated Alamy's skin and begun to suck blood out of her body. Her chest heaved as she sucked air into her oxygen-starved lungs, and Cato threw the loathsome animal at the opposite wall. The slither rolled itself into a ball during the flight, bounced off the wall without having suffered obvious damage, and rolled under the bed.

Meanwhile, slapping noises were heard as half a dozen of the leeches fell on Cato. Only four of them managed to connect, but that was enough as he struggled to peel the horrors off. "Fire!" he shouted, as hundreds of tiny teeth punctured his skin. "Try fire!"

It was a good suggestion, but Alamy didn't have a ready source of heat, so as Cato struggled to peel one of the monstrosities off his left shoulder, she ran to her dresser and opened the drawer where her sewing materials were kept. Then, scissors in hand, she ran back to the side of the bed and began to stab the loathsome creatures. The trick was to do damage without driving the point through the slither and into Cato.

The leeches squealed in pain, curled up into what looked like black-rubber balls, and bounced as they hit the floor. That was when Cato finally had the opportunity to snatch his pistol off the nightstand and fire at the creatures. Alamy placed her hands over her ears as he shot both the slithers that were still inching their way across the ceiling and those rolling around the floor. Each hit produced a fountain of blood followed by flapping movements as the animal died.

It wasn't long before Cato ran out of ammo, making it necessary to insert another magazine into his handgun, but most of the invaders were dead by then. That included the slither Rollo had killed and was ripping apart with his razor-sharp beak.

Cato was about to look under the bed when Alamy grabbed his arm. "Jak! What about Madam Faustus?"

Cato swore, made for the stairs, and raced downward. Then he went out the front door, and down another set of stairs, before running over to his landlady's door. There was no need to ring the bell or bang on the door. The gunfire had awoken Madam Faustus, and she was waiting for him. "Jak? What's wrong? Are you and Alamy okay?"

"Just barely," Cato replied. "May I come in? Someone sent some leechlike creatures into our apartment—and they could have entered your quarters as well."

Faustus let him in, and Cato found two slithers in her living room, both of which had probably gone astray. He speared them with a cooking fork, took the squirming bloodsuckers outside, and fired a single bullet through both.

A police car was circling above them by then, its lights strobing the night, but Cato sought to ignore everything except the mix of emotions that were swirling around him. There was fear, curiosity, and a strong sense of resentment that seemed to be emanating from the house next door. All of which was understandable. But, underlying all of it was a profound sense of sorrow, and that intrigued him. Who was in mourning? And why?

Weapon at the ready, Cato "followed" the emotion by the simple expedient of going to the point where it was strongest. The short journey took him through pools of light that fell from above, across the river of darkness that separated the two houses, and over to a large storage shed. The door was closed. Cato paused there, still "listening," and was surprised to hear someone sobbing inside.

Carefully, weapon at the ready, he took hold of the door and pulled. The barrier swung out of the way to reveal a hulking heavy-gravity-world variant. The breed had been created to perform physical labor on planets where most Umans could barely stand up straight. He was seated between what looked like two large suitcases, head in hands, shoulders shaking, as deep sobs racked his body.

Two street cops had caught up with Cato by that time, and as one of them aimed a flashlight at the suspect, the heavy brought his tear-stained face up to where Cato could see it. "You killed them!" the variant said accusingly. "They

were all I had—and you killed them! What am I supposed
to do now?"

"Who are you?" Cato demanded.

"My name is Korm, and I'm a beast master," the heavy
replied proudly.

"Well, beast master Korm," Cato said matter-of-factly,
"you are under arrest. The charge is attempted murder."

"It isn't right!" Korm objected. "All my children wanted
was something to eat."

"The bastard is crazy," one of the street cops observed.

"Yes," Cato agreed thoughtfully. "He sure as hell is. . . .
But someone sent Korm and his so-called children here. The
question is *who?*"

Tank three, as it was generally referred to, consisted of a
tiled room that was large enough to accommodate a six-man
lineup, and was equipped with vid cams, bright lights, and
a rather ominous floor drain that would make it easy to hose
blood off the floor. At the moment, a huge Cloque named
Emsay was seated on what appeared to be a dangerously
small bench as a police interrogator continued to grind away
at him.

The observation room was separated from the tank by a
pane of one-way glass so that people like Primus Pilus Inobo
could watch whatever interrogation was taking place, and
the policeman was pissed. And for what he considered to be
good reason. Because ever since Jak Cato had fallen out of
the sky and been assigned to his command, the errant Xeno
cop had been an unending source of trouble.

First there was the Emperor's Day episode, followed by a
wild-eyed assertion that Emor had been replaced by a shape
shifter, who was currently running the government. Then
came the hawala shoot-out in the X Quarter—closely followed by an effort to assassinate Cato on the job. And now,

after a *second* attempt on his life, Inobo was starting to wonder if his subordinate was immortal.

The good news, to the extent that there was some, was that beast master Korm had been willing to finger Emsay. Who, with assistance from a small army of police and a robotic cargo lifter, had been arrested and transported to tank three, where he was being interrogated. And now with Inobo, Usurlus, and Cato looking on, it appeared as though Emsay was about to spill his guts. No small task where the massively overweight Cloque was concerned.

The thought brought a smile to Inobo's face as the Xeno Corps interrogator took advantage of Emsay's emotional output to help break him. She had gray hair, a motherly demeanor, and was dressed in nonthreatening civilian clothes. "So you feel that you were used," she said sympathetically, as Emsay continued to bake under the hot lights.

"And now, based on testimony provided by beast master Korm, you are going to spend at least ten years on an Imperial prison planet. There won't be much to eat, I'm afraid. I understand meals consist of just enough calories to keep each prisoner alive. Meanwhile," she continued conversationally, "the person who hired you to assassinate Officer Cato will continue to live a life of luxury. It doesn't seem fair, does it?"

Emsay's saucerlike eyes blinked in an attempt to cope with the bright lights. He was hot, tired, and above all hungry. The mere thought of food caused his mouth tentacles to writhe uncontrollably. But it was important to remember who he was, *what* he was, and to hang tough. Because if he was going to sacrifice a client, especially one as powerful as Senator Nalomy, then there had to be some sort of quid pro quo. So he answered the question accordingly.

"No, it certainly doesn't," he croaked. "Let's say the accusations are true. . . . Let's say there *is* a client. . . . And let's say I was to provide you with a name. What would be in it for me?"

The interrogator had "felt" it coming and was ready with an answer. "First, there would be the satisfaction of knowing that you had done the right thing, thereby taking the first step on the road to rehabilitation. Then, were you to provide us with your client's name and testify against him or her as well, it's quite possible that you could serve your time on the Cloque home world rather than a prison planet. And, based on what I've heard, friends and relatives would be allowed to bring you extra food."

Emsay felt saliva flood his mouth. "Could my legal representative get that in writing? Especially the last part?"

"Of course," the interrogator replied smoothly. "So are you ready to talk?"

"Yes," Emsay replied reluctantly. "But I'm going to need something to eat first."

EIGHT

The city of Imperialus, on the planet Corin

A GROUP OF FIFTEEN PEOPLE HAD ASSEMBLED OUT-side the Imperial residence, four of whom were members of the Praetorian Guard, all equipped with the tools required to break in. But they couldn't do so without a final order from Chief of Staff Rolari, and he was waffling.

More than a day had passed since the Emperor had met with the Vord diplomats, and all attempts to communicate with him had been met with silence. So Rolari was faced with a terrible conundrum. It was his job to respect the Emperor's wishes, no matter how eccentric they might seem, and that included Emor's recent insistence on personal privacy. Because even if he was crazy, he was the Emperor.

If Rolari and the other top officials were wrong, and they forced their way into the residence only to discover that Emor was perfectly fine, then some very bad things were likely to happen. Especially to *him*. So Rolari felt a large empty place at the pit of his stomach as he made eye contact with the burly Centurion and gave the two-word order. "Break in."

The heavily embossed doors looked decorative but were made of solid durasteel and designed to hold off a concerted attack by a hypothetical force of armed insurgents long enough for the Emperor and his family to escape by air. So it was necessary for the soldiers to light cutting torches and go to work on the barrier's locking mechanisms before they could access the area beyond.

The first few minutes were the worst. Because as the yellow-orange lines sliced through vertical-locking rods and began to isolate the locks that controlled the horizontal bolts, Rolari feared that he would hear Emor's enraged voice over the intercom at any moment. But as the work continued without producing a response from within, the official became increasingly convinced that the Emperor was incapacitated in some way. Ill, perhaps? Or, God forbid, dead? There was always the possibility that he'd been struck down by an undiagnosed disease, or taken his own life, which would be consistent with the theory that Emor was mentally ill.

So Rolari experienced all sorts of emotions as the first rod was severed and the previously tight doors gave slightly. There was a momentary hiss, as if pressures were being equalized, followed by the outgassing of a very foul odor. One of the officials said, "My God, what's that?" and held his nose.

Rolari thought he knew the answer. But as the Praetorians pushed the doors open, and the Chief of Staff peered inside, he saw the debris-strewn floor and realized that something very unusual had taken place. Something very, very dark.

And that suspicion was soon confirmed as the group pushed its way farther into the residence—where a wealth of gruesome evidence was found. "There are bones scattered around the floor!" one of the soldiers announced.

"There's blood in the kitchen!" another voice said. "And what could be a body. . . . Oh, my God, I found a head! It's Ambassador Nusk!"

The claim was too outlandish to ignore, so Rolari went to see for himself, and was revolted to find that the official was correct. The head that had been left in one corner of the blood-smeared prep area *was* that of Ambassador Nusk! Who, judging from the expression frozen on his blackened face, had suffered a horrible death.

Rolari felt his lunch rise in his throat, stumbled out into the informal eating area where Emor traditionally had breakfast, and threw up in a vase worth five thousand Imperials. Others had similar reactions, and the crime scene would have been horribly compromised, had it not been for the businesslike Centurion who shooed everyone out of the residence. Then, under strict instructions not to touch anything, two of his men were assigned to search for Emperor Emor.

Fifteen minutes later, having completed their task, the battle-hardened Praetorians left through the front doors. Rolari and the others were outside waiting. "We looked everywhere, sir," the lead soldier reported as he removed wads of cloth from his nostrils. "There are bones here and there, some of which appear to have been there for quite a while, but no sign of the Emperor or his body."

Rolari took the news hard. Nearly all color left his face, his hands shook as if palsied, and beads of perspiration dotted his forehead. "Are you sure? *Completely* sure?"

The legionnaire nodded. "Yes, sir. Unless some of the loose body parts were those of the Emperor. I can't rule that out. But, if that was the case, who spread them around?"

Rolari's head began to swim, he felt weak in the knees, and he was about to collapse when two officials rushed to hold him up. "Inobo was correct," Rolari moaned pitifully. "I thought the story he told me was too fantastic to be true, but it *was* true, and I have only myself to blame!

"Call Primus Pilus Inobo, tell him to get over here, and to bring his best investigators with him. . . . Call Legate Usurlus as well. He tried to warn me, and I wouldn't listen."

"Yes, sire," an unctuous assistant promised. "Will there be anything else?"

"Yes," Rolari answered hoarsely, as his eyes darted from face to face. "There must be total secrecy until the investigation has been completed, the Emperor's son has been notified, and the succession is assured. Usurlus can help with that. Now, close the doors, post guards, and take me to my office. I need to lie down."

A swarm of silvery news cams swooped in to capture shots of Legate Usurlus as he stepped out onto the open veranda. And for good reason. It wasn't every day that a Senator was arrested and charged with agreeing to kill legislation in return for the death of a police officer and possibly a Legate as well, the same man credited with removing Nalomy's daughter from office on Dantha, thereby ending the corruption there.

But while the situation was breaking Usurlus's way, he was conscious of the fact that Senator Nalomy had lots of powerful friends and would soon be free on his personal recognizance. Not to mention the fact that the only evidence against him was the word of a Cloque crime lord. So even though Usurlus couldn't help but feel somewhat jubilant, he kept the emotion hidden and chose his words with care. "I was shocked and saddened to hear of Senator Nalomy's arrest," he told the hovering cameras. "The charges that have been brought against him are quite serious and, if true, would warrant severe punishment.

"However," Usurlus added sternly as he glanced from lens to lens, "each citizen is presumed to be innocent unless proven guilty in a court of law. It will be up to a tribunal and a jury to determine Senator Nalomy's guilt or innocence. I, of course, will be satisfied with whatever decision they reach."

There were lots of shouted questions from reporters who were watching the feeds from their various offices, but Usurlus waved them off and went back inside. That left the cameras to hover just off the veranda in hopes of getting more pictures of the Legate or, if they were lucky, a sound bite from a member of the Usurlus household. Meanwhile, Livius was waiting for Usurlus in the living room. "You have a visitor, sire. . . . Imperial Secretary Arla Armo is waiting in your study."

Usurlus was surprised and let it show. "Really? It usually works the other way around. What's the purpose of her visit? Did she say?"

Livius shook his head. "No, sire."

"It probably has something to do with Senator Nalomy's arrest," Usurlus mused. "Please ask Satha to bring some refreshments."

As Livius departed on his errand, Usurlus made his way down the hall and entered his office. Though not required to do so, Armo rose to greet him. A scarf covered her partially shaved skull, and she wore plain clothes, as if to avoid notice. And that was when Usurlus realized that rather than arrive by air car, as an official of her rank would normally do, Armo had chosen ground travel instead. Why?

"Please forgive me for dropping in this way," Armo said as they embraced. "But there is an urgent matter that I must discuss with you—and one that is very confidential as well. That's why I came by ground car, and judging from all of the news cams hanging around your home, it's a good thing I did."

"No apologies are required," Usurlus assured her, as Satha arrived with a tray and placed it on the desk. "Please," Usurlus said as his slave poured cups of hot caf, "have a seat. What is the matter you spoke of? And what can I do to help?"

Armo waited for Satha to leave before attempting to speak. And when she did, the tears began to well up. Usurlus offered a box of tissues, and she took two of them. "I'm sorry," Armo said, as she dabbed at her eyes. "But this is very difficult. As you probably know, given your connections, Emperor Emor has been somewhat reclusive of late. Frankly, many of us, myself included, feared that he had become mentally unstable.

"But late yesterday we discovered that a shape shifter not only managed to infiltrate the Imperial residence, kill Emperor Emor, and take his place. Worse yet," Armo said as she broke into tears, "it appears that the Sagathi ate him!"

Even though Usurlus not only was aware of the possibility but had attempted to warn authorities about it, he was still shocked and saddened. In spite of the fact that Emor had been tough, even ruthless at times, most of his initiatives had been selfless. Which was all a reasonable citizen could hope for. So his death was a real loss.

"I'm sorry," Usurlus said as he sat down next to Armo and tried to comfort her. "What about the shifter? Did they capture or kill him?"

Armo had regained control of her emotions by then and shook her head. "No," she responded. "It gets worse, I'm afraid. The investigation is still under way, but at this point it looks as though the Sagathi murdered a Vord diplomat as well and took his place! That allowed him to escape off planet."

Usurlus produced a low whistle. "That's bad. . . . Very bad."

Armo bit her lower lip and nodded in agreement. "There's more I'm afraid."

A look of disbelief appeared on Usurlus's face. "*More?* You must be joking."

"No," Armo said apologetically, "I'm not. Rolari ordered us to secure the Imperial residence and bring the Xeno Corps in to investigate. He also ordered us to notify you—in the hope that you could help.

"Then he went to his office," she continued, "tore down the curtain that blocked the windows, and went out onto the balcony. His body was found in the street below. Fortunately, it was unrecognizable, so the news combines don't know who the jumper was, and that gives us time. Not much, though, since everyone who works in the tower is a government employee, and they're clamoring for a name."

Usurlus swore softly. Emor's death wasn't Rolari's fault, although it might have been possible either to capture or kill Verafti had the Chief of Staff been courageous enough to take immediate action. But Rolari had been chosen for his ability to implement policy rather than create it, so the outcome was almost inevitable. "And Emor's son?" Usurlus wanted to know. "Has he been notified?"

"Yes," Armo replied. "Or he will be soon. He's on Inva II with the 8th Legion. A courier has been dispatched. We can expect Brunus to arrive on Corin roughly seven days from now."

"Good. . . . A smooth succession will be extremely important," Usurlus mused out loud. "What about the Vords? How much do they know?"

"Nothing yet," Armo answered. "We thought it best to keep them in the dark until the initial phase of the investigation is complete."

"I agree," Usurlus said. "In the meantime, we have a great deal to accomplish."

"Such as?" Armo inquired.

"I suggest that you begin by notifying members of the Senate that the Emperor died in his sleep. Then, about two hours later, put out a press release informing the public of the same thing. Tell them that Emor will be buried with full honors in two weeks' time. Rolari couldn't deal with the loss and committed suicide. Meanwhile, consistent with Imperial law, his son Brunus will take the throne assuming that the Senate confirms him. And I believe they will."

Armo was silent for a moment, as if giving the proposal some thought. "Yes," the official said as she came to her feet. "I agree. . . . Let's get to work."

The inside of the Imperial residence was much as it had been when the Praetorian Guards had broken in except that technicians in white clean-suits could be seen here and there, snapping hundreds of pictures, collecting bits of evidence, and recording their observations into hand corders. And standing in the middle of it all, watching them work, was Centurion Jak Cato.

Having survived an assassination attempt, and been witness to the lengthy interrogation that followed, Cato had been asleep on the squad-room couch when Shani shook him awake. Now, two hours later, he was in charge of a very high-profile murder investigation. By all rights it should have been carried out by members of the city's Xenocide team, but because of Cato's knowledge of Verafti and the need to limit the number of people who knew about the manner in which Emperor Emor had been killed, the job had fallen to him.

That was tough enough. But making the situation even more difficult was the fact that he was still working for Inobo, and having entered the residence from whatever meeting he'd been in, the senior officer had spotted Cato and was on his way over. The variant had a pretty good idea what would happen next and steeled himself against the coming onslaught.

As Inobo followed the "safe" path the technicians had established across the enormous living room, he was worried. Having given the report from Cato and Usurlus short shrift and failed to follow up after his initial meeting with Rolari, Inobo was in a very vulnerable position. Fortunately for him, however, the Chief of Staff had committed suicide, and in doing so, had effectively taken responsibility for the entire episode. Would that be enough to satisfy Brunus Emor? Inobo certainly hoped so and was eager to complete the investigation quickly, as a way to both look efficient and cover up his failure to pursue the Verafti threat.

So as he began to close with his subordinate, Inobo's priorities were clear: Wrap up the investigation, write a self-serving report, and send Cato to a place far, far away. "There you are," Inobo said. "What's taking so long? This is an open-and-shut case, for God's sake."

Cato frowned. "Sorry, sir. . . . I don't understand."

"I asked what the hell is taking so long," Inobo replied irritably. "Good God, man. . . . How many pictures do you need? Verafti killed Emor, took his place, and did the same thing to Nusk. Case closed."

"Not quite," Cato replied. "Based on what we've discovered so far, Verafti killed a Praetorian as well. . . . That's how he got access to the Imperial Residence in the first place. Then, posing as the guard, he could come and go freely."

"Terrific," Inobo put in sourly, "I'll make a note. But my comment stands. We know what happened, and we know who did it, so let's wrap it up."

"We know what happened," Cato agreed steadfastly, "and we know Verafti did it. What we don't know is *why*."

"Are you stupid?" Inobo demanded incredulously. "The answer is obvious. . . . Verafti killed Emor in order to become Emperor! Any fool can see that."

"I don't think so," Cato countered stubbornly. "I am very familiar with the Sagathies. . . . And this one in particular. Verafti has no interest in power or the trappings that go with it. He would hate this place. Look around. . . . See all the random destruction? That's Verafti venting his frustration. The residence was like a prison, and he wanted out."

"Assuming you're right, why come here at all?" Inobo wanted to know. "It doesn't make sense."

"No, it doesn't," Cato agreed. "And that brings us back to where we started. Verafti was looking for something, and if we want to catch him, we need to know what it was."

"Why bother?" Inobo replied dismissively. "The Vords are our enemies. . . . Let Verafti kill them for a change! Maybe we should give him a medal."

Inobo had been so fixated on Cato, he didn't realize that Usurlus was present until the Legate spoke from only a foot away. "I've heard some stupid comments during my life, Primus Pilus Inobo. . . . But that could be the worst of all. Has it occurred to you that in his role as Emperor Emor, Verafti had access to all of the government's most sensitive files? Including detailed information regarding the strength and disposition of our troops? What if he were to supply that information to the Vords? Or, worse yet, to seize control of their empire, just as he took over ours?"

It was clear from Inobo's horrified expression that neither one of those possibilities had occurred to him. Possibilities which, should they become reality, could easily be blamed on him!

Usurlus had a pretty good idea what the other man was thinking. He smiled thinly. "That's right, my friend. . . . There are some very good reasons why you should support Officer Cato's efforts! So I suggest that you return to your office and stay out of the way until such time as you are needed. Do we understand each other?"

Inobo tried to think of something to say, failed, and left without a word. Cato sighed. The outcome of the confrontation had been a victory of a sort. But what would happen once the whole thing was over? And Usurlus lost interest in him? He would be at Inobo's mercy then. . . . And payback would be a bitch.

Usurlus couldn't read emotions the way an empath could, but he could see that Cato was exhausted, and said as much. "You're tired, Jak. Go get a bite to eat and some sleep. That's an order."

Cato nodded stiffly, said, "Yes, sire," and followed the safe path out. He intended to go home but never made it past the neighboring reception hall, which had been transformed into a temporary office/laboratory for the investigative team. That was where Shani found him curled up on the floor. She threw a blanket over the Centurion. Then, having threatened to kill anyone who woke Cato up, she went back to work.

It was two in the morning, the forensic team had completed its work, and robots were busy preparing the residence for the new Emperor's arrival, as Cato sat at the same computer access point that Verafti had been using. For hours he and an artificial intelligence named Orl-48 had been hard at work sifting through the thousands of searches the shape shifter had carried out over the last couple of months, and certain things were becoming clear.

Among them was the fact that there was very little if any alignment between government priorities and the files the imposter had chosen to access. That seemed to support Cato's thesis that Verafti had little to no interest in actually running the government.

In fact, according to Orl-48, who was buried in an Imperial computer somewhere, most of Verafti's searches had to do with Sagathi shape shifters. And that made sense if the fugitive was trying to find out what efforts, if any, were directed at trying to find him.

But, because he had supposedly been killed on Dantha, there hadn't been any hits associated with his name. A fact which had probably been of considerable satisfaction to him. There were hits regarding other Sagathies, however, including two executions, and an escape that predated Verafti's. An extremely rare event in which a female shape shifter had been able to get off her home planet by posing as a human corpse. The question was whether Verafti was interested in the activities of *all* Sagathies or that individual in particular.

Even with all of the computing power that Orl-48 could bring to bear, because Verafti's searches were so varied it took another half hour to reach what Cato believed to be the answer. The search terms the shifter used included missing persons, cult activity, serial murders, fluctuations in the financial markets, crime statistics, and everything having to do with one Jak Cato. Including his assignment to the bunko squad and activities since.

Tempting though it was to focus on the personal threat, Cato knew that the *real* objective of Verafti's activities was buried somewhere inside all of the other searches. And, having focused on those, it wasn't long before the Xeno cop was able to assemble a working hypothesis that not only explained why the shape shifter had chosen to kill the Emperor but where he was likely to show up next.

So with that information in hand, Cato thanked Orl-48, signed off the system he would probably never be allowed to access again, and went looking for Usurlus. Because, if his theory was correct, the danger posed to the Empire by Sagathi shape shifters was double what it had been.

Once Cato was ordered to take control of the overlapping murder investigations in the Imperial Residence, leadership of the bunko squad fell to Section Leader Shani, who was determined to complete the pickpocket investigation and bring the ringleader to justice. The plants, none of which were judged to be sentient, were being returned to their home world for reintegration into the ecosystem from which they had been removed.

Meanwhile, the Kelf who was believed to be responsible for importing the plants to Corin and training them to become pickpockets was on the run. But now, thanks to information provided by a paid informant named Dybo, the squad knew where their suspect was hiding. And as Shani stood in the middle of a deserted street and peered down into the pitch-black storm drain below, she didn't like it one bit. "You're sure about this?" she inquired sternly. "Because if we go down there and come up empty-handed, I'm going to be *very* unhappy."

Dybo had a rounded head, one beady eye, and a short muzzle. His clothing consisted of a jeweled eye patch, a heavily embroidered satin jacket, and matching shorts. With the exception of a gold toe ring, his feet were bare. He was only three feet tall—and had to crane his neck in order to look up at Shani. "Taget is down there—I swear it."

Based on what Dybo felt, he was telling the truth as he knew it, but that was no guarantee of success, so Shani opted for an insurance policy. "Good," she replied, "because you're coming with us."

Dybo turned and ran, or tried to, but it was more of a waddle. A cop named Vium grabbed the Kelf by the scruff of the neck and jerked him off the ground. The criminal's face was partially lit by the spill from the streetlight above, and she could "feel" his fear. But fear of what? The storm drain itself? The creatures that were said to live down there? Or *her*? It was impossible to tell. She stared into Dybo's good eye. "You tried to run. . . . Why?"

"Everybody knows there are pipe crawlers down there," Dybo replied heatedly. "Some weigh as much as I do! If you were my size, you'd be scared, too. . . . Besides, I'm wearing my good clothes. I'll wait here."

"Like hell you will," Shani growled. "Cuff him, Siby. . . . And put him on a chain."

"Will do, SL," the cop said tightly, and went to get the necessary hardware out of the unmarked police van parked a few feet away.

"All right," Shani said as she eyed the rest of the squad. "Pair up, check each other's equipment, and don't forget gloves and kneepads. You're gonna need them. Three-Ball will be on point, and I'll take the two slot, followed by our furry friend. Siby, Vium, and Nutone will bring up the rear. Keep an eye on our six, Nute; otherwise, something nasty could crawl up your ass and nibble on your tonsils!"

The comment was meant to get a laugh, and did, which helped lighten the mood a bit. Then, with Dybo chained to Siby, it was time for Three-Ball to descend into the maze below. Like news cams, the robot could fly, although not as high, and was equipped with a powerful light. He was also packing a stunner, lots of com gear, and the capacity to feed live video to the team.

So as Three-Ball dropped down the vertical shaft and arrived in the pipe below, Shani could watch via her HUD as his light swept across badly pitted metal. Like so much of the city's infrastructure the tube had been there a long time and was overdue for replacement. Having checked the immediate area for heat signatures and come up empty, Three-Ball radioed the all clear.

Shani activated her helmet light before following Three-Ball down. Like the rest of the team, she was wearing black body armor, two pistols in shoulder holsters, and a hydration pack. Her cargo pockets were stuffed with ration bars, a first-aid kit, and miniflares.

Having cleared the vertical tube and followed Three-Ball a few yards north, she took the opportunity to look around as the rest of the team took their places behind her. The pipe was about four feet across. Large enough for a Kelf to walk through but not the Umans, who would be forced to duck-walk or crawl. "Okay, Dybo," Shani said. "We're here. . . . What should we look for?"

Dybo, who was equipped with a jury-rigged headset, was anything but happy. Something all of the empaths could pick up on. "It's hard to see," he complained. "And I've only been down here once before. Maybe we should get more lights and come back later."

A squeal was heard, followed by a sudden rush of words, as Dybo sought to forestall more of whatever Siby had done to him. "Go straight ahead," the Kelf instructed. "And watch for the luminescent arrows. They will lead you to Taget's hideout."

And that appeared to be the case because, as the team crawled along, a succession of glowing green arrows helped them navigate their way through a series of Y-shaped branchings. Yellow light washed the walls, their kneepads made squishing sounds, and on occasion a muffled rumble was heard as a subway train passed through a tunnel parallel to theirs.

Finally, Three-Ball sent the dimly lit video Shani had been waiting to see, along with a characteristically formal voice-over. "I see an empty catch basin directly ahead. It is fed by six pipes—including the one we are presently travel-ing through. Approximately three feet below the outlets a six-foot-wide ledge can be seen. It surrounds the reservoir, and judging from the number of sleeping platforms on it, I estimate that at least four individuals have been living in-side the chamber. None of them is visible at the present time. Over."

Shani eyed the video and swore softly. So much for her hopes that she could waltz in, arrest Taget, and put him in the slammer before breakfast. But it felt good to scrape past the point where a metal grate had been removed—and stand off to one side as the rest of the team followed her out. The inside of the chamber was quite spacious, and, by moving her head, Shani was able to sweep her helmet light back and forth across the domed ceiling.

That was when she saw three objects fall out of the vertical tubes that fed the catch basin from above and recognized them for what they were. "Grenades!"

The explosive devices were timed to explode in midair. Everyone hit the deck, but as three overlapping explosions shook the underground chamber, hundreds of pieces of razor-sharp shrapnel ricocheted back and forth off the duracrete walls. Siby and Nutone were killed instantly, a fact that quickly became apparent as their vital signs vanished from Shani's HUD, and Dybo began to yell while simultaneously jerking at his chain. "Taget! It's me! Don't shoot!"

Now it was clear that the informer had been in cahoots with Taget from the beginning, hadn't anticipated the possibility that the team would take him along, and was hoping that Taget would spare him. So Shani drew a pistol and shot Dybo in the head. The Kelf fell on top of Siby.

Conscious of the fact that each second was precious, Shani yelled, "Follow me!"

Vium, the only survivor other than Three-Ball, did as he was told. He could "see" Shani's heat signature thanks to his HUD—and "feel" the Section Leader's emotions as she dove into the closest pipe and scrambled to make room. He dove in behind her and scooted forward, as *more* grenades exploded and shrapnel rattled all around.

Shani was moving as quickly as she could by then, hoping to put some distance between what remained of her team and the chamber, before climbing up to the street above. Then she ran into the grate. It had thick durasteel bars that would clearly be impervious to anything less than a plasma torch.

Shani said, "Damn, damn, damn," as she turned back toward the chamber and ordered Vium to do likewise. That was when she realized that Three-Ball's icon had disappeared from her HUD.

A wash of light appeared in the chamber, somebody fired a gun, and Shani aimed for the muzzle flash. There was an almost deafening *boom* inside the pipe, followed by a cry of pain, which suggested a hit. But whatever satisfaction Shani might have felt was dulled by the knowledge that they were trapped. "Any unit, any unit, this is eight-five. I have two men down, and we're trapped. Do you read?"

But Shani was deep underground, and there was a lot of duracrete between her and the surface, so the chances of being heard were slim. The only reply was a moment of silence, followed by a maniacal giggle from the chamber, and the steady *drip*, *drip*, *drip* of water. They were alone.

Usurlus was ensconced in what had been Rolari's office. A chair had been brought in so that he could sit down, an open area had been created by clearing piles of printouts from the previously cluttered desk, and he was hard at work drafting a speech. Not for himself, but for Brunus Emor, who would have to seize the reins of power quickly lest some individual or group try to steal the throne out from under him.

Hardly anyone wrote by hand anymore, but Usurlus was one of the few, especially where first drafts were concerned. He enjoyed the feel of putting ink to paper, not to mention the freedom to scrawl text in the margins, with arrows to show where the additions should go. Now, having written the introduction, it was time to consider the main thrust of the speech.

The news of Emperor Emor's death had gone off like a bomb inside the Senate and was still sending political shock waves out across the Empire, just as Usurlus, Armo, and others had known that it would. Suddenly, everything had changed. Those who owed their livelihoods to Emor were without a sponsor—and those who believed themselves to be on good terms with Brunus were elated.

Others who had long been out of favor suddenly had reason to hope since a new Emperor meant new opportunities. And so it went from the top of the political food chain to the people stationed at the bottom. *His* job was to pen something lofty, something that would position Brunus as being above the fray, with his eyes firmly fixed on all of the important issues that had been so sadly neglected during Verafti's tenure.

Would Brunus accept the speech? And actually give it? If so, Usurlus would be able to count himself among those who would find a place in the new scheme of things. If not, it might be time to rejuvenate his military career or retire to some university, where he could lecture students about how things should have been.

Such were the Legate's thoughts when he heard a rap on the door, and Cato appeared. He looked rumpled and was badly in need of a shave. "Sorry to disturb you, sire. . . . But I believe I know where Verafti is headed—and why."

Usurlus hoped Cato was correct because Brunus would want revenge, and it would be best to give him that satisfaction immediately lest he focus his energies on finding his father's killer rather than the much-neglected affairs of state. So Usurlus put his stylus down and gestured toward the new guest chair. "Okay, I'll bite. . . . Where is Verafti headed? And why?"

Cato sat down, but on the edge of the chair, as if ready to get up and go. His expression was serious. "Well, sire, the simplest way to put it is that the bastard is in love. My research suggests that he had a relationship with a female named Affa Demeni on their home world of Sagatha. As you know, the entire planet is in permanent quarantine. But Demeni escaped by taking the place of a Uman corpse that was being shipped off-world for burial. The local CO was court-martialed for allowing that to happen.

"Three standard months later, Verafti followed her by killing a Sagathi who was being taken off planet for medical treatment and taking that individual's place. En route, he murdered the medical team *and* most of the ship's crew, before a handful of officers managed to fortify the control room and land on Oro.

"My team was there waiting for him. We took him into custody and were hauling his ass back to Sagatha, when we were forced to land on Dantha. You know what happened after that."

Usurlus shook his head in amazement. "So the whole point of killing Emor, and replacing him, was to find Demeni?"

"Yes, sire," Cato replied earnestly. "And, judging from an analysis of his computer usage, it worked. After running into hundreds of dead ends, he locked on to a trail of killings that led to the planet Therat."

Usurlus sat up straight. "The planet the Vords took over? *That* Therat?"

Cato nodded. "Yes, sire. . . . And that's why he murdered Ambassador Nusk. So he could work his way into the Vord hierarchy and travel to Therat."

"Damn him!" Usurlus said angrily as he brought his fist down on the desktop.

It was an unusual display of emotion on the Legate's part, and Cato could "feel" the extent of the other man's frustration. "Yes, sire," he agreed. "But it gets worse. . . . What if he finds Demeni? Imagine what *two* shape shifters, working in tandem, could accomplish."

"We've got to warn the Vords," Usurlus said grimly. "More than that, we've got to convince the ugly bastards to let us send a team of empaths to Therat and hunt both of those killers down."

"I agree," Cato put in soberly. "But with no previous experience of their own, would they believe that such a thing is even possible?"

"Oh, they'll believe us," Usurlus grated. "I'm going to call Inobo—and order him to—"

But Cato didn't get to hear what Usurlus was going to order Inobo to do because that was the moment when one of the Praetorian Guard's Centurions appeared in the doorway. A battered police bot was hovering next to him. "Excuse me," the officer said, "but could I speak to Centurion Cato? It's a police emergency."

The words were enough to bring Cato up out of the chair. Seconds later, courtesy of Three-Ball, he was watching a holo of the underground ambush. He winced as two members of his squad were cut down. "Did you call it in?" Cato wanted to know, once the robot's report came to an end.

"Yes, sir," Three-Ball responded unemotionally. "But hundreds of thousands of people are pouring into the streets in response to Emperor Emor's death. Off-duty officers have been notified and are coming in to work—but dispatch told me that it could be hours before the department can assemble a response team and send them down."

"That's bullshit," Cato replied grimly. "We're going in there even if it is just you and me."

"We aren't cops, but we know how to fight," the Praetorian put in. "And we owe you one for solving the Emperor's murder. Could you use some volunteers?"

"You bet your ass I could," Cato responded gratefully. "Let's go."

Usurlus had been forgotten but didn't mind. He had work to do, *lots* of it, beginning with a call to Inobo. The sun had risen by then and sent shafts of sunlight slanting into the office to clothe Usurlus in liquid gold. He was too busy to notice.

NINE

The city of Imperialus, on the planet Corin

TAGET AND HIS GANG COULDN'T FIRE DIRECTLY INTO
the pipe without standing directly opposite the opening—
which they quickly learned not to do. What they could do
was fire into the tube from an angle on the chance that their
bullets would bounce off the sides and hit the Xeno cops
hiding inside. Fortunately for Shani and Vium, they were far
enough back from the opening that the ricochet strategy had
been ineffective so far—although there had been two close
calls. Still, it made sense to keep their helmet lights turned
off to conserve power and make themselves harder to see. So,
viewed from inside the pipe, what little bit of illumination
there was came from what looked like a decim-sized hole
and the work lights beyond.

Now, hours after the ambush, Shani had begun to give
up hope. Because once her team failed to report within a
reasonable amount of time, the support team was supposed
to notify the shift boss, whose job it was to dispatch a quick-
reaction force to the scene. But in spite of what *should* be
happening, the two of them were still waiting.

Meanwhile, having peeked out of the darkened pipe from time to time, Shani knew that Taget was systematically removing both his belongings and loot from the pump room located just off the main chamber. An understandably lengthy process given the need for his full-sized henchmen to carry everything out via a maze of pipes.

So it was a standoff of sorts, or had been, until a trickle of water began to flow through the grate and along the bottom of the pipe. "What's going on?" Vium wondered out loud. "Is it raining topside?"

Shani tried to remember what the weather forecast had been but couldn't. "Beats me," she confessed. "But I hope it doesn't get any deeper. I forgot my towel."

Vium chuckled appreciatively. "Yeah," he said, "me too."

Taget couldn't hear them, of course, but clearly knew about the water because he called to them from somewhere in the chamber. His voice was high and squeaky. "Can you swim?" he demanded. "Because there's a ten-thousand-gallon holding tank up-system from your location, and one of my associates opened the main valve a minute ago. It won't be long before a whole lot of water is going to shoot through that pipe and blow you out into the catch basin! That's when we're going to shoot you. . . . Assuming you don't drown, that is."

The words were followed by a gale of maniacal laughter as the flow grew stronger and Vium's fear became almost palpable. "I don't know how to swim, SL. . . . I'm going to drown."

"Don't worry," Shani replied dismissively. "Taget is full of shit."

But she *was* worried, and being an empath, Vium could "feel" it.

"Okay," Shani said, as the water continued to rise. "Maybe this is for real. . . . Let's throw a couple of flash-bangs into the chamber and come out shooting. Given a little bit of luck, we'll take a couple of those assholes with us. Check your weapons."

Then, before either one of them could take action, they heard a sudden rattle of gunfire, followed by the equally le-thal *zing* of ricocheting bullets, as something round blocked the opening to the pipe. Then Three-Ball was inside and pushing his way upstream as the steadily increasing flow of water threatened to eject him. Shani recognized the voice that issued from the external speaker as Cato's. "Stay where you are. . . . We're coming in."

Shani felt her heart leap even as a solid column of water blew all three of them out into the chamber, where the Umans splashed into the pool of stagnant water below. Shani heard the muted sound of gunfire as she went under but was forced to let go of her pistols in order to grab Vium and try to keep the nonswimmer afloat. The pair surfaced long enough for Shani to catch a momentary glimpse of a snarling Kelf, a bald Uman, and a plug-ugly Ur, all of whom were firing down at her as the water from the pipe roiled the surface. Then, in spite of Shani's best efforts to keep both of them from sinking, cold water closed over her helmet.

The problem was that the weight of her gear, plus Vium's stuff, was pulling both of them down as bullets plunged into the pool around them. They were deadly as they entered the water but soon lost their force, as Vium produced a string of bubbles that followed each other toward the shimmery light above. That was when Three-Ball stunned the Ur, took two rounds through his housing, and burped black smoke before splashing into the catch basin. The entire team was down.

Emperor Emor was dead, the end of an era had arrived, and the streets were swarming with thousands of people. Most of the crowds were peaceful, but there had been opportunistic rioting in Port City, the neighboring Tank Farm, and the X Quarter. That, coupled with the fact that the streets were virtually impassable, meant the command structure had been more than happy to let Cato and the Praetorians handle what they saw as a comparatively simple problem.

So, as a century of uniformed soldiers struggled to keep the surging crowd back from the rope lines that had been used to cordon off the area where four streets converged, Cato and four members of the Praetorian Guard were about to drop straight down through the four vertical pipes that were equally spaced around the intersection. They were the same drains through which grenades had been dropped during the ambush hours earlier.

The circular lids had been removed, and makeshift tripods had been set up over each opening, where they stood ready to support Cato and his companions as they lowered themselves into the system below. The Xeno cop was arguably the least-prepared person on the team since, unlike members of the bunko squad, the Praetorians practiced such maneuvers on a regular basis.

Still, Cato knew how to rappel, and that was the main skill that would be required. That, and shooting straight while dangling from the end of a rope. Every second was precious, so having received ready signs from the rest of the team, Cato gave the necessary order. "Now!"

The interior of the tube was little more than a dark blur as Cato dropped through it. There was a sudden explosion of light as he entered the chamber, followed by a jerk as he came to a halt ten feet above the catch basin.

As Cato made a grab for the weapon hanging across his chest, he saw that a horizontal column of water was shooting out of a pipe and arcing into the roiling catch basin below. Meanwhile, having been surprised by the unexpected attack, a group of armed suspects fired up at the targets dangling above them.

That was a mistake. Two of the Praetorians got off sustained bursts before Cato even squeezed the trigger. The perps fell like wheat to a scythe—and the battle was over in a matter of seconds. But where were Shani and Vium? There was no sign of them until two heads broke the surface of the water.

Having shed her body armor, Shani managed to help Vium to the surface, where she fully expected to be killed. But as their heads emerged into a maelstrom of roiling water, and they hurried to suck air into their aching lungs, both variants were thrilled to discover that the shooting was over.

Three-Ball was floating half-submerged in the pool, having taken two rounds through his CPU, but he gave Vium something to hang on to as the rescue party lowered themselves onto the ledge below. Fifteen minutes later, Shani and Vium were out of the water and up on the street, where an air ambulance was waiting to whisk them away. "I'm sorry," Shani said miserably as she looked up into Cato's face.

"I know," Cato replied somberly. "It wasn't your fault."

Shani wasn't so sure. But there wasn't any point in saying that because Cato could "sense" it and already knew.

It was necessary to shout in order to be heard over the crowd noise. "What's going on?" Shani wanted to know, as Cato walked her over to the ambulance. By that time the government had preempted all of the city's video display walls in order to play carefully chosen clips of Emor's rise to power—and silvery news cams were cruising the crowd. Those who weren't out on the streets were watching from their homes.

"They made the announcement a few hours ago," Cato replied expressionlessly. "Emperor Emor died in his sleep."

Shani made a face. "Yeah, sure he did."

"I know where Verafti is," Cato said flatly.

"Are we going after him?"

"Yes, I hope so."

"I'll be ready," Shani promised.

"I know," Cato replied, as a medic took over. "But it isn't going to be easy."

"No," Shani agreed. "It never is." And with that she was gone.

More than two standard weeks had passed since Brunus Emor had arrived on Corin, ridden through the streets in an open limo, and made his obligatory appearance in the Senate, where he delivered the speech Usurlus had written for him.

There were those who would have preferred to see someone else on the throne, themselves, for example, but they knew that Brunus was extremely popular with the Legions, who would regard any other candidate as a usurper.

So Brunus's claim to the throne was approved by acclamation, and three days later his father was laid to rest in the Valley of the Greats, where each of the Empire's Emperors had a tomb.

Not only was the event witnessed by three billion people on Corin, but it would eventually be seen by trillions more as a fleet of courier ships raced to deliver video of the event to even the most remote colonies. Worlds which Brunus planned to visit as soon as possible to signal continuity, respect for his loyal subjects, and an interest in their problems.

But important though it was, the grand tour would have to wait while Brunus worked with the Senate to resolve a number of pressing issues, not the least of which was the threat represented by the Vords. And not just by the Vords, but by the presence of two Sagathi shape shifters hiding among them, where they could cause harm to *both* sides.

And that was why a group of three Vord diplomats and their so-called advisors had been invited to the Imperial Tower for what were being described as "follow-on talks." Although the actual agenda, as planned by the newly named Chief of Staff Isulu Usurlus and Secretary Arla Armo, was going to be somewhat different. That was where the Xeno Corps, Primus Pilus Inobo, and Centurion Jak Cato would come into play.

First, however, it was necessary to bring the Vords down from orbit and escort them up to the reception hall adjacent to the Imperial Residence, where Emperor Brunus was waiting to greet them. And Cato had a front-row seat because he was among the Praetorian Guards who were lined up against one wall.

Like his father, Brunus was a somewhat homely man but in good physical condition and possessed of a certain animal magnetism. Unlike the first Emor, however, he preferred plain military-style tunics and kilts to the court attire his father typically affected, and was less aloof. In fact, much to the amazement of his staff, the new Emperor had a disconcerting tendency to embrace people he took a liking to, slap the backs of people he barely knew, and occasionally challenge guests to soldierlike contests of strength.

But it was quickly becoming apparent that Brunus was capable of subtlety, too, as he delivered formal greetings to the Ya parasites as well as their Vord hosts, and was careful to seat his guests in order of clan precedence. A detail sure to be noticed and appreciated.

Once everyone was seated at the table, both sides began to spout what Cato considered to be worthless time-wasting bullshit, but that was the way of things, and all he and his comrades could do was wait. The previous two weeks had been spent writing, then rewriting after-action reports related to the Galaxus Hotel shoot-out, the attack on his home, and the underground ambush. All of which had been painful and frustrating to Cato, knowing that while he was feeding the police bureaucracy, Verafti was still on the loose.

The *good* news, if it could appropriately be classified as such, was that Inobo couldn't force him to fill out a single form regarding Emperor Emor's murder since every person who knew the truth had been sworn to secrecy! And, in the case of certain Praetorian Guards, promoted and sent to distant outposts. The veil of secrecy was about to be lifted, however, but only for a moment, and only for the Vord diplomats.

Finally, once the initial mumbo jumbo was over, it was Usurlus who took the meeting to the next level. He was seated directly across the conference table from a long-faced ambassador named Narwar Lyic Enynn. The Vord diplomat was attired in a shapeless hat to which a large jewel had been pinned, a mottled gray-green parasite that hugged his scrawny neck like a collar, and a severely cut coat that was decorated with two rows of gold buttons. "First," Usurlus said, "I would like to address an issue that while not a part of the formal agenda, should be of great concern to both parties and requires urgent action."

Enynn, who feared the statement was a prelude to some sort of Uman negotiating trick, produced the Vord equivalent of a frown. It made his already grave countenance look funeral. His voice was deep and gravelly. "My associates and I are not prepared to discuss subjects that are not already on the agenda."

"Of course," Usurlus said, "we understand. However, if you would permit us to make a short presentation, I think you'll agree that the urgency of this matter justifies a break in normal protocol."

Enynn was about to refuse, but his Ya had been listening and had other ideas. His name was Orery, and unlike his host, he was inclined to indulge his curiosity from time to time. *Let's see where the Umans are headed,* the Ya suggested. *We can always say no.*

Enynn swallowed his objections. "If you must," he said ungraciously, "but please remember our time constraints."

Usurlus nodded gravely. "Of course . . . Thank you. As you and your distinguished colleagues already know, the previous Emperor is dead, having been replaced by his son, who is with us today." All eyes went to Brunus at that point, and he smiled grimly.

"What you don't know," Usurlus added soberly, "is that rather than dying in his sleep as was announced . . . the Emperor was murdered."

It was startling news, and certainly of interest, especially if it pointed toward some sort of infighting within the Uman Empire. Infighting that could weaken the government and make it that much easier to defeat. But Enynn couldn't say that and didn't. "I hope Emperor Brunus Emor will accept our deepest condolences not only for his loss—but the unfortunate manner of his father's death."

Unlike the earlier comment, it was gracefully said, and Brunus acknowledged that with a half bow. "Thank you."

"Unfortunately," Usurlus continued bleakly, "we have reason to believe that the killer murdered Emperor Emor *prior* to the recent meeting with Ambassador Nusk, and was able to board one of your ships along with the returning diplomats."

"That's impossible," Enynn scoffed. "Our soldiers would never allow an unauthorized Uman to board one of our ships."

"Not one they knew about," Usurlus conceded, "but this was no ordinary criminal. Fiss Verafti is a Sagathi shape shifter, which is to say a member of a species which can adopt the appearance of any being of roughly the same mass. Which means Verafti was able to take Nusk's place, return to your ship without arousing suspicion, and subsequently shift identifies prior to merging with your population."

"That's absurd," Enynn objected tactlessly. "We have never heard of such creatures, but even if they exist, it would be impossible to trick us in such a manner. We would notice the difference."

"Really?" Usurlus inquired, as his eyes roamed the faces across from him. "Tell me something. . . . Where *is* Ambassador Nusk? Why isn't he here?"

There was a moment of silence as Enynn looked at his companions and they at him. *Take care,* Orery cautioned, *I sense the Umans are being truthful. . . . Why prevaricate where such a thing is concerned?*

Enynn swallowed the lump that had formed in his throat as the implications of the situation became increasingly clear. "We don't know where Ambassador Nusk is," he said hoarsely. "He disappeared."

"I'm afraid it's our turn to extend condolences," Usurlus replied sympathetically. "I suggest that you check to see if Nusk's disappearance was coincident with the discovery of a dead body. It may have been whole, or part of it may have been eaten, because the Sagathies are quite carnivorous."

Enynn was convinced by that time, because there *had* been a mysterious death, but one of his colleagues was still skeptical. His name was Inhor Atil Yoneb. "This has gone far enough. . . . We are here to discuss the relationship between two empires. Let's get on with it."

Usurlus smiled thinly as he turned to Brunus. "It seems our guests have doubts regarding the veracity of our claims, sire. . . . How would *you* respond?"

Slowly, so that the shocked Vords had plenty of time in which to appreciate what was taking place, Brunus morphed into a fearsome-looking reptile. "How would *I* respond?" the creature echoed. "I would eat them if given the chance! They look very tasty."

Having forced Inobo to bring the shape shifter in from Sagatha, Usurlus was anything but surprised by the transformation, but judging from the expressions on their faces, the Vords were clearly horrified. "I apologize for startling you," he said, "but we Umans have a saying: 'A picture is worth a thousand words.'"

And with that, Usurlus and the rest of the Uman delegation stood as the door to the Imperial Residence opened, and the *real* Brunus entered the reception hall. He bowed, as did his Sagathi twin. Then they began to circle each other until it became hard to know which was which.

"You can see the problem," Usurlus said gravely. "That's why we keep the Sagathies confined to their home planet— and our genetic engineers were ordered to develop a strain of variants specifically equipped to deal with exotic sentients. Individuals like Centurion Cato, who can identify a shape shifter no matter what form he or she might adopt. Cato," Usurlus said, "please point to the *real* Emperor Emor."

Cato "saw" the Uman's emotions, took a step forward, and pointed him out. That was the Sagathi's cue to revert to his true form, thereby concluding the agreement struck with his jailers. Once back on the surface of Sagatha, he would never be allowed to leave, but there was a huge difference between a prison cell and being allowed to roam the jungle, a freedom he missed and was looking forward to enjoying again.

"So," Usurlus said thoughtfully, "if such a creature could infiltrate the Imperial Tower here on Corin, and murder the Emperor's father, then imagine what *two* of them could do within your society."

"*Two* of them?" Enynn inquired hoarsely.

"Yes, I'm afraid so," Usurlus replied. "Both of whom are probably on Therat by now."

"It's a trick!" Yoneb objected. "They're trying to scare us! Trying to make us evacuate Therat."

Enynn was no fool. He looked at Yoneb, then back again. "What happened to Nusk's remains?" he demanded. "Do you have them?"

"We have some of them," the real Brunus replied as he spoke for the first time. "I'm sorry to say that the rest were eaten—just as my father's were. But, once you perform DNA tests, you'll know for sure. The being who boarded your ship was an imposter."

With that, Usurlus pressed a remote. That was the cue for a female slave bearing a beautifully wrought wooden box to enter the hall, approach the table, and place the container on the gleaming surface. Enynn, who had a hard time taking his eyes off the box, stood. "I apologize, but it will be necessary for us to withdraw and engage in private consultations."

"Of course," Brunus said understandingly. "It's a lot to absorb."

"Can I join you?" a *second* Enynn inquired, and laughed as the Vords hurried to escape the room.

"Get that thing out of here," Brunus ordered as he swung around to lock eyes with Inobo. "And if it escapes on the way to Sagatha, be sure to commit suicide. There won't be any point in coming back. Ambassador Nusk would be alive had you been doing your job."

Inobo's face turned pale, Cato smiled bleakly, and the meeting was over.

Having made arrangements to leave work early, Cato stopped by a store to buy a bouquet of flowers before starting the long climb that would take him home. The plan was to surprise Alamy and take her out to dinner, both because he hadn't been around much and had something important to tell her.

But once he arrived at Arbor House it was to discover that the upstairs apartment was empty. Thinking that Alamy might be downstairs, chatting with Madam Faustus, Cato went down to let her know he was home. When Faustus opened the door, she saw the flowers and smiled. "For me? How thoughtful!"

Cato grinned and plucked a flower out of the bouquet. "This one is for you."

Faustus held the blossom up to her nose. "It smells sweet. . . . Please come in."

Once inside, Cato took a quick look around. "Is Alamy here? She wasn't upstairs."

"No," Faustus replied, "she went shopping. She'll be home in an hour or so. Please. . . . Have a seat."

Cato didn't want to sit and chat with his landlady but couldn't figure out how to escape, so he sat in the chair that had once been her husband's. The flowers felt awkward in his hands. "Is there a problem with the rent or something?"

"No," Faustus said, "Alamy is very punctual. She always pays on time. In fact, if it wasn't for her taste in men, she would be an altogether perfect young woman."

Cato frowned as Faustus held up her hand. "Don't even think about leaving. . . . Not until you hear me out. I'll double your rent if you do!"

There was a disarming smile on her face, but Cato could "feel" how serious she was. "Okay," he said cautiously, "what's on your mind?"

"Somebody needs to tell you the truth," Faustus answered, "and since Alamy can't, I will. What you're doing to her is very cruel. You promised to free her, and to marry her, but that was months ago. Meanwhile, she's left to wait and wonder if you intend to keep your promises."

"I never promised to marry her," Cato countered defensively.

"It was implied," Faustus said primly. "You know Alamy. . . . Or you should. Given a choice, she wouldn't settle for anything less."

"I meant to free her," Cato said lamely. "I just never got around to it."

"Really?" Faustus demanded cynically, as her eyes bored into his. "You've been busy. I know that. . . . But Alamy is a human being. Not a project to be taken care of when you happen to have time."

Cato felt both embarrassed and ashamed. Some of his feelings must have been visible on his face because the expression on her face softened. "I know you mean well, Jak. . . . You bought Alamy in order to protect her, after all. But who can protect her from *you*? And whatever it is that keeps you from giving her a place in your life as well as in your bed?"

It was a tough question, and one that was still echoing through Cato's mind an hour later, when Alamy returned home. She was thrilled to receive the flowers, and her eyes sparkled with excitement as they set out to have dinner at a downslope restaurant that had good food and a magnificent view of the city.

Once they were seated on the terrace, with wineglasses in front of them, talk soon turned to the future and the need to acquire some more furniture. But, knowing what he did, Cato was forced to steer the conversation in an entirely different direction. "Alamy, there's something I need to tell you."

Cato "felt" the sudden surge of hope that followed his words, and with the criticism from Faustus fresh in his mind, he hurried to head off the possibility of a misunderstanding. "There's every reason to believe that Verafti not only escaped Corin but is making his way to Therat, where he hopes to find his mate."

Her hope having flared, Cato "felt" it start to fade as a look of concern appeared on Alamy's face. "You're going there, aren't you? To find Verafti and bring him in. Assuming such a thing is possible."

"Someone has to," Cato replied defensively. "You of all people know what he's capable of. And I'm the most qualified. Nobody knows the rotten bastard better than I do. And that's what I wanted to talk to you about. I could be gone for months. Or however long the process of finding him takes."

There was a long moment of silence during which she just stared at him. Finally, he saw a look of grim determination appear in her eyes. "All right, then," she said calmly. "I'm coming, too."

"No," Cato said firmly. "It wouldn't be safe."

Alamy's eyes narrowed. "Was it safe on Dantha? Was it safe in the motorcade? Was it safe when the slithers attacked our apartment?"

"No," Cato replied weakly, "but I couldn't predict those things. This is certain. Verafti will fight back—and there's his mate to consider as well."

Alamy was unconvinced. "So, is Section Leader Shani going to accompany you?"

"Yes," he admitted, "as part of my team."

"Then make me part of your team," Alamy insisted angrily. "Or sell me and bank the money. It will earn interest while you're gone."

"Alamy," Cato objected as he reached out to take her hand, "you can't mean that."

"But I *do* mean it," Alamy said stubbornly as she pulled her hand back out of reach. "I'm your slave, so I can't force you to do anything, but if you have any feelings for me whatsoever, you'll do as I request. Take me or sell me. And don't tell me you can't. Usurlus will give you anything you want at this point. Regulations be damned."

Cato shook his head and sighed. It seemed some battles were lost before they even began. "All right," he agreed. "You win. . . . But you may be sorry."

"Perhaps," Alamy conceded, "but it's what I want."

"I don't deserve you," Cato said contritely, as she allowed him to capture her hand.

"No," Alamy answered with a stiff smile, "you don't."

"But you deserve *this*," Cato countered as he pushed a small box across the table. "Go ahead—open it."

Alamy hadn't been on the receiving end of very many gifts during her life, so receiving one was special in and of itself, but the fact that it was from Cato made it doubly so. She removed the ribbon, fumbled the lid off, and looked within. And there, cradled in a nest of red velvet, was a necklace. It consisted of a stylized sun, complete with wavy points all around and a sizeable ruby at its center. Alamy looked up. Her face was flushed. "Really? For *me*?"

"Yes," Cato said gently, "for you. For the sun that rises in front of me every morning." Cato wasn't very good at coming up with such sentiments on the fly, so the words had a rehearsed quality, but that did nothing to lessen Alamy's pleasure as he came over to fasten the silver chain around her neck. And that was when the empath learned what it felt like to give a gift and receive it at the same time.

It was just past 6:00 AM, the morning was cold, and Usurlus was naked from the waist up as he started across the vast parade ground that the legionnaires referred to as "the grinder." The open area occupied the center of the huge military base that claimed the northwest quarter of the city. Usurlus normally rose about 10:00, so it was the last place he wanted to be at that time of day, but the new Emperor routinely rose at 4:30. Not only that, the ex-general was a fitness fanatic and expected everyone else to be one as well. Even reserve officers like Usurlus.

So Brunus thought nothing of combining meetings with exercise on the theory that doing so was more efficient and served to keep such gatherings short. Just one of the prices Usurlus had been forced to pay in order to take what was arguably the second-most-powerful position in the Empire.

Was it worth it? No, Usurlus decided as he arrived at an oval of green grass surrounded by an elliptical track. But it was too late to back out as Brunus turned to greet him.

Like Usurlus's, the Emperor's torso was bare. He had slablike pectorals, biceps as thick as an average man's thighs, and sinewy forearms. Scars could be seen here and there, along with a tattoo for each legion he had served with, nine of them. "There you are!" Brunus proclaimed cheerfully, as a small group of equally fit officers looked on. "Now there are six of us. Three against three. It will be the *pilum* this morning, gentlemen. . . . A rather primitive weapon to be sure, but useful in a pinch, and still used against us out on the rim.

"Team One will consist of Chief of Staff Usurlus, Tribune Oracus, and me. A rather creaky army that the rest of you should be able to defeat without difficulty. Any questions? No? Then let's get to it."

After flipping an Imperial, which came up heads, it was agreed that Team Two would throw first, with each member having the opportunity to hurl three javelins at a man-shaped target located sixty feet away. There were lots of good-natured insults as the first officer stepped up to the white line—then backed away to the point where his short run would begin. That gave Brunus and Usurlus an opportunity to talk. "So the Vords said yes," the Emperor observed as he began the process of selecting three *pila*.

"Yes, sire," Usurlus answered, as a cold breeze swept across the grinder, and he fought the impulse to shiver. "Thanks to our demonstration, they understand the danger and are eager to counter it. They insist on transporting our team to Therat, however—rather than allowing an Imperial ship to enter orbit."

"And after our empaths find the shape shifters? What then?" Brunus inquired.

Usurlus took note of the Emperor's nonchalant assumption and was glad that Cato wasn't present to hear it. "Based on the observations of Xeno Corps personnel who were present at the last meeting, the Vords are going to attack us," Usurlus responded as he examined a six-foot-long shaft. "Their emotional responses were quite clear. . . . Each time they spoke about peaceful coexistence, they were lying. The Vords have a burgeoning population, a warlike culture, and an economy based on conquest rather than commerce. So once the two empires came into contact with each other, war became inevitable. Then, once we allowed them to take Therat by force, the matter was settled."

"That's one of the things I like about you," Brunus said, as a javelin hit the mark and a cheer went up. "You're very direct in spite of all the years spent rubbing up against bureaucrats here on Corin."

Usurlus heard the gibe but chose to ignore it. "The good news is that while Centurion Cato and his team are on Therat, we will have additional time in which to prepare. But once their mission is complete, the Vords will have no further reason to delay."

"Tell me about Centurion Cato," Brunus said, as the third javelin nicked its target, and a communal groan was heard. "What kind of man is he?"

"He's brave," Usurlus answered honestly, "he tends to be very single-minded when pursuing a goal, and he cares about his subordinates. On the other hand, he has occasional problems dealing with alcohol, money, and authority. All of which explain why he's rather old for his rank."

"Yet you promoted him," Brunus observed, as his gunbarrel eyes bored into Usurlus. "Why?"

Usurlus shrugged. "Because in spite of his many flaws, Cato is a man of honor. And honorable men are hard to find."

Brunus tested a spearpoint with one of his blunt thumbs before turning to look at Usurlus. The look had a knowing quality about it—as if the Emperor was thinking about his newly named Chief of Staff rather than Cato. "Yes, honorable men *are* hard to find. Come. . . . Team Two is finished. Let's show them how it's done."

Brunus threw first. All three of his *pila* struck the target, with two strikes being classified as kills, while the third was scored as a hit.

Oracus went second. Two of his javelins penetrated the target, one qualifying as a kill and one as a hit.

Then it was time for Usurlus to throw. Each six-foot-long javelin had a sharp, three-edged point on a two-foot-long steel shank, which was attached to a four-foot-long composite shaft. Taken together, the weight of the various components added up to almost seven pounds—so a considerable amount of strength was required to use the weapon effectively. Throwing a *pilum* took skill as well, something Usurlus lacked because it had been at least ten years since he had participated in such a competition. And even then he hadn't been very good at it.

So as he stepped up to the line, then backed away, all he could do was try and maintain his dignity. And it wasn't easy. The first javelin fell three feet short. And the second *pilum* landed point down in the turf some six feet beyond the man-shaped target. The throws were so bad they were met with grim silence rather than the usual insults.

Having learned from his mistakes, Usurlus was fortunate enough to score a hit with the final shaft, thereby avoiding the ignominy of being the only officer to miss with every throw. Even if the other team still won.

Brunus laughed as the last javelin hit the target in the crotch—and slapped Usurlus on the back. "Right in the balls! Not bad for a rear-echelon stylus pusher."

The other officers laughed appreciatively and were about to follow Brunus to the chow hall for some breakfast, when the Emperor raised a hand. His expression was serious—and so were his words. "Tribune Didus. . . . Notify the procurement department that the Uman-shaped targets currently in use are to be replaced by Vord silhouettes as soon as possible. This order will apply to all units, in all sectors, on all planets. Understood?"

The Tribune's expression was suitably grim. "Sir, yes, sir."

"Good," Brunus said. "I'm hungry. Let's eat."

TEN

The city of Kybor, on the planet Therat

FROM HIS VANTAGE POINT ON THE BALCONY OF A spindly one-hundred-foot-tall prayer tower, Fiss Verafti could look out over the city and marvel at how industrious its residents were. Kybor wasn't especially beautiful, not by conventional Uman standards, but there was something about the steamy sprawl that he found to be appealing. Especially when compared to the sterile verticality of the skyscrapers clustered around the Imperial Tower on Corin. An environment he hated.

Verafti knew that some three hundred years earlier, Kybor had been founded as a penal colony where Emperor Titus II could send citizens who objected to the manner in which Titus I had been murdered. Eventually, new Emperors took the throne, criminals were no longer being sent to Therat, and the people who lived there were granted citizenship.

Since then, the discovery of zinc deposits containing high concentrations of the mineral sphalerite had brought a sort of shabby prosperity to Therat. Because sphalerite was the source of an important semiconductor named germanium, which was used in thousands of electronic devices and increasingly rare on the heavily mined core worlds.

That was the good news. Unfortunately for the citizens of Kybor, it was the abundance of both germanium and the refineries required to produce it that attracted the Vords to Therat and caused them to occupy it. That decision was also intended to test the Umans to see what they would do, which, under Verafti's questionable leadership, was nothing.

The thought brought a smile to a face that looked exactly like Jak Cato's. Except that his version of the Xeno cop was dressed in native garb that included a pillbox-style hat, a V-necked pullover shirt, a red vest complete with gold embroidery, trousers that were baggy at the thighs but tapered down to a tight fit at the ankles, and a pair of sturdy sandals. All of which helped him to blend in.

But now, after having impersonated Nusk and subsequently switched identities several times prior to landing on Therat, it was time to tackle the most difficult problem of all. And that was to find a member of his own species who didn't want to be found—and was hiding among the city's population of approximately three million sentients.

But as Verafti looked out over the city's patchwork quilt of tile, metal, and duracrete rooftops, and across some of the city's busy canals to the half-seen blur of germanium refineries to the north, he was looking forward to the task that confronted him. *I know you're out there, dearest,* he said to himself, *and I will find you. Then, with a whole planet to feed upon, we will eat our fill.*

Aboard the Vord destroyer Light of Yareel, in orbit around the planet Corin

Cato didn't like Vord police officer Pedor Umji, or Quati, his so-called advisor. And based on the emotional feedback coming his way, the feeling was mutual. But they were going to be stuck with each other during the three-week voyage to Therat, so Cato was determined to mask his contempt for Umji and keep the relationship civil. The task might prove to be difficult given the Vord's abrasive manner.

The Umans had just come aboard the destroyer and were standing in front of a pile of gray footlocker-sized trunks, when Umji spoke to them via a translator attached to his belt. There was a fraction of a second delay between the first version and the second. He was at least a foot shorter than most of his peers. Did that have something to do with what most Umans would regard as an obvious inferiority complex? Or was Vord psychology so completely different that comparisons couldn't be made? There was no way to know.

Umji's face had a gaunt appearance, mainly because of his deep-set eyes and the way his dusky gray skin was pulled tight over prominent cheekbones. His "advisor," a Ya named Quati, was midnight black. The parasite pulsated rhythmically as it injected both stimulants and waste products into Umji's bloodstream.

The Vord's uniform consisted of a shapeless cloth hat with a shiny zigzag-shaped lightning bolt pinned to the front of it, plus a broad-shouldered jacket and jodhpur-like trousers that were tucked into knee-high boots. Cato, Shani, and Officer Valentine Keen knew that Umji's true feelings were at odds with the words that came out of his mouth.

"Welcome to the warship *Light of Yareel*. Before I can show you to your quarters, it will first be necessary to surrender your weapons. As you can see," the Vord said as he gestured toward an open box, "a storage container has been provided for that purpose. It will remain sealed for the duration of the voyage. Once we reach Therat, your weapons will be returned to you. Are there any questions?"

Cato and Shani were reluctant to part with their sidearms and backup pistols. Still, they knew such a precaution was to be expected, so there was no point in complaining.

Keen had short blond hair, a moonlike face, and a stocky body. He looked to Cato and Shani for guidance, saw his superiors release their gun belts, and followed their example.

"I believe you brought other weapons as well?" Umji inquired. "In addition to body armor, com equipment, and related gear?"

"Yes," Cato conceded. "All of it is stored in the cases marked SQUAD 1 and SQUAD 2."

"Those containers will be sealed and locked away," Umji said sternly. "Now, please be so kind as to remove your clothing, so I can verify the fact that you are unarmed."

Cato glanced at Alamy and Shani, saw their disapproving expressions, and looked back again. "It was my understanding that we were to be treated as guests," he said. "And a strip search constitutes an insult within Uman culture."

"That may be," Umji allowed coldly, "but on the *Light of Yareel*, you are subject to *our* culture. So you will comply, and do so quickly, before I lose my patience. If it makes you feel any better, I can assure you that I have absolutely no interest in whatever passes for Uman sex."

"If we must, we must," Keen proclaimed cheerfully as he eyed Alamy and began to disrobe. Cato could "feel" the other man's unabashed interest in Alamy and wanted to intervene somehow. But to do so would reaffirm his status as her owner and signal the fact that they were lovers. Would that please Alamy? Or make her feel resentful? He wasn't sure.

Then there was the way such an admission might impact his relationship with Shani. They weren't lovers, but he knew she would be willing, and he wasn't ready to completely foreclose such a possibility. The situation was hellishly complicated, and as all four of them took their clothes off, Cato wished he was somewhere else.

Cato made a point out of looking away, but as he removed his clothing, he couldn't help but imagine what Shani would look like without hers. A bit more angular than Alamy, he imagined, with smaller breasts and skinny legs.

Then Cato remembered that Shani might be able to pick up on his emotions from the other side of the room and ordered himself to think about something else. But when he tried to do so, an image of Alamy without any clothes on popped up, and he was in trouble again. And so was Keen, whose thoughts were anything but pure, and he continued to eye Alamy out of the corner of his eye until Cato cleared his throat and sent him a dirty look.

Fortunately for the Umans, Umji's inspection was much less intrusive than a similar check by their own law-enforcement officers might have been, so it wasn't long before they were given permission to get dressed and place their luggage on a robo cart. It followed along behind as Umji led the Umans through a maze of passageways. It was a big ship, and there were lots of Vords in the corridors, most of whom radiated undisguised hostility. That made sense since the aliens had been raised to believe that their race was not only superior to all others but destined to rule the galaxy.

Cato knew that the *Light of Yareel* was far too large to pass through a planetary atmosphere and had an H-shaped hull. He made an attempt to memorize the path that took them across the bridge that connected Hull 1 to Hull 2, but there were far too many turns, and he was thoroughly lost by the time they arrived in front of a storage compartment.

Uman-style metal bed frames had been spot welded to the deck, along with a communal work/eating table and some bench seats. Four Vord-style lockers had been secured to a bulkhead, a large crate of field rations occupied the far corner, and the single sink was equipped with some sort of zero-gee hose arrangement that was unlike anything Cato had seen before. "What about the head?" Shani wanted to know.

Umji frowned. "The what?"

"A place to take a shit," Keen said helpfully.

"It's next door," Umji replied distastefully. "Other than that, you are to remain in this compartment at all times. Your actions will be monitored—and if you leave the area, I will know."

"Terrific," Cato replied sarcastically. "Is there anything else?"

"Yes," Umji replied without the slightest trace of irony. "Have a nice trip."

The city of Kybor, on the planet Therat

What had begun as a medium-sized cave hundreds of years before had been gradually enlarged until the domed room could accommodate more than five hundred true believers. Such a crowd was rare, of course, since most of the Rahati cult's thirty thousand members were busy working, but this was the "Day of the Feast," so the cavern was packed with worshippers.

What light there was emanated from the flickering oil lamps mounted on the rocky side walls, ropes of multicolored lights that crisscrossed the area over the supplicants' heads, and the green glow-rods that the heavily armed ushers wore thrust through their broad leather belts.

The result was a warm glow that glazed the surface of the massive altar that dominated the front of the space, while the corners of the room fell into darkness. Complex stonework served to frame the graven image of the goddess Rahati, complete with all three of her faces. The beast, its fangs bared, stared out at those who worshipped it. To either side of the central image, the idealized profiles of a man and a woman could be seen, looking in opposite directions.

Taken together, the three faces represented the various aspects of the Uman race, meaning male, female, and the sexless creature within. The latter was revered by the Rahaties as the "true" nature of the species, which should be held in check where fellow adherents were concerned but could legitimately be released in order to battle the unenlightened.

Now, as row after row of Rahaties knelt with their foreheads pressed against a patchwork quilt of expensive carpets, one of the sect's priests led them in chanting the poem of life, a journey that began with death in the spirit world, followed by birth in the physical world, and death yet again. So that each death became a birth, as the soul cycled between worlds, eventually accumulating the wisdom necessary to join the goddess Rahati in paradise.

Once the chant came to an end, a priest made his way up onto the platform that fronted the crowd and launched into an extensive rant against the Vord occupiers. Demons, to his mind, who were not only determined to eliminate the Rahati religion but were the very embodiment of evil.

The crowd was encouraged to participate in the denunciation by chanting *Ke-Ya* (we believe) in unison while bringing their heads up long enough to clap their hands before bowing again.

Then, the priest having made his point, it was time for the communal feast. It began, as it always did, with the screams of a terrified Vord as he was half carried, half dragged down the center aisle and up onto the platform. Umans had been used for the purpose prior to the occupation, but ever since the Vords had begun to systematically hunt Rahaties down, they had come to replace all others on the sacrificial platform.

Servos whined as a bloodstained ceremonial table rose out of a recess in the floor, and the crowd began to clap rhythmically. The alien fought back, or tried to, as practiced hands bound his wrists and ankles to each corner of the table.

The soldier's Ya was pulsating madly by that time as it attempted to free itself from the Vord's nervous and circulatory systems, but the connections had been forged over a period of twenty years and were too strong to sever quickly. The priests had seen it all before and ignored the parasite as they cut the Vord's uniform off.

By that time the crowd was chanting "*RA-HA-TI, RA-HA-TI, RA-HA-TI,*" over and over again as the god image came to sudden life. Though not of her invention, the role of goddess was one that Affa Demeni had learned to play to perfection, as three faces merged into one and the beast made its way forward. It was seven feet tall, very muscular, and possessed of prominent breasts and a large penis.

Having paused long enough for the audience to get a good look at her, Demeni held up her hands. The crowd roared its approval as long, thin fingers were miraculously transformed into razor-sharp claws. The goddess Rahati snarled menacingly as she bent over the helpless Vord, and he uttered a heartrending scream as her right index finger drew a line from a point just below his rib cage all the way down to his crotch. Though only half an inch deep, the incision was sufficient to slice through the alien's peritoneum and release an explosion of purplish organs. The soldier's scream was lost in the crowd noise as the chant "*Ke-Ya*" filled the chamber.

Then, knowing what her Uman followers expected of her, Demeni stuck her hand up under the alien's ribs, felt for his heart, and expertly cut it free. Then, having removed the still-squirting organ from the Vord's body, she held it up for the Rahati faithful to see. The response was a roar of approval, which grew even louder as Demeni took a big bite. The blood had a coppery taste, the flesh was soft and still quite warm. The morsel slid down her throat.

That was the cue for the priests to rush forward and butcher the dead body so that trays heaped with Vord tidbits could be passed through the chamber. Because to eat the flesh of an unbeliever was to consume demon energy to use against them. Meanwhile, having eaten her fill, the goddess

Rahati was transformed back into stone, or so it appeared to those in the audience. The miracle was complete.

Aboard the Light of Yareel, in hyperspace

More than a week had passed since the *Light of Yareel* had broken orbit, pushed her way out past the battle stations that stood guard over Corin, and entered the nowhere land of hyperspace. Things had gone reasonably well at first, but it wasn't long before the relatively small compartment began to feel like a prison, and nerves began to fray. And as Cato dealt himself another hand of Solo, he was painfully aware of the fact that he should be working. But as Shani pumped out seemingly endless push-ups, Alamy read the material *he* was supposed to read, and Keen eyed her longingly, Cato found that it was hard to focus.

Keen had been smart enough to check with Cato before hitting on Alamy. However, rather than tell Keen the complete truth, as he should have, Cato told the other officer that Alamy was free to enter relationships with whomever she chose, with predictable results. So that when Keen began to flirt with Alamy, and her owner did nothing to stop it, she knew his permission had been given. That made her feel hurt and angry.

Cato knew that, and wanted to talk to Alamy about it, but they were never alone. And having been abandoned by the man she had been ready to give her everything to, she was starting to laugh at Keen's jokes and perform small services for him. Cato could order her not to, of course, but that would make him look jealous and undermine his authority as the team leader. So he was sitting there, dealing cards he was only barely aware of, when Umji entered the compartment.

The Vord exchanged perfunctory greetings with Shani,

Keen, and Alamy before occupying the seat directly across from Cato. While the other police officer *looked* the same, none of the overt hostility that normally surrounded the Vord was present, which seemed to suggest that this visit was going to be different. "So," Umji began awkwardly, "it's my understanding that you have a special talent."

"Officer Shani, Officer Keen, and I are biologically engineered variants," Cato explained patiently. "And we can sense other people's emotions if that's what you mean. That's why we were chosen to go after Verafti. We will be able to recognize him regardless of the way he looks."

"Yes," Umji said dismissively, "I know all that. But, if my information is correct, you can tell if someone is lying."

"We can sense the emotions associated with lying," Cato replied, "and therefore infer that they might be lying. But we can't read minds. Why do you ask?"

"Nothing much," Umji lied. "This is a confined space. . . . In spite of our obvious differences, there are ways in which Vords and Umans are similar. Conflicts can arise in close quarters, and the results can be tragic."

Cato nodded knowingly and was conscious of the fact that the others were listening. "So you have a murder on your hands," he said matter-of-factly.

"I didn't say that," Umji objected.

"You didn't have to," Cato countered. "You're feeling stressed, worried, and fearful. Probably because it isn't clear who did what to whom, and the captain wants you to solve the murder in time for dinner."

"Yes, those in command are always impatient, aren't they?" Umji inquired rhetorically. "In any case, I thought you might be somewhat bored at this point. If so, perhaps you would welcome a chance to hone your skills and stretch your legs."

Cato knew that if he agreed to the proposal, Shani would want to come along, and by all rights should be allowed to come along, but that would mean leaving Alamy alone with Keen. Something he wasn't about to do. "Sure, that would be fine," Cato said casually. "Provided that the rest of my team can come as well. Otherwise, I'll have to pass."

Umji was silent for a moment, and Cato could "feel" the mishmash of emotions that swirled around him. Finally, it seemed as though Umji's need to solve the murder quickly was stronger than the other concerns he had. "Okay," the police officer said. "With the understanding that everyone will stay together, make no attempt to communicate with members of the crew unless given permission to do so, and won't be allowed to take pictures or make notes."

"We also promise to brush our teeth, eat our vegetables, and get plenty of exercise," Cato volunteered. "Now that we have that out of the way—who was murdered?"

"A Ya named Dancha," Umji answered. "His life partner is a Vord crewman named Esrothy Sayeska Heyavu."

"Which means Heyavu did it, or knows who did it," Cato observed pragmatically.

"Heyavu stabbed Dancha, he admits that," Umji replied soberly. "But he insists that it was in self-defense."

"How's that possible?" Shani wanted to know as she came over to join the conversation. "No offense, Officer Umji, but based on what I can see, it would be difficult if not impossible for a Ya to murder his host. They don't have hands, tentacles, or pseudopods. . . . So they couldn't hold a weapon."

"Ya don't require weapons to kill their companions," Umji responded bleakly. "Take my advisor Quati, for example. . . . In the same way that he can generate chemicals that are beneficial to me—he can produce toxins as well."

Cato frowned. "Excuse my ignorance of the Vord/Ya relationship, but if a Ya kills his host, isn't he committing suicide?"

"No," Umji answered simply. "Not initially anyway. A Ya can survive for weeks, even a month, entirely on his own.

Vords die of natural causes all the time, as do Ya, so both must be able to function until a new partner can be found."

"I see," Cato replied, although the truth was that he didn't. Not entirely, anyway. "So you want us to interview Heyavu and tell you if he's telling the truth."

"Yes," Umji said eagerly. "That would be very helpful."

"Okay," Cato said as he eyed the faces around him. "Is everyone ready?"

Shani nodded, Keen smirked, and Alamy gave him the same blank-faced look he had come to dread over the last few days. "I guess we're ready to go," Cato said ruefully. "Please lead the way."

As Alamy followed the rest of the group through the hatch and out into the dimly lit corridor beyond, she felt confused. Of course, that was nothing new since her relationship with Cato had been confusing from the start. He couldn't interact with her the way he usually did, not with Shani and Keen present all the time, she understood that. But when Keen began to flirt with her, she expected some sort of reaction from Cato. When none was forthcoming, she felt angry, because if Cato was willing to give her up to another man, then it was safe to say that he didn't care about her and was interested in Shani. And it didn't require an empath to know what *her* desires were.

The only problem with that theory was that Cato's interactions with the other officer had been strictly professional so far, and based on his nonverbal communications, it seemed as if Keen's continual advances troubled him. So with no opportunity for one of the private moments she treasured so much, there was nothing Alamy could do but push the other empath off and wonder what was going on.

The corridors were four Vords wide to facilitate the movement of personnel during an emergency, and wherever room allowed, side panels had been used to provide both decoration and structural integrity. Though not allowed to stop and inspect them, Alamy got the impression that the scenes stamped into the sheet metal were historical in nature because she caught glimpses of stylized Vord-on-Vord battles, elaborate hunting motifs, and sturdy castles that sat on islands or were perched high on hilltops. As if to suggest a long period of clan warfare prior to the creation of a ruling council and the subsequent conquest of other planets.

But as might be expected on a warship, most of what Alamy saw were the locks that led to secondary gun emplacements, what were obviously lifeboat bays, quick glimpses into berthing areas, what might have been the hydroponics section, and a space that smelled like a medical facility.

Then, after many twists and turns, the journey was over. A pair of armed guards came to the Vord version of attention, and there was an exchange of guttural words as the hatch irised open. "This is the ship's brig," Umji explained as he motioned for the Umans to enter. "Heyavu is the only prisoner at the moment."

The group entered a rectangular space that fronted a row of four cells. A forlorn-looking Vord sat head down in one of the barred compartments. Alamy noticed that the prisoner was hooked up to what looked like an intravenous drip. Was it providing him with at least some of the chemicals that a Ya normally would? Yes, that seemed logical.

"Bring him out," Umji ordered gruffly, and the cell door made a gentle rattling noise as it slid out of the way.

Heyavu was dressed in the Vord equivalent of blue overalls and wore slippers on his feet. A guard pushed the IV stand along as the prisoner shuffled out to the point where a metal table was welded to the deck. "Sit down," Umji ordered, and Heyavu obeyed. The mechanism that controlled the IV beeped every once in a while as if to prove it was still working.

Alamy looked at Cato and wondered what he was thinking as he took his place across from the accused murderer. Then, as she turned her head slightly, she saw that Keen was eyeballing her and *knew* what he was thinking. Maybe Madam Faustus was right. . . . Maybe all men *were* alike.

As Cato "looked" at Heyavu, he was immediately conscious of the fact that something was missing. It felt as if the Vord was a member of an entirely different race. Because while each individual member of a particular species was unique, there were often a lot of commonalities, which he thought of as "flavors." And the Vords were no exception.

Yet the prisoner in front of him "felt" more like a human than a Vord. Why? The obvious explanation was the absence of his Ya. Now that he was face-to-face with a parasite-free Vord, Cato realized the extent to which each Vord and Ya harmonized to project a single emotional "voice."

Still, with the second part of the emotional signature stripped away, Cato could "feel" the suspect's emotions even more clearly. He was frightened yet hopeful somehow. As if he believed that his current circumstances could eventually lead to something good. And that struck Cato as strange. Assuming the allegation regarding Dancha was true, and the parasite had attempted to kill his host, where was the anger one might expect Heyavu to feel?

Cato's thoughts were interrupted as Umji took the seat next to him. "Go ahead," the Vord instructed artlessly as he placed a translator in the middle of the table. "Ask Heyavu if he's guilty."

Cato made a face. "I'll tackle this my own way if you don't mind."

Then, turning to Heyavu, Cato introduced himself. "My name is Jak Cato. My companions and I are working with Officer Umji on a special assignment. And, because we happen to be aboard, we were asked to speak with you regarding Dancha's death. Whatever you say could be used against you. Do you understand?"

Heyavu looked up. He had a high forehead, prominent brows, and wary eyes. As he spoke, his thin-lipped mouth opened and closed like a trap. "Yes."

"As I understand it, you admit to killing Dancha with a knife. . . . Is that correct?"

Cato "felt" fear mixed with a sense of satisfaction as Heyavu answered. "Yes, I had no choice. He was going to kill me."

"Why?" Cato wanted to know.

Heyavu looked at Umji. "Answer him," the police officer ordered sternly.

At that point Heyavu felt something Cato wasn't entirely sure of. Embarrassment? Mixed with stress? And a vague yearning? Maybe or maybe not. "Dancha wanted me to mate with a female named Ryryl," he responded. "He said it would be good for the bloodline. But I didn't want to. So he tried to kill me."

Based on the suspect's emotions Cato knew that to be a lie. But, just to make sure, he directed a look to Shani and saw her nod. "You're lying," Cato said flatly as he brought his eyes back into contact with Heyavu's. "You killed Dancha— but for a reason other than the one you gave."

Heyavu was visibly angry. He turned toward Umji. "Why are you allowing a sub-Vord animal to question me? Aren't *you* supposed to conduct the investigation?"

"You will keep a civil tongue in your mouth," the police officer answered harshly, but Cato could "feel" how worried Umji was. Introducing Uman police officers into a Vord investigation was a risky thing to do.

"Put the prisoner back in his cage," Umji ordered. "And don't let him speak with anyone who hasn't been cleared by me."

Two minutes later, the entire group was out in the hall, where Umji convened an impromptu meeting. "So he lied," the Vord ventured.

"Yes," Cato agreed. "He did."

"You're sure?"

"Yes," Shani put in. "We are."

"But there's no physical evidence," Umji objected. "I have nothing more than your word. We'll need more than that."

"Yes, you will," Cato said soberly. "Emotions are tricky things. . . . And trying to read them is a subjective process. Whenever we use empathy as an investigative tool, we are required to produce corroborating proof."

"But how will we obtain it?" Umji demanded. "Heyavu will continue to lie."

"Find out who his friends are," Cato suggested. "Then we'll ask them what, if anything, they know. And if it looks like one of them is lying, *you* can drill down on that individual. Our job will be to narrow the field."

Umji was silent for a moment, as if to give the matter some thought, then he nodded. "It will be as you say."

Rather than interrogate the suspect's associates in front of him, Umji decided to take them to the compartment where the Umans were berthed. They arrived one at a time—and in no particular order insofar as Cato could tell. It was an unpleasant process because all of the interviewees were unfailingly hostile—and uniformly ignorant where the killing was concerned. Until a Vord named Nolex Dibir Tegat was shown into the compartment, that is, which was when everything changed.

The first thing Cato noticed about the lanky crewman was that he had dark eyes, broad cheekbones, and a pointy chin. He winced as he sat down, and the empath could "feel" the Vord's distress, and said as much. "I sense you aren't feeling well. . . . What's wrong?"

"I feel fine," Tegat lied, as both doubt and fear leaked into the ethers around him.

"Really?" Cato inquired cynically. "How about your Ya? How does *he* feel?"

"Layo feels fine, too," Tegat insisted. But as the Vord spoke, Cato "felt" something akin to emotional background noise. Was that the Ya? Expressing his own emotions? If so, the feeling of disgust that Layo felt regarding his life partner was both unexpected and unlike anything Cato had experienced during the previous interviews.

So as Cato asked the pair about Heyavu, and whether he had a reason to murder Dancha, the empath did the best he could to "hear" whatever feelings Layo might have. And when Tegat said, "No," an answer that he clearly believed to be true, Cato was surprised to discover that the Vord's Ya was experiencing the kind of stress normally associated with a lie!

Rather than confront the pair with his finding, and trigger some sort of cover-up, Cato let them go. Then, once they were out in the corridor, Cato turned to the others. "That was strange," Cato said. "Tegat is ill—but denies it. In spite of that, he seems to be telling the truth when he denies knowing anything about the killing. Yet, if I'm reading the feedback correctly, his Ya might be involved. It doesn't make sense."

There was a momentary silence, and much to Cato's surprise, it was Alamy who spoke first. Her question was addressed to Umji. "I've been reading about your civilization. . . . And it's my understanding that the pairing between a Vord and a Ya usually results in what we Umans would refer to as a love match—meaning the formation of a deep emotional bond between two individuals. Is that correct?"

Umji's expression was wooden, but Cato could "feel" agreement. "Yes," the Vord replied cautiously, "I think that's a fair description."

Alamy nodded. "And would you agree that while the typical relationship between a male and a female Vord may involve a significant friendship, it is primarily for the purpose of procreation?"

Umji nodded.

"In sharp contrast to that," Alamy said, as she seemed to gain confidence, "the Ya are self-replicating. That means a new Ya is something of a known quantity at the time of his birth. A fact that helps the clan elders pair him with a Vord when both are only a few months old. So is it possible that Heyavu fell in love with Tegat's Ya, and vice versa? Because if it is, that could explain both the killing and Tegat's illness since it's possible that Layo is trying to kill him."

"But how would Heyavu and Layo communicate?" Shani wanted to know.

"Chemically," Alamy answered. "Kind of like Uman males and females do when they meet for the first time."

It took a moment for the others to assimilate the theory Alamy had put forward. But once Umji processed it, he brought a bony fist down onto the tabletop. "Yes, damn it, yes! All of it is there. Quati and I should have seen it from the beginning. Late-life rejections are rare, quite rare, but not unknown. And in the close quarters of a ship, unfortunate things can happen. We will administer medical tests to Tegat in order to determine whether he's being poisoned—and reinterview Layo with one of you present. Thank you, my friends—you have been extremely helpful." And with that, Umji was gone.

Cato looked from Alamy to Shani. "Did he say, 'my friends'?"

"Yes," Shani replied gravely. "That's what I heard."

Cato nodded and turned to look at Alamy. "And did Alamy make both of us look like rookies?"

Alamy felt a sense of satisfaction as the other woman offered a reluctant smile. "Yes," Shani admitted ruefully, "she sure as hell did."

•

ELEVEN

The city of Kybor, on the planet Therat

THE NARROW STREETS OF KYBOR WERE CROWDED with Umanity and badly in need of maintenance. Horns beeped as brightly painted scooters bumped through potholes, heavily laden angens brayed loudly, and discordant music emanated from dozens of competing players. Shops crowded the street from both sides, jostled each other for space, and often spilled out over the sidewalks. That was the no-man's-land where raggedy children battled each other for customers. "Hey, mister," a grubby little girl said, as she ran out to tug at Fiss Verafti's waist-length jacket. "You wanna new pair of shoes? Come in! My uncle will make them for you."

On that particular day, Verafti was the spitting image of a reporter from Kybor's highest-rated news net. He paused to look down at her. "I've got an idea . . . Why don't you come home with me? Then I could eat you for dinner."

The little girl's eyes grew huge. She turned and ran for the safety of the shop. Verafti laughed and continued on his way. The street led to a dilapidated park. And there, right in the square, was a bronze likeness of Demius the Kind. The Emperor who was generally credited with giving Therat's population full citizenship. A bird was perched on his head.

Beyond the park, on the other side of the street, a blocky four-story building stood. It was at least a hundred years old and harkened back to the once-popular colonial style of architecture. The sign out front read, MUNICIPAL BUILDING, and Verafti noticed that a squad of Vord troopers were loitering outside. To "protect" it no doubt.

Verafti paused to examine his latest image in a convenient store window, was satisfied with what he saw, and made his way across the park. During the day, it was the province of shop workers, government bureaucrats, and nannies. But once darkness fell, a much rougher crowd would take over.

Having rounded the fountain in which half a dozen mostly naked children were playing, Verafti left the park and crossed the street. The Vord soldiers watched him warily but made no attempt to intercept the shape shifter as he climbed a short flight of stairs and entered a spacious lobby. Fluted columns supported the roof, the marble floor was spotless, and glassed-in cubicles lined three of the four walls. A sign hung over each booth so citizens would know where to go. Verafti saw stations labeled WATER, POWER, SEWER, GARBAGE, LICENSES, and half a dozen more. Each with its own line, some of which were twenty or thirty people long.

But the office Verafti wanted was labeled DEATHS, which logically enough was located right next to BIRTHS. And judging from the extremely short line that led up to the booth, death wasn't all that popular. Verafti took his place behind an elderly woman, waited until she had successfully paid her husband's death tax, and stepped up to the counter. The man beyond the glass had thinning black hair, large liquid eyes, and the look of a career bureaucrat. "Yes, sir . . ." he said politely. "How can I be of assistance?"

"My name is Vejee Saro," Verafti lied. "I'm a reporter with news eight. I have an appointment to see the coroner."

Verafti saw recognition in the bureaucrat's eyes and "felt" him perk up. Here was something to make this particular day different from all the rest. "Of course! My wife and I watch your show every evening. . . . Just a moment while I call down and have the coroner send someone up to get you."

That left Verafti to stand around and watch people come and go for a good five minutes before a tiny woman in a pristine lab coat appeared. The name tag over her left breast pocket read L. NAMJI, and there wasn't enough meat on her body to constitute anything more than a snack. "Hello," the woman said pleasantly, "I'm Lin Namji, the coroner's assistant."

As Verafti shook Namji's hand, he could feel her bones and knew he could easily crush them. "And I'm Vejee Saro," he replied. "Thank you for coming up to get me."

"It's a pleasure," Namji replied. What she actually felt was a mild sense of annoyance. Probably because she was busy, but there was no sign of her true emotions on her face. "How can I help you?"

"We're doing a story on the night stalker," Verafti answered. "And I would like to visit the morgue." The so-called night stalker was a serial killer who had been preying on young women. They were prostitutes for the most part, which meant they had to venture out at night. A situation which was bad for them but good for the news nets, who had been running the story around the clock. It was one of the few subjects they could report on without being censored by the Vords.

Despite the nearly nonstop coverage, Verafti had been unable to glean enough detailed information to rule Demeni in or out as the killer. The one-week interval between murders was about right for a feeding Sagathi, but what about the rest of it? The news stories were frustratingly vague. And that was why Verafti wanted to interview the coroner. He hoped to get more information and make a determination as to whether Demeni was involved or not.

"I see," Namji said cautiously. "You realize there are details about the killings that can't be released so long as the investigation is ongoing. Things that only the killer or killers would know."

"Yes, of course," Verafti replied smoothly. "What I'm looking for is background stuff . . . the look and feel of the place where the autopsies are carried out. That sort of thing."

Namji looked around. "Do you have a camera crew?"

"No, I have an implant," Verafti said as he pointed to his right eye. "Smile! I'm recording everything you say."

Namji produced something that looked more like a grimace than a smile. "Come with me," she said, and turned away.

Verafti followed her across what seemed like half an acre of marble to a door marked AUTHORIZED PERSONNEL ONLY, where Namji placed her palm on a reader. There was a soft hissing sound as the barrier slid out of the way, and she waved Verafti through. That was a relief. Because even though the shape shifter had a photographic memory and could produce a believable likeness of any being or part of a being he'd been exposed to, he couldn't replicate a palm print he'd never seen. So if the *real* newsman's prints were on file in the government's computers, as they almost certainly were, access would have been denied the moment he placed his hand on the scanner.

As Namji led Verafti down a tightly turning staircase, the air grew steadily cooler until it was verging on frigid by the time they arrived in the basement. A second door gave access to a long hallway. Namji ushered Verafti into the first office on the right. A man in a white lab coat was seated behind a desk. His back was to the door, and he was look-ing at a flat-panel screen. Verafti could see what he knew to be a Uman thighbone pictured next to some text. A report of some sort? Yes, he thought so. "Dr. Sintha?" Namji said. "Citizen Saro is here to see you."

As the coroner turned around, Verafti saw that the Uman was wearing a comb-over to hide his incipient baldness, had slightly protuberant ears and bright, inquisitive eyes. His face was smoothly shaved, and thin in keeping with a slen-der frame. "Citizen Saro," he said as he rose. "I watch your channel all the time. . . . At least I used to. However, it's mostly propaganda now. That isn't your fault, of course. These are difficult times for all of us. What can we do for you?"

Verafti shook the extended hand and accepted a seat. "I was hoping to learn more about the way the night stalker kills his victims," the shape shifter said honestly. "That kind of detail has been sadly missing from our reports."

Sintha nodded. "And for good reason. . . . We aren't al-lowed to disclose that kind of information lest it help the killer or hinder the police investigation."

Verafti glanced over his shoulder and was glad to see that Namji had closed the door behind her when she left the room. "That makes sense," he conceded, "but I'm hoping you'll tell me anyway."

The coroner frowned. "I'm sorry, Citizen Saro—but that's impossible."

"Okay," Verafti replied calmly. "I guess we'll have to do this the hard way."

Sintha's hand was halfway to the intercom when Verafti morphed into his true form and ripped the coroner's throat open. Then, as Sintha continued to bleed out, his killer went around to the other side of the messy desk. The blood-drenched chair was mounted on rollers, so Verafti towed the corpse out of the way and brought the guest chair around to sit on. Five experimental voice commands were required in order to bring the correct folder up on the screen. Once it was open, seven files could be seen. One for each of the night stalker's victims.

Verafti opened the files one after another, skimmed the notes associated with each autopsy, and felt an almost over-whelming sense of disappointment. There was a serial killer on the loose all right, but none of the prostitutes had been eaten. That meant his beloved Demeni was finding nour-ishment elsewhere. So the visit to the morgue had been for nothing, and the search would continue.

Verafti stood, morphed into Uman form, and went over to the door. He set the lock before pulling it closed. With that accomplished, it was a simple matter to return to the cav-ernous lobby and leave through the front door. By the time the sirens were heard, and guards rushed to seal the Munici-pal Building's doors, a man who looked completely different from Saro was examining a nice cut of meat in a shop two blocks away.

The governor's palace as well as the complex of buildings around it had been taken over by the Vords. And after land-ing at Kybor's dilapidated spaceport a day earlier, that was where Cato and his companions had been taken. The team was seated on a broad veranda that ran around all four sides of the colonial-style administration building. Overhead fans sent a cooling breeze down to caress them, verdant gardens served to screen off the not-altogether-pleasant sights that the city had to offer, and Uman refreshments were theirs for the asking.

But the living conditions did nothing to lessen Cato's anger. For the Umans were being held in what their hosts re-ferred to as "protective custody." Which meant they weren't allowed to carry their weapons, leave the mansion, or begin their investigation. A situation Cato had repeatedly objected to but to no avail.

So when Officer Umji and his Ya finally appeared on the veranda, Cato jumped to his feet. "What the hell is going on?" the police officer demanded angrily. "Why are we being held here?"

"Please," Umji said reasonably, "calm yourself. We realize this is inconvenient, but imagine how my superiors feel. A shape shifter may be on the loose in Kybor. They can't trust anyone. So before you leave the mansion, and begin the investigation, they insist that you vet all of the Vord personnel in Kybor. Once they're cleared, you can proceed."

"Did you say *all* of the personnel?" Cato inquired incredulously. "How many Vords are we talking about?"

"Three thousand, two hundred, and forty-three," Umji answered smoothly. "But never fear! Everything has been arranged. Tomorrow morning our personnel will parade past the table where you and your companions will be seated. Then, if you recognize the shape shifter, we'll nab him. Case closed."

"Let's not forget that there are *two* of them," Cato grated, "and what's to keep one of the Sagathi from impersonating a Vord *after* we inspect your personnel? Even if we inspected your people once a day for the next year, it wouldn't make you safe."

"We made much the same point," Umji replied stoically, "and we were overruled. The review *will* take place. At that point, you will be free to go."

There was a moment of silence as the cops confronted each other. That was when Cato realized that Umji and his Ya advisor had their own Inobo to deal with. Or Inobos plural, since each Vord had a parasite. A pair of superiors who weren't all that bright, wouldn't listen, or both. "You'll give me your word? If we participate in this farce, we'll be free to begin work?"

"We can't make a promise like that," Umji answered honestly. "But we believe you'll be free to go."

Umji and Quati were being honest. Or at least Umji was. Cato could "feel" it. So he nodded. "Okay, then. . . . Tomorrow morning it is."

Rather than let the team lounge around, Cato requested that three additional flat screens be brought up to the visitors' suite. Then, with four news nets blaring, the team members were forced to watch and learn what was going on. It quickly became apparent that the Vords were not only censoring the local news but largely unaware of what was taking place on Corin. So as far as the team could tell, the local population was completely unaware of Emor's death, the fact that his son had taken the throne, and the fact that an interstellar war was increasingly likely.

Most of that day's news was centered around the local coroner's death at the hands of an anchorman named Saro Vejee. He denied the charge, of course, but cameras don't lie, and pictures of his arrival and departure had been captured by security cams in both the Municipal Building's lobby and the morgue below.

For his part, Vejee claimed to have been home with his wife when the murder took place, but the local cops weren't buying that, and for obvious reasons. "The bastard is guilty as hell," Shani observed, and Cato saw no reason to disagree.

But even if the Vejee case was open-and-shut, there were other news items of interest. One of them was the illegal demonstration that had taken place earlier in the day. And because the voice-over was delivered by a so-called pacification monitor, meaning a Uman collaborator, it seemed safe to assume that the clip had been shot by the Vords for propaganda purposes.

The story opened with a wide shot of a plaza, where a large

group of people were gathered. The lettering on the signs they were holding had been blurred out. "In spite of rules prohibiting such gatherings," the collaborator said sternly, "criminal elements came together in an attempt to disseminate lies. Fortunately, members of Counterinsurgency Task Force Nine were present to disperse the troublemakers and make arrests."

At that point, Cato and the others saw half a dozen Vord military vehicles arrive and uniformed troops hit the ground. The *pop*, *pop*, *pop* of gunfire could be heard. A handful of demonstrators fell, and the rest ran. That was when more Vords arrived on the far side of the plaza, where they were in a perfect position to intercept the fugitives. Some were shot, others were beaten, and the rest were taken into custody.

"The entire population should give thanks," the off-camera narrator said self-righteously, "knowing that they are safe from those who wish to seize control of the city."

"It reminds me of Dantha," Alamy observed, "when Governor Nalomy was in control."

"Yeah," Cato agreed soberly. "Those people have guts, that's for sure."

"*Had* guts," Keen commented, as an armored troop carrier ran two people over. "The poor bastards."

But disturbing though that story was, the worst was yet to come. It was about twenty minutes later when Shani saw a familiar face appear, sat up straight, and pointed at the screen. "Look, Jak! It's you!"

As the rest of the team gathered around to look at the screen, they saw Cato, and themselves as well, all getting into a vehicle at the spaceport. A Uman pacification monitor provided the narration. "The interim government is pleased to announce that a law-enforcement team led by Centurion Jak Cato arrived today as part of a cooperative effort between the Uman Empire and the Vord Hegemony." Then the story was over. No further explanation was given.

"Damn it!" Cato exclaimed angrily. "What the hell is going on?" And with that he put in a call to Umji. Cato insisted on seeing the other police officer face-to-face, so he could gauge the Vord's reactions before sharing what they'd seen. And, judging from what Umji felt, he was just as shocked as they were. "We didn't know," Umji said, referring to both himself and his Ya. "I swear it."

"Verafti knows me," Cato grated. "He knows me very well indeed. So, if he sees that news story, he'll go into hiding, and it will be that much more difficult to find the bastard. Tell the idiots who authorized the story that if more people die, the blame will fall on them."

Umji was visibly shaken, and judging from the emotions that swirled around them, both he and Quati were frightened of the person or persons they assumed to be responsible. "We will look into it," Umji promised. "I can only suppose that the story was a misguided attempt to quell civil unrest by showing evidence of an amicable relationship between our governments."

The answer came so quickly, so easily, that it was as if Umji already knew what his investigation would turn up and who was behind the news story. "Well, tell them to stop it," Cato replied darkly. "Or Fiss Verafti might wind up sitting next to them at their next staff meeting."

Umji opened his mouth as if to speak, closed it again, and left.

The day dragged on, and by the time dinner was over, the Umans knew which sports teams were winning, that more hot and humid weather was on the way, and that the Vords had broken ground on a new Pacification Center. Except that judging from a computer-generated picture of the facility, it looked a lot like a fort. It seemed that the aliens were planning to stay.

*   *   *

The next morning, the Umans were transported to a sports arena, where they were invited to sit behind a table while thousands of hostile Vords paraded by. The sky was cloudy, the air was humid, and it felt as if it might rain as the processional began. Umji was present, as were a couple of his superiors, neither of whom was willing to communicate with the "animals" directly, and they chose to pass their wishes through the Vord police officer instead. So it was he who explained the way the system was supposed to work. "Once you spot an imposter, press the button," Umji said as he gave remotes to Cato, Shani, and Keen. "We'll take care of the rest."

"Okay," Cato agreed bleakly. "Let's get this over with."

For obvious reasons, none of the Vords who were being vetted knew why. So that added to the level of hostility that emanated from them as they were forced to parade by the Umans. And the feeling of dislike was so intense that it gave Cato a headache.

Cato could have requested a break, and might have been granted one, but that would have prolonged the unpleasant process. So he sat there and did the best he could to concentrate. At his request, a fifteen-foot interval separated the Vords so that he and the other empaths could isolate each set of emotions from the rest. Even so, it wasn't long before the seemingly endless line became something of a blur, and Cato found it difficult to focus. Finally, an hour later, the exercise was over, and Cato was able to deliver his report to Umji. "All of your people are clear. . . . There weren't any shape shifters among them."

Umji nodded gratefully. "That is very good to hear. I will pass it on."

"Terrific. Please give us our gear, including weapons, and we'll get to work."

Umji produced what might have been a grin, removed a key from his pocket, and handed it over. "See the vehicle parked over there? Your belongings are inside. You are free to go. I will contact you from time to time. If you need to call us, use this. Our number is programmed into it."

Cato accepted the pocket com, knew *it* could be tracked, and made a mental note to park it somewhere. "Thanks . . . We'll be in touch."

"Yes," Umji agreed gravely. "You will."

The van they had been given was a couple of years old, purported to belong to Havsu's Bakery, and was decorated with lots of graffiti. Something Cato actually approved of. The team's gear was already aboard and neatly stacked in the back. None of them said anything of consequence because they figured that the van was not only trackable but equipped with audio pickups as well. "Traffic's going to be a bitch," Shani predicted. And it was.

The sprawling house had been constructed ten miles south of Kybor, where it was a little bit cooler, thanks to evening breezes off Lake Boro. But the owner had been killed in a car accident, and there had been a host of legal problems related to his estate. So for the better part of two years, the property had deteriorated as the planet's heat, rain, and insects all took their toll. Finally, once the protracted legal battle was resolved, the estate came on the market and was immediately snapped up by a man who claimed to represent a benevolent association. Demeni moved into the house three days later.

There was at least one hole in the roof, a number of broken windows, and the interior furnishings had started to rot. None of which bothered her in the least since she typically slept in a corner of the great room, or out in the overgrown garden, where she could feel the rhythms of the surrounding jungle.

Others, the average Uman, for example, would have seen

a great many similarities between Therat's rain forests and those on Demeni's native planet. But the Sagathi was aware of hundreds of differences, starting with the fact that many of the local trees could kill parasites with discharges of solar-generated electricity and had leaves rather than the frothy structures she was accustomed to.

But alien or not, the house and the jungle that surrounded it was a much more friendly environment than the city of Kybor. So she spent as much time there as possible.

Of course, it was necessary to bring her work home from time to time. Like any other large organization, the cult required constant supervision. Especially now that the Vords had taken over and seemed determined to eradicate the group. The man who was suspended by his wrists in the middle of the garbage-strewn great room was an excellent example of their efforts to infiltrate the group. He was, or had been, a spy for the occupiers until a loyal Rahati had seen him enter a Vord vehicle and reported the incident. A priestess passed the information along to Demeni, who gave orders for the suspect to be brought in.

Two of Demeni's most fanatical adherents had been in charge of the interrogation. The red-hot irons hadn't been necessary, since Demeni could "feel" everything she needed to know, but her followers *wanted* to torture him, so why not? The result was a long sequence of screams, the pervasive odor of burning flesh, and a flood of words.

Yes, the man named Parakar admitted, he had been paid to spy on the Rahaties. But he didn't want to. The Vords *made* him do it, or so the informer claimed, which meant that the five cult members who had been arrested and executed weren't his fault.

Demeni could "feel" the surge of fear that she produced in him as she entered the great room. And for good reason. Having been witness to dozens of the blood-drenched ceremonies, Parakar knew what to expect. Or thought he did.

Demeni's smile looked more like a snarl. "I'm going to release you," she hissed.

Parakar's face was black-and-blue. One eye was swollen shut. Angry-looking burns were visible on his sweaty chest, and he stank of feces. His eyes blinked rapidly as he felt the first stirrings of hope and his tongue swept back and forth across dry lips. "Really?" he croaked. "That would be wonderful. Thank you."

"Then," Demeni continued, "I'm going to eat you. Unless you manage to get away, of course. In which case I will have to find someone else to feed on."

A look of horror appeared on Parakar's unshaven face. "Please! Don't do that. . . . The Vords trust me. I could be a spy! I'll tell you what they're up to."

"I already have spies," Demeni said clinically. "Ones I can trust. So shall I let you go? Or simply eat you here? I'd take the first choice if I were you. Who knows? You might get lucky."

A calculating look appeared on Parakar's badly abused face. "Okay . . . You want to have some fun. I can see that. So how 'bout a head start?"

Demeni's respect for the man went up a notch. He hadn't given up. He was still thinking, still plotting, still trying to stay alive. And that, insofar as she was concerned, was the essence of life. Even for lesser beings. So she nodded. "Five minutes. . . . I'll give you a five-minute head start."

"Ten," Parakar said hopefully. "I need ten."

"Five," Demeni replied sternly, as razor-sharp claws shot out of her fingers. There was no more than a whisper of sound as she cut him loose.

Parakar's feet hit the floor with a soft *thump*. In spite of the fact that he was a young man, and in good shape, he staggered and very nearly fell. Was that the result of the harsh treatment he had suffered? Or a trick intended to make her believe that he was weaker than he actually was? A routine execution was shaping up to be a memorable meal. "Shouldn't you run?" Demeni inquired mildly. "The five minutes starts *now*."

Parakar needed no additional urging. He bolted out through the open door, dashed through the garden, and made straight for the lake. Demeni, who had no intention of honoring her promise, was not only right behind him but impressed by Parakar's strategy. Because rather than head into the jungle, which he *knew* to be her element, he was gambling on reaching the water before she could. And the reason for that was obvious. Parakar believed that while Demeni might be able to swim, he could swim *better* than she could, which would give him an edge.

Had the Uman gone so far as to analyze her physiology? Demeni wondered. And taken note of the fact that she didn't have webbed feet or other aquatic adaptations? Or was he working off a hunch? Not that it made much difference, Demeni concluded, as her lithe body slipped through the vegetation, and all of her senses came wonderfully alive. That was the purpose of the exercise. To experience the thrill of the hunt *and* enjoy the rewards thereof.

There was a loud splash as Parakar broke through the foliage and threw himself into the water. Then, with a powerful overhead crawl, he made for the opposite side of the lake.

Demeni paused just short of the water to observe Parakar through a screen of vegetation. The Uman looked back from time to time, but it seemed unlikely that he could see her, not that it mattered. Parakar's gamble had paid off. Because while Demeni *could* swim if necessity demanded it, she preferred not to. So who would reach the other side of Lake Boro first? The Uman, who had the shortest distance to travel, or her? The foliage shivered, and Demeni disappeared.

* * *

Parakar felt as good as a hunted man could. The water was relatively warm, there were no signs of pursuit yet, and a steady trickle of adrenaline was providing him with some extra strength. Maybe, just maybe, the lizard bitch had chosen to let him go rather than enter the water. Some reptiles were born to swim. He knew that. But judging from the way her *real* body looked, the shape shifter wasn't one of them. So if he could reach the other side quickly enough, there was a pretty good chance that he'd be able to push through a half mile of jungle and reach the road beyond. Once there, he would hitch a ride, move to a small town somewhere, and change his name.

In the meantime, Parakar's light lace-up shoes were slowing him down. But he knew he was going to need them on the other side. So the only way to increase speed was to work even harder. He gave no consideration to style, only to power, being careful to rely on his legs as much as possible.

Fifteen long minutes passed before he began to close with the shore, and he caught momentary glimpses of it as his already strained heart began to pump even faster. Was the goddess Rahati waiting there, concealed in the lush undergrowth? Ready to rip his throat out? Parakar had seen her do it to Vords, heard their piteous screams, and knew he wouldn't stand a chance without some sort of weapon. But there weren't any weapons to be had as his feet made contact with the muddy bottom and his eyes probed the foliage for any sign of movement.

There weren't any. None he could detect anyway. So, conscious of the fact that his adversary might well be in the process of racing around the lake, the half-naked Uman battled his way up onto a steeply sloping beach. That was where he found a likely-looking rock. It was stupid. Parakar knew that, since the lizard was lightning fast and equipped with razor-sharp claws. But the stone's heft offered some comfort as he left the lakeshore and entered the sun-dappled jungle beyond.

Parakar's movements were tentative at first—knowing that the shape shifter could be lying in wait for him. But the farther he went, the less likely that seemed, since even if the lizard enjoyed toying with her prey, there was very little reason to delay her pleasure much longer. So Parakar let the rock fall and continued to push his way forward. He paused occasionally to listen, heard nothing other than his own heavy breathing, and moved on.

The sun was Parakar's guide. It was difficult to see, but thanks to gaps in the jungle canopy, he caught enough glimpses of the yellow-orange orb to stay on course. Once, as he crossed a clearing, he thought he heard the throaty growl of a truck engine. The sound gave him new reason to hope and brought new energy to his legs.

Five minutes later, he stumbled out of the jungle and onto a two-lane dirt road. The sight of it made his heart jump with joy. Parakar knew it might be difficult to flag down a vehicle because of his disheveled appearance, so he took a turn to the right and began to jog. Now he was thankful for the shoes because given the rough surface beneath his feet, it would have been impossible to run without them. Later, as soon as he could, he would steal some clothes.

Ten minutes later, Parakar heard the sound of a motor, looked back over his shoulder, and saw a car coming up on him from behind. So he paused, plastered a smile on his face, and waved. The car passed him by, then braked and came to a stop.

Parakar made his way forward, heard the passenger-side window whir down, and looked inside. A man with neatly combed hair and a pencil-thin mustache looked back at him. "Are you all right?" the man wanted to know. "Was there an accident or something?"

"Yes," Parakar agreed, "there was. Could you give me a lift to the next town? I need to file a report and send a wrecker back for my car."

"Of course," the man said politely. "Please get in."

So Parakar looked back over his shoulder and got in. That was when the driver morphed into a lizard, and Demeni laughed. It was the last thing Parakar heard.

TWELVE

The city of Kybor, on the planet Therat

DUST MOTES HUNG SUSPENDED IN THE SHAFTS OF sunlight that found their way down through cracks to probe the hundreds of booths crowded together under a common roof. Exotic birds trilled inside intricately woven cages, a huge mound of savory ola nuts threatened to cascade down off a table onto the duracrete floor, and racks of brightly colored children's clothing vied with each other to capture Alamy's attention.

Even though she wasn't an empath or a police officer, Alamy had been able to make a contribution to the team and felt proud of herself. Thanks to her efforts, and those of a local real-estate broker, the group had been able to move into a suite of rooms on the top floor of a slightly seedy apartment building. The whole idea was to disappear into the local population to whatever extent possible. Especially in the wake of the potentially disastrous news story announcing the team's arrival.

With that taken care of, Alamy had volunteered to handle the shopping. A chore that the rest of them were perfectly happy to rid themselves of. And that was okay with her because it felt good to support the team and get out on her own.

The first step was to identify vendors who sold high-quality meat, vegetables, and fruit at reasonable prices. Once that task was accomplished, she knew future shopping trips would go more quickly. So Alamy paused occasionally to examine piles of produce and sample the occasional piece of fruit. Had it been otherwise, she might have noticed the man and woman who were following her earlier.

It wasn't until Alamy emerged from the market with a full shopping bag dangling from each hand that she paused to look around. "Always check to see if you're being followed," Cato had admonished her. "And if you are followed, the last thing you should do is lead that person home. Stay in a public place, call me, and I'll come get you."

So when Alamy spotted the couple, and realized that she'd seen them earlier, she knew enough to be concerned. But not exceedingly so because the pair looked innocent enough and might have followed her outside by chance. Still, Alamy knew it was important to be careful.

With that in mind, she made her way over one block and began a systematic examination of shop windows, some of which were clean enough to reflect the area behind her. And the couple was still there!

Alamy felt the first stirrings of concern, put her bags down, and brought out one of four identical pocket coms that Cato had purchased for the team. Cato answered on the third ring. "Yeah?"

"It's me," Alamy said. "I'm on my way home from the market, and I think I have a tail. *Two* of them to be exact."

"Describe them."

Alamy studied the reflection in front of her. "One of them is a male in his early thirties. He's about six feet tall with an average build. He's wearing a red pillbox hat, a vest, and baggy pantaloons. The other person is female. She's wearing a white scarf, a wrap-style green dress, and carrying a drawstring purse."

"Location?"

"I'm on Imperial Way just north of the point where it intersects with Commerce."

"Okay," Cato said. "Continue your stroll. . . . We'll be there shortly."

Keen was out shopping for a van that wasn't loaded with Vord tracking devices, but both Cato and Shani were home, sitting in front of newly acquired computer consoles. The idea was to search public databases looking for the sort of patterns that might reveal the presence of a Sagathi shape shifter. Much as Verafti had done while posing as the Emperor.

So the need to venture out on what was probably a false alarm was something of an annoyance, and Shani said as much. But Cato, who was in the process of pulling a jacket on over his shoulder holster, was careful to counter the criticism. "We gave Alamy a hard time when she inadvertently told Verafti where to find us back on Corin. So give her some credit . . . She's learning."

That was fine except that Shani didn't *want* to give Alamy credit for anything more than the quality of her cooking. So she made a face but kept her mouth shut as Cato locked the door behind them and led the way down three flights of badly worn stairs to a grubby lobby and the busy street beyond. A wave of heat and a cacophony of noise reached out to greet the couple as they stepped onto the hot sidewalk.

The streets were busy as people of every possible description made their way to work, returned home, or kept appointments. There weren't any Vords in sight, but that wasn't unusual because the aliens had only about three thousand troops on the ground. Not that many, really, given the number of Umans on Therat, but enough thanks to the warships in orbit.

Ten minutes later, Cato and Shani were on heavily traveled Imperial Way and closing on what had been Alamy's position. There were so many people on the street it was difficult to sort them out, but thanks to Alamy's mention of a red hat, Cato was able to spot the couple. "Got 'em," Cato said from the corner of his mouth. "They're at two o'clock immediately behind the holy man with the frizzy hair. And I think I see Alamy about fifty feet in front of them."

Shani followed Cato's directions, located the couple in question, and was forced to give Alamy some grudging credit. At least the tails were real. "Let's close the gap," Cato suggested. "It's a long shot, but if that's Verafti and his girlfriend, then this could get interesting."

It *was* a long shot, but Shani found herself reaching in under her jacket to touch her handgun, in much the same way that a Reconstructionist priest might take comfort from his ankh. But as the variants began to close with the suspects, it quickly became clear that they were exactly what they appeared to be, which was Uman.

So why tail Alamy then? Were they thieves? Who were planning to rob her? If so, they were going to a lot of trouble for two bags of groceries. Cato made an effort to close the gap on the chance that he could pick up on some telltale emotions. But with so many people around, it was impossible to tell who was feeling what. So that left only one choice. "We'll have to take them off the street," Cato said. "Because if they're anything other than thieves, I want to know about it."

"That's just terrific," Shani replied sarcastically, "except how the hell are we going to accomplish that?"

"We'll stun 'em," Cato said pragmatically, "and hail a cab!"

Shani was about to raise the first of at least three objections when Cato drew a stubby stunner from a belt holster and began to walk more quickly. Then, while Shani hurried to catch up, Cato shot both suspects in the back. They jerked spasmodically, lost all motor control, and collapsed onto the filthy sidewalk.

"I'm a doctor!" Cato shouted loudly as he knelt next to the glassy-eyed victims. "Give them some air. . . . *You!*" Cato said authoritatively as he pointed at Shani. "Hail a cab! I'll take them to the hospital."

Shani, who was still reeling from the speed and ruthlessness with which her superior officer had immobilized two private citizens, managed to get a cab by the simple expedient of stepping out in front of one. Tires screeched as the vehicle came to a halt. The driver was swearing a blue streak when Shani held up her hand and willed her badge to appear. "Shut the hell up and help my partner load those people in the back," she ordered. "Or, if you prefer, I'll call down to city hall and have them jerk your ticket. You choose."

"But I have passengers!" the cabbie objected.

"No you don't," Shani said as she pulled the rear door open and stuck her head into the passenger compartment. Two brightly clad matrons were seated there, both wearing expressions of surprised disapproval. "This is a police emergency," Shani said gruffly. "Get out and find another ride."

The women, radiating anger, hurried to obey as Cato arrived with the female suspect cradled in his arms. "Good work," the Xeno cop said as he dumped his burden inside. "Search her. . . . And don't forget that purse. It felt heavy."

Shani discovered that the female suspect was carrying both a two-shot pistol and a flick blade as well. Both served to reinforce the notion that the couple had been up to something as they followed Alamy.

Cato and the taxi driver arrived moments later, with the male suspect slung between them. He went into the back with the two women. Then, as the driver slid behind the wheel, Cato got in beside him and began to rifle through the male suspect's wallet. "Take us to 4311 Orby Road," Cato instructed. "I want to make sure that these people arrive home safely."

"I thought we were going to the hospital," the cabbie objected.

"I changed my mind," Cato said unapologetically. "Now get going."

The cabbie saw lots of strange things on a daily basis and decided that the best thing to do was to say, "Yes, sir," and do as he was told.

Alamy was still wandering down Imperial Way. It was hot, but the first few drops of what promised to be a heavy shower were falling, and she was increasingly worried because it had been nearly half an hour since she had spoken with Cato. Then her pocket com rang, and she flipped it open. "Hello?"

"It's me," Cato said. "You were correct. Shani and I have the situation under control, and you can go home."

"Good," Alamy said as she stopped to look around. "All of my produce is starting to wilt."

"Heaven forbid," Cato said lightly. "And one more thing . . ."

"Yes?"

"Good job. Don't let up." The words were followed by a *click*.

The air was humid, and Alamy was getting wet, but she didn't care. She was happy, and for the moment, that was enough.

It was nearly noon, a warm rain had started to fall, and the streets were packed with umbrella-toting citizens. They jostled each other in an attempt to stay in under the slanting roofs that fronted many of the shops, and Verafti was there among them, the very picture of a store clerk on his way to work. His umbrella was black, the suit he wore was white, and his shoes were nicely polished.

Even before the Vords had occupied it, the city of Kybor had been aswirl with rumors, dangerous politics, and class warfare. Now, with armed aliens on the streets and members of a growing resistance movement trying to stir things up, the situation was even more volatile as Verafti continued his search.

Having concluded that Demeni wasn't responsible for killing the city's prostitutes, Verafti had turned his attention to other theories, the latest of which had to do with the Rahati religious cult. A group that worshipped a goddess who was said to have three faces.

Of course, the Umans had a seemingly endless capacity to invent religions. But if the rumors on the street were true, what made this cult different was the fact that the goddess Rahati was more than a graven image. She was a real flesh-and-blood being, one who could change shapes at will and had a taste for raw meat.

That suggested a need to investigate. . . . But how? The first step, or so it seemed to Verafti, was to visit a Rahati temple and see what, if anything, could be learned there. That was going to be difficult, however, since most of the Rahaties had been driven underground by the Vords. From what Verafti had been able to discover from online news archives, most of the Rahati temples had been raided, and dozens of the cult's adherents had been arrested. All in an attempt to shut down what the Vords called, "a vile and disgusting cult."

But the Rahaties were far from powerless. Or so it seemed. Because if Vord claims were true, more than twenty of their soldiers had been ambushed and murdered as part of what the occupiers called "unspeakable rites." Would Verafti be able to speak with one of the Rahaties? There was only one way to find out. The shape shifter paused on a corner, eyed the structure on the other side of the street, and waited for a pedicab to roll past.

One of the things that made Rahati temples different from the structures put up by other religions was the complete absence of external adornment. There were no spires, no statues, not even a window to break the building's box-like simplicity. Just a rectangular doorway, symbolizing the beginning of a new life, and the belief that everything a person needed to know lay within.

Having arrived in front of the temple, Verafti paused to shake the raindrops off his umbrella before lowering the canopy and tucking the damp implement under his arm. A gentle push was sufficient to open the door. After passing through a lobby with a colorful mural on the central wall, Verafti entered the large room beyond. If the outside of the building was austere, the interior was just the opposite. Ropes of multicolored lights crisscrossed the high ceiling, oil lamps flickered as an air current flowed around them, and the wall paint produced a luminescent glow. There were no benches on which to sit, just carpets of every possible color that overlapped each other.

Because of the relatively early hour, and the Vords' efforts to put the cult out of business, Verafti found himself alone with the goddess. Rahati, or an image of her, rested on a raised platform at the front of the room. And consistent with what he'd heard, the supernatural being had three faces. The one that faced the long, rectangular room was that of a beast with its fangs bared. Uman profiles could be seen to either side of it. The one on the left was unmistakably male—and the one on the right was female. All of which was emblematic of some nonsense or other. Verafti didn't care.

So, with no one to speak to, Verafti had little choice but to make his way up toward the front of the room and sit down. Then, with legs crossed, he settled in to wait. A person was present nearby. Verafti could "feel" the Uman's emotions. They consisted of boredom tinged with curiosity. Regarding him? Yes, most certainly. Visitors were probably rare that time of day, especially people the observer didn't already know, which would account for the way he or she felt.

Then why not come out of hiding? Verafti wondered. Unless he was being subjected to a test. A period of waiting intended to separate serious seekers from the merely curious. So he sat, and sat some more, even though the emotional presence came and went occasionally.

Finally, after the better part of two hours had passed, Verafti heard a momentary swish of fabric as a woman appeared. Her hair was pulled back into a ponytail, which served to emphasize a high forehead. She was dressed in a silky red fabric that was wrapped around her body in an artful manner with a small amount of excess cloth thrown back over her left shoulder. "Can I help you?" The words sounded like a challenge rather than an offer of assistance.

"That depends," Verafti answered evenly. "I have a message for Rahati. . . . Can you deliver it?"

Lamplight danced in the woman's almond-shaped eyes. "The goddess already knows that which lies within," she replied gravely. "There is no need for a messenger."

"My message is for the person rather than the goddess," Verafti countered. "If she is the person I think she is, we were friends once. Extremely good friends."

The woman was annoyed, and Verafti could "feel" it. "Rahati is there in front of you. Say what you will to her. Then I must ask you to leave."

When the shape shifter morphed into his *true* form, the woman screamed and attempted to run. But Verafti was fast, and she hadn't traveled more than a few feet before he caught up with her. He had only one hand, but that was sufficient. His fingers were like steel. "Go to Rahati," he commanded. "Communicate what you saw. And tell her that I would cross a thousand stars to be with her. She will know my name. Fail me, and I will kill you."

"I w-w-won't fail you," the woman said piteously. "Please don't hurt me."

"Tell her to meet me in the botanical gardens," Verafti said. "I will go there each night for the next two nights. Do you understand?"

"The b-b-botanical gardens," the woman said, "each night for the next two nights. I will tell her." She was telling the truth, he could "feel" it, and a feeling of joy bubbled up from deep within. Demeni was there! Somewhere nearby . . . Soon to be by his side.

"Good," Verafti said as he released his grip. And then, as suddenly as the first change had taken place, he was Uman again. "So, tell me," the shape shifter said pleasantly as he bent to retrieve his umbrella. "Is it still raining?"

Kybor's once-thriving warehouse district was located just south of the spaceport. But now, having been cut off from the Uman Empire for months, the only outbound cargoes were shipments of germanium bound for factories deep inside the Vord Hegemony.

The area had been hard hit during the Vord landings, and huge craters marked the spots where bombs had gone off or incoming missiles had struck. Many structures had been destroyed or were so damaged as to be useless.

There were survivors, however. Most of them were one-story metal-sheathed buildings that were locked up to keep vagrants out. Some were guarded by club-toting Urs— others had airborne drones for protection.

So the cabbie was understandably nervous as he turned onto Orby Road and began to watch for number 4311. "Are you sure this is where you want to go?" the driver inquired doubtfully. "I thought you were taking them home."

The male suspect groaned at that point and was in the process of trying to sit up when Shani stunned him again. "Nope," Cato answered. "This is the place all right. Rents are cheaper down here. There it is. . . . Number 4311."

The taxi slowed, passed through an already opened security gate, and came to a halt. There were no signs of life. Just a stripped truck, a lot of litter, and the head-high graffiti that decorated the front of the shabby warehouse. But appearances can be deceiving. Security cameras were mounted here and there all around the building, and as Cato got out of the car, he saw one of them move. The device might be synched up to a motion detector, but Cato thought he could "feel" emotional activity nearby and was pretty sure he was under surveillance.

"Okay," Cato said, as Shani got out to join him. "Let's pull them out of the cab. Assuming there are people inside, that should bring them out to speak with us."

Shani eyed the cameras, "felt" a rising sense of consternation, and nodded. Five minutes later, both of the suspects were laid out on the duracrete. Cato dropped three Imperials into the driver's hand and looked him in the eye. "I took your license number off the card in the back. That means I can find you. This trip never took place."

"What trip?" the cabbie responded as he made the Imperials disappear. Seconds later, he was behind the wheel, guiding the car out onto Orby Road. At that point, he gunned the engine and sped away.

"I don't mean to be critical," Shani put in as she eyed the warehouse. "But how will we make it home?"

"I'm not entirely sure," Cato answered, as a large sliding door rumbled open to reveal a pile of cargo modules. "But if things go well, the people in the warehouse will give us a lift."

"And if things *don't* go well?" Shani inquired, removing her weapon from its holster.

"Then we'll be in deep shit," Cato replied evenly, as a pair of heavily armed men walked out onto the loading platform and stood in front of the cargo modules.

"Who the hell are you?" the larger man demanded belligerently. He had a bulging forehead, piggy eyes, and an underthrust jaw.

"We're the people these idiots were sent to find," Cato answered as he placed a foot on the male suspect's posterior.

Piggy Eyes was silent for a moment. "Are they dead?"

"No, just stunned. I suggest that you send someone to carry them inside."

The man turned his head back toward the building's interior, spoke to a person Cato couldn't see, and turned back again. Then, as six men and women filed out onto the platform, Piggy Eyes jerked the submachine gun to the left. "Take your foot off my nephew's ass."

Cato grinned and took a step backward. "Sorry . . . So are you going to invite us in for a chat? Or should I call the Vords and ask them to join us?"

Piggy Eyes opened his mouth to respond but was overridden as a young woman appeared in the doorway. "Thank you, Bif. . . . I'll take it from here. Officer Cato? Officer Shani? Please come in. We have some pretty thick cloud cover at the moment, but the Vords keep a close eye on the city from orbit."

Cato returned his weapon to its holster, and Shani did the same as the semiconscious male suspect was carried into the building. The same young woman was waiting for them inside. Her blond hair was worn in a buzz cut, and outside of a pair of dangly earrings, she had a hard, almost masculine appearance. She was dressed in an olive drab shirt over baggy militia trousers and a pair of scuffed combat boots. A large pistol was strapped to her right thigh, and something about her stance suggested that she knew how to use it. "My name is Olivia Arrius," she said. "Welcome to Therat."

"Arrius?" Cato inquired. "As in *Governor* Arrius?"

"The same," the young woman responded gravely. "Governor Arrius is my father."

"We thought he was dead," Cato replied. "That's what the Vords told us."

"And they did their damnedest to kill me," a male voice said. "But I'm a cantankerous old bastard, and they missed."

Cato turned to discover that a man dressed in military fatigues had emerged from an office. He had a thick shock of white hair, the same sky blue eyes that Olivia had, and two days' worth of stubble on his cheeks. "Milo Demby was my personal assistant for more than twenty years. He took three bullets for me and lies buried in my grave."

"I'm sorry to hear that," Cato said respectfully. "So, are you leading the resistance? The people who stage demonstrations?"

"The people who commit suicide is more like it," Arrius replied sadly. "They are very brave—but foolish. No, my daughter and I lead another group. Rather than complain about the Vords, we think it makes more sense to kill them."

"No offense," Shani put in as she spoke for the first time. "But if the two people you sent to look for us are typical of your troops, you aren't going to get very far."

Arrius shrugged. "Most of our volunteers have little or no experience at this sort of thing. Once the Vords announced your arrival, we sent the best we had. How did you find us anyway?"

Cato fished a piece of cardboard out of his pocket and gave it over. "Your male operative was carrying this in his wallet."

Arrius looked at the business card. One of many that had been found in the office he was using. It read: ROSSI & SONS, 4311 ORBY ROAD, KYBOR SOUTH.

The governor made a face. "You can see what I'm up against. Please follow me."

So the police officers followed, with Olivia Arrius and Bif bringing up the rear. Cato could tell that both the governor and his daughter felt suspicious as Arrius led them into a makeshift living area. It was furnished with rows of sloppily made beds, racks of weapons, and two folding tables. "Welcome to our kitchen, dormitory, and conference room," Arrius said airily as he paused next to a circle of mismatched chairs. "Have a seat."

"Sorry, sire," Cato said as he turned and slipped in behind the governor. "But it appears that there are issues of mutual trust that need to be resolved before we can have a chat. Please instruct your daughter, Bif, and the rest of your people to place their weapons on the floor and step back from them."

Arrius sighed. "It seems we're outclassed. Olivia . . . Bif . . . the rest of you . . . Put your weapons down and step back."

Olivia obeyed, and, with obvious reluctance, the others did as well. "That's better," Cato said, as the freedom fighters glowered at him. "Now, let's get everything out into the open. The Vords ran a story about us, so you wonder if we're legit—or collaborators sent to help track you down.

"The answer is that the Vords told the truth. Or at least part of it. We're here at the behest of both governments, looking for a couple of criminals who represent a threat to sentients everywhere. That's all I can tell you for the moment since the exact nature of the threat is classified."

"That makes for an interesting story," Olivia Arrius said cynically, "but how do we know it's true?"

"Well, there is *this*," Cato said as he flashed his badge, "plus the fact that Xeno cops aren't all that common, so it's unlikely that the Vords would be able to subvert any."

Arrius looked quite interested. "So you can read our thoughts?"

"No, but we can sense your emotions," Cato replied. "That's why I have a gun to your head."

"Okay," Arrius said, "I believe you."

"His daughter doesn't," Shani put in.

"I'm starting to," Olivia allowed cautiously.

Cato "felt" Olivia's growing acceptance of the situation and holstered his weapon.

Shani did the same.

"So," Arrius said, once he was seated. "You can't tell us the exact nature of your mission."

"No," Cato agreed. "But I can tell you this . . . Other than arrest two criminals if we can—my team won't be providing any assistance to the Vords. And there's reason to hope that the Empire will send a task force to free Therat soon."

The resistance fighters listened with growing interest as Cato told them about Emperor Emor's unexpected death, how his son Brunus had taken the throne, and the increased likelihood of war. "Finally!" Governor Arrius said jubilantly, as the account came to an end. "Emor left us hanging out here, damn him to hell. I know Brunus, and he's just the kind of leader we need.

"And," Arrius continued, "that brings me back to the present situation. Help us, and we'll help you. We know this planet the way only a native can. So if the people you're looking for are hiding in Kybor, we'll find them. Meanwhile, you can provide us with some much-needed military advice. Most of our militia were either captured or killed during the initial fighting."

Cato was tempted. And for good reason. Because a force of locals could be extremely useful in locating Fiss Verafti and/or his lover. Of course, they could be a problem as well. Especially given how clumsy they were. The last thing Cato wanted to do was to tip the shifters off to the team's presence if they weren't already aware of it. "Okay," Cato responded cautiously. "It's a deal, providing you and your people understand that there are certain aspects of our mission that we can't reveal and that the Vords will not only continue to watch us but will show up on our doorstep from time to time."

"I'm glad you mentioned that," Arrius said as he directed a meaningful glance to his daughter. "We wouldn't want to have any misunderstandings."

And that was when the Vord air car landed out front. "We've got trouble!" one of the resistance fighters said as he looked up from a flat-panel monitor. "A carload of freaks just put down in the front yard."

"How many?" Cato demanded.

"Four. Three of them are headed for the front door. The pilot is still at the controls."

Cato turned to Shani. "Invite them in," he said grimly. "And don't let them get a message out. I'll take care of the pilot."

Nobody questioned the manner in which Cato had taken command, least of all Governor Arrius, who was up on his feet and headed for a rack of weapons. "We'll have to move again," he said grimly. "It looks like they spotted the place from orbit."

Shani thought the cab driver who had brought them to the warehouse was the likely culprit but didn't say so as she led Olivia, Arrius, Bif, and another man out front. "Unlock the door," she ordered, "and hide behind those crates. We'll use pistols unless things get out of hand. Olivia, what we need are head shots. . . . Are you any good with that thing?"

"Yes," the other woman replied as she held her weapon in the approved two-handed grip. And because Shani could "feel" Olivia's confidence, she believed it.

"Good. I'll take the two to the left—and you take the two to the right. And Bif, if we miss, then open up with the heavy artillery."

Shani could have said more, and wanted to say more, but there wasn't enough time as a Vord tried the door handle, and the Umans hurried to take their places behind the cargo containers.

A rectangle of sunlight invaded the warehouse as the door slid out of the way. The Vords weren't stupid enough to rush in; but with no one there to greet them, they were forced to enter or leave. So they entered. The soldiers were tall and somewhat grotesque by Uman standards because of the Ya parasites wrapped around the back of their necks. All three wore body armor and carried the long-barreled assault rifles that were standard-issue for Vord ground troops. They moved cautiously, clearly unsure of what they might find, which was consistent with Shani's theory regarding the cab driver.

Then, as the enemy troopers committed themselves, Shani stepped out from behind a large cargo module. As a police officer, she was expected to give a warning before she fired, but as a member of the 3rd Legion, she was under no such obligation. She chose the outside target first, firing two quick shots just to make sure, before swinging her weapon to the right.

The first body was already hitting the duracrete floor by the time Olivia Arrius triggered her weapon. But her aim was good. Her first bullet entered the trooper's left eye and blew the back of his head out. The second slug hit the Vord's soft-skinned Ya and tore it open. Purplish green organs spilled out onto the floor as the dead bodies fell.

Shani's second target was falling by then, having been hit three times, as Olivia shifted her aim to the sole survivor. The sound of her shot blended with the report from Shani's weapon as the Vord took *two* bullets fired within a fraction of a second of each other. The combination pulped the trooper's face and threw him backward. His body skidded out onto the surface of the loading dock, where the pilot would be able to see it.

Having exited via a back door, Cato made his way around the side of the building and out to the southwest corner of the warehouse. From there he had a clear view of the utilitarian air car, the pintle-mounted machine gun in back, and the Vord seated behind the controls. The engine was running, and the air shimmered as waves of heat came off the vehicle. It was located a good hundred feet away. Easy meat for a rifle but more difficult with a pistol, especially since the air car was hovering rather than grounded.

Cato was faced with two choices. He could remain where he was, steady his weapon by holding it against the corner of the building, and hope to put a couple of slugs through the spot between the pilot's bubble-shaped helmet and his body. Or he could charge the vehicle and close the range before the Vord could open a com link with his superiors.

The police officer chose the second option. He ran like hell, covered fifty feet as quickly as he could, and came to a stop. Then, as the pilot spotted him and muffled gunshots were heard from the warehouse, Cato fired all nineteen rounds at his target. The idea was to make up for any lack of accuracy with overwhelming firepower. At least three bullets hit the front of the pilot's helmet, shattered his visor, and smashed through his face. As he slumped backward, the air car lurched to one side, and sparks flew as it crashed to the ground.

Cato looked up, felt a couple of blood-warm raindrops hit his face, and gave thanks for increased cloud cover. But there were other dangers to consider, not the least of which was the possibility of an automated report sent out by the vehicle as it hit the ground.

So Cato reloaded his pistol, made his way forward, and put two bullets into the pilot's Ya. Then, satisfied that the parasite wouldn't have the opportunity to report on what its host had seen, he turned toward the warehouse. That location had clearly been compromised, and if the resistance fighters wanted to survive, they would have to leave in a hurry. Somehow, without intending to, Cato had acquired an army.

THIRTEEN

The city of Kybor, on the planet Therat

WHAT LIGHT THERE WAS ORIGINATED FROM THE SO-
lar reflector the Vords had placed in orbit around Therat.
The satellite's purpose was to focus the sun's light on Kybor
during the night, making it that much easier to patrol the
streets and maintain order. Still, as the dark-haired woman
paused in a shadow and removed her clothes, she knew it
was very unlikely that the eyes in the sky would be on her.
Not with so many other individuals to track. The cool night
air caused her nipples to harden, sent goose bumps racing
down her arms, and caused her to shiver.

Even with the wan light beamed down from above, it was
still mostly dark outside the botanical gardens. Even if Demeni couldn't see what lay beyond the tall steel-mesh fence,
she could smell the rich amalgam of odors associated with
the parklike facility. That included the sweet, sometimes-
cloying scent of exotic flowers, the thick, throat-clogging
muskiness of tree pollen, and the rich odor of decay that
reminded her of the planet Sagatha.

Was that why he had chosen to meet her in the botanical

gardens? she wondered. Because of the way the environment would remind her of home? And therefore of him? But who? Verafti? *Yes,* she thought, *of all my suitors, he was the most ardent. And now, having sought me out, he intends to seduce me here in this delicious darkness. But is he worthy?*

Demeni remembered the terrified priestess and the carefully memorized message. "I would cross a thousand stars to be with her." That was what he had said.

Yes, Demeni thought to herself, *he's worthy.* And with that, she launched herself at the fence. It rattled as Uman fingers and toes found purchase, and strong arms pulled her upward. Then, having swung herself over the top, Demeni dropped to the ground. Low-lying plants and soft loam absorbed most of the impact.

Conscious of the fact that there could be others, enemies even, roaming the darkness beyond, Demeni paused to "listen." Not so much with her ears as with that part of her mind that could "feel" what others felt. There were no clear emotions in the area. Just the static-like buzz produced by the surrounding plants and the faint emanations associated with small animals searching for food. They radiated hunger, with an overlay of fear and occasional spikes of curiosity.

Satisfied that she was momentarily safe, Demeni morphed into her true form. Then, with the surety of the jungle creature she was, she entered the maze of pathways, pools, and gardens that had so lovingly been laid out more than a hundred years earlier. The plantings were starting to suffer from neglect because the gardens had a very low priority where the Vords were concerned. But that was fine with Demeni, who preferred the chaotic growth.

Being careful to move as quietly as possible, Demeni followed a path between a pair of flowering creep-creep trees and out onto a slightly arched footbridge. Luminescent fish were visible below, bodies flashing as they shot out of the water to intercept low-flying insects before splashing back into the water.

From there the trail led past benches, the dark bulk of a slowly writhing snake-branch tree, and under a pergola hung with exotic air orchids. They looked deathly pale in the strange half-light projected from above.

That was where Demeni paused to listen and sniff the night air. Many of same scents were available to her nostrils, but there was a new flavor to be sampled, and that was the coppery smell of blood. It caused the shape shifter to growl softly as her lips pulled back and away from her teeth. A fresh kill had been left for her. It was both a present and a statement about her suitor's ability to provide for both her *and* their offspring. Should there be any.

Demeni snarled approvingly and followed the path into an open area, where a gazebo stood at the center of a circle bordered by tall, spindly trees. The structure's domed roof was supported by four columns. And there, hanging within, was a body.

Demeni knew he was out in the darkness somewhere, watching and waiting. Because that was part of the age-old ritual that predated sentience itself. Her suitor had played his part, and now it was time for her to either break off the courtship or take it to the next level.

With that in mind, Demeni went straight to the body. It was hanging head down and had been peeled, so that strips of clothes hung all around like the petals of an obscene flower. Most if not all of the night watchman's blood had been drained out of his body to form a black pool on the ground. Demeni didn't hesitate to step into it, grasp the corpse with both hands, and take a bite out of a meaty thigh.

She was hungry, and the flesh tasted good; but there was another need as well. One that hadn't been satisfied for a long time. The tacky blood pulled at Demeni's feet as she backed away. That was where the symbolic hunt began. The pheromones were present, still suspended in the air, and they led the way. But other senses were required as well, including her capacity to "feel" what he felt.

And suddenly there it was. A keen hunger, mixed with a strong yearning and a rising hopefulness. And because both Sagathies could "feel" each other's emotions, Verafti knew that Demeni was not only near but searching for him. So it was anything but a surprise as they came together in an open area.

No words were spoken, nor was there a need for any, as the two shape shifters came together. What followed was a very satisfying battle in which Demeni resisted and Verafti took what he knew to be his. It had been a long time for both of them, and the moment of mutual release was not only shattering but made all the more intense by the fact that they could "feel" each other's pleasure throughout.

Finally, having exhausted themselves, it was time to return to the kill and eat the first of many meals together. The world and everything that lived on it was theirs to share.

Cato was asleep in bed when the Vords came for him. There was a loud banging on the front door, followed by a heated exchange between Keen and whoever was outside, then a visit from Alamy. "Jak . . . Wake up! Umji's outside, and he wants you to attend some sort of meeting."

Cato swore, rolled over, and put his feet on the floor. That was when he realized he was fully dressed, glanced at his watch, and realized that his "nap" should have been over three hours earlier. And somehow, in spite of the team's best efforts to lose themselves in Kybor, the Vords knew exactly where they were.

Cato groaned, got to his feet, and made his way into the living room. A quick peek through one of the windows confirmed his worst fears. A Vord combat car was parked on the street below. "Those stupid bastards!"

Keen and Shani stood to either side of the front door, weapons in hand, as Cato came over to open it. "Did it ever occur to you that parking a combat car in front of our building would draw attention to us?" the police officer demanded. "Are you trying to get us killed?"

Umji looked both surprised and embarrassed as he entered the apartment. "We're sorry," he said contritely. "Our society is different from yours. Police don't have to hide. They go where they choose."

"I hope you have one helluva good reason for this visit," Cato said, as Keen and Shani holstered their guns.

"We were ordered to come," the Vord replied defensively. "There are new developments. The commissioners want to see you *now*."

Cato eyed the other law-enforcement officer skeptically. "Would this be the same pair who put video of our arrival on the local news nets?"

"Yes," he said apologetically. "But they are in charge."

Cato sighed and brought his wrists together in front of him. "Cuff me."

Umji was clearly bewildered. "Cuff you? What for?"

"So it will look like you arrested me," Cato answered patiently. "It isn't much, but it beats walking out of here looking like I'm your best friend."

Traffic had already begun to build but seemed to melt away as the Vord combat car pushed its way through Kybor's steamy streets. It seemed that no one wanted to get into a confrontation with the Vords.

A brief rainstorm had passed through an hour earlier, and as the sun rose higher in the sky, a ground mist rose and eddied gently as the car disturbed it. "You can take the cuffs off now," Cato said, extending his wrists.

"We might be better off if we left them on," Umji grumbled. But the restraints fell away as the electronic key made contact with them. At that point, Cato was about to ask what had prompted the early-morning meeting when something clanged against the roof. "What was that?" the Uman inquired as he looked upward.

"A sniper," Umji said crossly. "We capture or kill one or two of them a day, but they keep popping up. And they ambush our patrols as well. We lost four troopers yesterday. Eight, counting their advisors."

Having shot two of them himself, Cato was well aware of the incident. He thought about Governor Arrius, his daughter Olivia, and the group they led. The resistance fighters might be amateurs, but they were pretty well organized. Ten minutes after the gun battle, the entire group was aboard trucks and headed for another location.

Had the bullet that hit the roof been fired by one of their people? Or someone from another resistance group? There was no way to know.

The car slowed as it passed through a zigzag security checkpoint and entered the parking lot adjacent to what had been the Imperial palace and the surrounding administrative complex. Then, safe within the protective zone that surrounded the area, they got out and walked toward the building beyond. "Please surrender your weapon," Umji said. "If you don't, the commissioners' bodyguards will take it."

Cato was immediately suspicious. Was the meeting for real? Or part of a setup? But why bother? The Vords had clearly been aware of where the team was holed up and could have taken all of them into custody anytime they chose. Besides, Cato couldn't "feel" any of the agitation that Umji could be expected to project if a double cross was in the works. So he gave the pistol over. "It's loaded. Don't shoot yourself."

Umji accepted the weapon, stuck it into his waistband, and gave Cato the Vord equivalent of a dirty look. "What is it that you say? Go have sex with yourself?"

Cato grinned. "That's close enough. You're getting the hang of it."

Once inside the mansion, Cato was awash in a sea of emotions projected by the Vords who came and went through the halls. All of them were on errands of overwhelming importance judging from the way they felt.

The commissioners' office had probably been a conference room given the way it looked. Two stern-faced guards stood outside, *four* counting the Ya, and Cato had to submit to a pat-down before being allowed to enter.

Cato thought it was interesting that the commissioners felt a need for bodyguards inside a secured facility. Uman freedom fighters couldn't get at them, so *who* then? Vord rivals? Or, Sagathi shape shifters? Cato would have been willing to bet on the second possibility. The Vords weren't just worried about the Sagathies, they were *terrified* of them. Never mind the fact that either one of the guards could have been replaced by the very thing that the commissioners feared.

As Cato preceded Umji into the room, he saw a section of carpet, a table that had been pressed into service as a desk, and the single Vord/Ya entity behind it. They were backlit by an arched window, and Cato had to squint in order to see. "Commissioners Narth and Oomo," Umji said gravely. "Please allow me to introduce Centurion Cato."

By that time, Cato had learned that Vords were always introduced before their advisors. Most Vords were tall, but Narth was larger than most, and his Ya was exceptionally plump. It had olive drab skin, interrupted by orange spots, and Cato could see the parasite pulse rhythmically as it pumped chemicals into its host's bloodstream. "Explain *this*," Narth demanded harshly.

Cato was about to say, "Explain what?" when video appeared on a wall screen to his right. Cato had no idea what he was looking at as a spotlight swung back and forth across what appeared to be a path and eventually steadied on a small building. Then, after three or four seconds, the camera wobbled as the operator made his or her way forward, climbed a couple of steps, and stopped.

That was when Cato saw the bloody carcass hanging head down from the rafters. A great deal of the skin and flesh had been ripped away, leaving sections of bone to gleam from within. As the camera tilted down, Cato saw that the Uman's head was missing—and assumed that it had fallen off during the feeding frenzy. "Freeze the video," Cato ordered, and Narth did so.

"Tell me what you see," the Vord demanded.

"Footprints," Cato answered as he studied the bloody patterns that the camera had captured. "Sagathi footprints."

"So this is your Fiss Verafti?"

"No," Cato answered. "Judging from the size difference between many of them, I would say these footprints belong to Verafti *and* Demeni. It appears that his efforts to track her down were successful. They met wherever this footage was taken, had sex, and ate together. It's all part of the Sagathi mating ritual. This is what we were afraid might happen."

"You were sent to prevent such an occurrence," Narth said sternly. "You failed."

"The Sagathies are smart," Cato countered. "So the investigation is going to take time. And the fact that you told them about our presence was a big mistake."

Cato "felt" a surge of anger from Narth, and fear around Umji, but kept going. "*If* you want to capture or kill the Sagathies, you will leave my team alone and provide whatever support we ask for."

The commissioners were unmoved. "You would do well to show respect for your superiors," Narth responded coldly. "Deliver results soon or suffer the consequences. Dismissed."

A very frightened Umji led Cato out of the room and down the hall. "Well," Cato said, "you heard the man. Or 'men,' if that's the right term. It's time to quit goofing off and get to work! You're lucky to have such great leadership."

Meanwhile, back in the office, Narth and his advisor were standing in front of the big window looking out on the park-like setting beyond. *So,* Narth said, *do you think the Umans will be able to locate the shape shifters?*

I don't know, the Ya replied. *What if one or both of the creatures were to escape into space? As happened on Corin? We cannot allow such a thing to happen.*

But, if the Umans fail, how could we prevent such an escape? We have only three thousand troops. They should have given us ten times that many.

We need a backup plan, Oomo replied.

Such as?

It may be necessary to nuke Therat and everyone on it. That would eliminate the problem once and for all.

Narth was appalled. *Not our own people!*

Of course our people, Oomo replied. *It would be unfortunate, I acknowledge that, but casualties are a necessary part of war. Remember, even if the Umans were to vet our personnel every day, we still wouldn't be safe. One of the Sagathies could replace a soldier or administrator minutes after they were cleared.*

Narth was "silent" for a moment. *Yes, I see what you mean. Perhaps we should have a conversation with Admiral Trema. First, to ensure that none of the personnel on the ground are allowed to leave, and to prevent any more from being brought to the surface. After all, why increase the number of casualties that we might have to suffer? Secondly, should it be necessary to glass Therat, the Navy should be ready to act quickly.*

That's an excellent idea, Oomo agreed. *And while we're at it, let's make sure that you and I have the means to escape. After all, we know we aren't infected, and our guidance will be required.*

True, Narth agreed. *Very true. It feels good to have a plan.*

Near the town of Favela, on the planet Therat

There had been a time hundreds of years before when the Mocius Mining Company had operations on nine planets, Therat being one of the most important. But the company had changed many times since then, and what had once been state-of-the-art facilities weren't anymore, so processing plants like the one outside the town of Favela had been left to rust.

That was when the surrounding jungle launched a slow-motion effort to reclaim the land on which Plant 19 stood. First came an airborne assault by seeds and spores that birds, animals, and insects carried over or under the security fence. Then, once a crop of hardy sun-tolerant weeds had taken root, the *real* attack got under way.

It was innocuous at first, since the green feelers that the jungle sent out to embrace Plant 19 grew just two or three feet per year. But it was only a matter of twenty years or so before the green tendrils penetrated the fence, burrowed *under* the duracrete hardscape that surrounded the facility, and began to break it into sections.

Then, having established a good roothold, trees sought the sky, parasites took hold on them, and vines went to work tying the biomass together. So that fifty years after the last load of ore was removed from Plant 19, the structure was so much a part of the jungle, it was difficult to say where one started and the other left off.

Demeni, Verafti, and a group of bodyguards had just arrived on the crest of a heavily forested hill. "See?" she said proudly, as she pointed a very human finger at the valley below. "My temple is down there. . . . It's in an old ore-processing plant."

Verafti, who looked exactly like the man paid to polish his shoes the day before, nodded. Most of the building was obscured by thick foliage, but one corner of the metal-sheathed structure was visible from that vantage point, and an ancient com mast could be seen pointing impotently at the sky.

Two days had passed since the thrilling night inside the botanical gardens, and Verafti didn't know what to make of his mate's considerable accomplishments. Not only was Demeni the head of a Uman religious cult, she owned a private estate and was trying to push the Vords off Therat.

"It isn't that I *seek* such responsibilities," Demeni had explained the day before, "but I . . . That is to say, *we* need them in order to survive."

Verafti wasn't so sure. He believed that power, property, and wealth were Uman vices that were more likely to attract trouble than prevent it. But he couldn't say that. Not yet anyway. "The temple looks marvelous," he lied. "And the Umans built it for you. How clever you are!"

Both Sagathies were empaths, and both could block their emotions as well, so Demeni had no choice but to take Verafti's comments at face value. "Come on!" she said enthusiastically. "It's beautiful inside."

The steep trail switchbacked down along the verdant hillside, and a good forty-five minutes passed before Demeni, Verafti, and a group of twelve heavily armed bodyguards arrived on the flat ground below. More brightly clad Rahaties were waiting there. They lined both sides of the path and, having seen Demeni in human form before, showered the living goddess with flower petals as she walked past.

That struck Verafti as more than a little ironic since he knew that his mate would have eaten one of them for lunch had it suited her purposes to do so. In fact, it was only the presence of so many Vord oppressors that kept her from preying on her own followers.

The trail led through a tunnel of greenery and from there into the processing plant itself. It was at least ten degrees cooler inside, the air was sweet with incense, and there was no vegetation to be seen. Many hours of backbreaking labor had been required to cut the machinery that once occupied the space into smaller pieces and haul it away. But the effort had been worth it because the result was an open space equivalent to the largest Uman church that Verafti had ever been in.

Shafts of sunlight streamed down through skylights located three stories above and threw carpets of gold across the rugs that covered the floor. And there, chanting "*Ke-Ya*" (we believe), were at least a hundred of Demeni's followers.

The next hour or so passed slowly as Demeni met with administrators, received detailed reports from her spymasters, and resolved priestly disputes. So, finally, with nothing else to do, Verafti left the temple and faded into the sun-dappled jungle. The place where he *always* felt at home.

After casting about for a few minutes, Verafti came across an intriguing scent, wondered what sort of beast might be in the offing, and removed his clothes prior to morphing into his true form. Then, with blood pounding in his ears, he took off. Not because he was hungry but because the shape shifter wanted to do what he did best, which was to hunt.

It was dark by the time Verafti returned, took a quick bath in the nearby river, and morphed into Uman form. Then, having donned the clothing worn earlier, he reentered the temple. The ritual of life, which was actually all about death, was well under way by then. So Verafti had an excellent opportunity to watch the goddess Rahati disembowel a screaming Vord. Later, once the ritual was over, he knew Demeni would come to him, and the certainty of that felt good.

*   *   *

Hours had passed, night had fallen, and Verafti was sitting on the processing plant's flat roof, looking up at the stars, when he "felt" Demeni's presence. And she was angry. *Very* angry. The emotion fell on him like a blow from a hammer as he stood and turned to greet her. "Did I do something wrong?"

Demeni's *true* form was lithe and breathtakingly beautiful even if the emotions she projected were hard and cold. "Yes," she replied, "you did. First you killed the Uman Emperor and took his place. That was both rash and likely to cause even more trouble for our kind. But how could I complain since your impersonation of the Emperor was for the purpose of finding me?

"But now, based on information received from my spymasters, it looks as though the Umans followed you! Why else would the Vords allow a team of alien law-enforcement officers to land on Therat? They don't have empaths, and the Umans do."

Verafti felt the first stirrings of fear. "Your spies are wrong."

"The team's arrival was broadcast on all of the vid nets," Demeni countered angrily. "There were four of them—led by a Centurion."

Verafti felt a lump form in his throat. "Did they give his name?"

"I think it was Cato."

Verafti swore, and Demeni's eyes narrowed. "You know him?"

"He's the one," Verafti answered. "The only one who could follow me here."

"Yet you never told me," Demeni said accusingly.

"I didn't want to worry you," Verafti replied lamely.

"You didn't want me to *reject* you," Demeni shot back, "but it's too late for that now."

"I'll take care of it," Verafti said grimly. "Tell me where the empaths are, and I'll go there."

"My assassins will take care of it," she responded. "Then and only then will we know peace."

And that was when Verafti realized something he should have known all along. The last thing he wanted was peace.

The city of Kybor, on the planet Therat

Thanks to the arrangements put in place by Umji, a woman in a crisp lab coat was waiting to greet Cato and Alamy when they arrived in the Municipal Building's marble-floored lobby. She immediately led them through a checkpoint, where they were required to show identification and palm a scanner before being allowed to proceed.

The woman led them down a flight of tightly turning stairs to a door labeled MORGUE. The hallway beyond was both chilly and brightly lit. "This way please," the woman said, as she led her guests down the corridor to a room identified by the numeral "2." "I'll be nearby if you need me," the woman said as she pushed a button and the door slid out of the way.

The room had a white ceiling, the walls were covered with green tiles, and the floor consisted of polished dura-crete. Glass-fronted cabinets were mounted over a long countertop, on which gleaming instruments had been left to dry.

Umji was waiting next to one of two operating tables, and the Vord wasn't alone. A male corpse had been laid out on one of the stainless-steel surfaces, and there was no mistaking the look of horror permanently etched into his face. And no wonder . . . Half of his neck was missing, as were substantial chunks of shoulder and chest.

Cato said hello to Umji and immediately bent over to inspect the body more closely, while Alamy battled to keep her lunch down. The same lunch Cato had purchased for her only an hour earlier. Fortunately, Cato wasn't paying any attention as Alamy swallowed and looked away. "So, who *is* this guy?" he wanted to know.

"His name is Parakar," Umji answered. "Henro Parakar. He was found next to the road west of Lake Boro a few days ago but only came to our attention this morning."

"And the wounds? What does the coroner have to say about them?"

"Unfortunately, the senior coroner was murdered," Umji replied. "So we don't know what he would say. But the assistant coroner says the wounds are consistent with an attack by a wild animal."

"An attack that took place *prior* to Parakar's death? Or after it?"

"Prior," Umji said. "The coroner feels certain the bites and the subsequent blood loss were the cause of Parakar's death because he was in good physical health and no other wounds were found."

"So that's why you called us in," Cato said thoughtfully. "He fits the profile, I'll give you that. Are there large carnivores on Therat? The kind that could inflict such wounds?"

"Not in close proximity to Kybor," Umji answered. "We looked into that, and all such life-forms have been hunted to the edge of extinction in and around the city."

"So what was Parakar doing on the highway? Did they find his vehicle?"

"There wasn't any vehicle," Umji answered. "Although it's worth mentioning that when a passing motorist discovered the body, Parakar's clothes were wet. As if he'd been swimming in the lake. And, if you look at his face and what remains of his chest, you'll see injuries that might have been sustained before the fatal attack. A possibility that seems even more likely given the presence of what look like intentional burns.

"As for what he was doing in the area, that's hard to say," Umji continued. "Parakar was employed as one of our civilian consultants. As such, his duties required a certain amount of travel."

"So, he was an informer."

Umji frowned. "If you insist."

"Who was he ratting on?"

"Ratting on?"

"Informing on. What group, or groups, was he assigned to watch?"

Umji fished a hand comp out of a pocket and examined the screen. "A group called the Rahaties. They worship a goddess with three heads."

"Now that's interesting," Cato said gravely. "If our Sagathi friends are involved with the Rahaties, and they thought Parakar was ratting them out, they might torture him. That would account for the burn marks. Then, having confirmed their suspicions, they might very well rip his throat out Sagathi style and dump the body."

"That makes sense," Umji agreed. "The next logical step is to view all of his reports. Maybe we'll find something there."

"Can I ask a question?" Alamy put in as she spoke for the first time.

"Sure," Cato replied as he turned to look at her.

Alamy had her lunch under control at that point but was careful to keep her eyes off the body. "This is pretty unlikely, I know that," she said. "But the news nets have been running stories about the coroner's murder for days now. A reporter stands accused of killing him because his image was captured by security cams located here in the morgue. But the last I heard, no one has been able to come up with a motive. Maybe he doesn't have one."

The police officers stared at Alamy for a moment as both sought to understand what she was telling them. Cato was the first to respond. "You're saying that someone who looked exactly like the reporter might have committed the murder."

Alamy nodded.

"But *why?*" Umji wanted to know.

"That's a very good question," Cato said. "And, if Alamy is correct, the answer could be right here somewhere."

At that point, the police officers went in search of some help, and Alamy followed them out into the hall. Cato hadn't been surprised by the nature of her contribution, and that, insofar as Alamy was concerned, constituted a victory.

FOURTEEN

The city of Kybor, on the planet Therat

THE LAST VESTIGES OF A BEAUTIFUL SUNSET WERE STILL visible on the western horizon, and the previously warm air had begun to cool, as Alamy and Keen made their way down the sidewalk. Street vendors were hauling their carts away, and shop owners were taking racks of goods inside for the night, but restaurants that had been closed since two in the afternoon were open for business again.

Meanwhile, somewhere off in the distance the persistent *pop, pop, pop* of gunfire could be heard as members of a resistance group skirmished with Vord troops. Such clashes could be heard around the clock lately, and even though the Vords could bomb Kybor into dust if they chose to, they lacked enough troops to pacify it. A fact the rebels were clearly aware of. Meanwhile, most citizens, Alamy included, were alert to the possibility of trouble but sought to live as normally as they could. And with an armed policeman for an escort, she was reasonably safe from street thugs.

"How 'bout this place?" Keen inquired, as they paused in front of a restaurant known for its spicy cuisine.

"No, I'd rather not," Alamy replied honestly. "The one time I ate there, my stomach was upset all night. How about Bratci's? I know how much you like steak—and they have a menu any carnivore would love."

The Xeno cop brightened. Partly because he *was* carnivorous, but mostly because he had a tendency to interpret any sign of thoughtfulness on Alamy's part as the beginning of a burgeoning romance even though he could "feel" her emotions and knew the interest wasn't reciprocal. "Okay," Keen agreed, "a steak sounds good."

So they continued down the street and around a corner to the point where a green awning extended out over some nicely set tables and the sidewalk. It was the same restaurant Cato had taken Alamy to the day before. Alamy felt guilty about going there with another man, especially one who was hopelessly in love with her, even though that was silly. Especially since Cato had yet to make a true commitment.

Keen clearly saw it as a personal victory when they were seated out front even though they were early enough to get a good table regardless. That was when Alamy noticed the beggar on the other side of the street. He was dressed in raggedy clothes but looked too clean for his profession. And, more alarmingly, he was staring straight at her!

"Val," she said, "check the beggar on the other side of the street. Is he staring at us?"

Keen, who was engrossed in the menu, glanced up. "Nope . . . He's looking up the street right now."

Alamy checked, saw that Keen was correct, and concluded that life in Kybor was making her paranoid. The waiter arrived shortly thereafter, took their orders, and promised to bring drinks. When they arrived, Keen raised his beer in a mock toast. "To Centurion Cato, Section Leader Shani, and the jungle they're spending the night in!"

Alamy laughed politely. Cato and Shani had departed under the cover of darkness that morning for Lake Boro, where, if everything went according to plan, they were going to corner Verafti and Demeni. A prospect that terrified Alamy since she'd been witness to what Verafti could do back on Dantha and feared for Cato's life. The fact that he was spending so much time with Shani didn't please her either—since it was pretty clear that the police officer still hoped to get her hooks into Cato.

The meal was good even if Alamy's thoughts were mostly elsewhere. As they left the restaurant, she allowed Keen to take her arm, which pleased him greatly. Then, having just turned a corner, Alamy spotted the same beggar she'd seen earlier. "Look over there," she said as she gave Keen a nudge. "That's the man I saw earlier. I think he's watching us."

"Of course he is," Keen replied indulgently. "You're very pretty—so men look at you all the time."

Alamy knew Keen was referring to himself, and the comment made her feel uncomfortable, so she let the matter drop. It was dark by then, but the occasional glow of a streetlight, plus the added illumination provided by the orbital reflector, was enough to see by. There were still quite a few people on the street as Alamy and Keen entered the building and returned to their apartment.

Keen, who was quite diligent about such things, double-locked the front door and checked each room to make sure everything was as it should be, before sitting down in front of the vid screen to watch the news. It was something that Cato insisted the team continue to do as a way to monitor the overall situation. The fact that the Vords were in control of all media had to be taken into account, of course, but there were still things to be learned. Especially where crime was concerned—murders in particular.

With no meals to prepare, Alamy was free to take a tepid shower and go to bed in the room she normally shared with Shani. Once there, she discovered that it was too hot to sleep and lay staring up at the ceiling. Half an hour passed, then an hour, and Alamy was still awake when she heard glass shatter, followed by a soft *thump*.

Alamy was wearing nothing more than a T-shirt and panties, so she paused long enough to snatch her robe off the back of a chair before padding out into the living room. That was when she saw the broken window and Keen lying on the floor below it. A pool of blood was starting to form beneath him.

Alamy started to rush forward, thought better of it, and stopped long enough to kill the lights. Keen had clearly been shot by a sniper located on the other side of the street somewhere. There were at least a hundred windows over there, and the gunman could have been firing from any one of them. Had the street beggar been part of a plan to target the team? That seemed very likely. Alamy dropped to the floor and crawled to the other side of the room on hands and knees. She paused to pull her robe off. Maybe she could use it as a pressure bandage. "Val? Can you hear me? It's Alamy."

The answer was a rattling cough. "It hurts, Alamy. . . . It hurts really bad."

Alamy cradled Keen's head. She was kneeling in his blood. "I'll get my com . . . I'll call for help."

Keen coughed, and more blood dribbled down his chin. "It's too late," he insisted. "Take my gun . . . I can 'feel' them closing in. Kill them, Alamy, kill *all* of them, or they will kill you."

Keen's fingers found her arm, and it felt as if they were made of steel. The light in his eyes had already started to fade. "Alamy? Tell me . . . Was there a chance?"

"Yes, of course there was a chance," Alamy said softly. "You're a very special man."

Keen's lips twitched in what might have been a smile. "You're lying—but thank you." Then he was gone.

Alamy wanted to sit and cry, but there wasn't enough

time for that as someone tried the front door. She felt for Keen's pistol, found it, and wrestled the weapon free of the shoulder holster. She even had the presence of mind to take one of two extra magazines that dangled below the other arm. It was slippery with blood, and, with no pockets, Alamy stuck the clip into the waistband of her panties.

Cato had shown Alamy how to fire a pistol more than once, so she knew about the need to release the safety and pump a round into the chamber. That was as far as her thoughts took her before someone hit the door hard. Wood splintered, but the barrier held long enough for Alamy to bring the handgun up. She was holding the weapon with both hands, the way Cato said she should, when the door flew open and banged against the wall.

Alamy started to fire and kept firing, knowing that she wasn't a very good shot, so it would be a good idea to throw as much lead at the intruder as possible. And Alamy's strategy paid immediate dividends as the first assassin to enter the apartment took a slug in the chest and was thrown back against the man behind him. The second intruder stumbled and fired a burst of bullets into the ceiling before regaining his balance.

But death was already on the way as Alamy continued to pull on the pistol's trigger and the rhythmic *bang, bang, bang* it generated served to punctuate the momentary rattle of the automatic weapon. The second assassin jerked spastically as he took hits in the head, right shoulder, and arm. As he went down, Alamy's pistol *click*ed empty, and she felt a searing pain cut across the top of her shoulders.

The sniper! He or she was still out there. And firing a silenced weapon. Alamy dropped to the floor as *another* rifle bullet smacked into the wall to her right. Then, having scrabbled into Cato's bedroom, Alamy paused to eject the empty magazine and replace it with the one taken from her waistband.

She was scared at that point, but angry, too, and she surprised herself by yelling, "You want *more*? Come on, you bastards! Let's get it on."

Alamy's wish was granted as shots were fired somewhere above her, the skylight over the hallway shattered, and a man dropped through the hole. His feet made a loud *thump* as they hit the floor.

Alamy, who was still sitting on the floor, shoved the gun around the corner and fired. The heavy slugs shattered the man's ankles. He uttered a surprised grunt, crashed to the floor, and was curled up in the fetal position when Alamy shot him in the head.

Then she was up and headed for the closet. Alamy knew that Cato kept a shotgun in there, and with only a few rounds left in the handgun, she was going to need another weapon.

There were scuffling sounds out in the hall—as if more assassins had entered the apartment. Alamy gave thanks as her fingers closed around the shotgun's barrel. She brought the weapon up, found the pistol-style grip, and thumbed the safety. Then, having aimed the shotgun at the back wall of the closet, she pulled the trigger.

Alamy wasn't ready for the heavy recoil and was thrown back against the half-opened door, but the result was everything she could have hoped for. The double-ought buckshot punched a fist-sized hole in the wall and hit targets in the hall. Two of them, judging from the noises they made.

But the battle wasn't over as Alamy backed her way out of the closet and two bullets came straight down from above. They missed her toes by an inch and buried themselves in the floor.

Alamy tilted the shotgun up, pumped another shell into the chamber, and fired. Plaster showered down on her, but the blast had the desired effect in that she heard hurried footsteps up above and knew an assailant was on the run.

That was when an air car glided past, bright lights

strobed the apartment's interior, and Vord troopers opened fire. They didn't know who was shooting at whom and didn't care. Their sole motivation was to bring the battle to an end, which they did with brutal efficiency. It took them the better part of ten minutes to secure the area, land the air car, and enter the apartment's living room. That was where they found a half-naked Uman female sitting with her back against a wall. She was covered with blood, and the male on the floor next to her was clearly dead. "My name is CeCe Alamy," she said, as her chin trembled. "And this man is an Imperial police officer named Valentine Keen. He died in the line of duty. Please treat him with the respect he deserves."

Near the city of Kybor, on the planet Therat

The temporary command center was located just north of Lake Boro in an old hunting lodge. Dozens of beady-eyed trophies stared down at Cato, Shani, Umji, and five of his NCOs as the police officers bent to examine the map spread out on top of the massive dining table. "Parakar's body was found right about here," Cato said as he tapped a road with his right index finger. "And his clothes were wet. Yet he wasn't dressed for a swim. And, given the burns on his body, there's a very real possibility that he was tortured before being put to death."

"So," Shani said as she picked up the narrative, "maybe he was on the run. Perhaps he was tortured, managed to escape from his captors, and jumped in the lake in order to get away. Then, having emerged on the west side, he made his way to the highway, where he was recaptured."

"Exactly," Cato agreed. "So if our suspects have a hideout in the area, it could be located somewhere along the opposite shore. We're going to put a cordon around the entire area before we knock on doors. No one is to enter or leave without being cleared by Officer Shani or me. Are there any comments or questions?"

"Yes," Umji put in. "Parakar was posing as a member of the Rahati cult and providing us with regular reports about that group's activities. Now, having reread those documents, it seems clear that Demeni took control of the cult at some point prior to Verafti's arrival. So as we enter the search area, we might have to deal with an unknown number of Uman fanatics as well as the shape shifters themselves. That could pose an additional danger."

Umji had come a long way since Cato and the rest of the team first met him. In fact, there were indications that Umji liked and respected the Umans to some extent, even if his Ya didn't feel the same way. And Cato knew that the Vord noncoms standing around the table didn't agree with Umji. The possibility that they might have to contend with "fanatical" Umans fed the resentment they felt. But there wasn't anything he could do about it. "Officer Umji makes a very good point," Cato emphasized. "So pass the word to your subordinates.

"Okay, I think that's about it. Let's load the air cars, go in, and secure the area. The ground sweep will begin at 0500 hours. Good hunting."

Six military-style air cars were waiting behind the lodge. Cato, Shani, and Umji boarded the first vehicle, which carried four troopers as well. Each unit was headed for a preassigned landing point, and the air cars took off in quick succession. The homes along the east side of the lake were separated by swathes of thick vegetation. Hundreds of troops would have been required to seal the area off completely. And given constant attacks by the Uman resistance movement, there simply weren't enough Vords to do the job.

But by blocking all of the roads in and out, and using the air cars to monitor the jungle from above, Cato hoped to flush the Sagathies out of hiding and run them down. Then, once the fugitives were spotted, air cars would swoop in to contain them as ground forces rushed into the area. The rest would be up to the shape shifters themselves. They could surrender or die. The second option was preferable insofar as Cato was concerned.

The air cars were open to the elements, so as they rose to treetop level and sped south, Cato could feel the warm slipstream caressing his face. Like Shani, he was wearing a half helmet, body armor, and combat boots. In addition to his pistol, he was carrying a stunner, submachine gun, and a variety of grenades. And the Vords were heavily armed as well. But, if they were lucky enough to surround the Sagathies, would all of their weaponry be enough against such violent predators?

The question continued to haunt the back of Cato's mind as the aircraft slowed and all forward motion stopped. It was pitch-black below except for the moonlike glow projected by the solar reflector high above and a few isolated security lights mounted on the houses themselves. But Cato knew they were just east of Lake Boro and directly above the paved road that served the houses on that side of the lake.

An effort had been made to check on each owner. But if one of the homes belonged to Demeni or her Rahaties, it was through someone else. So with no way to narrow the field, the police had no choice but to check each residence. An unpleasant chore for both them and the homeowners who were about to be traumatized.

There was a gentle *thump* as the car landed, followed by terse orders from Umji. His troopers piled out as a thrumming noise was heard, and the rest of the air cars passed overhead on their way to various insertion points. "Okay," Cato said, as his boots hit the ground. "The first house should be a hundred yards to the southwest. Stay alert and stick to the plan. Execute. Over."

Thanks to an effort to bridge Uman and Vord com systems, each member of the team could hear Cato, and vice versa, even though their HUDs weren't linked. That would have required additional prep time. The troopers wore sculpted helmets, high collars that were designed to protect their Ya advisors, and clamshell-style body armor.

Cato didn't *like* the aliens, with the possible exception of Umji, but he couldn't help but respect them as they fanned out and began to close with a largely unseen target. The intervals between the Vords were correct, they were relatively quiet given their size, and there was no unnecessary radio traffic.

A security light could be glimpsed from time to time and seemed to switch on and off as the team advanced through a grove of trees. *If* the Sagathies were holed up in the house, and *if* they were asleep, there was a pretty good chance of catching them by surprise. Or, failing that, flushing them out. Which would open the fugitives to an attack from above.

As the team ghosted its way forward, Cato saw little blobs of body heat scurry away via the night-vision capability built into his HUD and "felt" spikes of fear. But none of the animals were large enough to represent a threat.

Then the fuzzy outline of a still-cooling house appeared. It was a two-story affair that had a peaked roof and a porch, which ran all the way around. Two ground cars were parked outside, and Umji made sure that both of them were secured before sending two troopers around to seal off the lakeside of the residence.

Once that was accomplished, Cato raised a megaphone borrowed from the Vords. "This house is surrounded by police officers representing both the Vord occupying forces and the Uman Empire. Please exit through the front door with your hands on your heads. If you own this property, and are not harboring any criminals, you have nothing to fear."

It was necessary to repeat the message two times before

a light came on in an upstairs window, the silhouette of a man was seen, and more lights appeared. Finally, after five minutes or so, the front door swung open, and two people emerged with hands on their heads. As soon as the couple were out on the porch, Shani led two troopers inside. Thanks to her ability to "feel" emotions, and thereby detect the presence of any sentients hidden within, the search went fairly quickly.

Meanwhile, Cato was able to confirm that neither the middle-aged man nor his wife was a Sagathi and was soon hard at work trying to placate them. He was still at it when Shani and her Vord troopers left the house. "You can go back inside now," Cato said soothingly. "But please don't call anyone until 0700 hours. If you do, we'll know and arrest you for interfering with a police investigation."

The man did what he could to look dignified in his pajamas. "If you insist . . . But please be aware that I intend to call police headquarters at seven o'clock and file a complaint with your supervisor."

"He's on Corin," Cato replied, "but go right ahead. In the meantime, lock all of your doors and call this number if anyone tries to break in. We can be here within a matter of minutes."

The homeowner accepted the slip of paper, looked as if he wanted to say something else, but apparently thought better of it as his wife pulled at his arm. She looked worried. Whether her concern stemmed from the presence of Vord troopers or the possibility that dangerous criminals might be lurking nearby wasn't clear. "Come on, Jorn . . . Let's go back inside."

"One down and four to go," Cato commented, as the couple reentered their home. "Let's move it."

Though separated, the houses weren't far enough apart to justify use of the air car, so it circled above as the team jogged down the road and turned into the next driveway.

Then it was time to repeat the procedure, except, having received no response from repeated requests to come out, the police officers were forced to break in.

A Vord trooper kicked the front door down, and Cato went in with his submachine gun at the ready. It was his belief that officers should lead from the front. But more than that, Cato knew that if someone was hiding within, he might be able to detect them *before* they could attack. And even a second or two could make an important difference.

But as the law officers searched the house, there were no emotional emanations to detect, and having come up empty, it was time to move on. A preprinted note was left on the door inviting the homeowners to contact the police regarding the forced entry, and, with the air car circling overhead, the team jogged toward the next house on the list.

Even though light from the orbital reflector was focused on Kybor, some of the pale illumination washed over the surrounding countryside as well. So as a couple of Vords led the team down a long, gently turning driveway, the leaves around them were glazed with silvery light. The area had a ghostly look as Cato's boots crunched on gravel, the air car hummed overhead, and the jungle shivered in response.

Then something broke cover, dashed across the driveway, and vanished into the undergrowth. Having been caught by surprise, one of the Vords accidentally fired a round. Clearly embarrassed, he said, "Sorry, sir. . . . It was an animal of some sort."

If Verafti and Demeni had been asleep in the house ahead, they weren't any longer. Cato swore, paused in the middle of the drive, and requested a slow-motion replay from his HUD. What he saw made his blood run cold. There had been *two* animals—both of which were native to Sagatha rather than Therat. "That was them, damn it! Umji . . . Order our air car to sweep the area to the east and stun anything larger than a dog. Then put in a call to units two, three, and four. I want them to position themselves to the east so as to block the possibility of escape in that direction. Over."

Having acknowledged the order, Umji went to work as Cato turned the team to the left and followed the fugitives into the jungle. It was slower going now, because of both the thick foliage and the very real possibility of an ambush. "Keep the formation tight," Cato ordered. "Stay within twenty feet of each other. Officer Shani will walk drag."

Cato knew Shani wouldn't like that, but it was critical to have an empath in the six slot, *and* a backup leader in case anything happened to him. Overlapping thrumming noises were heard, and beams of bright light slanted down through the jungle canopy to stab the ground ahead as the air cars crisscrossed the surrounding area. Given the infrared sensors aboard each aircraft, Cato expected to hear from one of the pilots fairly soon.

But as the minutes continued to crawl past, and branches reached out to caress his helmet and shoulders, nothing happened. And that was strange because, mutable though they were, the Sagathies were flesh-and-blood creatures who couldn't simply disappear. Their heat signatures would be visible no matter what shape they assumed. Then Shani's voice came in over the command frequency. "Echo-Five to Echo-Six . . . I suggest that you switch to the feed from air two and count heads. Over."

Cato frowned, eyed his HUD, and gave a voice command. The moment he did, the number of people in line abreast of him increased from seven to nine, with the ninth icon bringing up the rear. And that was wrong because there were only seven people on his team!

It seemed that Verafti and Demeni had taken up positions next to the team, and thanks to the thick vegetation, no one had seen them do it. And because the pilots were busy scanning the area ahead, they missed the additional blobs of green light and never thought to count. "Good work," Cato said grimly. "Which flank? Right or left? Over."

There was a brief pause as Shani played the external feed back looking for the moment when the extra blobs appeared. "Right flank," she said definitively. "Over."

"Okay," Cato said. "We don't have time to brief the team. . . . I'll wait for you to close the gap. Then, when you're in position, we'll pivot to the right and go after them. Stunners first . . . SMGs if we have to. Over."

Shani sent two *clicks* by way of an acknowledgment and was ready to break right, when one of the pilots spoke. "Echo-Ten to Echo-Six . . . A river is cutting across your line of advance. Do you plan to cross it? Over."

Cato swore as the two heat signatures on the far right-hand side of the line surged forward and suddenly disappeared off of his HUD. "They jumped into the river!"

But Shani was the only one who knew what Cato was talking about, and by the time the rest of the team came up to speed, it was too late. The river, which drained water out of Lake Boro, had carried Verafti and his mate to safety by that time. In spite of all the planning and hard work, the operation was a failure.

Verafti didn't like to swim. Few if any Sagathies did. But with the Umans and the Vords closing in from behind, the river was the only realistic way out. So he jumped, the cold water closed over his head, and the current took control of his body.

Thanks to the fact that he was an empath, Verafti knew that Demeni shared his discomfort as she, too, was pulled downstream at a steady two or three miles per hour. He paddled in the direction of her emotions, felt them strengthen, and was soon floating next to her. "This river joins the Punja," she said. "It's larger and will carry us all the way to Kybor."

"Is that a good idea?" Verafti inquired as he struggled to keep his head up. "They'll be looking for us there."

"There's a Rahati temple in the middle of the river," Demeni answered. "We'll hide there."

"Okay," Verafti agreed, as a large eddy turned them around. "But let's watch for some sort of boat."

The Sagathies were forced to duck under the surface of the river as a bright beam of light hit the river behind them and quickly sped their way. Verafti had been to an aquarium on Corin and seen various sea creatures there. So he morphed into an appropriate shape but discovered that he still felt uncomfortable and hurried to change back.

The air car had passed over by then, which allowed the pair to surface and take in big gulps of much-needed air. Ten minutes later, the current carried them through a sweeping curve, past a well-lit marker, and into the muddy Punja River. They were only twenty miles upstream from Kybor at that point, so there were lots of fishing boats, cargo vessels, and other small craft to pick from. Most were at anchor, but a few were under way, and visible thanks to their running lights.

Verafti spotted what appeared to be a small fishing boat anchored downstream and took a moment to warn Demeni of his intentions before paddling to the right. That served to align him with the low-lying vessel. Fortunately, the Punja's current was relatively slow, which made it possible to catch hold of the anchor rope and follow it to the boat. Demeni was right behind him.

Because the sides of the fishing scow were so low, Verafti was able to pull himself aboard with very little effort. The additional weight caused the bow to dip. That was enough to awaken the two men who were wrapped in blankets and curled around the tiny stove in the stern. One of them sat up, saw the glistening river monster, and screamed. But only for a second, because Demeni was behind him, and a

single swipe from her sicklelike claws was sufficient to cut
his throat. Blood splattered onto sun-bleached wood, and
the Uman's mostly severed head nearly fell off as he collapsed in a heap.

The second man was out from under his blanket by that
time and scrabbling toward the port side in a desperate attempt to escape. But Verafti was there to jump onto his back
and snap his spine well before the Uman reached the water.
"Sorry about the fish smell, dearest," Verafti said gallantly,
as the Uman went limp. "But even this humble craft is better than swimming."

Ten minutes later, the heavily weighted fishermen were
on the bottom of the river, and the anchor was back aboard.
Though neither of the Sagathies was an expert where boats
were concerned, the current was sufficient to propel them
downstream, and all Verafti had to do was swing the tiller back and forth to steer. Demeni, who had taken on the
appearance of the second fisherman, was seated in the bow,
watching for the island to appear.

A good fifteen minutes elapsed before Demeni spotted a
navigational light and the temple beyond. It had been constructed by fisherfolk and occupied the entirety of the island
it was resting on. Having visited the temple before, Demeni
knew that the only way to access it was via a flight of steps
that led up from the water. She pointed at them. "There!
Bring the boat in next to the stairs."

Verafti turned the boat so that the bow was pointed in
the correct direction but soon came to realize it would be
necessary to turn the boat upstream and *almost simultaneously* put a line ashore if he was going to successfully come
alongside the landing. And it was already too late to make
all of the necessary moves. "Get ready to jump!" he shouted.
"I won't be able to stop."

Demeni gave him a dirty look, and he could "feel" her
displeasure. But she gathered her strength, waited for the

bow to draw even with the stairs, and made the necessary leap.

There was a horrible grating sound as the side of the boat scraped against the rough stonework, and Verafti let go of the tiller and made his own jump as the scow continued downriver. Someone would intercept it and find all of the blood. But crimes were common on the river, so it would be a long time if ever before the Vords got around to investigating. "Wonderful," Demeni said sarcastically, as the boat slipped away. "How will we get off this island?"

"Someone will stop to worship you," Verafti predicted calmly. "And when they do, we'll eat them and take their boat."

It was a good plan, so Demeni led Verafti into the temple, where a dozen oil-fed lamps were burning. It was time. She could *feel* it. If he took her now, a new life would come into existence. And even though Verafti was something less than perfect, he was available and, above all else, committed to her. And that, Demeni concluded, would have to do.

Verafti watched Demeni morph into her true form, inhaled the pheromones that were floating in the air, and knew what they meant. The fisherman dissolved, a Sagathi warrior appeared, and he began to circle the female he loved. What followed was violent, brief by Uman standards, and very satisfying. Breakfast arrived two hours later.

FIFTEEN

The city of Kybor, on the planet Therat

THE FIERY ORANGE SUN HAD JUST BROKEN COMPANY with the eastern horizon, and a long, undulating call to prayer was echoing across the sleepy city as the Vord combat car screeched to a halt in front of the apartment building. Two police vehicles were parked out front. As Cato got out of the car and hurried toward the stairs, a uniformed Vord stepped forward to intercept him. But Umji and Quati were there to wave the other officer off as Cato pushed his way through the front door and took the stairs two at a time.

The landing was splattered with blood, the shattered door hung askew, and when Cato entered the shabby living room, he was forced to walk through puddles of blood. It was sticky and pulled at his boots. His heart was in his throat as he looked around. Keen had been killed. He knew that much. But Alamy was alive! Sorrow mixed with joy as he called for her. "Alamy? It's Jak."

Cato heard the quick patter of footsteps as Alamy emerged from the hallway. She was dressed in one of his shirts. It came down to just above her knees, and judging from the way her hair was slicked back, she had just emerged from the shower. He had never seen anything so beautiful.

"Oh, Jak," Alamy said as she entered the circle of his arms. "You're safe . . . I was so worried! I asked the police if you were all right, but they couldn't or wouldn't tell me. Is Shani okay?"

Cato pulled her close. She smelled of soap and flinched as his forearm touched the top of her shoulder. "Yes," he said. "Shani's fine. *You're* the one we were worried about. Umji told us that a gang of assassins attacked the apartment—and you killed four or five of them. I'm sorry you had to do that but very thankful that you did."

"They k-k-killed Keen," Alamy said, as she sobbed into Cato's shoulder. "They shot him from the other side of the street! I heard a *thump* and went into the living room. He was lying over there, by the window, and told me to take his gun. He said they were all around us, then he died."

Cato held her close and kissed her hair until the sobs came less frequently, and she backed away. "Look at you," she sniffed. "I got you all wet."

"Don't worry about that," Cato said as he looked around. The walls were riddled with bullet holes, and empty shell casings were scattered around the floor. The fact that Alamy had been able to fight the assassins off was nothing short of a miracle. And a testament to her courage. "Who were they?" he inquired. "Have the police told you anything?"

"A little bit," Alamy answered hesitantly. "All of the dead men had Rahati tattoos."

"That seems to confirm what we already suspected," Cato said thoughtfully. "Demeni has control of the cult and is using it for her own purposes."

Alamy nodded as Cato wrapped his arms around her.

Shani had witnessed the entire interchange from the front doorway. And even though she was standing on the other side of the room, she could "feel" what Cato felt. She turned, passed through what was left of the front door, and made her way down onto the street. Shani wanted to cry but was determined not to and knew she wouldn't if other people were around. So she put her cop face on and went looking for some breakfast. That, at least, was something the police officer could count on.

Nimji had been fishing the Punja River for about twelve years. He was a small man, with quick eyes and bad teeth. His body was strong but very lean and scarred here and there from work-related accidents. Thanks to his efforts, plus the blessings from the goddess Rahati, Nimji had been able to buy a small home and feed his family.

So now, having netted at least a hundred flash-fish during the early hours of the morning, he was headed downstream to sell his catch. But first it was necessary to stop at the island temple and give thanks. Because everyone knew that Rahati expected to hear from her devotees on a frequent basis—and could be quite vengeful if neglected.

So Nimji steered his boat downstream toward the island temple, turned the bow upstream at exactly the right moment, and dropped the lateen sail. As the tiny vessel drifted stern first along the edge of the landing, he stood ready to step ashore with a line. The end loop dropped over a rusty cleat, a few yards of line ran out, and the boat jerked to a halt.

Satisfied that everything was as it should be, Nimji went to fetch a small pot from the stern before going ashore once again. With the vessel held in both hands, he followed the well-worn path into the domed temple, where he paused to bow.

As Nimji's head came up, the goddess's coal black beast eyes met his and seemed to penetrate his very soul. What light there was came down through wedge-shaped strips of colored glass that had been set into the gently curved ceiling and the oil lamps that occupied niches all around the room. Most were running low on fuel and were starting to flicker.

One by one, Nimji filled each lamp with oil from his personal supply of fuel before placing the nearly empty container next to the door, where he would retrieve it on the way out. Then, having honored Rahati by ensuring that her likeness would remain lit for another day and night, he went forward to kneel in front of her.

It was then, as Nimji looked up at Rahati's beast face, that the miracle occurred. Slowly, as if in a dream, she came to life! Although Nimji had never witnessed such a quickening personally, he had heard about them and uttered a shout of exultation as the living embodiment of Rahati came forward to rip his throat out.

Nimji didn't live long enough to witness the moment when the goddess morphed into her true form, or to see her mate emerge from a dark alcove, but it didn't matter. He had already been borne away into the holy cycle of birth, death, and rebirth by the time razor-sharp teeth began to rip at his blood-drenched body.

It took Verafti and Demeni fifteen minutes to eat their fill. Then, with full stomachs, it was time to morph into Uman form and step out into the sunshine. Both were partially covered with blood, so they went down the stairs to the landing, and from there into the brownish water that gurgled below. Thousands bathed in the Punja each day, so the people on passing boats barely noticed the naked fishermen as they washed their faces and splashed around.

Then, still dripping, they hoisted themselves back onto the landing. The boat rocked gently as the Sagathies stepped aboard. A quick search produced very little in the way of clothes because most of the river's boatmen wore little more than loincloths while plying their trade. Fortunately, those were easy to improvise from the tattered towels found next to a woven sleeping mat.

But there was no way to disguise Verafti's lack of knowledge where small boats were concerned. So he did the best he could to steer the little vessel with rudder alone as the current carried them downstream. There were some very close calls. The worst of them was when the scow hit a small passenger boat a glancing blow, bounced off the port side, and Verafti was roundly cursed by the captain.

Fortunately, the trip to the outskirts of Kybor wasn't all that long. The moment Verafti spotted a gently shelving riverbank where other boats were beached, he made straight for it—and felt a sense of relief when the bow nudged up into a layer of mud. But then the current took hold of the stern, swung it around, and was threatening to suck the flat-bottomed scow downstream as the Sagathies went over the side.

It took the better part of a full hour for the pair to reach the city's largest Rahati temple and the apartment that Demeni maintained there. If three of the Sagathi's most trusted lieutenants were in any way nonplussed by their leader's sudden metamorphosis from male to female Uman, they gave no sign of it as they followed the half-naked beauty into a sparsely furnished living room.

As Demeni took her place on the thronelike chair positioned against one wall, she could "feel" her mate's impatience, as well as the other emotions that permeated the air. The Umans were frightened—very frightened indeed. Serious errors had been made, and they were worried about what she would do to them. And for good reason, too, since every single one of them had been present when others were punished and knew how unpleasant such sessions could be. "You're frightened," she said accusingly, as her eyes flicked from face to face. *"Why?"*

The most senior acolyte had short black hair, which she wore in a bowl cut. In spite of her efforts to appear composed, she was clearly terrified and barely able to meet Demeni's eyes. The woman was hesitant at first, but once she got going, the words came out in a flood. The essence of the story was that despite the team's painstaking efforts to prepare for the attack—the Rahati assassins had run into unexpectedly stiff resistance. At least fifteen heavily armed Vords had been waiting in the apartment, plus Cato and his team of Umans.

Demeni knew that wasn't true since Cato had been chasing Verafti and her through the jungle about the same time that the assassination attempt took place. The acolyte clearly *believed* what she was saying, however. Which indicated that the person or persons in charge of the attack had lied to her. "So some of our assassins survived?"

The acolyte nodded.

"They failed you," Demeni said harshly. "And more importantly, they failed *me*. Had they been true to the Rahati way, every single one of them would be dead. Kill them," she instructed. "And do it personally. From that point forward, your subordinates will understand that when you give an order, it must be carried out regardless of cost. Now, leave me while I think about the implications of this failure and how to compensate for your incompetence."

Heads hung low, the Rahaties left the pool area. "So," Verafti said, once they were gone. "We tried it your way, and it didn't work. So it's my turn."

Demeni eyed him skeptically. "Your turn to do *what?*"

"To attack the source of the Cato problem," Verafti replied, "and that's the Vords. They brought him here—so they should pay. And, who knows? If they feel sufficiently threatened, perhaps they will kill him for us!"

Shafts of late-afternoon sunshine streamed down through skylights mounted high overhead to probe the water reservoir below. The ground-level facility was the size of a small lake and protected by a duraplast dome designed to keep contaminants out. A twenty-foot-wide service platform ran all around the perfectly symmetrical container and made a good place for Governor Arrius and his resistance fighters to meet.

The air was muggy, and occasional drops of condensation fell from above as Cato addressed a group of about thirty men and women. They were seated on or around a cluster of color-coded manifolds that fed water to various underground pipes and from there to the entire city. Most of the guerrillas were middle-aged, some were relatively young, and a few were elderly.

Cato was reluctant to spend time with the resistance group since Verafti and Demeni were still on the loose— but had chosen to do so in hopes of reaping benefits later on. Because the men and women in front of him knew the planet much better than he did and could be very helpful if they mastered the skills necessary to survive. It had been necessary to brief Governor Arrius regarding the Sagathies. But the others didn't know the exact nature of the criminals Cato was chasing.

That day's lesson was on the subject of command and control. Specifically the need to break the larger organization down into four-person cells, each of which could function independently, or come together as military fire teams when the time came for an all-out battle with the Vords.

"So rather than meet as a group as you're doing today,"

Cato told them, "you will come together as individual cells. Then, if there's a need to feed information up the chain of command, you'll do so through your team leader. Once this system has been implemented, he or she will be the only person who knows how to contact top commanders. . . . And how to contact *you*. That means that a traitor, or a person who has been forced to divulge information, can't compromise more than four other people. Do you have any questions?"

A hand went up. Cato pointed toward a pleasant-looking middle-aged woman. "Yes?"

"What you say makes sense," the resistance fighter conceded, "but isn't the system pretty unwieldy? What if we need to communicate with each other quickly?"

"I'll respond to that one if you don't mind," Governor Arrius said as he stood. "Without getting into specific details, I can tell you that personnel within certain news organizations are working with us and will go on air in the case of a full-scale uprising. So any instruction preceded by my name and the appropriate code word should be obeyed.

"Unfortunately, we won't be able to communicate electronically because such calls can be intercepted and tracked. So be sure to delete all relevant numbers from your computers and pocket coms."

And so it went for the next half hour, until the meeting came to an end, and it was time for Cato to leave. Not to hunt the Sagathies, or to get some much-needed sleep, but to attend a funeral. Because he was an Imperial officer, one of his men had fallen, and it was time to say good-bye.

There was nothing subtle about the attack on the palace. Verafti was seated next to the Uman driver when she turned into the driveway that led toward the government complex and put her foot to the floor. The military truck had been stolen the day before, and the massive front bumper proved to be more than a match for the aluminum security gate, which flew into pieces as the vehicle hit it.

The truck was taking fire by then, which was to be expected, since the buildings that lay in front of them were the most heavily guarded structures on the planet. That made them a very tempting target for anyone willing to die to score a psychological victory. And, with the exception of Verafti himself, all of the other people riding in the vehicle were already dead insofar as their families were concerned. In fact, it had been the goddess Rahati herself who had presided over the elaborate death ceremonies held the night before—and promised each warrior a very fortuitous rebirth.

A hail of bullets pinged, spanged, and whined as they hit the well-armored truck. A series of white divots appeared on the windshield, but none of the projectiles was able to penetrate the reinforced glass as the huge tires rode up and over the front of a combat car and kept on going. "The stairs!" Verafti shouted. "Aim for the stairs."

There was another security point up ahead, so the grim-faced driver swerved around a concrete barrier onto the nicely landscaped median, smashed through an ornamental fountain, and turned back onto the road. The engine roared, and smoke belched out of twin stacks as she upshifted and ran over three troopers who were shooting at her. The truck bounced as the knobby tires hit the bodies.

Then all the driver had to do was turn the big steering wheel to the left and right again to line up on the stairs. The front tires hit hard, the vehicle bucked, and made it halfway up the formal stairs before stalling out. "Now!" Verafti yelled as he opened the passenger-side door.

The driver took a bullet between the eyes as she opened her door and fell while two dozen heavily armed Rahaties bailed out the back. "Follow me!" Verafti yelled as he ran up the stairs. A group of Vord troopers were there to defend the entrance, but when the first Uman morphed into a reptile, they stopped firing. And that was a serious mistake as he whirled and cut all of them down.

Verafti felt a sense of exultation as he arrived at the front door and nearly took a head off. There were plenty of security cams, so the Vords had pictures of him by then, which was half the battle insofar as Verafti was concerned. But just to make sure that they got the idea, he morphed into an exact likeness of Cato as he and the surviving Rahaties burst into the lobby beyond. "Kill them!" the Cato creature screamed. "Kill all of them!"

Meanwhile, as a Klaxon *beep*ed, and a series of flat-voiced orders were issued over the building's PA system, Commissioners Narth and Oomo had retreated to the heavily defended security center, where they were watching the attack via a bank of monitors. They were outwardly impassive, but that was deceptive given the dialogue within. *Did you see that?* Narth demanded. *It's one of the shape shifters! Right here in our headquarters building.*

Yes, the Ya agreed. *You read the report. . . . Officer Umji and the Umans came very close to capturing or killing the creatures a day ago but failed. And it's little wonder, seeing what they're capable of.*

But why? Narth wondered. *Why launch such a hopeless attack against us? Are they stupid?*

I don't think so, Oomo replied, as the Cato creature morphed into a Vord trooper and turned to attack the luckless Rahaties. *Did you see that?* the Ya inquired. *The shape shifter is sending us a message. He's bragging about what they can accomplish! It's an attempt to scare us into calling off the hunt for them.*

That's impossible, Narth said firmly. *Our home world is in danger so long as they exist.*

Yes, it is, came the reply, as the last of the Umans fell, and the Sagathi morphed into a different Vord likeness before slipping out the front door.

So, what should we do?

Think, Oomo replied. *And act in the best interest of both the Vord and the Ya.*

The graveyard was located just south of the city. It was a sprawling affair that covered more than a hundred acres of gently rolling land. As Cato looked out of the car's window, he saw a confusing maze of markers, headstones, and tombs. They came in a bewildering array of shapes, sizes, and styles. Some were no larger than a single flagstone. Others resembled ornate summerhouses.

The sun was low in the western sky by then, so the monuments threw long, hard shadows to the east as they followed a gently curving road past a family of nearly identical tombs and up over a rise. That was where six fire-blackened depressions came into view. A metal platform stood above each.

As the car turned in front of them, Cato saw that the first fire pit was empty, but smoke continued to drift away from the second, indicating that a cremation had taken place only a few hours earlier. The driver, who was a member of the undertaker's guild, brought the car to a gentle stop in front of the fifth pit, and that was where Cato, Shani, and Alamy got out.

A man-sized bundle could be seen resting on the metal platform that spanned the depression. Keen's body was wrapped in crimson cloth to symbolize his membership in the 3rd Legion. It wasn't much as honors went, but the only recognition that Cato could muster given the nature of the situation.

The Flame Master was waiting for them. He was a big man, with a considerable paunch and a suitably long face.

"Greetings," he said, as the mourners came forward to meet him. "Please accept my condolences regarding your loss."

That's what the man *said*. What he felt was a sense of boredom, which though understandable, was somewhat off-putting nevertheless. "We're ready," the Flame Master continued hopefully. "Will one of you say some words? Or should we light the pyre?"

Cato took note of the "we," saw motion down in the fire-blackened pit, and realized that what looked like a living scarecrow was making final adjustments to the pile of neatly stacked wood. He was dressed in raggedy black clothes and was clearly the person who did most of the work. "No," Cato replied. "Don't light it yet. I'll say a few words."

The Flame Master nodded respectfully, turned, and waddled away. Then, once he was out of earshot, the man turned to watch the informal ceremony. Cato could "feel" the weight of the man's stare as well as his growing impatience. That made Cato angry, and he sought to clear his mind by taking a moment to look around.

The graveyard had been carved out of raw jungle hundreds of years before. The edge of the verdant maze was about five hundred feet away. And now, having received less attention since the Vords' takeover, it was creeping steadily inward.

The jungle lacked the means to express emotions, but the creatures who lived in it could, and Cato was aware of the eternal tension that existed between hunters and their prey. At that range, it came across as a nonspecific buzz.

Cato knew that he was stalling, as if putting off the moment when he said good-bye to Keen would somehow forestall the other man's death. But it was too late for that because Keen was gone, and no one could bring him back.

Cato cleared his throat as both Shani and Alamy bowed their heads. "I didn't know Keen all that well," he began. "But I know he was willing to volunteer for a mission he didn't entirely understand. And I know that he gave it his very best, and when he was killed, it was in the line of duty, as part of an effort to protect the Empire."

Alamy was crying by then, and tears rolled down her cheeks as she held hands with Shani. "So," Cato continued, "Corporal Keen deserves our respect and that of every Imperial citizen. We'll miss him."

And with that he came to attention. Shani did likewise, and both of them saluted Keen as the Flame Master gave a signal to his assistant. The scarecrow had lit thousands of such fires in his time and knew exactly what to do. The blowtorch hissed as he turned on the small fuel tank. A single spark from his igniter produced a pencil-shaped blue flame. Then he circled the pile of wood while pausing occasionally to make sure that the pyre burned evenly. The Flame Master would be very unhappy if stray body parts fell free of the platform. Not because it did any harm but because most people found such sights disturbing and wouldn't tip if arms or legs were left over.

Then it was time for the scarecrow to back up the duracrete slope and out of the pit, as flames shot up through the metal framework to embrace the tightly wrapped corpse, making it disappear. There was a loud crackling noise, followed by intermittent *pop*s when bits of fat exploded, and a throaty roar as a column of smoke rose to merge with the quickly darkening sky. Cato completed the salute, and Shani did likewise, as Alamy made use of a handkerchief to wipe her tears away. And that was when the Rahati assassins struck.

They were led by a man named Kar Hotha. He was a hunter. A man known for his skill in the jungle—which he considered his friend. Like the rest, his face was decorated with death paint, and he was armed with a machine pistol and a razor-sharp bush knife. The idea was to close with the off-worlders quickly and do Rahati's bidding with a minimum of fuss.

It had been Rahati's idea to monitor the daily list of funerals, figure out which was related to the dead police officer, then lie in wait. "They will feel sad," she had predicted. "So sad that they will focus on little else. That will be your chance."

And, as with all things, the goddess was correct. Because as the funeral pyre was lit, and the off-worlders said good-bye to their friend, Hotha and his companions had been able to belly crawl to a point within fifty feet of the fire pit. And as the hunter uttered a low whistle, they rose and charged forward.

It was a good plan, and one that would have worked flawlessly had it not been for a sudden shift in the wind that sent a pall of smoke drifting out in front of them. But Hotha had a pretty good idea where his targets were and opened fire on them as he charged into the smoke. The rest of the seven-person team did likewise, which was unfortunate for the Flame Master, who jerked convulsively as he took half a dozen bullets. He then fell, rolling down the slope and into his own fire pit. The flames welcomed him, fed on his flesh, and crackled happily.

"We're taking fire!" Shani shouted, and grabbed onto Alamy's wrist with one hand as she drew her pistol with the other.

Cato turned toward the car and swore as it pulled away. Was that by design? Or was the driver simply trying to save his ass? There was no way to know. "The headstones!" he shouted. "We need some cover."

All three ran as the machine pistols rattled, and bullets threw up geysers of dirt all around them. Cato passed between two tombs, circled around behind one, and turned to face his attackers. The Rahaties were free of the smoke by then, still running, and still firing. Or some were anyway, because the fully automatic pistols ate ammo quickly, and a couple of assassins had paused to reload.

Cato took a marksman's stance, chose a target, and squeezed the trigger twice. The pistol jumped in his hands, and the man went down. Then it was time to turn and run as the assassins fired in return. Chips of granite stung the right side of his face as projectiles hit the tomb to his right and bounced away.

The markers, headstones, and tombs were like a vast maze, and as Cato dodged back and forth between them, he took occasional comfort from the distinctive bark of Shani's service pistol and the knowledge that Alamy was with her.

Shani slipped behind an obelisk-shaped monument, spotted a flash of movement, and fired. She heard someone cry out, smiled grimly, and gestured for Alamy to follow her. The slave obeyed, but as the police officer dashed between a row of identical headstones, she heard Alamy call out and looked back to see that she had fallen. A bullet in the back perhaps? No, the other woman was back on her feet and running again.

Shani rounded a huge piece of statuary and turned to look back. Two men were directly behind Alamy and closing with her. The police officer had a clean shot at one of them. She brought her weapon up, and was about to squeeze off a shot, when something kept her from pulling the trigger. What happened next seemed to occur in slow motion.

As Shani stood and watched, the men caught up with Alamy. One of them grabbed the slave, swore when she turned to claw his face, and hit her with his gun.

Alamy fell, giving Shani a clear shot at *both* assailants.

But even though she knew she *should* fire, the police officer couldn't bring herself to do so and knew why. Cato was in love with Alamy even if he wouldn't or couldn't admit it. Which meant that what she wanted most in the world wasn't going to happen. Not so long as the slave was alive.

The first man, the one who had three diagonal scratches across his face, took aim at Alamy. But, when he pulled the trigger, nothing happened. The magazine was empty.

So the man swore, drew his bush knife with the other hand, and raised it high. That was when Shani heard the second assassin say, *"No!"* as he raised his weapon to block the downward stroke.

Then Shani heard the familiar *blam, blam, blam* of Cato's pistol followed by the sound of his voice. Judging from the strength of it, he wasn't far away. "Shani? Alamy? If you can hear, don't answer. I think five of the bastards are down. Watch yourselves. . . . There are more of them. Two or three at a guess."

Shani opened her mouth to reply but closed it again as the men took the other woman by the arms and jerked her off the ground. Then, dragging her between them, they hauled Alamy away.

SIXTEEN

The city of Kybor, on the planet Therat

•

THE TRIP FROM THE GRAVEYARD INTO TOWN WAS both somber and dangerous. Somber because even though Shani had seen the assassins grab Alamy and given chase— she'd been unable to catch up with them as they had disappeared into the night and a maze of headstones. So there was a hole where the bottom of Cato's stomach should have been. And he was so preoccupied by all of the horrible things that could be happening to Alamy that he was barely aware of the fact that people were taking potshots at the Vord vehicle as it wound its way through the city. The aliens had responded to Cato's request for assistance, but the fighting had delayed them, and they had arrived too late to offer anything more than transportation.

The large-caliber bullets made a clanging sound as they struck the truck. The smaller stuff rattled insistently but bounced off the vehicle's armored skin as the turret gunner fired short bursts in response. But then there was a loud *boom* as something big slammed into the truck and threw the Umans against the left side of the passenger compartment.

The force of the impact lifted the tires on the right side of the vehicle off the ground and nearly tipped it over. "Sonofabitch," Cato said, as the run-flat tires slammed back down. "What the hell is going on?"

"That's what I've been trying to tell you," Shani replied irritably as she tightened her harness. "While we were at the graveyard, a Sagathi and a team of Rahati assassins attacked the governmental complex. All of the Umans were killed, but the shifter got away."

"Naturally," Cato commented sourly. "Who were they after? The commissioners?"

Shani nodded toward the driver's compartment, where a haughty-looking Vord officer and his Ya were seated on the passenger side. "All I know is what *they* told me . . . but it sounds like there wasn't any objective to speak of. They forced their way in, shot the place up, and got themselves killed."

"The Umans got killed," Cato observed grimly. "Our Sagathi friends aren't stupid. You can bet they had a reason. But never mind that . . . Why are people shooting at *us*?"

"It looks like the attack on the government complex brought all sorts of resistance groups out of the woodwork," Shani replied. "And they're shooting at every Vord they see. This vehicle included."

Cato's thoughts turned to Governor Arrius and *his* resistance fighters. Were they involved in the fighting? Or were they keeping their powder dry and waiting for a chance to do something meaningful? He feared the first possibility and hoped for the second. Because if Shani and he were to find the Sagathies, they would need more help than the hard-pressed Vords could possibly provide.

The combat car swerved in order to circumvent an improvised roadblock, lurched through a hail of rocks that rattled all around, and bounced over what might have been a Uman body. "We're almost there!" the officer shouted from the front seat. "Get ready to jump."

So Cato and Shani released their seat belts and positioned themselves next to the side opening. They were ready when the vehicle screeched to a halt. The door slid open, they hopped out, and Cato pushed it closed. Then the combat car was off and running as gunfire echoed throughout the city.

The police officers dashed across the sidewalk to the front door of the apartment building, ran upstairs, and opened the unpainted door. The living room was just as they had left it, which was to say messy, and empty without Alamy.

There was a distinct possibility that the apartment had been bugged by the Vords. So as Cato dropped into a chair, he was careful to keep his voice down. "There's a chance that the Rahaties killed Alamy. But the fact that they took her argues against that. And if she's alive, we're going to need help in order to find her. How many Rahati temples are there anyway? A dozen? *Two* dozen? I don't have a clue. She could be in any one of them—or at some other location."

"Should we look for Alamy?" Shani inquired innocently. "Or should we look for the shifters? On the theory that if she's alive, they'll be nearby."

"We'll look for both," Cato concluded. "And take whatever we get . . ."

He was about to say more, but someone banged on the front door and rattled the knob. The police officers made eye contact, drew their weapons, and took up positions to either side of the doorway. It was Cato who took a peek through the peephole, undid the lock, and pulled the barrier open. It quickly became apparent that Umji had been leaning on the door, as he fell inside.

Cato bent over to help the Vord police officer up onto his feet as Shani eyed both the landing and the stairs. They were clear, so she closed the door and locked it while Cato helped Umji across the room. "What's wrong?" the Xeno cop inquired. "Are you wounded?"

"Yes," Umji replied as he slumped into a chair. "Though

not in the way you mean. Now listen, and listen carefully, because the fate of the people living on this planet depends on you. And I mean *all* of the people. Vord and Umans alike."

Cato frowned as an explosion rattled the windows. "I don't see how that's possible—but I'm listening."

Umji doubled over, as if in pain, then straightened again. His words came in short bursts. "There was an attack. . . . On the government complex. It was led by a Sagathi. It got away. The commissioners are frightened. What if the shape shifters get off planet? No one would be safe. Not even our leaders. What happened to Emperor Emor could happen to them."

At that point, Umji jerked convulsively, as if an electric shock had been sent through his body, and the next words came through gritted teeth. "Sorry . . . Quati believes I'm a traitor. He's killing me. I don't have long to live."

Cato was kneeling next to the Vord's chair. He looked at Shani and back again. Because Umji spoke for both of them, he hadn't spent much time thinking about the fact that the sluglike Ya was a sentient being in its own right. And that, he realized now, had been a mistake. Judging from the rapid manner in which the parasite was contracting and expanding, it was pumping something into Umji's bloodstream. Toxins? Yes, that made sense.

Shani produced a knife, flicked it open, and pressed the point against the Ya's glistening skin. "No!" Umji said. "It's too late. Now listen . . . A convoy is going to take the commissioners to the spaceport at about four in the morning.

"Once the group boards the shuttle and lifts off the planet, they will be taken aboard the battle cruiser *Annihilator*. That's when the bombardment will begin. The plan is to glass Therat and everyone on the surface. Vords included."

"So that's why you came to us," Cato concluded. "Because the commissioners are willing to massacre their own people in order to kill the shifters."

"Yesss," Umji replied as his eyelids fluttered and another convulsion racked his body. "Quati and I were to lift with them . . . but I couldn't bring myself to do it. We're police officers. Our job is to protect people, not kill them."

"We'll get medical help," Cato said. "We'll . . ."

"No!" Umji said emphatically as his pain-filled eyes bored into Cato's. "Go . . . stop them. Find a way to save my people. And yours."

At that point, Umji's feet beat a brief tattoo on the floor before a final convulsion took his life. But the Ya was still alive, and Cato could "feel" the hatred that emanated from it until Shani pushed her knife in deep, and the emotional emanations came to an abrupt end. Green goo spurted out onto Umji's chest as the blade was withdrawn.

Cato looked up, and was about to chew Shani out, when he realized that it wouldn't do any good. Shani was Shani. Not to mention the fact that Quati was a murderer. "All right," Cato said as he lurched to his feet. "If we had a need to contact Governor Arrius earlier—we need him even more now. We've got to intercept the commissioners and prevent the *Annihilator* from dropping those bombs."

"But what about Alamy?" Shani inquired. "Shouldn't we go looking for her?"

"I want to," Cato answered. "Believe me, I do. But that will have to wait."

Shani nodded obediently, and replied, "Yes, sir. . . . That makes sense."

It was a little past three in the morning, and the city was in a state of chaos. The Vords were trying to keep the lid on, but there weren't enough of them to keep the city under control, and there was fighting in the streets. Not just between Umans and Vords, but among criminal gangs, and competing resistance groups. Because even though the presence of the occupying Vords should have been enough to unite them, some of the Umans wanted complete independence and saw the current situation as an opportunity to break free of the Empire.

So as Governor Arrius and his fighters drove through the city, their vehicles came under occasional fire. But given the importance of the mission they were on, they didn't fire back.

It had taken hours to contact Arrius, gather all of the necessary supplies, and put everything in motion. So, as precious minutes continued to come off the clock, Cato battled the desire to start yelling at people. Because that would not only be pointless but counterproductive in a situation where he was trying to build unit cohesion, not destroy it. Still, meaningless as it was, Cato found himself turning to Arrius and asking the same question all over again. "How much longer?"

"About ten minutes," Arrius assured him, as the five-vehicle convoy turned a corner and something heavy hit the roof. "Don't worry, Centurion Cato, we'll get there in time."

Cato believed the politician but knew that reaching the ambush site in time, and destroying the Vord convoy, were two different things. However, there was no point in saying that, so he didn't.

True to the governor's word, the vehicles came to a halt one block away from the ambush site with forty-five seconds to spare. "Keep a sharp lookout," Cato said over the jury-rigged radio system as he opened the door to get out of the car. "And be ready to leave on a moment's notice. Section Leader Shani will be in command while I'm gone." Cato heard a series of *click*s and "Okays" by way of replies.

Even though some of them had been shot out, most of the city's streetlights were still on, as was the orbital reflector. Though a layer of clouds was blocking some of the illumination the big mirror would otherwise provide. So as Cato, Governor Arrius, and the man called Bif got out of the Vord-manufactured vehicle, there was enough light to see by.

They were in among the strip of five- to ten-story buildings that lined the south side of Commerce Avenue, the road that led from the governmental complex to the spaceport. Most of the structures belonged to businesses—and were therefore dark given the early hour. So there was no foot traffic to contend with as the three men jogged around the corner, ran half a block, and arrived on Commerce. An orange maintenance truck was parked in the middle of the street. Its hazard lights were flashing, luminescent barriers had been set up, and it looked as though the crew was working down below street level.

"There they are!" Arrius said happily, "just like I told you. Lots of the city's workers belong to the resistance movement."

"You told me they'd be done by now and clear of the area," Cato said critically as he glanced at his watch. "We have no way to know if the commissioners will leave early."

"I'll talk to them," Arrius said soothingly. "Take cover by that building, and I'll be back in a minute or two."

It was a full ten minutes before Arrius came back from the middle of the street. "The wiring is taking longer than expected," he said. "But another five minutes will do. That's when the crew will pack up and pull out. Here's the remote."

"Excuse me, sire," Cato responded, "but that's bullshit! Because if the convoy appears, I'm going to press this button! You tell them to finish up and run like hell."

Arrius wasn't used to taking orders from junior officers, felt a surge of anger, and was about say something when Cato smiled. The expression took on a ghastly appearance thanks to the glow of the green-blue streetlights. "Sorry, sire. . . . *Please* tell them to run like hell."

Arrius laughed, took off at a jog, and was back in the middle of the street when a thrumming noise was heard. A Vord air car flashed overhead, clearly headed for the spaceport. "It's a scout!" Cato shouted. "The convoy will be right behind it. Tell everyone to get out of there!"

Arrius could be seen bending over the open manhole. Then half a dozen people came boiling up out of the ground and took off in a variety of directions. "Good work," Cato said, as Arrius arrived back on the street corner.

"Here they come," Arrius said, as the two men peered around the corner of the building where they had taken shelter. "May they rot in hell."

There was nothing wrong with that sentiment insofar as Cato was concerned. But his attention was focused on the headlights that grew brighter with each passing second. The objective was to trigger the explosives at exactly the right moment and destroy the vehicles before the occupants could broadcast a distress signal.

So as the lights grew brighter, and the first vehicle changed lanes in order to avoid the utility truck, Cato already had his thumb on the button. He was about to detonate the charges when he realized that the oncoming headlights belonged to a delivery van! A bread truck which, based on appearances, was making the usual rounds in spite of the fighting. At some point the driver had pulled out in front of the Vord convoy and unknowingly taken the lead.

Cato was careful to lift his thumb as the bread truck rolled by, then he eyed the following vehicles and counted four sets of headlights. As the second combat car, the one Cato figured the commissioners were in, approached the manhole, Cato pushed the button. Nothing happened. A second passed. Then two. He swore. "God damn it. . . . You—"

The rest of what Cato was going to say was lost as a series of powerful explosions pursued the Vords. The detonations started farther back, where the convoy had been, and blew a series of huge holes in Commerce Avenue. One of them consumed the maintenance truck as steel manhole covers soared into the air, underground pipes were severed, and a geyser of water shot straight up.

BOOM! BOOM! BOOM! The sound reverberated and echoed between the buildings as the sequence of explosions caught up with the speeding vehicles, and an abyss opened up directly under them. One moment they were there, speeding along, and the next they were gone, as if snatched into some other dimension.

There was a loud *clang* as a manhole cover landed twenty feet away, followed by a muffled *thump* as one of the vehicles caught fire below street level and the far-off chatter of machine-gun fire as the battle for the city continued. Then came a couple of seconds of complete silence before Cato gave a low whistle. "Damn . . . That was incredible. Who set those charges anyway?"

"Her name is Lola," Arrius replied. "And she's a mining engineer. I told you everything was under control."

"And you were right," Cato conceded. "I'd like to buy Lola a beer. But first we need to get our convoy onto Commerce before that air car circles back to see what's going on. There were four cars in the *real* convoy. We have three cars and two trucks. We'll leave one truck here. Let's hope the Vords don't notice the difference."

With Bif bringing up the rear, the two men ran back to the fake convoy, where they hurried to jump aboard the first vehicle. The engine was already running. "Hit it!" Cato ordered, and the driver obeyed. Tires screeched as the car pulled out. With the exception of the second truck, which Arrius ordered to hang back, the rest of the vehicles followed.

"All right," Cato said over the radio, as the driver made a left, then a right onto Commerce. "Stage one was a success. But stage two will be even harder. Lock and load. The Vords won't let us aboard that ship without a fight.

"I understand we have a naval officer with us," Cato continued. "Please identify yourself."

"My name is Tracius," a male voice said. "I was a naval officer, a Captain to be exact, but I came here to retire. Good choice, huh?"

Cato chuckled. "I don't know about•that, sir, but we're lucky to have you. Assuming all goes well, you and your crew people will board the shuttle and the ship last. Once we take control of the *Annihilator*, I'm counting on you to make sure that the Vords don't drop any bombs."

"Roger that," Tracius answered. "But there are only six of us . . . So we'll need some help."

"You heard the Captain," Cato said over the radio. "Once we have control, *he* will assume command, and the rest of us will report to him."

There was a flurry of acknowledgments followed by radio silence as the convoy sped toward the airport. As Cato peered up through the windshield, he saw the lights on the front of the Vord air car coming straight at him and knew the pilot had seen and/or heard the explosions. Would he accept the fake convoy as real? Or would he notice the fact that one of the cars had been replaced by a truck? If he did, the convoy would be under attack soon.

There was a moment of suspense as the air car flashed overhead—followed by a feeling of relief as it circled around and took the lead. The Vords were buying it!

The spaceport's lights became visible three minutes later, and thanks to the fact that the guards were expecting the commissioners, the gates were open wide.

The air car banked away as the convoy sped up the access road and out onto the tarmac beyond. Three shuttles were lined up side by side, but only one of them was lit up with the boarding hatch opened. "Remember," Cato said, as the car began to slow. "Surprise is critical. If we allow the shuttle crew to warn the *Annihilator*, we're screwed. So move quickly and use your knives."

There wasn't enough time for a response as the car stopped within feet of the shuttle. By the time Cato rounded the front end of the vehicle and arrived at the hatch, two Vords already lay dead on the ground. Olivia Arrius had just wiped a bloody blade on one the bodies as she came to her feet. "Shani and Bif are already aboard," Olivia said woodenly. "So the pilots are either cooperating or dead."

"The first option would be best," Governor Arrius said as he placed an arm across his daughter's shoulders. "We want things to appear as normal as possible."

"That's right," Cato agreed. "Let's get everyone on board and out of sight. It's dark, but if one of the Vords sees a Uman hanging around the shuttle, alarms will go off right away."

It took less than three minutes to bring everyone aboard and get them strapped into the oversized Vord-style seats. The single exception was Captain Tracius, who, along with an experienced merchant-marine engineering officer, had gone forward to take over if it was necessary to kill one or both of the pilots. The Vord-style controls would be different from what they were used to, but as Tracius put it, "At the end of the day, a bicycle is a bicycle. And handlebars are handlebars."

Cato wasn't so sure about that but welcomed the chance to brief the boarding party as retros fired and the shuttle lifted off. He stood at the front of the cabin with his back to the cockpit and scanned the faces in front of him. Most of them looked a little bit scared, which was completely understandable. "Believe it or not, I had an opportunity to board a Vord ship once before," he began, "although it was smaller than the *Annihilator*. And both sides were wearing space armor. So this situation will be different.

"Still, I can tell you that the Vords have an understandable preference for energy weapons when fighting on one of their own ships since they are less likely to puncture the hull. And you may face a battle-axe or two. Not because of a need to hack a hole in armor we aren't wearing—but because they will be widely available.

"And don't underestimate the bastards," Cato added. "The Vords are smart, they're brave, and we'll be fighting on *their* ground. Oh, yeah, and did I mention they'll outnumber us ten to one?"

One of the resistance fighters groaned as the shuttle continued to gain altitude. "Great . . . Maybe we should surrender the moment we board!"

That got a chorus of chuckles, and Cato grinned sympathetically. "Let's give this thing a try first. We have some advantages, too . . . including surprise. But remember, we don't have enough people to take and hold prisoners. Not off the top, anyway. So it's going to be necessary to kill every Vord who shows any sign of resistance. And if that makes you feel queasy, remember this: The bastards are getting ready to kill thousands of their own people as well as millions of ours. Questions?"

There weren't any questions, and a sober silence settled over the passenger compartment as the citizen soldiers checked their weapons and prepared to take part in a battle none of them had ever imagined possible.

Cato took a seat next to Governor Arrius and wondered if it had been wise to let the politician come along since there was a very real possibility that he would be killed. But, given the reality of what would happen if the attempt to take over the *Annihilator* failed, Cato concluded that it wouldn't matter much.

Then his thoughts turned to Alamy. Was she still alive? And if so, what sort of horrors had she been forced to endure? There was no way to know, but the questions continued to haunt him as the ship entered space and Cato felt his body float up against the six-point harness.

But then, as Tracius came on the PA, it was time to focus on the task at hand. "Okay, people," the retired naval officer said. "The Vords are expecting a shuttle, so once we catch up with the *Annihilator*, we'll be allowed to land inside the ship's launch bay. Then, because they think the commissioners are on board, they're going to pressurize the compartment. Which is a damned good thing because we don't have any space armor. What happens after that will be part skill and part luck. We're about fifteen minutes out. That will be all."

Now, as the shuttle began to close on the larger ship, Cato began to have serious misgivings about his plan. Trying to take over an entire battle cruiser with a handful of people was an act born of desperation. Or was it? How much did the *Annihilator*'s captain know about what Commissioners Narth and Oomo planned to do?

Maybe he had been briefed, or maybe it had been the commissioners' intention to give him the order to nuke Therat *after* they boarded the ship, to lessen the possibility of a leak. So maybe the bombs were prepped and ready to drop, or maybe they weren't. But one thing seemed certain. Once the *Annihilator* came under attack, the commanding officer's primary concern would be for the safety of his ship. His natural reaction would be to secure the bridge and control room *before* turning his attention elsewhere.

So what did that suggest? One possible answer was to try to take control of the engineering spaces rather than the bridge as originally planned. Because if the Umans could control the battle cruiser's life-support systems, they could force the ship's crew to do whatever they wanted!

Zero-gee gravity wasn't a problem for most of the resistance fighters, but some were feeling sick, and globules of vomit drifted around the cabin. The smell of if was making even more people ill, and Cato waved some beige-colored droplets away as he began a hurried briefing in which he told the boarding party about the new strategy. "So," he concluded, as the shuttle came alongside the battle cruiser, "the immediate objective is different, but the tactics are the same. And please keep Captain Tracius and his crew alive. We're going to need them."

Then the time for talking was over as the seconds ticked away. The *Annihilator* was more than a mile long, and, because she was too large to negotiate a planetary atmosphere, her designers had been free to let form follow function. So no effort had been made to streamline her wedge-shaped hull.

As Cato and the others looked out through the view ports that lined the shuttle's starboard side, they caught glimpses of cooling fins, weapons blisters, and dozens of other dimly lit installations. Then, as the little vessel banked and passed through a rectangular opening, the passengers had a momentary view of the brightly lit launch bay. Space-suited figures could be seen moving around below as they went about the endless task of servicing the ship's fleet of fighters, shuttles, and other auxiliary craft.

Suddenly, gravity was restored as the smaller vessel came under the influence of the *Annihilator*'s argrav generators. Something the spacesick Umans welcomed, but the shuttle's pilot had to compensate for, as his previously weightless ship was pulled down toward the steel deck.

But with Shani's knife pressed against his very frightened Ya, the Vord had every reason to perform well, which he did. As the shuttle settled onto its skids, there were a number of routine radio interactions to take care of as the massive doors closed.

It was going to take at least ten minutes to pump an atmosphere into the bay, and Cato could "feel" nervousness and fear all around him as the boarding party was forced to wait. Governor Arrius couldn't access emotions directly the way the empaths could, but he knew how he felt and made it a point to crack a few jokes.

Having made his way back from the control compartment, Captain Tracius offered Cato a small sphere. He was of average height and had a full head of white hair, which he kept military short. There were deep lines in his face, but his eyes sparkled with intelligence. The empath couldn't "feel" any fear around him, just a sense of excitement. "Here," the other man said with a grin, "check this out."

"What is it?" Cato inquired as he examined what appeared to be a chromed ball.

"Squeeze it," Tracius instructed. "You know how you can download a map of an Imperial city when you land at a spaceport? Well, the Vords thought of that, too, and they sent this to the commissioners seconds after we arrived. Section Leader Shani forced the pilot to make a copy."

Cato gave the sphere a squeeze and was rewarded with an explosion of light motes which immediately coalesced into a 3-D cutaway image of the *Annihilator*. All of the most important spaces were clear to see, as were the corridors that connected them. And that included an area toward the stern that had to be the engineering section!

"Nice job, sir," Cato said admiringly as he eyed the most direct path from the landing bay to the engineering section. "Let's pass it around. I want everyone to memorize the route."

Five minutes later, Tracius announced that the bay was pressurized, and the boarding party could depart. That was Cato's signal to take charge again. "All right," he said grimly. "Open the hatch. Let's do this thing."

There was a loud whirring noise as the hatch cycled open, stairs unfolded, and Cato stepped out into the cold, ozone-laced air. He had a vague impression of a huge space, rows of neatly parked aerospace fighters, and a vast expanse of metal decking as he began to run. The immediate objective was an open hatch located about five hundred feet away.

A number of Vord technicians had entered the bay by then. All of them were wearing bright orange suits and clearly on their way to perform various maintenance activities. There was a delegation of senior officers as well, probably sent down to greet the commissioners and escort them to the bridge. None of the Vords were armed, and they stared in openmouthed amazement as a column of Umans jogged past them headed for parts unknown.

While the Vords rushed to contact the bridge for instructions, Cato led the resistance fighters into a spacious lock and slapped a large button. Precious minutes came off the mission clock as they cycled through, but it seemed as if the Vords were still trying to sort things out because the only people waiting for them on the other side were two very surprised crewmen.

Cato knew he should probably shoot them, but they weren't armed, and he couldn't bring himself to kill them in cold blood. He took a right, then a left, and began the long run to the ship's stern. Klaxons were beginning to sound by that time, orders could be heard pouring out of the PA system, and the first signs of organized resistance appeared up ahead.

When two crewmen stepped out of a side corridor and raised their energy weapons Cato didn't hesitate. He fired two long bursts from the stubby submachine gun (SMG) the resistance fighters had given him and didn't even pause as both of the Vords staggered and fell.

As with Uman vessels, all of the corridors were monitored by cameras, so Cato knew that the people on the bridge were watching by then and calling for reinforcements. That made it very important to keep the Vords off-balance and continue to move, lest they establish some sort of barricade. So he yelled, "Come on!" and waved the team forward as somebody fired on them from a darkened compartment, and a resistance fighter went down.

It was tempting to pause and try to give aid, but that was impossible given the importance of speed. So when a man tried to stop, Olivia was there to grab his elbow as Shani yelled, "Keep going!"

Meanwhile, Captain Tracius and his bodyguards were bringing up the rear. And, because of his age, they were forced to slow down, thereby opening a gap between Cato's group and the rear guard. Shani was in charge of the tail end of the column. She understood the danger and was quick to warn Cato. "This is Shani," she said over the radio. "We can't keep up. We're falling behind."

Cato didn't want to slow down but had no choice since Captain Tracius and his team were critical to success. So he decreased his speed, and was busy wondering why the Vords hadn't responded to the invasion more forcefully when energy bolts slagged four ventilator grills some thirty feet in front of him. A succession of armed security drones poured out of the overhead ducts. It seemed that some smart sonofabitch was making use of the ship's air-distribution system as a speedy way to move the machines into position! All the drones had to do was pin the Umans down until reinforcements could arrive.

"Governor Arrius!" Cato shouted, as an energy beam cut one of the Umans down. "Take two men and make a run for the engineering section! If the hatch is open, figure out a way to keep it that way!"

Arrius gave a short jerky nod as a sizzling beam missed him by inches and left a black scorch mark on the bulkhead behind him. Then he and his escorts were off, firing as they ran, even as the robots tried to burn them down.

"Kill those drones!" Cato ordered as he put a sustained burst into one of the machines and had the satisfaction of seeing it blow up. But more drones were arriving, there was nowhere to hide, and the Umans were forced to retreat as three ruby red beams converged on Olivia Arrius. One hit her in the shoulder, one cut a leg out from under her, and the third spilled her brains onto the deck. She went down like a rag doll.

Bif screamed his rage. He was carrying a rotary three-barreled minigun. A belt of ammo was draped over his right shoulder, and his tombstone-shaped teeth were bared as he stopped retreating and began to advance.

The minigun roared, and a stream of empty casings arced away from it as Bif filled the air with bullets. A robot disappeared in a flash of light, followed by another, each explosion being accompanied by a loud *boom*.

The rest of the boarding party was advancing as well, adding their fire to Bif's, so by the time he ran out of ammo, only one robot remained. It fired a bolt that took one of Bif's legs off at the knee. The machine fell as Cato put a dozen rounds in it, and produced a loud *clang* as it hit the deck.

"Keep going," Bif said through gritted teeth as he held on to the neatly cauterized stump. "But leave a shotgun."

Cato didn't want to leave him but knew he had to and waved the rest of them forward. "We're almost there! Follow me!"

After that it was a mad dash past the burned-out remains of at least a dozen drones, down the hall, and up to the point where a sturdy toolbox had been jammed between two sliding doors. One of the resistance fighters was down, but the other was still on his feet, as was Arrius. "I took the toolbox out of the damage-control locker over there," the governor said proudly as he pointed across the corridor. "It was meant for emergencies, right?"

The governor had no way to know about his daughter's death, and it was too early to tell him, so Cato forced a grin. "Well done, sire! What's the situation on the other side of the doors?"

"One of the engineers shot Decius," Arrius said regretfully. "But I think we nailed the bastard."

"Okay," Cato said as he readied a police-style flash-bang grenade. "It's a narrow opening, so we'll have to go through one at a time. Let's get everyone in there before some Vord reinforcements arrive."

The grenade flew through the opening, bounced once, and went off with a *bang*. Cato was the first one through the gap, saw two dazed engineers raising their weapons, and cut both down with one sweeping burst.

Then more people were sliding through one after the other until Captain Tracius entered, followed by Shani. "Pull the toolbox," Cato ordered. "And lock the doors. If the Vords try to force them open, let me know. Meanwhile, we'll try to get the rest of the ship under control."

"*You,*" Cato said as he gestured to a youngster who couldn't have been a day over eighteen. "And *you,*" he added as he pointed at a middle-aged woman. "Stay here and do whatever the Section Leader tells you to do." Both fighters nodded.

Then it was time to send teams into the various engineering spaces, kill the Vords who put up a fight, and capture those who didn't. Fortunately, most of them weren't armed and surrendered peacefully.

While that was taking place, Cato, Arrius, and Captain Tracius entered the control room, where all of the ship's various life-support systems were controlled. It was a circular space surrounded by banks of screens, some of which morphed from shot to shot while data scrolled across others.

Only one Vord was present, and he was seated in a high-backed chair that was sculpted to accommodate a Ya as well. His back was turned, and there was no sign of a response as Cato told the engineer to place his hands on top of his head.

That was when a stern-looking Vord appeared on the centermost video screen. A green Ya with black striations was wrapped around the back of his neck. "Officers Hordu and

Zank committed suicide rather than allow themselves to be captured," the officer said flatly.

Cato took hold of the chair, turned it around, and saw that both the engineer and his Ya were dead. A pistol lay in the Vord's lap. "That works for me," Cato said coldly as he looked up at the screen. "Maybe you and your parasite should do the same."

The Vord laughed humorlessly. "*You're* the one who's going to die, Uman. You're trapped—and there's no way out."

Captain Tracius and his experts were seated in some of the control slots by then. They couldn't shut the intersystem engines down, or break orbit, not without codes they didn't have. But that left a whole lot of other options, which quickly became apparent. "Oxygen is no longer flowing to the bridge," Tracius announced matter-of-factly, as one of his people took over control of the *Annihilator*'s life-support system.

"You can evacuate the bridge, of course," Tracius continued as he looked up at the Vord. "But we can cut off air to whatever part of the ship you take refuge in. So, why waste a lot of energy running from place to place? It would be much more practical to simply surrender the *Annihilator* now. As a member of the Emperor's naval reserve, I promise that you and your crew will be afforded the protections extended to prisoners of war."

It took the *Annihilator*'s commanding officer more than three hours, the last of which was spent wearing space armor, to finally come around and surrender his ship. The *only* ship in orbit that was armed with nuclear weapons—and one that was far too powerful for lesser vessels to take back. Especially once the defensive shields were up.

The smaller ships could run for home, however, and most did, as the Umans took full control of not only the *Annihilator* but its weapons systems as well. A reality that became apparent when experimental salvos from the battle cruiser's main armament scored direct hits on a military transport and a destroyer escort. Both were rendered useless.

Subsequent to that, the ship's crew was taken down to Therat while a crew of volunteers was brought up to man the battle cruiser, and Governor Arrius took theoretical control of the planet. There were still thousands of Vord troops to deal with, not to mention competing resistance groups, but the *Annihilator* gave him the literal as well as figurative high ground. So there wasn't much doubt as to how the situation was going to turn out as a courier ship was dispatched to Corin with news of the victory and an urgent request for a naval task force. A request Brunus was sure to grant.

Victory came at a price, however, as Arrius, Cato, and Shani stood before the same row of fire pits where Keen had been cremated and watched as flames consumed Olivia's body. It was a sad moment which was made even sadder by the fact that Alamy had been taken from that very spot. Something which Cato was very conscious of as the ceremony came to an end. "So," Shani said, as she looked up at him. "Don't tell me . . . Let me guess. We're going after the shifters."

"Yes," Cato answered simply. "We are."

Shani could "feel" his pain, his determination, and something more. Was it love? Yes, the empath thought it was, but not for her.

SEVENTEEN

The city of Kybor, on the planet Therat

IN THE WAKE OF THE RAHATI ATTACK ON THE PALACE
complex, and the subsequent capture of the *Annihilator*, the
surviving Vords had been forced to retreat into a few well-
defended fortresses, where they remained under siege. Now
that the Umans owned the sky, it would have been easy to
bomb the aliens into paste, but Arrius wouldn't allow it.
"We're better than that," he insisted. "And the Vords aren't
going anywhere."

Still, even though Kybor was back in Uman hands, there
was a good deal of civil unrest. Now that Arrius had reoccu-
pied the palace, the competing resistance groups were starting to fall into line. But various criminal gangs continued
to battle each other over territory—hoping to expand their
various kingdoms before order was completely restored.

So, as the carload of resistance fighters left the graveyard
and reentered the city, sporadic gunfire could be heard, and
the streets were less crowded than usual. Fortunately, the
clearly marked combat car was able to make its way through
the maze of streets and arrive at the apartment house with-

out being fired on. Cato thanked the driver, slid over to the other side of the vehicle, and got out. The car departed as they entered the building, made their way upstairs, and unlocked the door.

It was getting dark outside, and as Cato pushed his way inside, he noticed that the air was hot and muggy. When Shani flipped the lights on he saw something shiny dangling from a light fixture located at the center of the room, an item that hadn't been there before. "It looks like we had visitors," Cato said tightly as he drew his weapon. "Check all of the rooms." Shani drew her pistol, veered off to the left, and entered the hallway.

As Cato went over to grab the object, he recognized it immediately. There, in the palm of his hand, was the silver sun he had given Alamy. After conducting a quick tour of all the rooms, Shani was back. "Look!" Cato said excitedly, as the other cop came over to join him. "I gave this to Alamy back on Corin—and somebody left it here for us to find. She's alive!"

"Maybe," Shani said cautiously, "or maybe they took it off her dead body."

Shani's words caused Cato's suddenly high hopes to come crashing down. The other police officer was correct. The necklace *could* have been taken off Alamy's body. So who left it dangling in the middle of the room? And more importantly, *why*?

Then Cato realized that something else was attached to the necklace. And the image that had been stamped into the cheap metal disk looked very familiar. "It's the goddess Rahati," Shani said, as he held it up for her to look at. "There must be thousands of those floating around Therat."

"So it's a message from Verafti and Demeni," Cato said thoughtfully. "Odds are that it was one of the Rahaties who picked the lock and left the necklace. The shifters *want* us to come after them."

"More than that, they want us to walk into a trap so they can kill us," Shani observed bleakly. "Now that the Vords are on the run, we're the only thing standing between them and control of the planet. One of the shifters could replace Arrius, and who would know? It might be months or even years before a Xeno cop saw the governor and realized who he was looking at. That's what happened with Emperor Emor."

"Everything you say is true," Cato conceded. "But it doesn't alter the fact that we have an obligation to go after them. Trap or no trap."

Shani sighed. "Yeah . . . I know. So how are we going to find them?"

"It shouldn't be too hard," Cato mused. "Not if they *want* to be found. Let's start with some basic police work. Umji told us that the Rahaties were targeting Vords before we arrived. Parakar said as much before the shifters killed him. So let's take a look at police reports for that period and see if there are any interesting patterns. Chances are that the shifters will want to confront us in a place where they feel safe and know every inch of the killing ground."

"Okay," Shani agreed. "In the meantime, let's get the hell out of here. Or would you rather wake up dead?"

Cato knew she was correct. If the Rahaties could pick the lock once—they could pick it twice. He nodded. "Let's pack."

Cato freed the chain from the light fixture, passed it over his head, and dropped the silvery sun under his shirt. The metal felt cool and came to rest directly above his heart.

After gathering all of their belongings and transferring them to what had been one of the resistance's safe houses, Cato and Shani had been able to get a fairly good night's sleep, knowing that armed guards were on duty. That wouldn't stop

Verafti and Demeni if they wanted to infiltrate the home, but it was better than nothing and a chance they had to take in order to get some rest.

Having showered and eaten a hearty breakfast prepared by the home's owner, the Xeno cops went down to police headquarters. The building had not only been occupied by the Vords but trashed by them as well. So as Cato and Shani went looking for the person in charge, it was easy to see that chaos ruled as people struggled to bring critical systems back online. Meanwhile, warring gangs were shooting at each other, and the city's murderers, rapists, and burglars were having a field day.

The harried Centurion who was in charge of all the craziness was anything but thrilled to have two off-planet Xeno freaks show up and make demands on his scarce resources. But their badges were clearly real. And a quick call to the palace confirmed that they were operating at the behest of Governor Arrius *and* the Imperial government. That left the Centurion with no way to say no. So he sent them off to see a civilian database administrator named Marci. She had long black hair worn in a braid, serious brown eyes, and chromed temple implants.

Marci's cramped domain consisted of a small cubicle in the building's basement, a computer terminal, and a beat-up chair. It was elevated as high as it could go because she was so small. Most of the interactions between Marci and the Artificial Intelligence (AI) in charge of the local databases weren't accessible to Cato and Shani because they took place electronically. So Marci gave them a running narration as they looked on.

"Here's a map of the city," Marci said, as the graphic appeared on the screen in front of her. "Now I'll add a star for each unresolved disappearance during the twelve months prior to your arrival."

Cato watched dozens of stars appear. They were sprinkled

across the city. "Okay," he said. "But we're looking at Umans *and* Vords, correct? Can you subtract the Umans?"

"Of course," Marci said matter-of-factly, as three-quarters of the symbols disappeared.

"Look at that!" Shani said, as she pointed at the screen. "Of the sixteen Vords who disappeared, eleven of them were in the old town area."

Cato nodded. "Good work. Now, can you drop an overlay of Rahati temples onto the screen?"

"Of course," Marci replied, and a series of temple icons populated the screen.

"There it is," Cato said grimly, as one of the symbols appeared inside the area where eleven Vords had gone missing. "Ten to one that's where they will be waiting for us. Let's see what the interior layout of the building looks like."

"Here's the file," Marci said, "but you aren't going to like it. This isn't Corin, you know." Once the map disappeared, the screen was blank.

The attack was slated for two in the morning. A time chosen because guards were likely to be sleepy, most of the city's citizens were home in bed, and civil authorities could provide the Xeno cops with the maximum amount of support.

The box-shaped temple had no windows and no external lights other than the one directly above the front door. So what illumination there was came from the solar reflector and nearby streetlights. They combined to form a blue-green glaze that washed the front of the building with a spooky iridescence. A force of civilian workers had erected an electrified wire-mesh fence to contain any Rahaties within. The fence stretched all around the block and had one gate.

With the barrier in place, two companies of resistance fighters moved into position and were stationed at fifteen-foot intervals, so that each one would be visible to at least two other fighters. The precaution was intended to prevent the Sagathies from impersonating any one of them—even though it was hard to imagine how Verafti or Demeni would be able to get over the fence without being electrocuted.

Ideally, Cato and Shani would have been accompanied by a squad of empaths like themselves, all capable of "seeing" the shifters for what they were. But, since that kind of support wasn't available, the Xeno cops were faced with a difficult decision: They could enter the temple with a squad of volunteers or go in by themselves.

The first option was tempting, but, knowing how easy it was for the shifters to confuse and manipulate nonempaths, Cato chose the second possibility. Even though that meant Shani and he would be on their own. And there was no way to know how many adversaries they might face. It was a sobering thought.

It was about two in the morning and raining. Water was running off the corners of the mobile command post's extendable awning as Cato stood under a spotlight and made final adjustments to his body armor. It was equipped with two built-in shoulder holsters, pockets for extra magazines, and a slot for a radio.

Governor Arrius had chosen to take personal command of the operation and stood a couple of feet away. "Are you sure about this, son?" he inquired. "Maybe we should wait."

Cato made a face. "I wish we could, sire. . . . Believe me, I do. But the Vords were right about one thing. If Verafti and Demeni get off planet, there will be hell to pay. Right now they think they can seize control of Therat by getting rid of Shani and me. So this could be our only chance for a head-on confrontation. Assuming they're inside the temple."

"I'm starting to wonder about that," Arrius put in doubtfully. "If the shape shifters are present, they must be aware of our preparations. Yet there hasn't been a response. Maybe they're somewhere else."

"That's a distinct possibility," Cato conceded. "But if they're inside, they want Shani and me to enter, and they have some sort of escape plan.

"Now remember, sire," Cato added as he settled a bandolier of shotgun shells across his right shoulder. "If you hear fighting, and you can't raise either one of us on the radio, be sure to keep the entire block sealed off until you can bring a team of Xeno cops in from Corin. And whatever you do, don't send any nonempaths in. If you do, Verafti and Demeni will literally eat them for lunch. Promise?"

Arrius gave a reluctant nod. "I promise."

"Good," Cato said as he checked the eight-round shotgun to make sure that the tubular magazine was full. "And there's one more thing. Something personal."

Arrius's eyebrows rose. "Yes?"

"You'll recall that the Rahaties took my slave. A young woman named Alamy. Verafti met her on Corin, so he knows I care about her. She's probably dead by now. But if it turns out that she's alive, and I fail to make it back, it's my wish that she be freed. And whatever there is of my estate should go to her." Cato forced a grin. "I'd file all the proper forms, but I'm a little short of time."

Arrius nodded. "I pray that both of you will be reunited—but if the worst happens, I will take care of it."

"Thank you, sire," Cato said as he fastened the half helmet's chinstrap. "And one last thing . . . Don't let officer Shani or me out through the fence unless we provide the correct password."

"Which is?"

"Olivia."

The governor swallowed. "I won't forget."

"Good," Cato replied as he turned away. "Shani? Are you ready?"

Shani was about ten feet away. Like her superior officer, she was wearing body armor and carrying plenty of extra ammo for both her pistols and a shotgun. She produced a cheerful thumbs-up. "I was born ready!"

Cato knew she was frightened, just as he was, and was impressed by her courage. In all his years as both a legionnaire and a cop, he had never been paired with a better partner. He grinned. "Were you born? Or issued? Come on. . . . Let's drop in on the goddess Rahati and say hello."

Governor Arrius and the Centurion in charge of the police cordon were there to escort the pair as they walked up the street, through the pool of light at the intersection, and over to the heavily guarded gate. Cato could "feel" what the nearest cops felt—which was happy that they weren't going in. He looked from face to face. "Any signs of activity?"

"No, sir," a burly cop answered. "It's quiet as a tomb."

"Just what I wanted to hear," Shani deadpanned, as Cato turned to the Centurion.

"Order everyone to come out with their hands on top of their heads. It's ridiculous, I realize that, but we're going by the book."

So the Centurion raised his megaphone, gave the necessary orders, and told whoever might be listening that they had three minutes to come out with their hands on their heads. Time seemed to slow as all 180 came off the clock. Finally, having timed the interval with his wrist chron, the Centurion nodded. "Time's up. . . . You can go in."

"Lucky us," Shani said, as the gate squealed open. "This should be fun."

As they crossed the open area beyond, Cato half expected a group of murderous Rahaties to burst through the door, guns blazing. But, with the exception of the distant *pop, pop, pop* of gunfire from gang warfare, everything was quiet.

Once they had taken up positions to either side of the

door, Shani pumped a shell into the chamber of her shotgun. "Shall I knock on the door?"

"Hold that thought," Cato replied as he reached out to try the lever-style handle. The door opened easily.

"Damn," Shani said. "Either we came to the wrong place—or the shifters can't wait to see us."

"Yeah," Cato answered laconically as he pushed the door open. "Cover me."

The blob of white light thrown by Cato's helmet preceded him as he slipped through the door into a dimly lit lobby. His visor was down and the only sources of heat visible on his HUD were two oil lamps, one located to the left and one to the right, each marking a doorway.

Cato's headlamp played across a colorful painting that covered the wall between the doors. From what he could see, the well-executed mural was meant to show how wonderful life on Therat would be if the goddess Rahati were in charge. Her throne was sitting on top of a flat-topped pyramid. Each of her three faces was looking in a different direction as the sun rose directly behind her and thousands of adoring worshippers looked on.

"Left?" Shani inquired pragmatically. "Or right?"

"Left," Cato answered as he angled across the lobby to the open door. So far nothing was the way he had imagined it. No forced entry, no gun battle with a group of fanatical Rahaties, and no confrontation with the shifters. Maybe his central assumption was wrong. Perhaps the Sagathies wanted to hide rather than fight.

That theory seemed all the more likely as Cato entered the large room beyond. It had a high ceiling supported by thick pillars. Widely spaced lamps threw arcs of light onto the splotchy green walls. The floor was covered with dozens of overlapping area rugs. But judging from the absence of heat signatures, none of the Rahaties were present. "Damn it," Cato said as he lowered his shotgun. "It looks like—"

That was when a whirring noise was heard, and a silvery sphere drifted out from behind one of the columns. Light from Cato's headlamp reflected off the drone's metal skin as it hovered over their heads. "Officer Cato?" a masculine voice said, as Shani tracked the ball with her shotgun. "Is that *you*?"

"Yes," Cato responded gravely. "It's me."

"Good," the voice replied. "Even though you aren't especially intelligent, you are persistent. Or should I say 'were'? Since Demeni and I plan to eat you for breakfast."

Cato was about to respond when a single spot came on. The previously dark altar was flooded with light. "Look!" Shani said. "There's an opening in the floor."

Cato brought the shotgun up. "There's a saying where I come from," he said. "Be careful what you ask for." And with that, he pulled the trigger. There was a loud *boom* as the drone exploded and showered the room with metal confetti.

At that point Cato pressed the transmit button on his radio. "This is Cato. Do you read me? Over."

"We read you," Governor Arrius replied. "And we heard a muffled *thump*. Over."

"We have contact," Cato replied as he approached the altar. "There's an opening in the floor. We're going down. I suggest that you put some people to work sealing off the surrounding sewers and storm drains. Over."

"Understood," Arrius replied. "But that will take hours if not an entire day. Over."

"Roger that, but do the best you can," Cato said. "It's my guess that the shifters plan to use an underground escape route. That's why they let us surround the temple without a fight. Over."

"Be careful," came the reply. "We'll seal everything off as quickly as we can."

Cato clicked the transmit button twice by way of a reply. Then, knowing who and what he was up against, the Xeno cop brought the shotgun around so that it was pointed at the lifelike replica of the goddess Rahati. She was seated just beyond the black rectangle. A single blast was enough to blow her head off. An unnecessary precaution, perhaps, given that he couldn't "feel" any emotions emanating from the statue, but it felt good nevertheless.

Then, secure in the knowledge that the graven image wasn't going to come to life, Cato removed a ball-bearing-sized flash-bang from a pocket in his vest, squeezed it twice, and dropped the device into the black hole. There was a flash of light followed by a loud *bang*. Hopefully, if someone was lurking down below, they would be momentarily blinded and disoriented as well.

Cato went down the stairs first, fully expecting some sort of attack. It was pitch-black down below, or would have been without his night-vision capability and the beam from his helmet light. The air was not only stale but smelled bad. The foul odor reminded Cato of Emperor Emor's apartment after Verafti had been in residence.

Shani joined him, and the beams from their headlamps crisscrossed as they followed the narrow corridor toward what Cato's HUD claimed was west. Three inches of water covered the floor, and Cato's boots made splashing noises as he pushed on. The ceiling was oppressively low, and the walls were made of brick, suggesting that the structure might date back to the colonial period. The toe of Cato's right boot made contact with something and sent the object skittering ahead. A blob of light splashed the floor as he tilted his head down. That was when he realized that the object in question was a bone. It was too long and too thick to be Uman. Vord then? Quite possibly—although there was no way to be sure.

A wall appeared ahead, leaving Cato with no choice but to turn left and hope for the best. Something slithered through the water, entered a hole between two bricks, and disappeared. Cato had the momentary impression of a dim intelligence eternally driven by hunger.

Then it was time to peek around another corner to make sure there wasn't an ambush waiting for him, before making the necessary turn. This corridor was wider, and as Cato's headlamp threw a wash of light across the wall to the right, he saw an unexpected sign. The white letters were faded but still legible. FADO'S BAR & GRILL.

Had there been stairs down from street level in the distant past? That appeared to be the case as a double-wide doorway appeared. "Careful," Shani cautioned. "I can't get a clear reading yet . . . but I'm pretty sure we have company."

Cato could feel it, too. A seething cocktail of volatile emotions. He slipped two shells into the shotgun's magazine to replace those fired earlier. His heart skipped a beat as Verafti spoke. The hoarse-sounding voice seemed to come from nowhere and everywhere at the same time. "Demeni said you wouldn't come. She said nobody, not even a Uman, could be that stupid. I told her she was wrong, that you *are* that stupid, and I was right!" he said triumphantly.

Shani pulled a flare and held it up for Cato to see. He shook his head. Tempting though the idea was, a flare would illuminate everything, including *them*. With that in mind, he reached up to kill the headlamp, and Shani did likewise. The night-vision technology built in their helmets would have to do.

Water sloshed away from Cato's boots as he stepped into the blackness beyond. He looked left, then right, as lights at the far end of the rectangular room came on. Cato brought the shotgun up, saw three people standing on what had once been a stage, and froze. All three of them looked like Alamy! Naked Alamys, wrists tied to hooks in the ceiling, all of whom were clearly terrified. Cato's heart soared as he realized that one of them was the real thing. Alamy was alive! But which one? It was impossible to tell the beings apart given the way their emotions overlapped each other's.

The Sagathies wanted him to come closer. Then they would strike. In the meantime he couldn't fire for fear of hitting the woman he loved. That was when the Alamy on the right spoke. *"Jak? Is that you? Kill all of us! It's the only way."*

There was a splash as the shotgun fell, followed by a soft whisper as Cato drew a pistol. Alamy was the only one of the three who would say something like that, so he knew it was safe to fire at the woman to her right. But the shot was hurried, and the bullet hit Demeni in the shoulder rather than the chest. In spite of appearances to the contrary, her wrists *weren't* tied. That became apparent as she staggered and fell over backward. Verafti produced a roar of bestial outrage and threw himself forward.

Cato fired, but missed, and felt the pistol fly from his hand as an exact likeness of Alamy crashed into him. Except that this was a *stronger* Alamy, one who had razor-sharp teeth and three-inch claws. The impact sent Cato reeling.

He'd never seen a shifter half morph before, but knew Verafti couldn't revert to his true form without losing his right hand, thereby placing himself at a tremendous disadvantage. Cato was grateful for the helmet as he fell, hit the back of his head on the concrete floor, and felt the fake Alamy pin his wrists. Then her teeth were at his throat as she brought her right knee up between his legs. Cato felt an explosion of pain as the quickly gathering darkness threatened to pull him down.

As Verafti charged off the stage and threw himself at Cato, Demeni was already getting up off the floor. Like Cato, Shani couldn't fire the shotgun without running the risk of hitting Alamy as well. So she dropped the weapon and ran forward. Shani had had the opportunity to kill *both* Alamys and wasn't entirely sure why she hadn't as she jumped onto the stage.

Unlike the other two, Alamy's wrists were tied to a ceiling-mounted hook, which meant she couldn't escape. Demeni morphed into her true form and turned in her direction. Blood was dribbling out of the hole in her shoulder, but the Sagathi was in no way disabled as she threw herself at Alamy.

Time seemed to slow as Shani entered the gap. Not for Alamy, but for the man who loved Alamy and could never be happy without her. The pistol was out, and about to come into alignment, but not soon enough.

Demeni stopped. Her right hand went back. Razor-sharp claws cleaved the air. Shani felt something tug at her throat. She saw a curtain of blood spray the stage and "felt" Demeni's bloodlust. The lights went out of focus. Shani fell *through* the floor. Or that was the way it felt. There was no pain. Just a wistfulness. Why Alamy? Why not *her*? Then it was over.

As Alamy reared back, blood dripping from her razor sharp teeth, Cato saw his chance. The pink-tipped breast was only inches from his mouth. He bit into her nipple, heard Verafti scream, and threw the shape shifter off. Then, ignoring the pain where his neck had been ripped open, Cato scrambled to his feet.

What looked like Alamy stood as well, one hand cupping her bloody breast, as Cato drew the second pistol. He had already fired once and missed by the time Verafti shifted into the form of an Esselon Dire Beast.

But the second, third, and fourth bullets were on target as the vicious carnivore took to the air and launched itself at Cato. There was a mighty splash as it fell, twitched once, and lay motionless in the water.

That was when Cato looked up, saw Demeni step in front of Alamy, and knew there wasn't time to save her. Or so it seemed until Alamy brought both of her bare feet up and kicked the shape shifter in the chest!

Demeni toppled over backward and was still in the process of falling when Cato shot her four times. Each bullet threw up a geyser of blood, until the Sagathi landed and the water seemed to explode. Demeni's eyes stared sightlessly into the bright lights, and as *she* died, *another* shape shifter died, deep within her body.

Cato pushed the visor up as he made his way onto the stage. His knife made quick work of the ropes on Alamy's wrists. Then she was in his arms, sobbing convulsively and shaking like a leaf. "You came! You really came. I prayed that you would. . . . Then I prayed that you wouldn't, knowing they would try to kill you. I'm so sorry."

Cato held her close. "There's nothing to be sorry about," he said gently, "other than the fact that it took us so long to get here."

"Shani saved me," Alamy said sadly, as she turned to look at the Xeno cop's body. "I didn't think she liked me—but I guess I was wrong."

"Yeah," Cato said regretfully. "I'm going to miss her. Come on. . . . Let's get out of here."

"Not yet," Alamy said firmly, as she bent to scoop up one of Shani's pistols. Then, gun in hand, she shot both shape shifters once in the head. "There," she said, as the echoes of the second shot died away. "Now I'll be able to sleep at night."

"Good," Cato said. "Jump on my back . . . I'll carry you out of here."

Alamy wrapped her arms around herself. "Are people waiting up above?"

Cato nodded. "*Lots* of people. Out on the street."

"Then I need some clothes."

"We'll find something on the floor above," Cato pre-dicted. "It's my guess that you and the goddess Rahati are about the same size."

The city of Imperialus, on the planet Corin

More than three months had passed since the harrowing night under the streets of old town in Kybor, the restoration of Imperial rule on Therat, and the subsequent arrival of a naval battle group. Unfortunately, war with the aliens was still extremely likely, but thanks to Emperor Brunus, the Empire had strong leadership and was more prepared with each passing day.

All of that was important, but not as important as the ceremony about to take place on a raised platform in front of the smartly uniformed 3rd Legion. The much-celebrated organization of which the Xeno Corps was part.

Alamy was seated next to Chief of Staff Isulu Usurlus, along with half a dozen senior officers and as many poli-ticians, all of whom were present to honor Centurion Jak Cato. *Her* Jak Cato.

As Alamy looked out over the glittering troops to the lake and the crater wall beyond, she felt a tremendous sense of pride and wonder. Because somehow, unlikely though such an outcome seemed, she had been elevated from sandal maker to the head of a household on Corin. A place where even slaves such as her could earn a modicum of respect.

Alamy's thoughts were interrupted by a blare of trumpets as Tribune Hathis completed his introduction, and Emperor Brunus Emor stood. He was a sturdy man, who had fought on many worlds, and was much loved by his troops. There was a noise similar to rolling thunder as thousands of fists made contact with brightly polished chest plates.

The real Brunus smiled as news cams hovered all around him—and the giant images on screens to either side of him smiled as well. "Greetings," Brunus said as he looked out over the assembled legionnaires. "The men and women of the 3rd have had many proud days, the defense of Maago, the charge at Cylon, and the taking of Tygo being excellent examples.

"But *this* day, and *this* victory are especially noteworthy, as are the actions of Legionnaire Valentine Keen, Section Leader Yar Shani, and Centurion Jak Cato. Together, they tracked two dangerous criminals to an enemy-held planet where, with assistance from Governor Arrius and his valiant resistance fighters, Centurion Cato and Section Leader Shani led a successful assault on the Vord battle cruiser *Annihilator*.

"That accomplishment alone is worth celebrating," Brunus continued, "but consistent with the 3rd's motto 'never give up' these military police officers went on to find, battle, and ultimately kill two escaped criminals. Unfortunately, both Legionnaire Keen and Section Leader Shani were killed in action. But it is my honor to call Centurion Cato forward to be recognized by a grateful Empire."

Cato heard his fellow legionnaires pound their chests and felt slightly dizzy as he stood and crossed the platform to the spot where the Emperor was standing. Like it or not, he could "feel" what Brunus felt, which was a genuine sense of pride. He was about to bow when the Emperor preempted the move with a soldierly forearm-to-forearm grip. "Centurion Cato," Brunus said formally, as Usurlus appeared at his side, "it is my pleasure to award you the *Legion of Honor*. As you know, it's the highest decoration that a member of the military can receive for actions above and beyond the call of duty."

Cato felt a profound sense of embarrassment and pride as he bent his head so that Usurlus could place the ribbon and medal around his neck.

"Furthermore," Brunus continued, "I would like to be the first to congratulate you on your promotion to Primus Pilus with responsibility for all Xeno Corps operations on Corin."

That announcement was sufficient to elicit another round of chest pounding from all of the assembled legionnaires, except for Tuso Inobo, who, having been left in place up until that point, had been hoping that his failures would go unpunished.

There were posthumous medals for both Keen and Shani as well, both received by saddened relatives, some of whom had been brought in from distant planets to take part in the ceremony.

Alamy watched the entire thing with tears brimming in her eyes as memories of both Keen and Shani came flooding back, and was therefore somewhat distracted when her own name was called. "Now," Brunus said, "it is my honor to welcome a new citizen into the Empire. Would CeCe Alamy please come forward?"

Alamy was frozen in place, but a smiling Usurlus was there to help her to her feet and escort her over to the podium. She knew how to curtsy, having served Governor Nalomy on Dantha, so she did so, and might have held that position forever had Usurlus not been there to take her elbow. "You can straighten up now."

Brunus smiled understandingly. "CeCe Alamy, on behalf of Primus Pilus Cato, it is my pleasure to announce that your freedom has been restored and that you are a full citizen of the Empire, with all of the rights, privileges, and responsibilities attendant thereto, including the opportunity to pay taxes."

That got a good laugh from all of those on the platform as Brunus gave Alamy a scroll certifying her citizenship. "Now," he said, "I believe Primus Pilus Cato has something to say."

Tears were streaming down Alamy's cheeks as Cato stepped forward to take both of her hands in his. He looked very handsome in his crested helmet and ceremonial armor. "CeCe Alamy," he said, as hundreds of thousands of people looked on, "will you marry me?"

Alamy's answer was forever lost in the thunder that followed. But there was no doubt about the look of joy on her face—or the passionate kiss that followed. So the next thing the citizens of the Empire heard was the Emperor, who turned to one of the hovering cameras and grinned. "I don't know about you," he said, "but I think Primus Pilus Cato is a very lucky man."

M903OA0511